Also by John Whitbourn from Earthlight

The Royal Changeling

DOWNS-LORD DAWN

JOHN WHITBOURN

Panel One of the Downs-Lord Triptych

EARTHLIGHT

LONDON · SYDNEY · NEW YORK · TOKYO · SINGAPORE · TORONTO

www.earthlight.co.uk

First published in Great Britain by Earthlight, 1999
An imprint of Simon & Schuster UK Ltd
A Viacom Company

Copyright © John Whitbourn 1999

This book is copyright under the Berne Convention
No reproduction without permission
® and © 1999 Simon & Schuster Inc. All rights reserved
Earthlight & Design is a registered trademark of
Simon & Schuster Inc.

The right of John Whitbourn to be identified as author of this work
has been asserted in accordance with sections 77 and 78 of the
Copyright Designs and Patents Act 1988

Simon & Schuster UK Ltd
Africa House
64–78 Kingsway
London WC2B 6AH

Simon & Schuster Australia
Sydney

A CIP catalogue record for this book is available
from the British Library.

1 3 5 7 9 10 8 6 4 2

0-671-03300-X

This book is a work of fiction. Names, characters, places and
incidents either are products of the author's imagination or are used
fictitiously. Any resemblance to actual people living or dead, events
or locales is entirely coincidental

Typeset in Goudy by SX Composing DTP, Rayleigh, Essex
Printed and bound in the UK by
Caledonian International Book Manufacturing, Glasgow

DEDICATION

For my daughter, who (aged 8) asked (Binscombe, 8:10 a.m., Monday 2nd February 1998) *'Dad, what are Downs-Lords?'* – before I knew the answer.

Thus, to: Rebecca Rose, *Downs-Lady*, who thought of it, Joseph Robert, who walked it and Esther Amy, who will (Dv) walk it.

Bless you.

A POLITE NOTICE AND PLEA

Would there have been *silk* to outline Jezebel's divine form? **Was** there *enough* shaggy-men to make it all possible? **Were** the fleeting years sufficient for *New-Wessex* – itself a child of the implausible clock? And **whence** the iron ore to forge all those swords . . .?

Gentle reader, spurn accountancy's cold calculations. Emigrate from mean-spirited Mundania. A new world awaits, a gift horse.

Thomas Blades, first of the *Downs-Lords* but once far more timid than yourself, found all those things – and more – within. So might you.

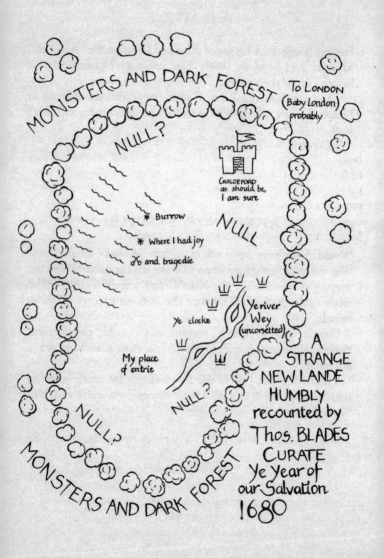

'Pennies for a poor man, sir?'

'Get a job, damn y' eyes!'

And there Captain Theophilus Oglethorpe (jnr.) would have left it, their divergent life-paths intersecting never to cross again. But then he realised the beggar had spoken in English. In Capri, indeed, in all eighteenth-century Italy, that was rare enough to command attention. The sparkling blue sea, the crumbling headlong path down to the piazza and dinner still beckoned but they could wait. He backtracked.

'Say again, sirrah.'

Joanna, his mistress of the moment, frowned unbecomingly. She did not understand her lover's moderation towards street-scum. A true native of seething Naples, she no longer even saw them.

Conversely, Oglethorpe deplored that lack of charity, waving her on with his swordstick. In his English-naive opinion, seventeen-year-olds should retain some of the innocence of youth. Fine legs and skilful lips wouldn't save her from displacement if she didn't sweeten soon. Her sister was poised, waiting in the wings. Her tongue could tie a knot in a cherry stalk: he'd seen her do it.

'Come, come, my man. I heard you plain. Speak English once more.'

The appalling figure considered the request. He was not as humble as a broken oldster by the wayside ought to be. His grime and rags and wrinkles should have engendered servility. Finally, the toothless mouth cracked.

'Very well. How do you do, sir? Could you possibly spare a coin or two?'

1

Theophilus was so amazed that a hand was on its way to his pocketbook before he knew it. Just to hear the exquisite mother tongue spoken so far from home deserved reward alone – but to encounter its cultured version was veritable rain in the desert.

'Here,' he showered piastres and pennies mixed, down into the proffered hat. Thanks were nodded but not spoken.

Oglethorpe stirred the dust with his stick. Motes rose briefly, glorified to significance by the Caprisi sun.

'And so, my man, how came you here – and why?'

It was the least of requests. He was willing to waste a minute or two – and tighten the pout on Joanna's face. There might be a story therein to sprinkle zest on the waiting flagons of wine. It didn't arrive.

'I might ask you the same question,' came the sole reply.

Back home, the Oglethorpes were renowned for their tempers, for duels and falls from grace. It was through just such, and Jacobite opinions spoken boldly without thought for cost, that Theophilus now trod the path of exile, from Surrey home to France and then China and Sicily – and finally sybarite Capri. The easy south had relaxed him somewhat. He'd acquired a patina of the Mediterranean life-cycle outlook, learnt the easy-going resigned shrug, and draped both over the sharp *get-things-done* angles of an Anglo-Saxon upbringing. People liked him better, even as they became wary of his new charm. To themselves the locals recalled a medieval proverb: *'Inglese Italianato è un Diavolo incarnato'* – *'An Italianised Englishman is a Devil incarnate'*.

Now, his native nature reasserted itself, a unsuspected sea-monster rearing from the suave waters. Oglethorpe's whole universe telescoped down until it was exclusively outrage.

Joanna came hurtling back, a silk centre to a dust storm. She didn't want to lose this fountain of generosity just yet. Murder was still murder – even on Capri.

Her shapely boot connected with the beggar.

'Speak, dog! Answer the *Inglese* Lord!'

That did the trick, proving her tough wisdom nicely. The old man was broken: abject. He'd learned her language right enough.

He looked up into Oglethorpe's face, silently surrendering his story. He was read: he was understood. His eyes held all the sadness there ever was.

Theophilus had seen the like before. In Canton he'd observed a forger boiled alive. Before the cauldron even grew tepid the felon had peered out upon the world like that. The Englishman had hoped to reach life's end without witnessing it again.

'Actually, I'm not sure I want to h . . .' Oglethorpe's words were involuntary, instinct overridden and foreign to his nature. Accordingly, Joanna didn't recognise or acknowledge his fear. She booted again – and the deed was done. Speech poured forth: there was no point in protest, no lid to fit the box.

The consoling fragrance of the wayside flowers was lost: overshadowed; the sun shone less bright. Theophilus steeled himself.

'I have fallen far,' said the beggar, humbly; fearful of another blow – from any direction. 'I am the first of a long line of kings . . .'

Oglethorpe frowned – thinking he might as well get in that mode.

'The last in the line, surely?' he corrected.

For an instant there was backbone in the beggar, but it was fleeting, like a stillbirth's soul. Whilst it still lived he spoke.

'What I have *said*, I have *said*,' he told them firmly.

'*The Null are a disgusting and oppressive race. I have decided to exterminate them all.*'

The god-king set down the diary. At last: something to cheer the heart and agree with.

'*Yesterday they caught and ate my third-favourite concubine. A Mrs Speed look-a-like, no less. Her sucked bones were sent to me with the blinded survivor of her thousand man escort. I thought well on't.*

'*I **concluded** that if it be jests they require they shall have them.*

3

People – and monsters – should be given what they want . . .'

Ah now, the god-king remembered this from history: the marvellous blood-eagle sacrifices of year 23. All the Null captives, awaiting transformation into nourishing pig-feed (once drained and diced) in the secure-corral, were set down, one by one, and cut open, their ribs being drawn back and out, in mockery of wings. A Null-queen, one of the first captured, was likewise treated. Now, *that* was a sizeable job. Even today no grass grew where her blood had flowed.

After that, when they found their dishonoured brood-mates strewn on the Man–Null frontier, they treated humanity with more respect. They paid their prisoners the honour of unbelievable torture before dining on them. Men were no longer mere food-beasts but *opponents*.

'The Vikings treated their enemies thus and I think it a salutary policy. Compared to the torments my imagination frames for my foes I consider I have been full merciful . . .'

One of the problems with the diary were the frequent references to the first god-king's previous life in Paradise. For popular consumption his successors claimed omnipotence and all-knowledge. In practice they obviously had to await the chrysalis transformation of earthly death. *This* god-king freely admitted to himself he'd no idea who or what a *'Viking'* was.

His attention wavered from the echoing throne-room, where ninety-nine wide-spaced silken veils separated him from the nearest worshippers. Their prayers were conveyed by voice-tubes snaking all through the palace, a ceaseless whisper of supplication and praise. There were even mouthpieces in the castle walls so that the lower orders might approach their Lord and (alleged) creator.

The god-king paused upon that thought. He had no recollection of creating anybody. If he *was* responsible then what had he been thinking of? Why so many types of beetle? How many did you strictly need? And why that priest-cantor he

4

saw yesterday, with unsightly, sticky-out, ears? Could he now alter that or create new and better life; less big beetles that crunched sickeningly when you accidentally trod on them? Universally attractive humans? No, he couldn't. It was a puzzle.

Another was why he couldn't have a cushion on his throne. Carved from one vast quartz crystal it was cool and hard – a penance to the backside during prolonged adoration. Why shouldn't he opt for comfort when no one would see it and he was a god who could do as he willed?

Because, came the inner, divine, answer, a god-king – who should have all that he wilt etc. etc. – didn't ought to need cushions or acquire a sore arse. One notion thus negated the other in an annoying circular argument. He chased his tail round that circuit till his head hurt. The god-king was minded to execute someone.

Resisting that temptation (too wearisome, too messy) there was the possibly of seeking other diversion. His 'Companions of the Silken Passages' were waiting, poised, in various secret side-chambers, raring to go and terrified, waiting for a sign. Relays of them were kept in readiness twenty-four hours a day, unsleeping candidates for the honour of his lustful attentions. Nowadays, they were less and less troubled, as the urge played *will o' the wisp* with him. For some whole shifts passed without incident. Such a waste . . .

Well, waste it would have to be. He felt sorry for them, poised and cramped on their starting blocks, all oiled and painted up for nothing, but he hadn't the wherewithal. Even the most mettlesome *Maiden of the Back Passage* or *Lady of the Silken Lips* didn't strike a spark at present.

Nor did he feel like pot-shots at the Null-corral, though his musket-of-gold sat temptingly on its window rest, aimed directly at the hapless giant captives below. Likewise, the leathery reptiles the first god-king had christened 'Parliaments' wheeled and cawed round the tower in no danger today.

Should gods have moods he wondered?

He wished he'd never heard of the diary, never out of bored curiosity ordered it extracted from beneath the Holy of Holies.

5

There was much within that was . . . subversive.

Whole pages were mere levity and lack of seriousness. The section on accumulating the first harem was disfigured by what the god-king strongly suspected to be drool. The book was no stranger to wine-glass rings and fingerprints and the ghosts of long ago suppers. It wasn't what he expected from the original and model god-king, the revered source of a broad and mighty river.

Far along the succeeding centuries, **this** god-king felt vaguely . . . let down: disappointed.

He looked round, through one of the slit windows and out into the green land beyond. Such settlements, such peace, such beauty. Supposedly, it was all his, by maker's rights – supposedly.

He sighed, and wished the sound could carry back down the voice-tubes. His worshippers ought to know that he doubted.

There are few things sadder than an atheist god-king.

The future 'first god-king' shut the Bible with a crash. Most of the congregation re-awoke.

'In the name of Almighty God, *Amen*.'

Some replied in kind, others mumbled sullen affirmation. A few, the real black-clad malcontents, gave him equally black looks.

'*Canting dogs!*' he said – more or less – to himself, but the front row, they heard it.

'And you – and your mother,' countered one of them, a known Anabaptist dragged unwillingly to Anglican worship.

His poor sermon over, Curate Blades retreated from pulpit prominence to decent obscurity. In the sideline shadow by the high altar there should have been comfort but he found none. What he did find was the Reverend Speed writing furiously – as in fast and angry. The Curate hated that memorandum book; he dreamed of a pack of hounds savaging it with dribblesome *grrrrs*.

He met a dashed clerical stare asking: '*Was that **it**?*'

'*Fraid so,*' he shrugged back.

'Stupid boy!' came the response, not troubling who heard.

Speed, a proper priest, arose, magnificently oblivious to the waves of hatred coming from at least a quarter of the worshippers. He approached the altar and the waiting communion vessels. He was a moving statue called '*Confidence*'. There was no danger of adverse comment when Fighting Sam Speed was about his trade.

'Beloved brethren . . .' he began.

> '*His chaplayne he plyed his wonted work.*
> *He prayed like a Christian and fought like a Turk.*
> *Crying now for the King and the Duke of York*
> *with a thump, a thump thump . . .*'

regarding Reverend Samuel Speed, MA. From a ballad of the Dutch Wars by Sir John Birkenhead.

'Not to mention overtones of Pelagianism, Solipsism and Unitarianism.'

The Reverend Speed ticked off the notes in his notes, anointing his pencil between each accusation with a coating of bile.

'A rich harvest of heresy indeed, Mr Blades, for so short and thin a sermon.'

The Curate knew better than to protest: least said the sooner the bombardment ended. In dealing with the Reverend it was vital to recall he had never really ceased to be a *soldier*. In fighting the Dutch or fighting 'the Good Fight' he brought the same principles to bear: no prisoners and no wasting sword-strokes on fallen foes. Curate Blades bowed his head, feigning shame.

'I should hope so, sirrah. Sort your ideas out!' He was poked in the coat buttons, hard enough to evict breath. 'And sort 'em short-ish: before next Sabbath, for then you shall ride again!'

In the purple thunderstorm that was his intellect, the Reverend Speed saw purpose in thrusting his curate forward under fire. He entertained wild hopes of reform for both minister and unwilling audience in their fumbling intercourse. That neither wanted the other he held to be 'a notion of straw'.

'More *rage*, man!' he told him, the jabbing finger like the officer's half-pike he used to use. 'Less milk and water! Tell 'em about the wailing and gnashing of teeth! Recount the torments to come!'

Curate Blades was miles and centuries away. There was countryside visible through the bubbled glass of the vestry window. Out there, he didn't doubt, were people, peace, knowledge, experience – fun, even. At the moment it seemed a long way away . . . but so, so, desirable.

Coincidentally, desire saved him, arriving in the form of Mrs Speed. That '*soft palmed and full-bottomed*' (Blades's summary) form, those hinted-at hills and valleys, invited appraisal. Likewise her sweet-to-everyone smile. Curate Blades appreciated God's Creation even as he doubted the Creator's love for it. He saw no bar to gorging his eyes on the feast of nubility. As always, Rector Speed was part flattered, part enraged. Before the Curate's gaze had even tracked up to her ankles he was dismissed.

Speed had no real grounds for complaint but knew very well what had shimmied through Blades's mind. Damned cheek.

'The trouble with him,' he told his wife, 'is that he lives in another world.'

The *so-what?* glance from Mrs Speed was fielded and fired back.

'And I don't mean the next one,' he explained.

Blades didn't catch Speed's diagnosis but wouldn't have demurred. If enough people say a thing there must be something to it.

A Godalming schoolroom: somewhen whilst '*the English*

Monster', Cromwell, was smashing the Monarchy and Scotland.

The junior Blades could not command his eyes to attend to Caesar's words. If Gaul was indeed once '*divided into three parts*' he did not care.

Way beyond the dust-mote bearing air within, the window showed a better view. The green North Downs beckoned him to days of delight. Caesar was dead, young Blades was not. Why should the long-gone hamstring the living?

The master noticed – for the umpteenth time. He had the persistence of the gentle – and wisdom enough to know when to despair.

'The trouble with you, boy,' he roared (for form's sake),'is that you live in a world of your own!'

Blades jumped – as was proper and required and polite – and readdressed his text. *Three parts . . . three parts . . . Gaul is divided . . .* He tried to recall that his mother paid good money for this nonsense. Childhood tedium and terror were the required price for avoiding hard work and poverty in adulthood. Logically, it made sense.

Gaul is . . . divided . . .

The wider world – the verdant and interesting bit of it – was no longer visible but its siren call continued. Fragrant fingers tapped his brain and said '*come and play . . .*'

'A *world of my own*,' he thought on. '*If only . . .*'

Years later it all came back to him – in another place that was also the same place. The first real victory.

They had recaptured the Long Barrow of *Those Before*. It was black-coated with dead Null, their golden eyes turned lifeless to the sky. Some remaining bones of the ancestors were discovered, unsullied, unsucked by Null lips, in its deepest, darkest, recesses. They were brought forth and shown the sun for the first time in generations.

The *People* forgot their drill and sergeants for one mad

moment and returned to a state of Nature once more. Muskets were fired in the air and the regimental musicians greeted the day with throbbing music from their weirdly carved air tubes. He'd tried to wean them off those in favour of the more martial fife and drum, but then they were not happy and Curate Blades wanted his children to be happy. The relevant *Princely* (he'd promoted himself) *Proclamation* was quietly dropped. Today was a day for joy and he would let them play.

The redcoats swarmed over the battlefield and bit the Null corpses to show their hatred. The sun winked on shiny new knives as they were drawn to slice off trophies. That was both vengeance and good policy: dried Null tokens or necklets of Null fangs brought honour and marriage offers to the homestead they adorned.

Restraint was not totally abandoned. His *huscarl* regiments, drawn from the sturdiest and best and first-met, stood firm. He was well pleased: they had earned the gold braid and lace on their scarlet. Bred up fierce, they continued to scan the distance with burning eyes. A few Null lancers, circling restlessly, well out of gunshot, still observed them. It was as well to keep a stone in your sling, just in case. He felt sure that the monsters were now broken in Sussex, but there remained the chance of a fresh purple tide from beyond the Thames.

He was not a god-king yet. Even the Imperium was still a gleam in his eye, left unspoken. Those good ideas were quite a few triumphs and disasters away. Still, in keeping with his new position, he'd promoted himself to Bishop a while back. The Apostolic Succession question had been set aside along with propriety and what-the-neighbours-might-think. Those hurdles were cleared and well behind him now.

In that guise he passed hands over the knights and cavaliers, the cream and prime spirits of his army who'd galloped to him for his blessing. He signalled they might rise from their knees.

'May God be between you and harm,' he told them, his words instantly repeated and spread right along the line by schools of *scop*-bards, 'in all the empty places you tread.'

It was something he'd read in the before time, in the previous place. The pagan Egyptians had prayed thus but the sentiments were still fitting.

Even the huscarls were caught up in the mood now, looking upon him with love. He had brought them out of slavery and beastdom, he had woken their hearts with the gift of hope and now he had led them to the promised land. It was all prophesied in the black book he carried. Great Blades freely admitted that it was not of *his* authorship – but fewer and fewer listened when he said so. When they thought of the Almighty, when he spoke of a 'Saviour', the People's mind's-eye saw *him*.

Curate – or Bishop – Blades looked over the nation he had forged and wondered what the Reverend Speed would have thought. He had a shrewd idea – but it no longer mattered.

There could be an even better notion of *Mrs* Speed's opinion. He's scoured the People for look-a-likes of her and found half a dozen quite passable. With voice coaching and gowns brought from the other place the similarity grew astounding. 'Her' satisfied smile now lit up many a morning or bedtime. She was – would be – supportive and . . . delicious.

Everything was delicious in this, his own, world.

'No, Thomas, it must be no.'

'Why *no*?' He didn't want to ask and didn't wish an answer: the grovelling phrase was drawn out of him by some stranger.

She too was a stranger now: no longer smiling eyes and pleased-to-see-you. He'd misjudged: she was merciless.

'You'd not suit I. Let it be.'

He couldn't: the wound must be held open to receive salt. Thomas barred her path.

'I must know. Tell me.'

The maid was angry and quick starting about it, willing to lash out. There would be comfort in that later: relief at being rejected.

'Leave off the boy, Tom Blades. Play the man – if y' can!'

'Boy? I'm twenty!'

11

'*Boy* I said and *boy* I meant. I want a husband who's lusty – and providing. That you'll never be. So let me go!'

He stood aside, temporarily a featherweight creature, and she was gone, a rustle of gown and contempt.

'Go forever,' he blessed her retreating back – and an entire pathway of life, and all those future beings dwelling in it – shrivelled and died and became nothing.

Hands like cold lead grasped his shoulders and guided him. The Angel of Failure, his lifelong companion, would see him safely home.

'*"Go forth, Christian soul, from this world"*,' said the Reverend Speed,

'*"in the name of God the Almighty Father who created you,
in the name of Jesus Christ, the Son of the living God, who suffered for you,
in the name of the Holy Spirit, who was poured out upon you.
Go forth, faithful Christian.
May you live in peace this day, may your home be with God in Zion,
with Mary, the virgin Mother of God,
with Joseph, and all the angels and saints.
May you return to your Creator who formed you from the dust of the earth.
May Holy Mary, the angels and all the saints come to meet you as you go forth from this life.
May Christ, the Good Shepherd, give you a place within his flock.
May He forgive your sins and keep you among his People.
May you see your Redeemer face to face and enjoy the sight of God for ever.
Go forth!"*'

'No,' answered Mr Blades senior. 'Not till I've got me clock sorted.'

A dying man should have better things to think of than timepieces. The precise monitoring of time was no longer his concern. Or so thought the Reverend Speed as he urged him on to God. However, in deference to the man's family there gathered, he restricted his words to those of the prayer book.

'Master Blades?' Speed transferred his puzzlement to the man's son, his Curate, standing, red-eyed, nearby.

'His clock,' came the reply: clipped and poised for blows – though not the usual sort. 'His *Grandfather*. Very special to him: only he touches it – winds it himself religiously. He wants me to have it.'

'And so?'

'I've been terrible busy lately. There's not been time to shift the . . .'

Reverend Speed leaned confidingly close. Curate Blades flinched and then recovered. Surely there'd be no violence beside a death-bed?

'Lie, Mr Blades,' the Rector whispered to him. 'Matthew 10: 16. *"Be ye therefore cunning as serpents and harmless as doves."* Lie!'

Blades was suddenly reminded of another phrase from scripture – or somewhere: '*Peace I leave with you, my peace I give unto you . . .*' There was one last gift he could give his beloved Dad. His *peace* was worth spitting in Truth's eye.

'I moved 'er yesterday, Da.' In his distress the country accent swung far and wide. 'She's there now, wound and working.'

Blades senior wanted to believe. His whole frame visibly relaxed.

'I'll go forth, then,' he said, 'and now so can you . . .'

For a fleeting second there was one more presence in the room – and then one less.

Peaceful as you like, the patriarch of the Blades had left the world behind.

'What did 'ee mean by that? Weren't nice.'

'Was if he said so,' Thomas Blades told his brother. 'When did he ever do us ill?'

Silas Blades pondered on it and could come up with no example. If he could have he would have.

'Still, weren't nice. Gave I a fair turn.'

This was getting out of hand. Not only were they conversing in the slow, '*long-a'ed*' southern-speak supposedly bred out of them by school and church, but there was implicit criticism of the dead within. It wasn't on. Their father was no less their father for no longer being beside them. He'd been a good man and was now in a better place, his just reward, listening to every word. And even if he wasn't, it still weren't right.

'Spit it out straight,' he told his brother, 'or not at all!'

Silas thought on – and then thought better of it.

'Mebbe so,' he conceded – he was a carpenter, doing very well thank you and had no need for learned better-talk – 'Mebbe not. I'll say no more. Spit on y' hands and let's shift this thing or we'll be 'ere all day.'

Tom Blades would do no such thing. For one, spittle might mark the Grandfather's polished wood and secondly it was a coarse habit to get out of for fear of repetition somewhere inappropriate. Nowadays, even some of the gentry offered to shake hands with him and imagine it if he'd just . . . '*He's the man who put a pavement oyster in General Oglethorpe's hand . . .*' that sort of story could haunt a family for generations.

Silas shifted the weight to him and Thomas put his shoulder beneath it. Despite Mrs Silas's earlier efforts a blizzard of ancient dust came down to adorn and age them. No one could recollect when the clock was last moved: probably somewhen back during the Great Rebellion, when Grandfather Blades, a martial sort of man, had put the house into defensive shape. Father had often recalled to them how each substantial bit of furniture had been designated a place in a barricade for 'when the cavaliers come'.

They'd disengaged the pendulum and rope and such innards as could be shifted separate, but even so it was still a prodigious weight. The brothers had hoped to show some respect in the carrying but that idea went home as soon as they took the strain.

'Bugger I!' heaved Silas as they struggled, splayed-legged, to six doors down the High Street, 'what's it got in here? The whole world?' Ever after, in all that followed, Curate Blades remembered that.

If it had been night there he would never have noticed. He'd have gone on being a trodden-on curate and died the same way: not a *bad* life as such – but nothing special.

In walking the thing down Godalming High Street there'd been no occasion to look. Staying upright with a little dignity had been the summit of ambition then. Silas in particular had been punished with splinters in tender parts and was in a hurry to be out of company to tend them. Thomas likewise didn't relish his burden for a moment more than necessary. Blundering past the family reception committee at his door they man-handled the weight according to their shouted, contradictory, instructions. Some wall plaster went, a plate was dislodged to its death, but otherwise they made it without undue harm.

A spot beside the stairs had been prepared for the monster and they slid it into place, vowing residence until doomsday. The clock's back was reversed into the already shady corner, sealing it into eternal dark.

'Down ye go and fare ye well!' said Silas, all dust and sweat slicked, expressing his true opinions with a look. Then he limped away. Everyone went away now the fun was over. Only the Curate remained, as always the slave of duty. There was the matter of the rope and pendulum and the winding to complete. He had to launch the clock at this, the start of its new life, and set it running true, just as his father had wanted.

A brass catch held fast the door. He flicked it and peered within expecting only more dark and dust. The second he found aplenty, but of the first not much: nowhere near as much as there should be.

15

Minutes passed. Curate Blades looked – and looked again – and then gently closed the door.

He collected his thoughts over ale and brandy in the *Red Lion*. That alone was testament to his confusion, for the Reverend Speed lived hard by there and he would not have rejoiced to find his Curate tippling in broad daylight.

Daylight . . . daylight: that was the crux of the quandary, the stubborn stain on the sheet of his contentment. Like Cromwell's *Ironsides* at Naseby, it just wouldn't desist. *Daylight . . .*

When he last enquired within the clock there had only been what there should be: he was sure of that. In extracting the pendulum and winding-rope he'd seen mere darkness and machinery and wood-scented confined space. Had there been aught else he would surely have recalled. Then, calling to mind all other occasions he'd seen inside he found no other, contrary, memory: not even a hint of one.

There again, his father had been such a jealous guardian of the clock that there were few such occasions *to* recall. Maybe there was guidance in that.

If so, it was guidance of the will o' the wisp variety: no damn help at all. Curate Blades downed his drinks under the wondering, suspicious eye of the landlord, none the wiser than when he entered – but marvellously more resolved.

More times than he cared to recall he'd exhorted his flock to 'find the light'. He'd instructed them and they'd looked back at him, neither of them sure what precisely to seek. Now, after a fashion, he knew.

A new day had dawned within his Grandfather clock, a sunrise independent of that which mankind enjoyed. Tom Blades recalled it was said that 'every dog must have its day'. Stiffened with a little Dutch courage he proposed to see if this one was his.

The point of first entry was the Empire's holiest shrine: that

16

spot where heaven had condescended to kiss the mundane world. This was where the Divine fire had bestowed a spark of itself, concealed in human form. It was left alone in awe throughout the year, save only on the anniversary of the current god-king's nativity. Then, he and only he entered in to . . . well, probably worship himself. Nobody knew or dreamed to enquire.

In recent times a puzzling difficulty had been found in securing the requisite Null to sacrifice. True, they were all scoured out of New-Wessex and getting rarer in the Marcher lands beyond, but that couldn't fully account for the lack. The Empire was obliged to send out special squads early in the year to infiltrate the wild north and even, on one memorable occasion, the tip of Scotland to catch their prey.

The god-king's hymnists had been inspired by this change of fortunes and composed an inspired work to reinforce the point.

'The hunted is now the hunter,'

ran the chorus, appearing intermittently through a long orchestral work,

'The meal is now the master;
Let every child rejoice . . .'

Looking back, people saw that day, that concert, as a fulcrum upon which History turned. It was the moment of realisation, the real end of the struggle, the moment when mankind finally got up off its knees. Afterwards all that was left was a warfare of detail: mere pockets and mopping up. Within a few generations, in the British Isles at least, humanity would be uncontested top dog. A new confidence – and in due course, arrogance – alighted gently on the species's shoulder. Pride strode boldly forth to find a fall and it proved to be just a short space down the path. They would soon learn that there were far worse enemies than the Null.

Meanwhile, even in those days of innocence, many of the 'squads' failed to return, for the Null and their brethren still had teeth, and each such loss was a blow, for they were drawn from the very cream of youth.

Smeared dark like their quarry and dressed in the greens and

17

browns of earth, they crawled into the nights of Null-land and plucked out choice specimens to honour their god-king's birthday. Fear of them must have entered the enemy's scented sleeping heaps: fear of puny, flimsy humans! That pleasing notion was put abroad and the squads never wanted for volunteers, clamouring for admission.

This year they had done well and harvested plenteously from the Mendips and Cumbria. Hamstrung and de-fanged and clawed, their captives awaited mankind's pleasure in steel cages hung high up the walls of the Cathedral. They were sullen and resigned, well aware of the role of a Null in Church.

The god-king traditionally entered at dawn – though, speaking for himself, he'd have much preferred a lie-in on his birthday. Then, progressing eastwards towards his kinsman, the rising sun, he acknowledged the subjects and worshippers abasing themselves in waves as he passed. Rampant music from the twin organs either side of the nave filled the air space, rebounding off the crowded women's galleries right up to the carved bosses of the roof.

Before the first high altar he would pause and then commence the basic, first-taught, formula of praise to himself. That was always bellowed with fervour, a suitable whipping-up of frenzy for the service to follow. The massed choirs of boys and girls and castrati shadowed the response in higher octaves, rendering it uncanny.

Next, the complicated machinery of chains and pulleys would operate, clanking the protest of age, to invert the cages and deposit their captives on to the floor below. Stunned and already crippled they were drawn to centre stage with lassoes and pole-mounted hooks, some howling hatred and pain, others past caring. The Null clove-reek was overpowering.

Soldier-priests then moulded them into a heap reminiscent of the intertwined masses in which they rested in the wild. Pike jabs maintained the sculpture just so.

Some early god-kings felt obliged to do everything themselves, even to the extent of getting in a terrible mess and then changing robes. Their successors had grown fastidious and delegated the

18

work to others, happy volunteers for the role. Even so, there was no escaping the task of commencement. He had to accept the sickle of sacrifice from the High Priest and slit at least one Null throat. The gore must then be directed at the symbol at the Eastern end, the cross painted above the High Altar and door to the Holy of Holies. He did it well enough and then stepped lively to prevent his slippers from being fouled by the flow.

Priests-for-a-day butcher-boys and slaughtermen now moved in to make a holocaust of Null. The flash of blades and inhuman moans competed with the wider spectacle and music.

The precise significance of that cross had become somewhat hazy over the decades. That it was a sign dictated by Heaven, and brought from there by the very first god-king, was not disputed. He had often spoken many fine words regarding it. Thereafter, however, it was discussed less and less till opinions varied – and were freely allowed to. Now it was hallowed by the reverence of age, if not clarity of purpose.

The god-king avoided the splashes and other unpleasantries by walking round the Null-pile, one unique occasion when he would condescend to deviate from the straightest path. Even his castle, first constructed with nothing but stark defence in mind, had been altered so that Holy feet should never be detoured or inconvenienced. Nowadays it hardly mattered of course, for the evil races were far away and whimpering, but that hadn't always been so. There were greybeards still living who'd cowered in their cradles as the frontier-hymen was breached each 'Null-summer', the terrible breeding season when their blood was up.

Right now their blood was up in another fashion: up in the air and up the walls, but the god-king had left that behind and passed on to even greater things. He (he!) knelt in due reverence before the golden door and then broke last year's seal. The pious shielded their faces from the backwash of god-essence as the diamond handle obeyed his touch.

Prising it open only a sliver, he slipped through and out of view.

It was a boring little room, dusty through lack of use and

made oppressive by the thickness of its walls. Supposedly, the divine dwelt within, focused like sunlight on to paper but if so, it did nothing for him. The god-king never felt any more or less a god by lingering within, sensed no augmentation of powers, but sadly an hour's stay was the expected minimum. Many times he'd been tempted to bring a book.

The only feature was the gash: otherwise the place was bare. That had been wonder enough in early years but now he took it for granted. It hung there glowing and unnatural but otherwise passive: just a slightly unusual window into . . . somewhere else.

He'd since seen others elsewhere and they were no different than this. Sometimes new ones came into being and old ones flicked shut. Suitably guarded and reverenced they posed no threat to stability. The god-king couldn't understand all the fuss.

Just for form's sake he went to look through. There was the usual, impudent tingling of the divine head as he observed. Nothing had changed. It never did. Heaven was still a dark small space, dominated by a ticking sound.

Fifty-five minutes to go . . .

The light streamed through cracks in the back panel. The way to one was through the other.

Curate Blades looked guiltily behind him. He didn't care to be caught headfirst into the Grandfather clock with no good explanation. There was also the chilling thought of his father's shade silently behind him, glowering disapproval born of knowledge of all he planned to do. Blades checked that wasn't so and then applied the hammer's claw.

The nails were old and well content with their homes. They'd thought to abide there forever and only came forth under protest. Blades forced himself not to ponder developments whilst he was about the work. '*Load y' musket afore y' observe y' kill*' was one of the collection of clichés belonging to

20

an old 'New Model . . .' soldier who vented his disillusion in the Rose and Crown in Mint Street.

There were two long back-panels: good, thick, seasoned wood, not the 'put-your-fist-through-it' nonsense modern clocks were made from. They put up a fair struggle but the Curate was implacable. He had every encouragement to be. With each extracted nail and pull upon the planks fresh light streamed into the dark.

At last the job was done and the barrier lay forgotten beside his feet. He allowed himself to consider the work of his hands.

Curate Blades looked within – and beheld the light of new day in a new world.

Its air was as sweet, its grass as green, the summer as beautiful, as any in the old world. Curate Blades trod its turf with joy. His father's final words blossomed with meaning.

Somehow it was easier than he thought it would be. One brief moment of confinement, one instant of confusion, and he was through the clock, squeezing his narrow shoulders into the gap. It bordered on to a void of light.

There was light where there should have been wall. It continued forever where his house ought to be. Curate Blades hesitated only a moment. He didn't account himself a courageous man and quailed before even the merely verbal assaults of Sam Speed. Yet, poised on the lip of a new creation, he struck out like a conquistador. That proved just the first of many self-revelations.

Amidst the splendours of the new world it went unnoticed. Just being there was wonder enough without pondering the why and wherefores. They could wait. For the moment he just wanted to *be*.

A torn paper edge of light remained behind him, motionless and crackling sullenly in mid-air. He'd emerged from it in mid-step: one foot still pushing forward upon the ground of the old world. The leading shoe meanwhile alighted on fresh soil – and kept going.

Curate Blades was on a hillside and could survey the

panorama. It was green and people-free and smelt of Eden.

The first hour was like a good day on the Downs: brisk, breeze-blessed, striding with only God's creation for company and that happy analogy just kept on fitting, as the two landscapes proved to be kith and kin. These too were rolling hills of grass-topped chalk, though more scrub-colonised, less sheep cropped, than the Downs he knew. All the same, they were close cousins at least.

He ascended to the heights and then an absence of paths and the wealth of woods down below made him stick to the hilltops. From there nothing of the surrounding miles was hid from him. He looked and learned and when walking palled, ever so slightly, he paused to ponder.

Of sheep there was – proxy – sight and sign, in the forms of stray wool and turds and their teeth-work upon the grass. Likewise the birds and minor fauna wheeled and crawled about as they should. But of man or his works there was nothing: not even a shepherd's bower or distant chimney's plume. At first he'd approved but now it oppressed. With that change of heart came riding first thoughts of return.

He'd not neglected to well mark the route back to . . . the light. Looking round with the eye of faith he thought he could just discern its sparkle far off. There was the comfort that within a short hour he could be beside it and a thus a pace away from home. On the other hand a lot could happen in an hour, even in the settled world he was used to. Whereas, in this quiet, unknown place . . .

He retraced his steps at more sprightly pace than when first exploring. Vivid wild flowers and other exuberances of nature no longer seemed worth diverting for. The (or *a*) sun still poured its welcome on his back but had lost its power to induce gambolling. There'd always be another day to sample these delights, he told himself, so long as he make it back from this very first of days.

Enlightenment came halfway along and, as so often happens,

whilst not being sought. All the previous long gazes had told him nothing but when he ceased to think suddenly all became clear.

He breasted one rise and looked sideways to another. Unasked, all the disparate parts fell together, meshed and shuddered into life.

'Hang on,' he told the indifferent air, 'I know this place. This is Surrey!'

And so it was. Indeed it was: he had no doubt. The dips and bumps, the horizon and everything, matched exactly. He had stood here before: only then man had worn a track atop the Downs and ravished the forest, making ships and cannon from or with it. A road had then skirted the worst of the steepness and made its way towards Guildford Town – and there was traffic upon it, even on the quietest of days. Now there was none of that: it had gone or never been and trees and quiet and Nature took their place.

All the same he *knew* where he was and what a walk in any direction should show. He was only a mile or so from home – and at the same time a very long way away indeed. The portal had conveyed him both distances.

Recognition and the increased loneliness it brought only strengthened the desire to return to a restored England; that same and yet more bustling land he'd walked a short time before and sort-of walked now. Only company would have detained him – and so that's what he got.

A squeal of shock – his own – and then razor swift assessment of risk. Looking all round, once, twice, thrice even. Stern messages to a heaving heart to get a grip and behave itself. Then the recovery of hat and composure and dignity. At length, Blades addressed his new friend.

'Come forth, shaggy one: be not afraid.'

He – or it – *was* however, and no honeyed words from the Curate were going to change that. It was only curiosity that kept the hairy head in sight, dipping in and out of view from its burrow.

'Here boy, don't worry.' He held out his hand as he would to a hound. Bad manners aside it seemed to do the trick. Head and shoulders now emerged the better to sniff for proffered food.

It was a man, after a fashion: man in savage and unwashed state. Its animal odour preceded it like a calling card. Blades could now see that this kindred breed had not totally joined ranks with the beasts: it had draped its body, or at least the most needful parts thereof, with a covering of fur or wool. This evidence of delicacy reconciled the Curate to staying put. He evidently stood before a man enquiring what might be in his hand, not a dumb brute planning to devour the limb.

'This way, friend, come and see.'

In fact the ploy was a cheat: he carried no food to fulfil expectations, but the savage seemed not to mind. It did not retrace its creeping, nervous path to its hole but lingered on, surveying the greater wonder of the vision standing before him.

Curate Blades's clean hand held enormous fascination, if nothing else; and the cuff of his black coat was held worthy of sniffing and tasting. Growing bold, the scrutiny continued on and up until their eyes met.

The gaze was held for mere seconds: a guilt-troubled dog might stand up to a contest of stares better. The savage conceded straightaway and flung himself cowering to the ground.

The true Christian thing to do would have been to raise the man and assure him of the equality of all God's – sentient – creatures. Sadly though, positions of uncontested advantage were too rare in Curate Blades's life for him to just relinquish one. He decided to savour it for a moment or two. He little thought then how long that 'moment' would extend or where it would lead to. Even had he known he wouldn't have acted differently. When the meek do inherit the earth they have a lot of ground to make up.

'Where – you – live?' Blades asked, in the voice of an emperor, not a curate. It was wasted breath: the sound of his voice, loud in the open air, made the primitive only more fearful.

Blades considered his next step and then called to mind the

24

old proverb: '*act like a sheep and you'll find a wolf next door*'. Normally he was the butt end of its employment but today there seemed more than usual truth in that cold wisdom. He felt . . . justified.

Prodding the man the man with his boot he enquired again. 'Where – *live?*' and his tone caused reluctant eyes to lift. The Curate's hand mimicked his question and succeeded where words did not.

The savage pointed first to himself and then to the spot from which he'd emerged. That done he lowered his face again.

Blades didn't so much raise the man as drag him up. Where he touched the filthy form it shrank from him in abject fear.

'Go on, show me, don't be shy.'

Again, a shove and imperious gesture proved worth a thousand words. His companion scurried back to his lair, keeping low. Blades followed on.

It was as well he followed close for the man seemed suddenly to disappear, swallowed up into the earth. A close peer at the relevant spot revealed only the tiniest of portals. Without forewarning he could have passed within feet of it, never knowing.

Since the natives appeared so craven no objection occurred to a good look round. He parted the overgrowing turf and thrust his head into the gap.

There was a chute cut into the chalk, barely man-sized, and steep-pitched into the hill. Sunlight revealed its start and then some other, internal, source of illumination took over, revealing a portion more up to a sharp turn.

Blades looked back: the world was empty again and the loneliness returned. A stiffer breeze now stirred, inviting the grass into sprightly dance. The sun went into purdah behind a cloud. He wished for company – especially deferential company – again, even more than he wanted home. That desire was augmented by reason's support in noting the closeness of the portal now. Its yellow glow was clearly visible, ten minutes march away.

For the second time that day Curate Blades surprised himself.

He *wanted* to investigate this burrow and that sufficed. Whereas normally a thousand difficulties would have presented themselves for inspection and the same number of fears arrive, all clamouring for inaction, today they did not show. He was proud of this new resolve and made the most of it. Booted-feet first he clambered in.

There were footholds cut into the smoothed chalk and those aids made him wonder why they didn't make the passage a little more than man-sized, for comfort's sake. And even at his modest height, the sharp turn in direction a few feet in made matters more difficult than necessary. The Curate resolved to take the matter up, as best impatient gestures would allow, when he met his new friend again.

It was the spears that prompted a change of heart: that and the reinforcements in the arrival chamber.

The Curate literally fell into their midst, a drop enough to wind and floor him. He'd been expecting that as little as the reception committee, blithely assuming the continuance of footholds until he could stand and command again. The burrow's designers had other plans.

They stood around him in a circle with a spear apiece, all aimed purposefully at his eye. Tension rose off them like an oncoming storm. He could not rise for fear of impalement.

Initial thoughts, once breath was regained, was to locate the first encountered savage. With him there'd been some or other rapport and thus hope of mercy. The Curate looked round the ring of them but in their timidity and dirt all resembled one another. They threatened violence but at the same time gave the impression of holding little hope of it. He found encouragement in them being such defeated curs.

Likewise, they were all the same in the weakness of their gaze. Every advantage was theirs, in numbers and weaponry and location but not one could hold his glance. A few made feeble jabs at him as looks collided, but none connected and each gave way.

The Curate found that if he held the stare they were abashed, subdued even, and driven back. He swept the ring with one of the Reverend Speed's specials and thereby widened the circle, giving himself freedom to rise.

A third self-shocking incident in one day. Rather than flee or beg he just dusted himself down, removing the worst of the chalk from his coat and breeches. He made time to re-dress his wig and generally resume a presentable picture. Only then did he reach out to seize a spear – and snap its flimsy shaft over his knee.

They gasped – a universal term requiring no translation – and, as a man, bolted away.

Only one savage remained, prostrate in supplication before the invader. Blades recognised him as the human-facsimile he'd first met.

By his gentleness of spirit and forgiveness he took the first step to Empire. The Curate threw away the flint-tipped spearhead. He stepped forward and raised the trembling savage up. Cupping his head between two hands he obliged him to look eye to eye.

'Show me round,' he said – or commanded.

There was a surprising number of them, perhaps hundreds, though of the majority – womenfolk and babies (plainly fast but poor breeders) – he caught only the most fleeting glimpse, as they occupied the deepest tunnels. For this was a labyrinth, a well organised habitation extending far out along and deep below these pseudo-Downs.

Beyond the entrance area the tunnels were hollowed high and wide and could be walked in ease in those few places where they were well-lit. The Curate supposed they restricted the number of rush-torches to minimise the irritation of smoke. A few narrow shafts supplemented them, filtering tight bands of sun down into the depths but, all the same, he desired greater generosity in illumination: Downs-bred eyeballs could only acclimatise so far. Commandeering an unused flare he lit it with his pocket tinder-box, causing fresh paroxysms of wonder. The combined light imperfectly revealed a sad and dingy city.

In fact, sadness and its cousins, fear and melancholy, seemed

27

the burrow's prevailing theme. One and all shied away from him, though they were many and at home and could have throttled him in a trice. The poor females of the breed set up a wail at the sight of him till a few examples were cuffed (not by Curate Blades, of course) to silence. Even the leading males with their stick-spears and axes of flint kept their distance and did as Blades – best he could – directed, as though by centuries of rough training. Beneath the tangled locks and grime they looked both terribly young – and terrible, without the resilient bloom of youth. Eventually the lowness of spirits got to even Blades's sunny disposition.

'I think I should go.'

That meant nothing to them but they deciphered his accompanying vigorous gestures between his torso and straight up. They looked cast down by the prospect. Some shook their shaggy heads.

'Oh, yes I must. Lead on, grubby ones.'

After a grunting conference some, the younger males, including the first found savage, seemed disposed to escort him. Blades, ever a company sort of person, saw no harm in it.

'As you wish: the more the merrier!'

They made a great business about actually leaving the earth-hold: snuffing the air and taking an age to scramble forth. Some of their nervousness transferred itself to the Curate till he emerged into blessed sunshine and the brightness of day. As before, these new Downs held nothing but beauty: there were no good grounds for fear.

'Step lively, gentlemen,' he told them – just for something to say. 'Or else I shall be missed.'

In fact that was unlikely. Wifeless and childless and a clergy-man on a weekday, his time was his own to account for – for a few hours on end at least. What really goaded his thoughts was dinner and the widening gap between it and breakfast time. In their childlike kindness these primitives had offered him sustenance but he'd spurned the rations. He couldn't conceive what degree of famine it would take to make him consume such wretched vegetables and rank mystery-meat as was proffered. He only hoped his refusal had been couched with sufficient courtesy.

They formed an honour guard around him as he walked, though he set the direction; a respectful circle of armed men, sniffing the air in high alertness. Their twitchy, rabbit-like, timidity amused him. Then, in making fresh identifications, he ceased to notice.

That, surely, must be the river Wey. Uncorsetted by man with his banking and revetments it meandered and spread over a new, more generous, flood plain, lapping right up to where Godalming ought to be. And *that* valley was where an afternoon had turned golden when Joy from the Ladies Academy had kindly donated the usage of her fleshy canyons. Beside it should be the inn where he'd – with all discretion – celebrated afterwards . . .

Far off, he now noticed great herds and flocks, like brown and white chequers pieces, cropping the hills. They looked wild, stringy creatures, unmodified by man, free to choose their own mates. Here no one had bred their horns out and respect for humans in. Blades was vaguely glad of their distance and some company.

His escort shrieked, just like the rabbits of recent metaphor. In his distraction he hadn't noticed their growing discomfort with the route.

They stopped and squatted on their heels, eyeing him with fear and sorrow.

The Curate pointed towards the weird portal, close up and comfortingly achievable now.

'Look, it's not far. A few more minutes and I can show you where I . . .'

He realised that that was the problem. They did not wish to approach his destination.

'Don't worry,' he told them, accompanying his words with the most '*don't worry*'-ing of expressions. 'It won't hurt you.'

Since it was their world they ought to know best but their subservience led the Curate to lean unto his own judgement.

His urgings on, by word and gesture, had partway convinced them till a fresh wave of terror arrived. Again they squealed but this time in greater extremity. One of them pissed himself,

quite unashamed, whilst the Curate curled his lip in disapproval at the steaming arc. As someone who'd oft reproached
himself for cowardice he doubly disapproved of it in others.

'Look: come with me and I'll show . . .'

He then took his own advice and *looked* – and found they had
excuse for their lily-liveredness. Across the sward, still way off,
dark dots were heading in their direction. '*Wild cattle?*'
wondered Blades. That would account for the speed of
approach, if not the arrow-like sense of purpose. Bovines, wild
or otherwise, were not hunting beasts – not in his world at least.

Maintaining that identification for the moment, he tried to
amend his friends' interpretation of events. They had spears –
of sorts; they had numbers and the advantage of the slope: even
the most skittish of troops ought to be able to make a fight of it.
As self-appointed general he indicated they should *stand*.

And so they did – just, though every indicator showed a
preference for flight. Some were trying to tell him something,
voicing urgent, puffed-out noises. '*Null! Null! Null!*' they
pleaded, pointing madly. He jumped to the obvious conclusion
whilst graciously overlooking such indiscipline. Let these '*Null*'
come or not as they wished. Curate Blades's new army would
pause to await developments.

They were not kept waiting long, for the arrivals moved at
pace. The purple conglomerate resolved itself into individual
figures and the Curate partook of some of the festival of fear.
Either they were implausibly close or else they were . . . large.

He continued to entertain the hope that these were just
more men, of the naked, Negroid variety; another freakish
happenstance of this new world. If so, he looked forward to the
encounter for '*Sons of Ham*' were a novelty to him. Once, in
Southwark, he'd glimpsed a little black servant-boy – all the
rage amongst the nobility, so he'd heard. And, not long ago and
remarkably, some Indians of the Yamacraw tribe had been
brought to Godalming from Georgia, till smallpox claimed a
couple and the rest took sanctuary in General Oglethorpe's
House at Westbrook. Before they fled, he'd made several
goggle-eyed studies of them.

The Curate persisted in hopes of such novelty but doubts developed. He'd never heard that the sons of Africa grew so prodigiously . . .

Order amongst his fresh-raised militia was ebbing away, a trickle of lost resolve turning into a flood. Piteous looks were directed at him every second.

'Steady . . .' he told them, as he would a dog.

The giant 'Negroids' moved in step; long loping steps that ate up distance with ease. Curate Blades tried not to prejudge any man but he could not help but think he was being regarded with hunger.

'Have it your way, off you go then!'

He dismissed them with a wave of his hand and they didn't wait for second bidding. The savages dispersed at the sprint, every man for himself. Blades wondered, with a chill, if there wasn't old wisdom in their scattering like chaff in every direction. When no resistance could be offered such tactics made it likely at least some would escape.

A few seconds on Blades embraced their example. Close up he accepted the unpleasant truth. The *Null* were large and fanged and ravenous and had not come to bless him.

Some of the troop peeled off to address the matter of the fugitives. Most remained on track, shot-like, straight at him.

He now saw they were more purplish than black, perfectly formed, though one-and-one-half times man-sized; hawser muscles filling out the flesh like lush hothouse grapes. Almond eyes, of leprous yellow, colour mismatched by their maker, looked confident, even humorous, about their business.

The Curate decided not to make their acquaintance in any form. He turned on his heels and scorched the turf. They increased their pace.

Hat and then wig were lost, without regret, in haste to be away. He'd have discarded his frock coat, trailing behind him like the wings he wished he had, save for the precious second that would have wasted. Much the worse of the ordeal, viler even than the molten breath and needles in his guts, was the silence. That they were gaining on him he knew, through sundry senses, but they chose to give no token of it. He imagined those white-teethed smiles widening. He hated them.

Screams enlivened the outing. Some of his former friends had been caught. He'd heard similar sounds from rabbits under a fox, octave-ascending songs in the night, ending suddenly.

Now he heard the *pad pad pad* of their feet on the ground. A hot scent of cloves preceded them. He begrudged his tormentors their lack of breathlessness. He was a little boy at school again: bigger bullies, hunting in packs, were on his trail. The portal was painfully close; painfully far away.

But – it transpired – close enough. Just as he visualised claws in reach to rake his back, they were gone. He could sense their absence as he had their threat. The Curate, a sweating frantic beast, stumbled on alone. Damning dignity to mind its own business he pressed on a space further, just to make sure. Only then, weeping with exhaustion, did he turn.

They'd halted at some invisible frontier. Unused to failure, the purple titans regarded neither him or the portal – the true source of their defeat. They shunned it and thus him, wheeling away like a well practised troupe off to fresh entertainment.

Unable to believe his fortune, Blades surveyed his realm: the wide berth of empty grass round the gateway. Within its invisible bounds he was both master and sole subject. The primitives had shunned it and now so did their predators. Winded, arms resting on his knees, he was glad to just credit the happy fact, for there was now no chase left in him.

The abominations moved like monarchs themselves, every one a joyful celebrant of its own powers. They herded and toyed with the scattered savages as if it were a game and their ancient privilege. They were merciless as cats.

Some of his hosts escaped. They'd scampered in too many directions to all be caught. There was a bountiful harvest nevertheless.

The Curate stood and watched. He had little choice in it whilst his chest still heaved like a duchess under her sovereign. Exhaustion was gradually replaced with nausea.

32

There seemed a point when discipline was relaxed amongst the Null. When a kill was made it was now permitted to remain and feed, stripping living flesh from its bones. Blades shuddered as if struck with every truncated shriek. There also seemed no question of resistance: any warding spear or limb being casually brushed aside. He saw a few survivors regain the safety of the burrow or else disappear over distant hills and he rejoiced on their behalf. For the majority though there was only death, and not always a speedy one.

When the pack had fed to their content they turned on still-living captives, held pinioned like lambs. They were then jointed with teeth and claw and borne away for later or some others' consumption.

They did not favour him with so much as a look, either in triumph or contempt. As far as they were concerned, in their pride and satiety, he had ceased to exist: never had existed. They loped away.

Fourth self-surprise of the day: Curate Blades hated them and always would. They *would* know that he existed or he would never rest again. At long last, after thinking it would never come, he had found his vocation. Traditionally it should precede ordination but now would do.

With greater things on his mind he returned to the portal as though crossing his front door. A last look was bestowed on the sullied green-scape.

'Beginning, not end,' he told that world, and then, for the time, rejoined his own.

'What for?'

'Because.'

'Not good enough, brother.'

To the Curate's mind requests within the family shouldn't require an inquisition. It wasn't as though Silas hugged the musket to his breast. As best Blades knew it lived in its cupboard from one year's Kingston militia muster to the next.

They fired off a few rounds to please the Sheriff and then retired to drain the inns and strike bargains – the true meaning of the moot. In fact, that was a thought: the piece was likely so ill-maintained it might go off in his face. The Curate made a mental note to give her a good clean before embarking. It wouldn't do to start a crusade with a misfire.

'All right then, for shooting.'

'Ah, me, and I thought you wanted 'er for stirring the pudding. Shootin' what?'

Blades had foreseen that question and given thought to an acceptable half-truth.

'Vermin.'

Silas looked at him and then showed unsuspected knowledge of his brother's true nature: wisdom all the more impressive for mapping a yet invisible continent.

'Two or four-legged vermin?'

The Curate feigned outrage at such aspersions against a man of the cloth but its hooks failed to grapple. Therefore honesty seemed the best policy.

'Either.'

'Hmmm . . .' He wasn't won over.

'Peddlers then.'

That might strike home. Gangs of tinkers and 'sturdy beggars', sometimes four-score strong, were the terror of rural farmsteads. Popular songs were rich in mentions of Irish raiders.

Silas rubbed his scratchy chin.

'Peddlin' what?'

The Curate looked him in the eye, hoping to convey what he couldn't speak.

'Peddlin' meddling.'

The brothers pinned each other with their gazes. Trust flared into life and travelled along the exchange.

Silas resumed his normal self with an old-fashioned look.

'She's in 'er cupboard. Best clean 'er first.'

Curate Blades was away up the stairs, taking the first step to god-head.

The new world's first gunpowder – as best he knew – arrived in all of a fluster: determined to be so, spurning all encouragement.

It should have been no small matter to squeeze a primed piece *and* himself through the tiny keyhole. Yet somehow he was accommodated, some pliant force easing the passage. The crossing was achieved with ease. Then, still refusing to arrive carefree, he wondered whether the glowing cord might be extinguished by transit between dimensions, thus delivering himself impotent into the hands – and teeth – of enemies.

When that fear proved false Blades looked around for fresh worry, unwilling to accept the new world's smile. Its beauty when he saw and felt it on his face seemed false, no longer reminding him of Eden. Here the serpent had the upper hand. But now an ordained curate of the Church of England '*by law appointed*', had come to remedy matters. Moreover he was armed – with his brother's militia gun. It was cocked and primed. Vengeance – or restitution – was only a matter of time.

That thought stopped him in his tracks, two paces into the land-beyond-the-clock. Such confidence! Such pride! Where had it all come from? Blades paused and considered the question – for a moment only. He shook his head. Did it really matter? He was just glad to see it. What was it his father said about gift horses and their mouths? If at home he was downtrodden and here a hero so what? Who was to say which was the true he?

No one, that was who – quite literally. Curate Blades looked over the empty landscape and saw not a soul to contradict him. Nor was there anyone to shoot – so he stood down the musket he found clutched high to his chest.

For further reassurance he poked his head back through the portal. Beyond the dissonance there was the expected gloom of the clock-case, then light in his Godalming hallway. Blades was pleased but felt no call of home. He was where he should be and had his vocation to think of.

A changed sky matched his new perception of the land: grey, leaden and threatening. When a novel notion occurred he tried to change the weather with thought alone – and then laughed at his presumption. Nothing happened of course, save that land heard its first honest amusement for some time – perhaps ever.

Blades thrust that mood aside: no time for soft considerations yet. He patted the heavy satchel of musket balls for reassurance: the wisdom of his own world in a bag – easy to carry yet never known to fail.

He knew the way and strode along it like Alexander. Tokens amidst the grass – clean bone and rejected gristle – of the beasts' feeding did not distract or slow him. He had come to make amends like a true Christian should and that sufficed. The manly way was to rectify, not wail over, wrongs and no would-be wife could now fault him.

The burrow's entrance took a bit of searching, and plunging down it some of his store of spine. But once committed there was no going back and thus no doubts. Feet-first he went to meet the future.

It was there in the form of his former friends: cowed and timorous as before. Blades had wondered if events might have revised their opinion of him. One – unfair – perspective blamed him for leading them into, and not saving them from, massacre. He recalled the feeble, but plentiful, spears and recognised the possibility that his crusade might end at its beginning, aborted by those it was designed to aid.

He need not have worried: that night of fitful bad dreams had been just wasted effort. To them he remained a wondrous visitation, an erect version of themselves. No fault attached itself to passive surrender to the teeth or fleeing like bunnies. Their subservience to the Null was of such long standing that the notion of resistance didn't occur.

Curate Blades smiled. He would preach them a new gospel.

Eventually their fear grew so great they withdrew below ground. One by one the savages shrank from his implacable preparations, slinking off, gibbering their concern, down to the deepest levels. Only 'First-met', happily a survivor of the Downs-feeding, remained; as scared as the rest but more faithful. The Curate would have shaken his hand but for the shrieking anxiety it provoked. Blades just had to reconcile himself to some autocratic loftiness – for the time being.

He'd brought kindling, and the burrow-people's scant supply of wood – spear shafts and clubs torn out of dirty hands – bulked it out. His tinderbox produced a spark and utter wonder from the witnesses. Though a rough wind was blowing over the imitation-Downs he persevered and soon that world's first beacon was blazing its message far and wide.

They'd never seen a proper blaze – or at least not the man-produced variety – and he lost most of his audience when it crackled into life. The rest went when they thought on beyond enjoyment of heat and novelty, realising their existence, their very location, was being advertised. Some besieged his feet, begging eloquently that he extinguish the wonder-light but Blades was merciless. He shooed them back into the bowels of the earth.

The Curate followed on, in more dignified fashion, to await developments.

They came with the dawn, when he'd twice had to go forth to replenish the bonfire. From this he surmised they were not night travellers: an useful nugget of knowledge for the future – should he have one.

When the drum of their feet were heard amidst the silence of the new day, he re-lit the musket's slow match. When the purple troop, moving in unison, became visible he reviewed his position for perhaps the thousandth time. He looked and saw that it was good.

The burrow's entrance would not admit a beast – they were too broad in the shoulder and long of limb. To come in they would have to dig and by then he would be waiting below to welcome them. He would have occasion for a last stand and opportunity to acquire company for the trip to the afterlife. If so, he trusted their paths would soon diverge.

Meanwhile, he stood in God's clean air before the burrow and the dying blaze. He was alone, not even 'First-met' lingering beyond the earliest whiff of enemy.

Rather than ponder that enemy he recited the musketeer's litany out of Silas's Soldier's Bible, painfully committed to heart since his last trip.

Have a Care. Order arms.

Hold your match 'tween first and second fingers of your left hand and third and fourth of the left hand.

Poize.

Prime your musket (left-hand flask – the finer powder)

Blow off your loose powder

Place home your bullet and charge. (from your apostle's bandoleer for the first twelve shots – please God – and then the right flask and bullet-bag)

Draw forth your scouring stick

Ram home your bullet and charge.

Sentinel posture.

Shoulder your musket (the drill-book said *present upon your rest* but the new lighter guns didn't need them any more)

Give fire.

He reckoned he could do that once every couple of minutes if he didn't panic or get eaten.

He'd become so engrossed he'd lost track of how close they'd approached, how fast their purple feet travelled over the green. He looked up. He was ready – and so were they.

They observed the faltering beacon with nothing more than amusement. They studied him with even less respect. Curate Blades now saw exactly how things stood between the two species. He was just meat with some fancy wrapping: hardly worth their journey.

The white teeth flashed and so did the musket.

The Curate had been offended by their attitude and so shot the nearest one.

Actually, with firearms of that era and vintage, it took a professional – and a lucky one at that – to prefer one target over another. In the warfare of the Curate's world, regiments stood close to and blazed away at handy, hard to miss, blocks of men. Sniping was for specialists, poachers and gamekeepers and shades between the two, specially equipped, whereas the Curate's skill was bounded by youthful duck-hunting and recent days of intensive practice. However, his debut death-dealing was smiled upon, his aim was true, the powder proportions just right. A beast in the centre of their formation ceased grinning: ceased everything. A rosette of deeper purple sprouted on its purple chest and it sank gracefully to decorate the sward.

Curate Blades resisted the temptation to celebrate with gawking. He set to feverish reloading amidst the smoke.

There proved to be no cause for hurry. The creatures did not understand what had happened and stood to debate. Powerful arms tried to raise their dead comrade but he slid sinuously from each grasp.

They were puzzled and looked from fallen friend to the sky and all around: the Curate and his gun no greater suspect than any other.

He shot another – and another.

They began to grasp something of cause and effect now, most purple faces turning to regard Blades. Some of their offensive confidence had evaporated. The Curate liked that.

One shot missed somehow, whistling between the ranks. He made amends by felling a fourth in swift succession.

They still didn't really comprehend: only that they were standing in a bad place which somehow killed. The brighter amongst the troop connected that with him and their smirks turned to savagery. In their own babble, an incongruously liquid, gentle sound, they began to explain to the rest, supplementing the story with gestures.

Blades wasn't having that and so shot one of the quicker-on-the-uptakes.

They were maybe thirty of them – well, twenty-five now –

and they could have been on him in under a minute: less time than needed for one shot. In that event it would have been twenty-four to one and thus the end were it not for the burrow behind him. He could be down that in even swifter time and so safe for a while. He had it in mind to linger in the bend of the entrance and fight on from there. It ought to be just possible to reload in that confined space and if a beast should hang its head over the outlined circle of sky . . .

It never happened. They came to a collective decision and turned their backs on him. In celebration and defiance of chivalry, he put a hole in one of them. Then they loped off, no more hurried than on their approach, never looking back, a dwindling, diminished, clump of colour.

Curate Blades was left alone, master of all he surveyed.

When the first, tentative, hairy head showed above ground they found him making sure of each beast with a bullet apiece. He shot from a respectful distance, in case any should be shamming.

The burrow people could not accept the sight as reality. Each spectator would dive back to safety, later returning for confirmation of what their eyes saw but their mind could not comprehend. Curate Blades chuckled to imagine the underground discussions.

When his work was done he drew out the leading fainthearts, dragging them over to the dead. With the first it was hard work but later arrivals came more readily. At last a ring of burrow menfolk stood saucer-eyed round the closest corpse.

The Curate stirred it with his boot to show there was no harm left, no life within. They shied back.

What happened next shocked him. All at once they *believed* and untold ages of oppression came hurtling up like vomit. They fell upon the fallen beast and rent it. They extracted its dulled yellow eyes with fingernails, they ripped off its gross, dangling privates and then fought their way within its chest, clawing and pounding, to dishonour what had lately powered the owner.

Blades retreated, appalled by, powerless before, such ancient hatred. He felt its raw breath arrive and bowed before it. Instinctively, he removed himself from the demonic zone, knowing it to be no place for a Christian man. The dangerous energies he'd so carelessly released must be left to play themselves out.

It was then he knew he could never leave – not permanently at any rate. With the best of intentions he had allowed Satan a fingerhold in this new world, introducing cold slaughter and vengeance into the previous rule of Nature. Watching what he now thought of as his children 'at play' he realised it would always be his duty to be there to guide them.

It transpired he was not the only one observing.

She had no name – not yet – but in spirit was the foremost of them. Even knowing no other way, she had always chafed against the round of servicing the hunters: their hunger, their babies, their urges. Yet when she wished for better there were no notions to frame. Life had always been fear outside and rough words underground. Until the covered stranger and his killing stick appeared she could not conceive of anything but dirt and dark and being taken on all fours and the babies that ensued. The woman did not know what he was, only that he was everything different and wonderful.

She had a hunter's spirit. She'd watched the menfolk fall on the dead Null and wished herself amongst them. Half in, half out of the burrow, contrary to every taboo, her teeth and talons moved in sympathetic tandem.

The beautiful visitor was standing apart, smiling on the scene. She felt fear, she wished him closer, she wanted that he should never go.

The female-folk were not supposed to leave the burrow save under escort. The more fastidious hunters sometimes drew her out into the sun, to breed on the Downs in some privacy, but that was rare. Otherwise, her experience of the upper world was wary foraging for fruits and berries, or nervous guarding of children's play. Only on this day of high strangeness, with normality stunned or diverted, could she direct her own feet into the great void.

The other womenfolk gasped as she scrambled out of the entrance. She raced, unsteady and blinking at first, towards the vision. The grass felt like pure pleasure under her feet. Too busy with their post-mortem vengeance the hunters did not notice.

She had no idea what she wanted; she was unused to even considering what she wanted. Hunters and womenfolk alike led stunted lives. All she knew was that she must be closer to him, to be near in case he vanished like dawn mist, to stand by him and drink in the power.

The visitor marked her. He made a sound – to her! She heard it as '*haloo*'. He was looking straight at her; with no hint of a threat or blow.

The woman's vocabulary of pleasing was limited. This hunter didn't look hungry, he showed no signs of thirst. His astounding bright body-cover hardly needed her repairs. That left little else. She turned and knelt and offered herself.

Instead of the expected part, it was her hand that was taken. He drew her up and round and moved his own head – for her! – to catch her elusive eyes.

She'd seen kindness before, but not that often, and never for nothing.

'You . . . jezebel!' he reproached her – but smiled.

Before the hunters could intervene, she repeated it – and so, inadvertently, became the first named.

Journal of Tom Blades Esq. Minister of Religion.

July ye Second: Ye Year of Our Salvation 1680.

. . . so I located the first-met male savage and raised him up and mayde him my lieutenant and trusted right hand before all ye assembled tribe. A forward wench likewise.

Then I had a choice set before me – should one learn their barbarous tongue thereby to converse – or should I bless them with the sweet pliability of Englysshe?

A second's indecision and then I embraced the latter option. When one has learned a parcel sufficient he shall be set to teach two others – and so on and on till they shall all equally favoured. And 'twill be good plain saxon-englssye too. No Norman-yoke lawyer-latin speak will trouble this world as it has subjected my own.

'GUN,' say I to the male to commence, displaying said object. 'GUN! BANG BANG!'

It is difficult to teach a soul anything when he clings to the floor like a Frenchman . . .

His two days absence were not easily explained, even had the Reverend Speed cared to listen to explanations. Curate Blades rode out the storm, removing his mind elsewhere and thinking far ahead. Even a clipped ear, previously the ultimate degradation, did not distract him.

Noting that – for Speed wasn't only bluster and hard thoughts – the tempest blew over sooner than usual. The Curate was sent on his way not with the intended boot up the backside, but an narrow-eyed gaze.

It didn't matter. He wouldn't have noticed either. He was thinking . . .

He was thinking '*if I sell Silas my share in our fields **and** hawk my theology books, then . . .*'

The equations fell into place as they never had at school.

*A little land here = muskets here = a lot of land **there** . . .*

What he planned on was teaching 'First-met' and a few best others to reload guns. With them feeding him he could keep up such a rate of fire that the Null, no matter how numerous, couldn't get near. In that way they'd clear a zone round the burrow where they were left in peace and in that peace he'd enlighten the primitives' gloom.

He'd also teach them planting and husbandry and then weaving, the better to cover the decencies; and then the rudiments of religion. When conditions were meet he'd have them build dwellings outdoors and above ground, under God's endless sky as was proper and intended. In those houses he'd have them marry one mate with whom to cleave together and be companionable, raising little savages who were less savage than their sires.

The Curate had glimpsed the downtrodden females held in common in the deepest parts of the burrow, them and the skinny infants that clutched silently to them. His heart had been touched and their raising up to humanity was amongst his first priorities.

As best their beginner pidgin-Anglo grunts could convey, it seemed they knew of other human burrows; many, many, of them. They sometimes met their brethren, at night and other slack Null spells, to trade and breed, sensibly mixing the blood for fear of 'burrow-idiots'. For they were not total barbarians: in some areas they had understanding. There were even hints of communal worship, when the scattered tribes gathered for their moots. Alas, it seemed they prayed to an angry god shaped in Null form.

The time would come to contact these lost children, instruct them and gather them in, augmenting their strength. Spread fingers were merely digits: drawn together they formed a fist. All that Curate Blades had learned through his life and studies indicated that the true, living God shone his favour on the big battalions. Therefore, to organise was to obey His commands.

First and foremost, though, was the matter of firearms. There was little use in cultivating mere beast-fodder. Nor would either side thank him for arranging slightly more civilised dinners.

So, first mayhem, then civilisation, then kindness. From what he recalled of his history texts that had always been the natural order with 'progress'. Who was he to differ?

The master of all you survey, that's who! came the inner answer. Here there was no *history* – or none till he strode upon the land. Here there need be no labouring under history's chain, maybe no more hamstringing by 'original sin'! Here was a fresh start – for himself and everything!

Silas had ummed and ahhed over the rock-bottom price for

half the family land and then paid over the coin as if he was giving blood. The books went easier, at the price of raising eyebrows and suspicions. Curates only sold their holy books when they went apostate or were in hock to wenches or gambling. He had to travel to Kingston to sell for fear of word wafting back to Sam Speed.

Likewise he was obliged to patronise Guildford for his weaponry: two flintlocks and a brace of pistols were a lot for a mere Godalming Curate to treat himself to unless he was planning insurrection. The times were touchy: everyone scented after Papist conspiracies and Jesuit legions awaiting their day in cellars under London. Blades had to emphasise low-church credentials to allay suspicion. The 'vermin' story was deployed again – locals seemed to lap that up.

He planned a further few days away, the project being worth another sore ear from Speed. With him would go the rudiments of a new life: a small handcart load of civilisation's basics: firearms, Bible, tinderbox, clothing and food. Second strands of refinement, the glorious adornments of culture, all called out to him from bookshelf and cupboard in vain. Culpeper's *Herbal*, Holinshed's *Chronicles*, even Elias's *Pork Butchery* were ignored or fobbed off – told to follow on later. A missionary pioneer ought to travel light and he was strict with himself.

Even so, being by no means a rich man, by the time packing was finished, his cottage had acquired a thin and unlived-in appearance. Blades looked around and failed to repine. It merely seemed appropriate.

A handcart through a Grandfather clock ought not to go. At best it takes the contents passed in item by item and then the cart after them, with much tilting and profanity. Finally, the owner and propellant follows on and reverses the process. It was no way for a King to enter his realm and Blades pondered the problem as he proposed to traverse the dimensions. Maybe if one or both side panels were dispensed with and the head of the timepiece *nailed* to the wall? That wouldn't be in accord with his father's wishes but already that voice was growing dim and distant. Time and changed circumstances altered cases. It was the way of the world – any world.

The decision was made: he'd see to it during his next – and maybe last – visit to the old universe.

And then, at first attempt, he and his burden were accepted whole. One corner introduced to the *'gap'* was enough to admit all. Both driver and vehicle were through.

Blades marvelled at it – but only for a while. Like some well-stretched Portsmouth whore, the thing accepted any size of visitor, perhaps any number of sailors. That was nice.

Already changed but not noticing, he failed to prod the good luck *'just to be sure'*. He just took it as his due and moved on.

Reality's breached hymen was left behind, hanging there dependably like it always did. Curate Blades gave it barely a thought as he trundled his cart across the Downs. He was looking forward to his hero's welcome, he felt in celebratory mood. There was claret in the provisions before him – and maybe, if asked politely, one of the savage women, bathed and combed, might care to carouse with him. It was just a thought – he wouldn't insist: he wasn't *that* sort of king.

The dead cannot welcome or embrace anyone. Their devoured remains, the unsavoured parts and the 'kills-just-for-sport' littered the front of the burrow. Its entrance was widened, raped into a cavity dug out by relentless claws. Blades could have entered standing erect, with room to spare. He could have but didn't care to.

They'd come for his trusting subjects whilst he was preparing their salvation. They'd come for revenge.

Whilst he haggled in Guildford or Kingston, they'd cowered in the tunnels as the Null clawed their angry way towards them. He hadn't been with them at the end. Perhaps they had prayed that he might appear, even in the final moments, to make all right with his thunder stick – but he had not. Brother Silas had been muttering about the shortage of coinage and Speed had insisted on Thursday evensong. He hadn't been there – where it mattered, when it mattered. The barrowload of civilisation fell from nerveless hands. Curate Blades bowed his head, not in prayer but shame.

For a long while he stayed thus, not much caring if the Null returned to finish the job. He knew he could go home – complete with bloody barrow – and restock his shelves and cupboards. He could be a Curate again – forever – and no one would know any different. He thought all those things and accepted them but they were made of mist. They held no appeal. Sooner the swift (ish) fangs of the Null than return to . . . littleness.

Then he noticed the dead monster. Thought of them had made him look closer and better. There was only one but it lay there, huge and purple: incontrovertible. A stick spear protruded from its eye socket. The breeze gently moved the shaft and thus the head attached. The lifeless thing appeared to be nodding agreement to something.

Thomas Blades took it as a sign and gave thanks for it. He *had* taught them a new dignity, he had made a difference! They'd fought and gone to their maker with honour.

It was a lacy sort of compensation: one to handle gently for fear of tearing, but better than nothing. Therein was a spark to light the fire of carrying on.

Blades tore free of the tempting waves of despair, denied himself the pleasure of surrender and took a step. From that one could come another and then many.

He entered the sundered barrow – an easy stroll now – and lit a rush taper when growing gloom obliged. He wanted to read the story of the end, discern it from the pattern of digging and death, before he pressed on to . . . somewhere.

Blades had attended a single badger hunt and imagined this to have been much the same – but from Brock's perspective. They'd tunnelled furiously, driving straight to the deepest levels and the heart of the matter, leaving side rooms and other nooks for later attention. On reaching bottom the Null had killed luxuriantly, ravaging the womenfolk and infants, then drawing out the remaining males to feast upon above. Those were the remains he'd first seen: the remnants of either butchery or torture. With them they must have dragged their own sole casualty and Blades hoped that innovation robbed relish from the feeding.

There was nothing here for him: what wasn't dead was smashed and the torchlight revealed only sprays of blood: a repetitive tale that swiftly grew tedious. The Curate turned on his heels.

They must have smelt *him*, not the reverse, which wasn't very flattering when you thought about it. Blades didn't think about it till long after. He was too preoccupied with joy.

A section of the earth wall collapsed. Blades had his pistol trained on it in an instant. A bereaved man is a dangerous opponent, being streamlined and focused by events. The Curate was surprised by the steadiness of both torch and gun grip.Behind the false covering of packed soil there was a trellis of woven split-sticks. Hands grasped it from behind, wrestling it free from firm placing. Human hands.

Finally the barrier shot forth and to the ground. Humanity literally leapt from the hidden cavity behind. *First-met* was amongst them, *Jezebel* also. They were pitiful, rank and few and weeping, but glad. Curate Blades had to suppress his own pleasure to be strong for their sake. That would become the pattern of the years to come.

Some had wonderfully evaded the Null: at the last they'd hidden and waited, in silence and in faith, for his return. He had not failed them.

He so far forgot himself as to embrace the leaders, ignoring the stink of confinement and fear. That never occurred again and so it lived on in tribal legend. Unwittingly, the Curate had selected his apostles and anointed them. Since there was no present means of discourse it was as good a method as any.

They besieged his ankles and soaked his shoes with tears – for what had happened and what would. The braver ones touched the pistol to share in its power. Already he had changed them. Not even the Null's terrible reprisal could restore them to the old ways. They treasured dreams of restitution.

48

Blades saw that and concurred.

'That's right,' he told them, even though they couldn't understand. 'Never again. That I swear to you. *Never* again!'

' "*Go forth and multiply. Replenish the earth, and subdue it: and have dominion over the fish of the sea and over the fowl of the air, and over every living thing that moveth upon the earth*" – and the Null!'

He read from, and amended, the Good Book not because he needed to – there were whole sections of it securely shelved in the library of his mind – but because the shaggies found it terribly impressive.

True, they might not know what '*fish*' and '*the sea*' were but it still did the trick. He'd explain the fullness of it some other time. Meanwhile, the poor creatures needed all the encouragement he could provide to venture forth in broad day.

That same bright, crisp, sunshine was auspicious. Blades lifted his head to its touch and expressed thanks.

It was felt important that they did not arrive by skulking night. The unenlightened far-burrows needed to be impressed by a human out and about by day. There was a tall-sounding story for them to swallow, requiring every assistance to help it to go down and inspire delegates to return for instruction.

Blades raised his hand in blessing. He looked and saw that they were joyous, for all their – only natural – fears. These evangelists were eager to harvest men.

He was proud of them – and himself. Some would be Null-eaten, some would be disbelieved and enslaved, sewing their seed on stony ground. Yet surely some would return with reinforcements from the other tribes.

If not, if need be, he'd take musket in hand and go fetch them personally, like the Reverend Speed dragging Quakers to church. Despite himself, he now almost saw the bellowing-man's point. There was *good news* to spread, news of a new dispensation . Like it or not, no one should miss it.

He waved them away and his missionaries scattered to all four points of the compass.

To the Reverend Samuel Speed, Esq.
The Vicarage,
By St. Peter and St Pauls'
Godalminge
Ye County of Surrey
ye 23 daye of March, the year of our salvation 1681.

Sir,

I have had the surly privilege of being yor Curate this last two year but now I shall trouble you no moor.

I resign, relinquish and lay aside my post forthwith, this very minute.

There is much I would wish to say to you but its recitation would not be Christian. In-stead, I shall recount to you a curious dream which came to me last night: viz.

I 'magined that I had dyed and gone to Hell. I did not think that right but bore the injustice judgement meekly – as I have borne all your 'damn you's and 'damn your eyes'. Hell, I shall tell you, that you may be prepared, is a vast array of chairs laid out in lines before the infernal fire. The nearest are the most afflicted. I looked and looked for a place for myself but could find none: all were occupied by sinners in torment. At last I came to the front and there, in the very epicentre most close to the blaze, was one seat, all empty. I took it and roasted but soon enough the devil came up to me and quoth:

'What do you here, Tom Blades, you dog? You are allotted to the other place. Vacate that seat right now! 'tis reserved for the Reverend Speed!'

Suffice to say, as I hope never to set eyes on you again in this life, so am I confident that I, a blameless man, shall not see you in the next.

I only conclude in affirming I wished your wife had been as open to me as your roaring mouth ever was. She owns, if you will excuse *me, the finest bum in Surrey – fit enough for fame in London – and quite wasted on a eunuch such as you.*

I am no longer, sir, your faithful servant

Thos. Blades

'Anglo-Saxon,' he concluded, at length. 'Not yet Alfred the Great and a flowering of culture – but not pagan pirates either. We're midway between the two ages, but definitely on our way up.'

It wasn't bad going – a mere decade ago they had been stone age, no argument – and grim stone age at that. It still didn't look pretty but you had to compare with what went before. They had *books* here now – albeit a few and those well secured in a chained library, naturally.

To himself, in his own thoughts, he would always be *curate* but others bestowed more *regal* titles now – and he graciously allowed them their way. The scene before him entirely justified such tolerance. Curate or Bishop or King Blades swept a drink-softened eye over his people at play . . . They weren't so awful, he thought. He could – just – recall many worse communities: Godalming's Councillors and Aldermen for instance – and say what you like: this lot were at least loyal.

As if to prove his unspoken point, the nearest (and soberest) warriors, his own guard, the *huscarls*, raised their drinking-horns and voices in his praise. Roared and slurred the words were indistinct but still plain to him through a thousand repetitions.

'Hail Blades, visitor from Heaven!
Bane of the Null and saviour of Mankind!
Bring us muskets! Bring us powder!
We swear to you our aim is true!
'Hail Blades, Hope from God-al-ming!
Shitter on the Null and protector of our babes!

51

Bring us sharp swords! Bring us daggers!
We swear to you our blows shall bite!'

And so on through as many verses as weapon types he'd brought through. He thought it rough, deficient in melody – but rather touching for all that.

It was warm in the Great Hall, a delicious contrast to the winter gale outside. The central hearth roasted those too close and froze the unfavoured by the outer walls, but on the raised dais, round Curate Blades and his nobles it was just right, entirely as planned. Young warriors considered it a signal honour – and promise of possible favour if they continued in heroism – to be invited to warm themselves in that cosy zone.

His senior wives, proven breeders of sons, sat beside him, all haughty and beautiful, shimmering and liquid-curved in other-world silks. The lady Jezebel presided over all. Through long intimacy they'd each learned of his kind heart and given trouble of late accordingly. The Curate had had to remind them that ten years back they were mud-covered chattels cowering in tunnels. Some chose to listen to him – or pretended to.

More pliable were his trusted lieutenants, likewise gathered about him behind the high table; those he embraced that fateful day, those he'd later chosen. Firstmet – he'd taken it as name, not description – was chief amongst them, a scarred veteran of the struggle to stay above ground. He'd lost an ear and eye in the process but, overall, gained in the bargain. No one was fiercer in battle or more subtle in tribal management than Firstmet; no one had more Null tokens pinned to his cabin, yet no one had greater love than he for the man who'd first raised him to his feet. He dogged Curate Blades like a second shadow, learning and loving.

Blades called for more barley-beer and beef. It was with him in an instant, pages jostling each other to be the one. He wasn't really that fussed, but heroic consumption seemed expected by the ever-watching throng. Most of it went surreptitiously down into the absorbent floor-rushes or ditto hunting dogs. If anyone noticed nothing was said.

Being uncharitable, they were a barbaric sight: all pelt and leather clad, treasured weapons close to hand. The company was not much leavened by the civilising presence of the fairer sex, who were mostly outside in the weaving sheds or with their babies or doing something useful when they weren't sleeping. King Blades I deplored that even as he recognised its sad necessity. When they were above mere subsistence and bred to sufficient numbers, he had *plans* to do something or other about it.

Meanwhile he tried to steer his amorous propensities away from the lickable-as-a-plate serving girl carting round the ale-jugs. It didn't do to take advantage – not too often or blatantly anyway. Sadly, she'd noted his sly glance and, desirous of wifedom and glory, used hips and eyes to answer *yes, yes, yes!*

It wasn't all plain sailing being a god-king in the making.

All the same, the years had been good: a bit of a haze maybe, blood-flecked and gut-churning certainly, but on the whole, in the round, not too bad.

They'd established themselves under God's open sky (or rather, he had), enjoying His Sun and rain when it suited them, as their maker intended. The jump had been made from overgrown-rabbit rabbitdom to full humanity. There had been pain and reverses in the process but now a fortified village stated their right to be above ground all the time. The Null assailed it constantly but had not prevailed. They'd grown to respect the whiff of black powder . . .

Things were getting raucous down amongst the lower benches: the younger warriors growing beer-brave and boastful. The Curate saw them comparing the beautiful guns and swords he'd bestowed on them, spinning tales, true or not, of their exploits. Spaces were swept clear of food remnants to recreate battles past, pots and knives serving as Men and Null. Beer was spilt and blood likewise – in memory.

The Curate did not discourage them. His huscarls would watch but ignore all but the grossest of behaviour. The vanguard of the people must be allowed their head, however painful the noise and sight to higher sensitivities, the better to hone them through long winter nights for the summer's campaigns.

Humanity was now off its knees and Curate Blades fully intended it should soon stand erect, looking whoever – or whatever – may be straight in the eye. That prize was worth almost any price. Afterwards, he could always make amends to God and morality, patching up some or other peace. Necessity was an implacable mistress: the Divinity would surely know that and so be at least as indulgent a Lord as Blades was. Surely.

Knowing that his presence inhibited them Curate Blades left his people to their play. Besides, the hall was now smoky, an irritant to eyes and nose: he would benefit from a stroll, a head-clearing, interlude before the intriguing prospects of bed.

His wives and concubines and huscarls rose with him. He considered and then signalled which of each should accompany him – in their own separate roles – for the night ahead.

Two huscarls unbarred the thick door at the rear of the hall and he slipped out as quiet as possible, into the starry dark. There were the signs and sounds of industry to greet him. Lights shone in the factory huts, musketeers patrolled the stockade walls. Beyond, teams of humans toiled, taking advantage of the Null-free night. Master of all, he sighed with pleasure. Everything was as it should be.

Curate Blades then thought he'd go and inspect the slaves' labours before he turned in. Whilst he strolled he sought not to recall their recruitment.

The *Ancient and Honourable Armourers Company* of the City of London really pushed the boat out for their annual dinner. First there was communion in St Ethelrelda's, processing there in order of precedence – which was always good for a laugh and a scuffle. Then followed a business meeting to rack up next year's prices and admit the new apprentices at one end and incorporate the freshly qualified at the other. There was also the question of the Company's extensive investments and property holdings to discuss and have a good wrangle over; its wide farms in Kent and Essex and rented-out shops and dwellings in the Home Counties, towns like . . . Godalming, for instance.

After that they could doff their heavy robes and chains of honour and were one speech away from the best drink-up and dinner of the year. The Company got the silver cutlery out and hired in flunkies. In the days beforehand, out in the Company's farms, there was a holocaust of cattle, lambs, geese and chicken, destined for their laden table. They pulled in favours from London Docks and secured exotic fruit and other delicacies out of ships new in from all over the world. Generally, there was also a conversation piece, a really special surprise, some huge and appropriate confection: maybe a currant-pudding like a cannon or muskets made of marzipan.

In sum, if they weren't fed and watered to bursting point, if there wasn't enough to talk about all through next year, then the departing Master of the Company, whose responsibility it was, would leave office head hung in shame. The annual feast made or broke a Master's reputation, never mind how good his guns were.

The wives took themselves and their new-purchased finery away after church and the formal Company meeting. Then the men could prime their appetites over an ale or four. A lot of real business got done – no contract signing or lawyers amongst trade-brothers; their simple word sufficient to seal a deal.

Also around that time, their specially invited guests from the Army and Navy, and all the associated trade Guilds would trickle in one by one. There seemed more than last year, enough to be remarked upon. The more single-minded 'guts' amongst the Armourers wondered if there would be enough feast to go round.

That was later remembered – by the survivors.

' . . . whereas the Portuguese levy duty *after* the affixing of the firelock, which if you tot it all up and compare the final price the makers get, makes further comment on my part superfluous, don't you think, brothers? I urge that the Company most urgently lobbies his Majesty to reconsider the infamous and iniquitous system of taxing by his Customs House. And since he has graciously relinquished responsibility for this part of government to his . . .'

The wine had flowed well, even through the Master's speech, and he permitted himself a jocular little pause. It got the hoped for laughs and shouted alternatives.

'. . . *friend*, the Duchess of Portsmouth, I suggest we first approach her . . .'

'Not like he does!' yelled one wag. The Master *looked*. It proved to be tolerable: a drunken mastercraftsman, not some pudding-head apprentice.

'. . . with our humble suggestions – and a modicum of gold. Now, turning to the vexed question of solder prices . . .'

'Actually,' said a slim figure, rising to his feet, 'I wanted to make a suggestion here.'

It was unprecedented. Right back into the days when the Armourers contested with the Bowyers for death-dealing supremacy, it had always been the Master's privilege to speak uninterrupted at the annual dinner, on any subject that came into his head. Heckling: yes, in moderation; groans and sighs; not unknown – but a takeover bid: never!

The gathering turned as one to face the sacrilegious speaker. As it happened that suited him very well: he wouldn't have to raise his voice.

'What I'd like to suggest, if you don't mind,' Curate Blades said softly, unfastening his long coat, 'is that you raise your hands and follow me.'

That got a better laugh than the Master's witticism – until it was backed up by a brace of pistols. Other men dotted round the room's outer fringes, presumed servants till now, also revealed themselves as armed. At the same moment the vast double doors of the dining hall crashed open, to admit a cloud of hairy men bearing muskets.

That the Master spotted one as of his own manufacture only added insult to injury.

'Stand you. Stand you still. If you please.'

The coachman didn't please and made as if to whip the horses on. The Highwayman shot him.

His sincerity thus proven, he was obeyed. The coach guard reined in and let fall all thoughts of his blunderbuss stowed under the top seat. He then climbed down to join the passengers standing out on the Great West Road.

Other armed and black-clad figures reinforced their compatriot but only he seemed to have the authority to speak.

'You now tell me what you do – what *work* you do?' he ordered his dejected prisoners, emphasising his wish with a wave of an unfired pistol.

They couldn't place him at all. His English wasn't child-learned but a language late come to. A foreigner accordingly, and so all the more deserving the noose each victim now visualised. The accent, though, was even more puzzling: it was English from nowhere, a mangled mating of all sorts of dialects.

'Heaven forfend,' said one of the passengers, an elegant young fop, 'I should try to teach you your job, but isn't it our money you should be after, not our ranks or profession?'

He held out his (second) purse. The first and real one was cunningly stowed in a false lining to his coat. The road west across Heath Row was notorious and travellers knew to take precautions.

The Highwayman brushed it clinkingly aside and rested his gun upon the young brow.

'No. Not gold, not coin: what job?'

'Well, I . . . I don't actually . . . there's no call for me to . . . Father's allowance . . .'

A growl shut him up. His assailant moved on down the line.

'You – what you do?'

'Merchant: molasses mostly, but some spices and . . .'

'You?'

'Master tailor.'

57

'Surgeon.'

'Foundrymaster.'

Some things had to be explained to him: his vocabulary was strangely lacking. Nevertheless, quick on the uptake, some definitions were roughly curtailed, others plainly welcomed. In his own curious, foreign way, he was separating sheep from goats.

'You lot, no good. Stay here. You lot come.'

There was only-to-be-expected consternation and tearful partings but the criminal emphasised the strength of his desires and secured obedience, by shooting – one, two, three, four – the horses; primed pistols being passed to him in quick succession. A tear adorned the coachguard's eye.

'Am sorry, the Highwayman told them. 'Good cause. Goodbye.'

The rich, the idle, the ladies of leisure were left behind, unrobbed, with nothing worse to fear than a long walk across Heath Row.

The rest, the skilled and useful, were escorted away to start a much longer journey.

'In this little pleasant valley, the Springs serve not only to water the Grounds, but for the driving of 18 powder Mills. 'tis a little commonwealth of powdermakers, who are as black as Negroes. Here is a nursery of Earth for the making of Salt-Petre: There is also here a Boyling-House, where the Salt-Petre is made, and shoots: a Corneing House, and separating and finishing Houses, all very well worth the seeing of the Ingenious. I had almost forgot the Brimstone Mill, and the Engine to search it.

'Many of the Mills were blown up in a little more than half a year's time of my seeing them, the cause a mystery though but a slighte one . . .'

Chilworth Powder Mills. Circa 1680s. From John Aubrey's 'Natural History and Antiquities of the County of Surrey'. published 1718 – 19.

'. . . whatever the cause, the late Seventeenth century disaster seems to have been a thorough-going one. When the shrewd Sarah Churchill, Duchess of Marlborough and lesbian lover of Queen Anne, commissioned a survey of the site after buying Chilworth Manor, she cavilled at the extent of investment required. The pulverising and incorporating and stamping mills, not to mention the skilled workforce, all seem entirely gone . . .'

Dr Wayne Cocroft PhD (Cambrensis) FSA.
'A Dangerous Energy – Towards a Post-Processualist Archaeology of the English Gunpowder Industry and Stuart Patriarchal Militarist-Mercantile Complex'.
The Royal Commission for England and Wales, 1998.

Being an interview with Sir Polycarpus Wharton, gent. Proprietor of ye Chilworth Gunpowder Company, Surrey. Contractor to ye English board of Ordnance. Rendered into good New-Wessex tongue by Lord Null-ear Firstmet at the command of his sovereign Lord, Emperor Blades I, ruler under Divine sanction of New-Wessex and the Protectorates. Closer of the Burrows, Sanctioner of Sunlight, Defender of the Faith.

Q: What is gunpowder?
A: 'tis a mixture, made up of 7½ parts saltpetre to 1½ parts charcoal to 1 part of brimstone.
Q: What is saltpetre?
A: It's made on site. We have our own boiling house.
[pause]
A: AAAAAAA
Q: Answer the question.
A: May your mother's pimp desert her. You are the scraping of Satan's nostrils. You . . . AAAAAA. Do not hurt me any more, I pray you.
Q: Answer the question.

Blades set the document aside. He didn't know whether to feel guilty or exasperated or both.

'When I asked for a transcript,' he told Firstmet, 'I meant of salient matters, not every *um* and *ah* – or AAAAA, for that matter.'

Blades could tell that Firstmet was hurt, despite his stoical expression. He relented. The man had only been obeying orders – and to the letter as usual.

'Never mind. I'm sure it will contain just what we want. You did well.'

That swelled Firstmet's chest and the Curate returned to the task. It was a funny thing when a till-recent savage's handwriting was better than his tutor's. He deserved praise for that as well. He didn't get it.

A: *Saltpetre comes from manure. Pigeon houses give the best stuff. You make a distillation . . .*

Q: *What is charcoal?*

A: *Don't you know what char . . . OWWWWW. Charcoal is part-burnt wood, done real slow. We use alder or willow from special coppices . . .*

Q: *What are alder, willow and coppices?*

A: *They're bloody trees, man. How much longer . . .*

Blades skipped the next few pages. The *People*'s vocabulary didn't presently distinguish between types of tree.

Q: *What is brimstone?*

A: *Damned if I know. It comes from Sicily. You can't get it nowhere else. It just arrives in casks. I don't ask, I just uses it.*

'Damn, damn, damn.' That put the proverbial bung in the barrel.

Q: *What is Sicily? . . .*

Well, they'd have to find that out for themselves soon enough.

You couldn't rely on supplies from the old world for ever. They must become self-sufficient.

'Next trip over,' he told Firstmet, 'I've a new task for you. Kidnap shipbuilders. Oh, – and a ship's crew or two.'

There were surely bits of that he didn't understand but the Curate could be confident he'd find out. Lord Firstmet was reliability personified: just right for the pioneer visit to New-Sicily – and thus too useful to be spared for it.

Talking of 'sparing' things made him consider his useful servant's feelings. Though he had what he wanted he skimmed diligently to the end of the document.

Q: *One final question. Where is your stock of prepared powder?*
A: *In that fortified store there. Why?*
Q: *After you help us dismantle some mills, we must cover the loss with explosions. You will assist.*
A: *Never! Never!*
Q: *Then you will accompany us home to your new position and managership. Chil-worth shall be reborn elsewhere. Thank you for your cooperation, Sir Polycarpus.*
A: *Help! Help! Infamy! [and etc. etc.]*

Curate Blades looked up. The former protester, now glorious in gold braid, looked well reconciled: even thriving. What a difference a few days and second thoughts make.

'There, there, Sir Polycarpus. It didn't turn out so bad, did it?'

Earl Chilworth, as he now was, couldn't argue.

'T'wasn't well explained,' he replied, excusing himself and beaming. 'My lord Firstmet should have said. There, I only had debtors prison to look forward to. Business wasn't good, and the Government paid late and poor. Whereas here . . .'

He spread his hands wide, indicating his present health and wealth and, beyond the Castle, the broad lands and properties in New-Wessex instantly his. Thanks to the Null, 'business' in this new world looked wonderfully promising: he would be valued. No slave he, but a partner in the enterprise, a vital cog to be kept well oiled and cared for. It was all more than fair exchange for 'democracy'. Much good that had done him.

Curate Blades returned the smile, looking down from his high throne.

'There you are then,' he said, finally settling the balance between them, 'All's well that ends well.'

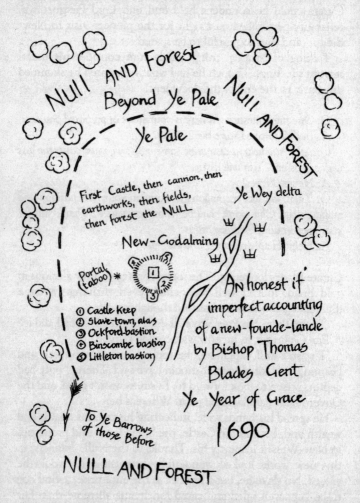

Null AND Forest
Beyond Ye Pale   Null AND FOREST
Ye Pale

First Castle, then cannon, then earthworks, then fields, then forest the NULL

Ye Wey delta

New-Godalming

Portal (taboo) *

① Castle keep
② Slave-town, alas
③ Ockford-bastion
④ Binscombe bastion
⑤ Littleton bastion

An honest if imperfect accounting of a new-founde-lande by Bishop Thomas Blades Gent Ye Year of Grace 1690

To Ye Barrows of those Before

NULL AND FOREST

Had he not been trussed like a chicken, the Captain would have kicked himself. There was ample opportunity for reflection and retrospect now.

At the time he'd had major doubts about those dockside recruits but avarice had overruled good instinct. The shaggy mongrel-men had been willing to work dirt-cheap and their weird English and unguessable origins were as nothing to that. Hadn't he once had an Eskimo sign up on a Newfoundland run? He'd proved all right – in the end.

So he'd taken them on, no questions asked. They'd come as a job-lot: his crew problems solved in one swoop. He'd had confidence a bit of shouting and the bosun's boot would soon teach them seamanship.

It turned out they had lessons to teach him. Like how to smuggle weapons aboard without his knowledge and take over a ship in short order. They were barely out of Portsmouth before there was a pistol shoved up his nostril. It was all very efficient; obviously pre-planned – rehearsed even. Surprise was total, and ruthlessly exploited. The Captain doubted Bosun even got to realise he was dead. His was the only resistance. He was long overboard now.

On reflection, the Captain wondered whether he actually wanted to survive. He didn't wish to be recalled in every south coast tavern as the master who lost his ship before it cleared the Solent.

Even deep down in the hold, he could tell they were heading back to shore. Every shoal and wreck from Portsmouth to Dover appeared for inspection in his mind. He just couldn't conceive where they might be aiming at. A Kent or Sussex harbour was out of the question. Everyone knew *The Lady Bridget*: her looks, her master and business. The pirates would be detected in minutes. Could they be that stupid or audacious? Yet, Gospel-convinced of their bearing, he could think of no other alternative.

The vital missing clue, not available to him in his confinement, was already hoving into sight. A horde of men – as 'shaggy' and mysterious as their comrades aboard – were waiting on Pevensey strand as the ship sped to shore. Their first glimpse of it was accompanied by a jig of joy. They knew just what to do: cranes and blocks and tackle were ready. The great Blades had so commanded. Within an hour of its beaching the ship would be de-fleshed; stripped of all things useful; left as skeletal puzzlement for the tide to deal with. With luck no one would ever know. Ships often went down without trace and enquiries weren't unduly prolonged.

Everything: from cannon and sails and mast and reusable timbers, to ropes and gear and saucy full-bosomed figurehead, went into waiting covered wagons en route to the capacious portal. Likewise, (bound and gagged) the seamen with their many skills and talents. Soon enough, when they'd taught their trade to sufficient others, they'd be off on the New-Sicily brimstone run. Everything and everyone would find a good home in the new world.

Unaware of the exciting fate life held in store for him, deep in the damp hold, the Captain dreamt dreams of his tormentors on the end of a rope – and him tugging on their legs, just to make sure of it.

Meanwhile, *The Lady Bridget* sped on to ravishment on Pevensey beach.

'Ye Shaggy Men in London Againe

Reports continue this week to abound – from men and women of sober countenance and known God-afeared, non-tippling, station – of ye so-called shaggy-men padding the streets of the City, privily by night or dusk, on errands known only to them and the Almighty.

After the outraging of the Armourers' dinner, and intrusions into the domestic bosoms of divers mechanicals, 'tis feared that Jesuits and Papists have commissioned the gradual disarming of the English nation, employing savage serviles from the furthest reaches of their dark empire to abduct those most useful in our defence.

The City militia and guardians of the Docks have doubled their sentinels to thwart the machinations of the Pope's emissaries in these Isles but, to date, none of the invaders have been detained to be put to question. One of such ilk, apprehended on Surrey Quay last Thursday week, and suspected of ill, cast himself into the depths, preferring watery death to capture. Such is the thrall in which Papistry casts a man's – even a shaggy man's – soul.

The Duke of York, James Stuart, a open and proclaimed Papist, was closely quizzed by THIS REPORTER *as he attended ye House of Lords two days gone, but he claimed no knowledge of the strange invasion: denying to this face, that he hid and succoured the said shaggy men in his own rooms . . .'*

'The Protestant Flail & Gazette' July 1681

'And you, brother?'

'There are no *brothers* here, slaves have no *brothers*.'

The weary man steeled himself to another try.

'Then, fellow slave, tell me: how long have you slaved?'

The smith paused in his hammering to consider. He dared not stop too long. The other-worlder guards were vigilant and merciless. By now he had taught untold apprentices his trade; he was no longer indispensable.

'You lose tracks of days; this furnace is my sun: it still shines whilst I sleep. Other smiths serve it as I rest. Maybe ten years: I call to mind ten Christmases.'

The enquirer faltered at the bellows. The smith noted it – and the guard's sudden attention.

'Ever onward, bellow-slave. Ever onward. 'tis the first year that's the worst.'

He realised his assistant was fresh into this Hell world, new into a blurred life of labour in sunken huts under harsh masters. Residual charity led the smith to try and save him the guardian's lash.

'More air! Faster! That's better. Keep it going. Now, slave, what were ye in the before place?'

'Where?' He was distracted: lost in surveying the landscape of his despair.

'Earth: England. You are there no longer. Accept it. What were you?'

65

Rather than think on and sip bitter conclusions, the man decided just to answer.

'A lawyer.'

The smith laughed – a rare sound in the forge, attracting dark glances. He stifled it.

'A lawyer? A land-pirate? What did they want *you* for?'

That question had apparently already occurred. The man shook his sweat-streaked head.

'I know not. I was at my brother's manufactory . . .'

'Ahh . . .' said the smith, as though that explained all.

'. . . he is – was – a barrel cooper. He would not come: they ran him through . . .'

'As they will you if y' don't bellow harder.'

The memory made him redouble his efforts.

'I told them: "*I have no **dextrous** skill. I plead in the assizes*". They smiled – smiled at me over my brother's corpse – and said "*come along in any case.*"'

The smith should have had more sympathy but he was jealously husbanding the last drops in the jar. There was none to spare on strangers.

'You're here now; best get used to it. No more "*m' luds*" and "*my client pleads*" for you. You're a labourer, nothing more: no skills to teach – and that's a hard road hereabouts.'

'But . . . why . . . why?' He might have been addressing either the smith or the Almighty, it was hard to say. The smith answered anyway – it being far from sure that God had any presence in this realm.

'Because we're building a mighty empire, that's why: not that you'll see much of it from a slave hut. There's great things going on outside: fruits of our knowledge and labour.'

The ragged ex-lawyer looked at the wattle walls as though he could pierce them by wish alone.

'I hadn't thought to die in servitude . . .' he mumbled wistfully.

The smith barked harsh amusement.

''Spose not: that what lawyers put other souls in, 'ain't it?'

The gibe bounced off his distraction.

'We could escape. We are not chained. I have glimpsed open countryside.'

The notion sponsored an especially hard hammer blow.

'Oh aye, you try it; they'll not hinder a mere labourer constructing an example to others. It'll be your last service to them.'

'Why not? We are many, we could take arms. Spartacus . . .'

'Think on, widow-robber.' The smith spoke harshly: the reciting of their joint predicament had soured his temper. 'Consider why we toil at guns and swords and halberds, ponder why earth-ramparts and fort making are all your future till exhaustion claims ye. No, bellow-man: he yonder with the lash is your best friend, poor as it is. He stands before ye and something worse.'

The lawyer couldn't comprehend it: this was surely the worst of places. Jealous of such innocence the smith wished to rob him of any remaining comfort. He knew it was unworthy, a petty slave feeling, but what did that matter in *this* place?

'Go and see,' he told him. 'Walk out: no one will stop 'ee. Go on – the Null are everywhere. They're waiting for you!'

'High Medieval,' Curate Blades told the world. The wind carried his words away; no one heard. 'Richard Lion-Heart maybe: early Plantagenet, pre-cathedrals.'

He looked on. First there was castle, then cannon and earthworks, then fields, then forest, then Null. It was progress. Better than just burrows, then Null.

Other than in the land he'd carved out, that was the situation elsewhere, as far as was known. They were too busy for idle exploration but even in the dense forests of New-Sicily *they* were reported, besieging the fortified brimstone works. The ships plying the seas between, carrying the precious cargo, reported Null on the lonely coastlines they tacked along; beasts who stupidly chased the ships, screaming fury at the inexplicable sight. Free-standing humanity was beleaguered, a fact that could reconcile you to many things.

Chance insisted he be looking down upon the smithy at that very moment. The distance – real and social – between the hut and high tower barred him from the conversation within. He'd never know what was passing between the two doomed men, not that he'd have disagreed with a single word. It didn't matter. There were weightier things on his mind than slave chatter.

The castle was solidity enough, stone firmness, crystallised effort, to support a wealth of – necessary – injustice. Blades saw it as an achievement, bought with blood and sweat, not fit to be undermined by whining conscience. He'd slapped all that nonsense down till it stopped moving. Its sole residue was regret. He regretted the antlike activity of slave-town even as he oversaw it.

As the Good Book that he no longer preached suggested, he raised his eyes to the hills. There was his justification. The North Downs, the Wey valley; both were green just now, but often enough they were black with Null.

King – or Curate – Blades sighed, but not hard and not for long.

'Harsh necessity . . .' he lamented, and fastidiously withdrew from the scene.

Behind the balcony lay still further excuse for a modicum of cruelty – like spacious apartments, books, paintings, refinements; all the panned-gold of being alive. Burton's *Melancholia* sat – alas, unread – on the shelf, a stolen Lely oil observed the scene. The bedroom was warm and inviting, and its occupants likewise.

The Anglo-Saxon phase had had no opportunity, no place for *love*. Then they were still precarious invaders, forced to single-mindedly address life's demands. When existence was just food and fighting and sleep; mere survival, then *love* was only breeding and the satisfying of an urge, hurriedly assuaged, without sophistication. He blamed the Null for that.

But now they were High Medieval and the Curate recalled

'courtly love' and 'chivalry'. He had explained the concepts to his courtiers and the *Corps of Cultural Diffusers* and they'd set to work. At first there were some memorable disasters: unconsummated marriages, maidenheads neglected and maidens rampant, but gradually the good drove out the bad. Now, fine examples of high ideals were known – even if they didn't abound – and they set a tone even for those who chose not to follow.

As for the earlier excesses; constant war whittled them away. Those ladies who'd gained a taste for command were left to forge their own, new way. The Curate instituted a unit of Amazons amongst his knights for them and ensured they saw their fair share of battle amidst the greater struggle. God – the real one, not the temporary Bladian version – would decide if the experiment should prevail or perish.

For himself, the Curate preferred a middle way between the brutish and over-sophistication. A true marriage, he knew, came from long trial and error and practice. Accordingly, he married often in order to acquire perfection.

The dress code he'd promulgated over recent years tended towards the black: stern fashions out of his puritan youth crossbred with the fancy style of the Spanish Counter-Reformation – as imagined by a Surrey village boy. By day it represented decorum, by night (or whenever else his fancy rose) the snowy miracles of the female form were thereby enhanced. The nice thing about absolute rule was the ability to form the visual landscape. Curate Blades now moved amongst a lacy-gothic paradise of his own creation.

Two wives awaited him: on his schedule and with schedules of their own.

'First me,' said one. 'I have something to ask.'

As his first-wife, Jezebel had that right – as well as sons by him and proxy-ambitions. She was the rounder of the two, the most Mrs Speed-like. And though he'd largely sated that fixation by now and cast his nets of lust wider, it remained hard to refuse her anything since, once placated, she'd likewise offer *anything*. The Curate was like putty – then a ramrod, then putty again – in her hands.

'So be it, sister.' Wife two was reticent, retiring. 'But do not drain him: I wish to converse.'

Surprisingly, Boudicca was the more desirable. She was mild and irregularly formed. She limped badly. Tireless efforts had not raised a child from her but she was kind. Likewise, only kindness stirred her to passion. It made for hard work but was very arousing. Blades had transformed Boudicca's life by introducing spectacles into the Empire. For the first time her world ceased to be mist and the first true-visage she greeted was the Curate's long face.

'*Shorter than a woman's gratitude*' was a proverb from his world but she was its disproof. Boudicca quietly remembered.

Blades trailed affectionate fingers across Boudicca's starched ruff, across to tickle her sharp chin. Jezebel's face directly soured and he had to reach across to placate her in the same way. There was no choosing between them and, now he reflected on it, no need to choose.

'Both,' he said, and drew them together. The two women exchanged looks he would treasure forever.

Far below, the swivel gunners on the castle walls looked out into the gloom for Null. Beneath them and their surveillance one slave shift wearily replaced another.

Come new-light the *meat* were dozy, easier to catch, less likely to wield the fire-sticks. Older warriors said their flesh was better, sweeter, when fully roused, wide awake, stretch-eyed after a chase. Maybe so but that was before. The chance was rarer now. Older Null often fell to the fire-sticks; they grew less and less. Young Null had learned better, relearned sneaking, clever-hunter skills.

He'd disengaged himself from the sleep huddle even before light. Once that would have earned him fang marks. The Null frowned on initiative. The Null were as one, did as one. Now discipline was weaker, the young did not always obey, the old did not always know best. Some even caught and fed alone, as though *individual*. Before, that would not have happened, would have meant death-by-claws. Even now, the Null-mothers would not open themselves to such as that, denying the innovators any posterity. They would not future-tread the lovely world.

Deplorable: worrying. Only in the night-huddle were they whole now, sweat-bound in species-love. And even then some slipped away early, as he had.

The Null did not know guilt, only unworthiness; a tightening of the stomach, much the same as the hunger that overwhelmed it. They always acted upon the victorious emotion: submission to the strongest, within or without, was their concept of the right. But any troubling lack could be made up for. He would hunt alone first, and then – harder, to kill that pain – with the brood.

The *meat* felled trees – by night for fear of the Null. They tidied them and reset them aloft in places of their choosing. Arrayed together they made a tall barrier the Null found hard to climb. They now did the same with the hard stones from under-soil. Those barriers were even worse than the dead trees: bruising to Null talons: anger-making.

To stock *meat* just out of reach was a provocation, a tantalising, a temptation that roused hunger even when there was no hunger. The *meat* brought their death upon themselves. It was better for them when they were more obliging to the questing teeth. The Null did not take so many then; they conserved the *meat* for future feeds. The *meat* were stupid creatures, not knowing when they were well off.

Now, even the four-legged *meat* were taken away by the selfish two legs. They rounded them up and kept them for themselves alone, hidden away behind stone and stockade. There were great herds and flocks of them accumulated. Their delicious, fearful, smell wafted on the breeze. The two-leg *meat* were no longer as savour-some. They took off their proper scent with water, they draped themselves in coverings. But there were other good reasons to still find them the best of *meat*. Hatred sprinkled relish on a mouthful.

The Null youth looked up at the high walls from his cover. The bushes irked his fine skin, there was the whiff of the killing powder that went in the fire-sticks. He had patience but he also had hunger. Some Null could not take hunger, not even for short spans. They went frenzied and fed on their own infants. That old-style spirit was approved of but it was also visible sign of decay. It had not been necessary once.

He took comfort. In the castle there were signs of waking. It was known that they had . . . tasks they performed, inexplicable things, very often early in their day. They ate, then made fire, relieved themselves. They were inattentive. And best of all, every so often . . .

The Nulls' movements were fluid but easy; their musculature well up to anything demanded of it. His face was addressing the sight as soon as it was half-glanced.

Sometimes, there was *meat* that did not wish to live with *meat*: perhaps did not wish to live at all. In ones and twos they left the habitations and work-parties and fled away. The Null loved them: for then it was like the old days. They were all fear and lively feeding. Also they were the easiest, the least likely to carry fire-sticks.

The lone figure lowered itself over the walls, clinging inexpertly to a rope; a too short rope. It dangled awhile, the essence of temptation, feebly postponing the inevitable. The ground was hard, it winded itself in landing and lay helpless a moment. The Null could have taken it there, bearing it away to feed in cover but that was to risk the creature's friends aloft. They might point a stick.

In commanding his hunger to wait the Null was punished with anger. For his kind it was like fire in the veins; all-consuming: insupportable.

The lone *meat* was up and running. The Null found the strength to wait, to postpone pleasure. That was a new facility in the species: mankind was sponsoring swift evolution amongst them. Rising on one knee, talons flexing, he let the man go past.

The lawyer-slave raced from Castle Blades thinking to find freedom. Imminent freedom from all cares followed on fast behind him.

'Angels.'

'Pardon?'

'A thousand pardons, majesty – I meant to say "majesty".'

He didn't mind, since she was new. A spot of informality, even from very junior wives, wasn't resented – in moderation, naturally. It was the substance of her response that had brought him up short.

'I'm sure you did, Guinevere. Let that pass. But what did you say about the ruins?'

She was a simpering thing, not destined to last long – hence the ill-omened nickname. After catching his eye at the coronation of all times and places, exactly when his thoughts should have been strictly Imperial and elsewhere, one thing led to another and he'd married her – a childless war-widow – out of charity, as a favour to her deserving family. They'd lost grievously to the Null lately, beyond all proportion. Now, sanctified by a brief marriage to him they'd be able to pass her on, post divorce, for a spectacular dowry. It seemed the least he could do, though right now she was proving to be hard work.

'I don't know, majesty. I can't recall.'

'You said *angels*.'

'Oh yes, that's right. The angels must have made them.'

They both turned again to the excavations. The slave hordes constructing a third defensive ditch round New-Godalming had uncovered old work in the lowest levels. One slave had earned his freedom by proclaiming the fact rather than just hacking it out. His message slowly trickled upwards towards Imperial levels and, joy of joys, news came back the same route of *his* interest.

Now the workers were stowed away in their corral so that the Emperor might see. He'd come and duly seen; and still the crumbling foundation walls told him nothing. He'd always assumed his people's past was just burrows right back to the creation and 'long-barrows' for the dead the height of their above-ground achievement. But poor though they now were, these cyclopean blocks went a long way back and once were something better. He found the notion vaguely disturbing: plainly the People didn't owe him quite everything.

She looked at him slyly. It failed to arouse, being more calculation than come-on.

'Weren't you there at the building, majesty?'

The less educated thought he was eternal: omnipresent. When time and energy permitted he disabused them of the ridiculous notion. Right now he was too tired.

'No. I must have been elsewhere that day.'

'Oh . . .'

He was no god but he *had* given them their English and all the terms in it. The notion of 'angels' must be an approximation to something from their former grunt-speak.

She was still at the early stage where his sighs frightened her. He resisted the temptation of one as a prefix to his probes.

'And who are the *angels*, Guinevere?'

'I don't know, majesty.'

'What do they look like?'

'I don't know, majesty.'

'Don't know much, do you, lady?'

'I don't know, majesty.'

The Emperor turned in despair to Firstmet.

'Do I have to cast myself on to these rocks in order to learn their secrets? What is the matter with you all?'

Firstmet recognised a joke as well as any man but still stepped between his Emperor and the precipice – just in case.

'The answer truly is not known, majesty. We have found them at rare intervals, back in below-ground days.' He turned to spit at the turf, although one of the most cultured of the new nobility. Memory of the age of humiliation was still fresh and so abhorrent to them. 'They occur only in the deepest delvings. The grannies term them *angel-craft* but no one knows.'

'As you said. How very frustrating. And these *angels*?'

'More granny talk, lord. Long ago and like unto us, only strong against the Null. One once led us against the monsters,

74

back when the barrows of *Those Before* were built. That's the tale. But I've never seen one . . . not as such.'

He faltered because he had fallen from absolute honesty in the service of their salvation. The truth was that the People believed the Emperor was angelic himself, returned to save them. Firstmet himself didn't disbelieve it. He knew Blades insisted on his plain humanity but that might just be modesty. He also didn't like those occasions when the Emperor felt the need to proclaim his mundanity. There was a feeling of . . . disappointment to it. When he saw one coming he found excuses to be elsewhere.

'*If* they lived, they left long ago,' he ended lamely. 'No one knows.'

Blades wasn't Emperor just by virtue of muskets and know-how.

'I understand now,' he placated his lieutenant, metaphorically backing off. 'You've told me all that's needful.'

That swelled out Firstmet's chest again.

'Unlike this minx,' added Blades, 'even though she's forgiven!'

Guinevere got a playful slap on the wrist and she played along, mimicking a squeal. Both wife and chief noble were happy with what they'd received.

'Why can't you be more like Lord Firstmet?' he asked her.

She considered her husband's proposition, studied the maimed and bearded soldier – and for the first time revealed hidden depths.

'I'll remind you of that tonight,' she replied with a smile – to which the Emperor of humanity had no reply.

In the event, there was no '*tonight*' – not in the sense Guinevere meant. Blades forsook her and any other's bed to return to the diggings in minimal company. Some slaves held torches, a few huscarls provided incurious security. By Imperial standards he was practically alone.

Helping hands lowered him down the scarp of the ditch and

a former publican kidnapped out of the old world positioned a
light. Otherwise he wanted no one. He was thinking.

The structure was all mud and crumble now. With no means
of telling what span separated it from former glories, there were
no lessons he could draw from it, other than the mere fact of
existence. Time passed in silence.

'Tomorrow you may dig it out,' he told a huscarl at last,
blithely confident the order would be passed on to a more
relevant person. Then he prepared to ascend back to normality.

So what, even if it were all true? There'd been *angels* in his
home world once, according to the Bible he'd preached. It was
they who'd driven Adam out of the garden, slew the first-born
of Egypt and delivered all of God's most important revelations.
Powerful beasts – but he'd ignored their existence over there, to
all intents and purposes. He could do just the same here.

'Please excuse me.'

It felt the disturbance of its last material home. Intangible
links of sentiment remained with that former fixed point, lines
gossamer-light across the years and light years.

It was from there it had launched, had first flown. Now those
fragile skeins were pulled, the '*angel*' was vaguely drawn. It felt
inclined to answer the call. There was nothing better to do for
the present. The choir of painted virgins were decades off doing
justice to the symphony it had composed upon them. They
would wait: they had no choice.

Opening ways between the worlds at will, it came and saw
and drew no conclusions. There was some surprise at certain
features, a little . . . sadness at others, but nothing untoward. No
feelings flared: it was all rather a disappointment.

That spectral petulance was perhaps why it passed among the
workmen as an angel of death. They felt the brush of its wings
and then nothing more, ever again.

A foreman saw it, the flash of its arrival; the same as it went.
He knelt – to be on the safe side – but knew in his heart he was
only a spectator. He had not been noticed.

To keep it that way he resolved not to report the matter. It was dawn; only slaves and slave masters were abroad. This was an age of wonders: they fell promiscuously from the sky. What else was the Emperor who commanded these delvings if not a gift from the One God, if not participating of his essence himself? Wonders had dragged them from burrows, had set them above ground armed with sticks that killed. Nowadays, even the Null knew fear, had learned its metal taste. Amidst all these wonders might not even a lowly foreman aspire to his very own miracle, and hug it close to the chest?

He surveyed the dead slaves and decided to say nothing.

'Dusk approaches: they will do it soon.'

Blades sincerely hoped so: his bladder was giving him stern reprimands for being so long pinned to the cold soil. It wouldn't do for the leader of humanity to wet himself. Position carried responsibilities – and many of them. Like the blessed martyr King Charles, he'd worn two vests today, lest others mistake honest shivering for cowardice.

'What if they don't?' It was a natural question. His urine couldn't be stockpiled indefinitely. There must be a contingency plan for escape from this blighted place.

Emperor Blades's chief scout, a grim hard-bitten man, winced – till he recalled who spoke. The deep lined features were rearranged.

'They will, majesty. They be beasts of habit. They can do no other. I seen it a thousand times.'

He probably had. His job, deservedly honoured and well rewarded, was to seek out the Null, to ascertain their nearest approach. He'd survived the risks it entailed for three whole years: his longest-serving colleague couldn't boast one third that. In mankind's present state his was accounted the most important subject of study there could be, more, far more, than philosophy or even the word of God. What was the use of refinement or piety if only practised during a short life in a burrow?

'When light fails the hunters come in,' the scout whispered in Blades's ear (the impertinent proximity was specially sanctioned). 'Then they feast on what they bring – live usually:

they prefer it screaming. Afterwards, the young 'uns are shepherded up round the brood mother. You see 'er there? Yon fat bloated thing: she's the size of a dozen normals, specially when 'er's laying. Otherwise there don't seem male and female like us. Can't leave 'er alone during breeding time; swive her raw, they do, go mad, fight over every 'ole: I seen it. Then rest of the year she drops cubs all the time and they're more respectful: treat her sweet. Funny arrangement. Anyhow, come nightfall they layer and mingle 'emselves on top o' 'er, writhing about like worms till they're interlinked and comfy. The best beasts toil aloft the lot and keep a weather eye out. Leastways they do nowadays, ho ho. I recall . . .'

Blades studied Scout, considered him, shut him up: tuned him out. A meditation on his life might serve to occupy the long wait, but not, please God, his anecdotes. They were the unlovely by-products of a lonely occupation.

Scout's speciality was sniping at the – comparatively – vulnerable Null sleeping piles and then haring away. Slowly but surely it took a toll of them. Perhaps his dimly glimpsed figure haunted Null dreams, spoiling the careless slumber of untold centuries past. His wiry flesh would taste especially sweet between their teeth.

Presumably that day would come, when age narrowed the margin between his start and speed and the Null's hatred. Till then he accumulated a heroic total and though there were no trophies to adorn his hut, he had young wives within, in numbers and beauty to match his daring. And even if he were caught, Scout professed not to care. His coat had patches of poison sewn within. He'd be an indigestible meal and die happy, '*taking one with him*'.

With such people to serve him, and there were legions and legions of them now, Curate Blades could have rested easy on his throne and left things to the experts. Scouts told him when the Null were coming, a hereditary caste of soldiers met them when they did. His mines and manufactories were admirably managed by specialist slaves or the replacement managers they'd trained. By rights he could have sat back in the time honoured manner of incipient god-kings and taken credit for every success (or lashed out for each failing) and not troubled his head at all.

That wasn't the Curate's way – or not yet anyway. It just struck him one day, and at the oddest moment too, when tying his cravat and being obliged by an exceptionally velvet-mouthed wench (two crucial preludes to his day), that he, he himself, didn't know enough about the Null. He hadn't actually faced them, gun in hand, since the battle of the *Those Before* barrow. No one would dream of criticising him for that: he'd acquired enough hero points in the people's eyes to be able to draw on them eternally without ever going in the red. No, it was self-reproach that he heard, whispered gibes on the very edge of internal hearing.

So, he had shed his gowns of gold, his silken slippers, and put on the brown and green of the scouts. He'd drawn a carbine from their armoury, just like a plain man, and walked on his own two feet, palanquin, coach and sedan chair left behind. He had gone forth to see – and it felt good.

The Curate was smuggled out of New-Godalming before dawn and through an obscure gate. His courtiers had pleaded for that, once they saw he would not be swayed from the larger folly. 'At the very least,' they begged, 'do not be seen to be embracing mundanity: think of your position!'

Blades was still wise enough to see that *their* position, as his closest intimates, was intimately linked to his, but he did not like to see them pained. He indulged them and left his capital like a criminal. A glorious hero's return was doubtless being arranged even as he went.

For many miles now there were fields, and fortified farms to mind them. They could be abandoned and then reoccupied if the Null overran. The beasts did not think to scour captured land with fire: they did not have that skill and saw no reason to acquire it. Homesteaders reported the beasts pausing in their attack and gazing with entranced hatred at hearth fires. They were fascinated but would not learn. The wisdom of ages past said that claws and teeth sufficed.

After a day's journey, the wild, uncleared country began: ancient wood and heath, the wide, marshy, expanse of the Thames. They crossed on a ferry where Kingston ought to be, humanity's furthest flung outpost. The ferrymen lived in a stone tower and did not expect long life. They flung themselves at Blades's feet, weeping for joy, thinking themselves forgotten. He blessed them.

Beyond that there was nothing – or almost so. Inexplicably, some few men forsook life under the Curate's dispensation and ran away. Scouts reported that some survived in obscure places, waiting for the first Null to happen on them. It seemed a novel enough – if slow – way of committing suicide. Their Emperor was happy to assist. Where he saw these signs of life the little group detoured to destroy them. Blades could not abide ingratitude.

Null land commenced a day beyond there. Bands of braves ventured further south but now they were wary. Their relaxed life was pushed up into Bedfordshire and points north. Thanks to Curate Blades you had to go up there to see the full horror.

They found what they wanted in a valley where Biggleswade should have been. For a while it had been a fascinating, skin-crawling, sight, like watching a spider on the face of your first-born. Then like every other shock in life it palled. There was . . . repetition to what the beasts did, an aimless chasing round a dull cycle. The Null had no *history*.

Still, finally tired of his own thoughts, Curate Blades risked another peek, and almost threw down the perspective-glass in disgust. The Null were scattered all about, indolent at end of day, the warriors mock brawling or lazily sodomising one another.

'Aye, they do that – out of the breeding time,' confirmed Scout, daring to break the silence. 'Old on young for preference, but old on old at a pinch.'

'"*The sin of the Cities of the Plain*",' agreed Blades, lip curling.

Scout saw no '*city*' , nor any plain for that matter, but if the god-king decreed a valley was flat, then so it was. It was a '*mystery*', a subject for pondering humbly in your heart at worship. He'd no more contest it than raise the alarm.

The Curate's telescope was raised again.

The Null cubs were closer in, keeping out of the way of their elders but desirous of the remains of their meals. Occasionally, a braver type would dash out and retrieve some gnawed bones or unappetising gristle and then junior battle would ensue for possession of that.

Curate Blades was gratified. This trip was not just a dangerous whim, the guilt-born bravado of a cowardly man. He had learned something. He now saw how the Null were trained to *be*. They had little mercy even amongst themselves and his own harsh measures appeared all the more moderate. He would sign that waiting list of death warrants after all.

Prompted by dusk, the Null troop simultaneously received the internal signal to muster. Or else there was some call beyond the ears of man. If so, the evening birdsong from the trees went uninterrupted. Blades could not accept that peculiar contrast in creation. One came from God, the other, surely, an accident or treachery when the Almighty's back was turned. They were not fit companions to be experienced together. He tuned the music out.

The brood-mother subsided vilely into her blubber; parts and genitals and nipples protruding everywhere, a new dark hillock upon green grass. Then her children began to mount her as Scout had predicted, leisurely forming a mountain of purple flesh like so many maggots in a bowl. Compounded, their acrid clove scent wafted over to the peeping toms.

The warriors came last, with darting backward glances. Some squatted on their heels at the hummock's base, looking outwards. The rest went aloft and locked themselves into intimacy. The family was now gathered.

'They slumber like falling off a cliff,' whispered Scout. His breath was rabbit – raw rabbit – flavoured. 'You can't put a knife 'tween sleep and wake.'

Blades looked and saw it was so. Like the beasts he didn't doubt they were, they had no thoughts to detain them from rest. In the space of seconds the pile's muscular tautness had gone; only the basal ring of shining guardian eyes remained to evidence life.

The Emperor wondered if they dreamed. It was likely: he recalled his hounds whimpering and dribbling in sleep, off on imaginary pursuits. The Null probably had their own dreams. A likely theme was his rib-cage being drawn out – slowly and to the accompaniment of screams – by bright, white teeth. The thought made him shudder, undoing all his two-vest precautions.

A soldier-courtier noted it and rushed to drape a shawl over him. Scout hissed at him to get down but Blades did not echo the rebuke. A bit of solicitude was nice during a delicate moment. He welcomed the material's warmth and weight securing him to the turf. His ribcage was still there, at home, undivided, supportive.

Scout was reaching for his long-barrelled musket.

'Shall I take one now, majesty?'

Blades considered. One less Null to ravage Christendom or a unhurried retreat? One uneaten farmer somewhere in the future or a dignified return home?

He started to push himself back down the slope. He felt wiser – and that sufficed.

'No, thank you, Scout, not today. Let us wait until they come nearer home.'

As it turned out, that day wasn't long delayed. If they'd pressed on but one valley further they'd have seen all the gathered Null they could wish – and more.

It was a shame to send him to his death: wild-faced, sweat-streaked, the man was enjoying himself too much.

''tis their last throw! The world is black with them!'

He meant well: the great enemy were all assembled in one place, he'd lost an ear: the lack of respect could be overlooked.

'Attend the left wing. Tell them they must hold.'

Curate Blades directed with his polished-granite baton and was obeyed. The messenger-page left immediately for that cauldron. It was unlikely he would return. In the absence of the requested reinforcements those over-tested regiments, mere flesh and blood for all their armour and carbines, would break. Then the Null runners, the younger, fleeter, beasts, would be amongst the scattered ranks, gouging and rending in pursuit – and that would be the gallant footmen's last service to the greater army.

A provocative vanguard, they'd held the bulk of the Null tide down in the valley, grimly retreating from one prepared position to another. The lines of sharp stakes and island emplacements served their purpose even as they were swamped and overcome. Elsewhere, marvellous things were being set in train. Behind them, out of sight behind the hill, the army waited. Whilst the fiercest, most lithesome of the beasts preoccupied themselves, the forces of humanity drew back its fist to deliver a deathblow. The cannon had been trundled forward: they were ready.

Even the slaves, unchained and armed bar a few less-trusted tethered to the guns, were proud of their works. They had forged the mighty armaments of mankind-militant: their skill and labour were in all those muskets and artillery. Now they were granted the honour of marching alongside them, albeit with humbler weaponry, to see their sorrows blossom into glorious fruit.

Blades had thought it charitable to grant them this holiday. Better they should die with a knife in a Null than await the battle's outcome – and certain death either way – confined in the factories. The knives and spears they'd been permitted were some small addition to the army and their participation would ease one post-battle problem.

It grieved Blades to do it, but few of the other-worlders could long survive the struggle. They'd taught and mined and trained but now were redundant. In this new Eden Curate Blades was trying to construct they were just so many serpents, rich in troublesome memories of another place. He could hardly send them back through the portal, not with the lack of affection they now bore him. Alas, his reluctant resolution was the simplest solution.

So, Blades made sure that the slave regiments saw the hottest part of battle. They would die with honour at least. Regarding those that didn't so oblige, instructions had been given . . .

The Null had eaten the outlying villages, consumed the Empire's frontier posts. The far-flung mines and quarries were lost. A purple tide had washed over them and they were no more. At least, that's what Blades presumed. Doubtless, if humanity prevailed today a few of the more sensible miners and prospectors would turn up in due course, having gone to ground faced with innumerable Null. They would be welcomed back with no questions asked.

The same was not true of any who conformed to instinct here in the centre of things. Gallows were set up waiting in the courtyards of Castle Blades for those who sought sanctuary under mother earth. It was bred in them to burrow when the Null arrived but the Curate was determined to dig out that habit. They had to learn to stand erect, steadfastly accepting the vice-regentship of God. If changing the practice of millennia took a little parental severity, then so be it.

But that was all for later – if there was to be one. This sunny summer's day on the Downs where Epsom ought to be, would decide that.

Over the brow of the hill they went. The Null did not scout or devise strategy. When they saw food – even prickly human food – they went for it. The sacrificial lamb of the left wing had absorbed all their attention and most of their strength. When the main body of mankind appeared on the skyline there were only the older and lazier and more replete Null directly facing them in the valley below.

The scarlet-coated regiments marched towards the maw of death without demur, air-tubes, pipes and drums preceding them. They ignored the dying scrum of combat over to their left. The hearts of Blades's lace-frilled generals swelled with pride.

The cannon were placed between the regiments. Slaves toiled at their wheels, keeping pace with the infantry. The army halted, newly revealed to the enemy. A low growl rose from the thin line of Null. They sang betrayal and anger at the cunning shown by mere *meat*.

Curate-cum-Emperor Blades was too precious to risk and a cloud of golden cavaliers surrounded him at all times. He could barely glimpse the action, but it was all pre-planned in any case. He could run the last great battle by his personal, Emperor's only, timepiece.

'Speak, gentlemen, if you please.'

He addressed the masters of artillery via his corps of signallers. The giant flags passed on his indulgence.

All the guns, from culverins to falcons, spoke as one. They had their range already. It had been calculated and paced out to the last degree in the days before. The Null lines erupted.

'At will, gentlemen, at will. Let our creations play . . .'

It was a temptation to long-distance bathe the Null in death for ever. Their distant screams were music to human ears. Too few, too surprised, for the moment, the monsters dared not close. Instead they took revenge on their human prisoners, pointedly slow-devouring them where all could see. The human gunners, trained to chilly calculation, did not let that affect their choice of target.

Already, elements of the main Null force were peeling off from the won struggle over on the left. Their long legs were carrying them across the sward. The elders amongst them probably understood the deception must be addressed, and soon at that.

Emperor Blades agreed. The human army too must close quickly before the odds became more equal. He gave the order for the bombardment to cease. The gun crews rushed to break out the mortars with which they could continue to lob shells over the heads of the advance. Later, when the infantry were engaged, they would traverse the cannon to face the enemy entering stage left. Null reinforcements would not have a free passage in.

His command went down the line, the drums played more frantically. The standards of each regiment, bearing the name of their original, now blocked-up, burrow were waved aloft. Slowly at first, and then more briskly, the footmen of humanity advanced down the valley in a bristle of pike and shot.

The nearest Null did not disappoint, for all they'd suffered gravely from the poorly understood distance-weapons and though broken purple bodies liberally festooned the green. The survivors should have stood to face the onslaught, retaining the advantage of the opposite slope and awaiting their brood-brothers who were hurrying to the rescue. Instead they charged to meet mankind. The insolence of food that fought back could not be patiently endured.

They met in the hollow between the hills; their would-be salvation still far away, strung out and already troubled by cannon. Mere seconds before they clashed the human front line vanished in clouds of powder smoke. At that range there could be few misses. The Null went down like corn but their impetus carried the remainder on. They impaled themselves uselessly on the hedgehog of levelled pikes, a few struggling to draw their pierced bodies up the shaft to strike just one dying blow.

The humans redressed their ranks, the musketeers reloaded. When all was ready their guns spoke again and the advance resumed. Certain officers, whose job it was, dissuaded any from looking behind. Shouts and the occasional blow sufficed, the veil of smoke assisted. Their sole business should be with the dissolving enemy in front. It was nothing to them – for the moment – if an oil-slick of Null was entering the valley below.

The immediate foe shrank from the tidy lines, step by step, duel by duel, retracing their steps back up the hill. Gradually, by death or flight, they faded away. The army gained the high ground across the valley from their starting point. An equally good position. They turned about.

Of course, the cannon had to be abandoned – and the slave handlers manacled to them likewise. Those gunners who could do so shifted – hopefully faster than a Null – down into the valley and then up the opposite slope in the wake of their comrades.

The Curate knew this was to be the real struggle: the diversion on the left wing, the slaughter just meted out, were a mere evening of the odds. The Null had emptied the south and midlands of every troop and band to assemble this host. Their brood-mothers had rightly concluded that supremacy was in the air, waiting to fall into one lap or the other.

'Rather like Hastings in fact,' mused the Curate – earning solicitous glances from his aides. It hardly mattered. He defined normality here and his eccentricities were material for respectful ponderings amongst his subjects.

'Always did disapprove of the outcome of that. Shan't fall for the old "feigned retreat" trick this time either. Fire at will, please. Let's try and deal with as many as we can at a distance.'

Early on in the wars the Null had often ridden a kind of scaly lizard beast, adopting crude branch-lances in imitation of human ingenuity. Whether they were too easy a musket target or rare or sacred was not divulged to mankind, but of late they'd become an uncommon sight. The few horses imported from 'the other place' that could be spared from intensive breeding usually still outnumbered the Null cavalry.

Not so today. The resources scrimped in previous battles were now released in luxuriant flood. In the van of the oncoming Null tide rode rank after rank of the lancers. The carrying beasts were swifter than a horse and had appetites fiercer than their riders.

Maybe these troopers were chosen for their greater wisdom. They reined in their rainbow-coloured steeds and waited for numbers to amass before attacking.

The cavalry of humanity were fewer but just as colourful. Blades had allowed the flower of his new nobility to monopolise the available silk and horses and develop a bond with both. They and their children and favoured servants were graciously permitted to form his lifeguard. They had a reputation to forge.

'Majesty, let us charge now: t'would blunt their advance.'

'And furnish us with passports to Paradise.'

The comments came from Firstmet's offspring, a son by his second wife, an Amazon from his eighth, respectively. Curate Blades smiled but did not answer them.

By now his order had reached the ranks and each man was selecting his own target. Tiny notches were being knocked in the wall of Null.

The Curate took out his perspective-glass, but then thought better of it. His stomach was already in turmoil enough after a night of nerves, without revisiting its nightmares in close-up. Let them linger down there, slowly diminishing, for as long as they like. Mankind wouldn't run out of powder or of the appetite for killing Null. He, Emperor Blades, had constructed a society that would never lack for either.

Of course, they could see that just as well as he. Null elders were passing in front of the horde, trying to marshal them. Each passing moment brought fresh diminishment of their strength from the cowardly far-killers. Time was not on their side.

Numbers were, though. The valley bottom was lost to sight under their close packed force. The world was indeed turned black, exactly as the sadly departed messenger had said, the artillery train now quite invisible amidst the swarm. If the Null only had the wit and humble spirit of humanity they might have learned to turn those guns against their creators, but Blades knew, from long observation, there was no danger of it. If man prevailed today the cannon could be recovered, undamaged. If not there'd be no further need for them.

The liquid voice of the Null raised in anger and in number sounded like an incoming tide. Likewise, the sight of their rolling advance. In the normal course of things water cannot ascend hills but this advance had nothing of normality about it. On they came up the slope.

In years past Curate Blades wondered what had become of the Null in his original world and queried their absence there. Observing them now he concluded that the Almighty had been merciful – in some places.

The ground was shaking. Lizard hoofs and bare Null feet pounded. They were in step. The gradient was nothing to them: they saw only impertinent cattle, overdue for slaughter.

The humans were firing by volley. There was just time for two discharges. Each shook the oncomers, peeling away the foremost, tripping those behind. There was hope on each occasion – but when the Downland breeze cleared the smoke, the Null were still there: undeterred: closer.

The first line hit the levelled pikes and sacrificed themselves upon them, dragging down the shafts with the weight of each great speared body. Their luckier brethren darted amongst the gaps. Men started to fall, ripped by claw or fang.

After that there was only clamour and tumult and the push of the throng. The Generals of humanity had no cause to fear flanking movements or other subtle manoeuvres by the Null, for they were too arrogant to pay mankind that tribute. Their overlordship had only been challenged during the last few seconds of a long historical day. They'd seen no reason to learn.

There were detachments of chosen human youth held back, boys and Amazons mixed, the cream of the first generation raised under freedom, the best armed, the most furious about their fathers' subjection. From time to time Blades ordered them to plug a gap or stiffen resolve. For the most part they did the trick. When not, slave battalions were whip-driven in to absorb the worst the Null could do.

A second line of foot stood behind the first, edgily observing, not knowing whether to wish for involvement or not. There was no one behind them: they were the last.

Individual Null and some riders began to appear in the space between the two lines. They had fought their way through and bore trophies of parts of men. Roaring victory they flung their prizes at the waiting ranks. Where possible they were shot down, but failing that clouds of youngsters fell on them. A dozen striplings – more for the lizard beasts – usually sufficed to down a Null, so long as they were happy for half their number not to rise again.

And then there were no more reserve units to cast in. The Null had carved avenues in the first line and were pouring through. The commander beasts were directing some to tear down men from behind, weakening those regiments still resisting. Meanwhile, others were rallied ready to assault the second line in force.

Blades's bodyguard gathered closer to him. Ravenous almond eyes were already being cast in his direction. Seen from the vantage point of horseback, that second line looked awfully thin. He knew what those regiments were thinking now: the dawn-time urge to be beneath earth was upon them. He saw it in downcast looks and irresolution. Fortunately, the age of burrow-hiding was gone. The issue was to be decided today, one way or another.

Blades was glad of it, resolving not to quit the field, come what may. Better that humanity should fall in God's clean sunlight, living on as chill memory to its enemies, than skulk-exist a million years, slow-devoured like rabbits. He had lived that way once, a timid curate in Godalming, prey to any passing predator and now perceived the shame of it. Nowadays, he definitely *knew*. Rather stand for a short space than cower for ever. Blades swung his horse round.

One of the nobility dared to grasp his reins.

'No, master, don't hazard your death! This is not for you.'

The Curate looked at the buzzing combat and all the death. The first line was now mere die-hard remnants, the second was bracing itself. He brushed the – kindly meant – restraining hand aside.

On the contrary,' he said, and smiled, 'It's *all* for me!'

Drawing his jewelled sword he charged.

'Brought me musket back have you?' Silas continued planing the plank. ''Bout time too.'

Actually he hadn't. Emperor Blades hadn't given it a thought in years. Presumably one of his legionaries toted the thing, if it hadn't broken through hard use long ago. Stolen militia guns were a consideration from way back penny-pinching days, best forgotten. His own gun shops churned them out by the thousand now.

'No, I haven't. Sorry.'

'So, what you here for, then? Apologies don't pay no fine.'

Blades wasn't expecting much of a welcome from his brother. Two decades without a word wasn't exactly calculated to warm the heart. And even at the best of times Silas would have rather slept with a he-Quaker than show emotion.

The Emperor leant on the workshop door and looked around. Little was changed. Silas Blades had neither fallen or prospered: he'd just . . . gone on. Blades gave thanks that hadn't been his fate.

'I just came to say hello . . .'

'She's easy done, then. You've said it. Don't let I detain you.'

'And goodbye.'

That got his attention. Silas ceased to shave great slivers of pale wood. He looked at his brother, carpenter fixing eyes with an Emperor. There was no contest: Silas had always been the stronger of the two.

'Off for good, now, are you?'

'That's about the shape of it.'

Silas considered the unfinished plank, pondering some deep question. At length he placed the plane down.

'Then you'd best 'ave a bite to eat 'fore you go.'

'I always wondered 'bout Dad's attachment to that clock.'

'You believe me then?'

'Why not? You weren't much of a clergyman, but not a liar either. God's got a good imagination: miracles lurk round all sorts of corners.'

Blades put down his platter: he'd done justice to the bread and cheese; messing it up enough to simulate consumption. It was years since he'd had such humble rations and they were no longer to his taste. He could now politely ignore the tankard of cider.

'Good. That's saved a wealth of talking.'

Silas was still tucking in. 'I'm all for that,' he said between mouthfuls. 'There's a cabinet to be finished by evening. Special order – for the *gentry*.'

The carpenter screwed his face up to express disdain. Blades couldn't help but smile. His brother was a 'Cromwell man', too young to have fought for him, old enough to lament the return of Kings. The *quality*'s money was serviceable enough but not service *to* them. Once, under the influence of ale, he'd confessed to etching Roundhead sentiments on certain of his commissions, tucked away in back-panels and under-seats: places only he would ever see. It amused him to think of grand cavalier backsides sitting upon subversive verse.

For a worrying moment Blades wondered whether any of his artisans dared to do the same to him – and concluded probably not. He held his place through gratitude: not succession or oppression. The People loved him – or moved on and learned how the Null rewarded ingratitude.

Between brothers there can be thought-reading.

'Mind you,' said Silas, 'you're gentry yourself now: royalty even.'

In this place only, that truth seemed improper: an affront to his upbringing. Another reason for leaving.

'In a manner of speaking. There was no other way.'

Silas said 'hmmm . . .' and had another drink. Blades hated those *hmmm*s. It wouldn't be tolerated from his normal company. He wondered why he'd come.

'Where's the clock now?'

That was another, more agreeable, tack. He let the flare of resentment go.

'In Southwark: a goldsmith's safe house – for security's sake. I've paid him liberally; he asks no questions, even under the grossest provocation.'

'Eh?'

'We are obliged to ferry all sorts through the portal. For instance, the new land lacks good breeding stock, so sheep and cattle and ducks and geese – even rabbits – must be driven thence. Getting a prize bull through even an accommodating and expansive clock is the very devil, I can assure you. They pop in readily enough, under duress, but the noise! The mess! He must think I am making a hecatomb of sacrifice down there, what with all the beasts that go in but fail to emerge.'

'How d'ye pay for him – and them? I can't even afford a milk cow.'

Silas had always had the better eye for commercial realities. But for his ethics he could have been comfortably off.

'We "shop by night", brother,' – and Thomas Blades had travelled so far that the admission of rustling brought not a blush – 'and in number, and well armed. Strange to relate, no one thinks to detain us. Also we're no longer so abstemious in our highway robberies. Nowadays a certain amount of coin comes our way along with the people: enough to pay the goldsmith.'

He paused to rearrange his silken cravat. It had become less than perfect but he couldn't restore it to his satisfaction. Normally there were valets to oblige. The kingly lips pursed.

'I suppose you'd have me trade and barter, would you? Well, one could readily undercut grain prices with other-world imports. My labourers work for free. But would that be fair dealing, eh? And the tedium of it, the delay! Don't you wrinkle your nose at me, brother. I ask you, did the nobility do different when they came to this land? Did the Normans stop to pay a fair price when they carved out a kingdom?'

'No, they didn't,' growled Silas – and spat heartily into the straw. He'd read all 'Freeborn John' Lilburne's incendiary pamphlets. He knew all about 'the Norman Yoke' laid upon the poor oppressed Saxon. He believed they still laboured under it.

'Well, there you are then; and our cause is infinitely more just.'

'That's not saying much: t'would be difficult to be less.'

Blades conceded the point with a shrug. He'd gone beyond that sort of pettifogging, *Non-conformist*, conscience-bothering. It merely made him impatient.

'Be that as it may, but you'll allow that we require a person of the utmost discretion to husband the portal. The Goldsmith is one such. He's a good man, for all that we test him.'

A snort and sneer queried the ripeness of 'good' in such contexts. Most goldsmiths were Hebrews. Then Silas recalled that Cromwell had favoured the Hebrews. The one and only time Oliver had overruled his Council was to permit the Jews back into England after 500 years away. The Carpenter thought on – and then stealthily relented.

'Just as well. You need an upright man to guard rarities – assuming it is so rare.'

Silas *looked* at him again and Blades wondered just how much his brother had worked out for himself. He was a clever – wasted – man.

'I mean,' Silas expanded, apparently in all innocence, 'in my experience the Creator can't abide one-offs. Even miracles have close relatives.'

The Curate drew in breath – and decided to confide his inmost thoughts.

'Good point, brother. I've often wondered if other clocks – maybe most – don't communicate in that way. Accordingly my people are not allowed them: sundials and water and candle clocks suffice.'

'People never enquire, do they?' agreed Silas, kindly riding over the sudden imperiousness. 'When do you ever go peering round the back or into the guts of clocks? Clockmenders, maybe – but they're dry-as-dust mechanicals. Would they even see?'

'And, of course, most clocks are too small to be useful in that respect. It takes a grandfather or town timepiece to permit a man access. The rest would only give you a useless glimpse – if that.'

'Happen the workings must be a certain size to tear time like that.'

'That's what I've been thinking.' Blades was moving swift in his enthusiasm. There'd been no one he dared share his ideas with up to now. 'Maybe measuring time alters it, or, going awry, puts it into alignment with other times.'

'Or maybe our grandfather was made with planks from the tree in Eden?'

Swept up in the debate, Blades was going to concur – but now he paused. His thoughts had moved on in recent years. Ample leisure had given him space to study the Book of his faith. Lack of the Reverend Speed's supervision permitted him to draw his own conclusions. Studying the Bible he found inconsistencies, unpalatable passages and grounds for *doubt*.

'I don't know about that so much, brother.' He spoke wary: Silas had always been suspected of Anabaptist opinions. He knew and loved his Good Book as much as he despised the

Church of England. 'Eden was a fair while ago – and I reckon there's much of the allegory about it. I mean, if Adam and Eve had two sons only, then . . .'

'You've found other portals, ain't you?'

That derailed conversation like a musket-butt to the chops. Blades had been keeping that to himself. There'd seemed no need to volunteer the disquieting intelligence. He studied his brother with renewed respect.

'How did you . . .'

'I can read 'ee like a song sheet, so I can. Good job I'm not in your world. I'd always be catching you out. End up on a rope, I dare say.'

Blades gaped in shock. It was the undeniable truth of it that appalled, that sudden vision of an occupied scaffold. He'd travelled further than he suspected. Here, now, in this place of memories, he did not like where he'd arrived.

There seemed little point in anything but stark honesty.

'The furthest scouts have reported such. Rips in reality. Two or three. I warned them away. No one may approach.'

'Why the surprise. Where one man goes, why not another?'

Blades recalled the terror of the news. He had thought himself unique. The portals were far away in Null territory. He had banished them from his mind as he had to his people.

'My new folk think I am given them for a purpose. I do not want their belief threatened.'

'You should still go see.'

'I do not care to.'

From a pouch by his side Silas took out his favourite yellowed old churchwarden pipe and began to fill it with tobacco. He looked sidelong at his brother.

'Thomas,' he mused – it was so long since Blades had been so called that it lacked connection to him and failed to grasp. 'Thomas, my brother, I do declare you've grown unused to reversal . . .'

Emperor Blades rejoiced to have something he knew he was in the right about.

'Now *there*, brother Silas, is where you're wrong.'

His legions were melting, like rock-sugar assaulted by tea. The Null had the measure of them now; lapping round their shrinking edges, pulling away at their substance strand by strand, man by man. The killing mood was on them, they did not stop to taste each execution.

Each regiment was an island set in a purple sea; his household cavalry in no better plight than the lowest slave formation. The glittering cavaliers were growing less, plucked from their embroidered saddles by eager claws, the red-hot poker of their charge dulled to cold, bludgeoning iron. Soon they would be at a stop and the Null able to wash over them. Even Emperor Blades had occasion to deal blows as individual beasts penetrated the clump of horsemen. His noblemen were all fear on his behalf. They sheltered him with their bodies.

Amidst the tumult the Curate reflected. It was not he or they that were at fault but circumstances. His army had done all that might be reasonably required but the Null were simply too many. They would be less after this day, their presence upon the land thinned, but they were *too many*. It was the twilight of humankind. Night would soon fall: here and on humanity.

Unless . . . there was a phrase back in the old world: *better a live jackal than a dead lion*. He considered the notion. The Reverend Speed would not have agreed with it. A dead lion is still a lion in memory, a jackal is never more than a jackal: the slinking, most cowardly of beasts.

And yet it might change – if it but lived – to be a fiercer jackal next time or the time after that. He knew what he'd earlier resolved but things *change*.

He gave the order to the trumpeters: full retreat. They, the noblest of youths, full of youthful ardour, *looked* – for a mere second – but then complied. It didn't matter. Few enough would hear the signal. Those that did would need freakish luck to cut themselves out. Horsemen, though, they had a better chance . . .

Blades's cavalry turned and strove against the tide to free themselves. Borne along in the throng the Emperor had space and time to look over his shoulder at the abandoned. The circles of men grew tighter, gaps grew in the walls of pikes: the Null poured in.

'Ride! Ride, gentlemen – and each look to himself!'

It was the one order that they would not take from him. The horsemen moved at his direction but stayed close. It was hard going, in every sense. The Null resisted, the foot regiments they passed cried dismay. Emperor Blades winced at every despairing glance he caught.

At the dying army's fringe some of the looks grew reproachful. They knew he was leaving them. The Emperor took back control of his feelings, as emperors should. It was as well, he thought, that few would survive this day. Clearly, many had lost faith. Better they should go taking Null with them, easing the lot of a successor people.

When the diminished band of cavalry burst clear, a great groan broke from the doomed army: their last collective action. Blades then had a choice: he could let that sound break him or not.

He felt movement – a liquid flow down the length of his back. It was his tender conscience and better nature sliding off him like Christian's burden or some peddler's pack of cheap rubbish. At last it lay at his feet and he moved on, leaving it, unregarded, behind. He wouldn't be needing *that* anymore.

Emperor Blades rode into wide open country.

'T'weren't heroic exactly, were it?' Silas's face was wry. 'I'm surprised you care to tell.'

Blades glared at his brother. The cider grew sourer still in his mouth.

'So you'd have generals die with their army, would you?' Blades knew the heat in his voice and face signalled false outrage. Truly they sprang from deeper wells within.

Silas set down his crust.

'I would. They *start* all the dying: how come they then daintily abstain?'

'You do not understand.' His voice was imperious. 'You command a shop of shavings and one apprentice: what do you know of harsh decisions?'

The carpenter shrugged, un-awed.

'I have some experience. I'm making a few about you at the moment.'

'Suspend judgement, brother: Matthew chapter seven, verse one: *'Judge not, that ye be not judged'*.'

'Oh, scripture now, is it? And I thought you'd quite abandoned your former profession . . .'

'Not so. And you should walk in my shoes a while before rushing to condemn.'

'*Ride* in them, more likely, brother – and on a fine steed too. Or were palanquins more your style by then?'

How did he *know*? Whence came all this annoying intuition? An unbidden image of the glorious gold slave-borne chair flashed into memory. He'd excused himself by saying elevation helped him see more of the throng. Here and now he knew that was just self-deceiving dung.

'There was still bravery!' he protested. 'I made a stand!'

At the portal the last of his companions peeled away. One by one the horsemen left him. Some wept. They knew he was leaving them, going back to whence he came. Truly, that day they had lost everything.

None stayed to watch. Separately they rode away to Castle Blades to await the end.

The grass grew luxuriant round the shimmering tear. At that stage he'd not yet thought to centre a cathedral around it and, though not far off, New-Godalming was not yet expanded to there. His word alone was enough to preserve its sanctity. It had been taboo to the People even in their days of savagery and the Emperor had since reinforced that with layers of proscription. No one walked here save the cropping sheep and rabbits that kept it free of brush. It was as he had left it all those years before.

The Downs never looked more beautiful than today but it was all a lie: the Null were coming. A dark tide would sweep over the hills and when it drew back there would be nothing left but emptiness. Beauty unbeheld is not beauty.

Emperor – soon to be Curate again – Blades edged his nervous horse closer. He'd made his decision during the wild ride, turned the page and closed the book. The sense of failure was unendurable. He wished to put a world between him and it.

Fallible memory would be his friend, his only friend. In time he would doubt his history. It would be as a dream against the dusty reality of curacy. He would remember where he *should* be, the life he had truanted from just like school lessons long ago. It was settled and so was he.

Therefore, he wondered why he retained his seat: the horse could not come with him, he had no use for a war steed there. Why didn't he just dismount . . . step down?

Because he couldn't. Truth blossomed within like a sunburst. Blades knew, with all the certitude of a saint, that he couldn't be small again. It wouldn't fit him or he it. He'd grown; Godalming had shrunk to impossible proportions. His tastes had become ungovernable: he thirsted for experience and command. He commanded his experiences: he thought and things *happened*: and even now that might still be so, for a while longer. Back there, no one listened: they smiled at him. There, he'd live a lifetime. Here, a Null jaw was only days away. It was a simple, stark, choice.

He surprised himself by not wavering. There was no doubt.

Blades wheeled his horse round and fled from the portal as though it were contagion.

The drop was sheer, dizzying, but he would not show fear. He stood at the rampart's very edge.

There was a sea of faces, more women and infants than men, thanks to the defeat. They were all that were left to him, beaten survivors, the skeleton garrison, civilians: their eyes upturned to the Castle wall.

Blades was wild and still streaked with the tokens of battle. He stood alone to address the remnant.

'They come!' he told them. Trained cantors amplified and repeated his words. Others dutifully recorded them. Not everything had gone by the wayside. 'They come!'

A lament started on the edge of the crowd. He killed it with a chop of his hand.

'And we live! We shall live!'

They believed him. He only had to speak and it would be so.

'They are many,' – that was always true – 'we are few,' – new but undeniable – 'but we will live. We shall be many again.'

They were glad to hear it, for most were mourning sons or fathers.

'Women, divest yourselves!'

There was surprise, but only a little and not for long. Such was their belief that many started to comply. Gowns and dresses fell.

'Go breed! Go now to your homes – be brief but be fruitful. Breed!'

The generation set on the slow path to the light that day would be forever treasured, a chosen nation of brothers and sisters commissioned amidst the darkest hour, a symbol of hope.

They could easily give each other babies but only Blades could give them hope.

At the Castle there'd been wild rejoicing equal to their earlier despair. Some of the army remnants who'd announced the god-king's flight were lynched for their lies. Blades did not intervene. There was need of every fighting man but still more requirement for *faith*.

He was all energy, inspiring the garrison to defence and storing and preparation. Before, they had drooped like dead men, looking their last on everything. Even the gates were open when their Emperor rode in. Uncertain of welcome he'd awaited a sign. There was a second's silence in the courtyard until Firstmet broke through the crowd. *He'd* never doubted. He flung himself at Blades's bridle and howled with joy: an odd reversion to a lost, animal past. The rest took their lead from him and the joy became general.

Now there was purposeful activity. Powder barrels were hidden in New-Godalming to await the Null, and doomed volunteers found to ignite them in the fullness of time. Other subtle traps were set in the emptying houses and abandoned town: the cack-smeared spear in the concealed pit, the throat-level wire and whiplashing spiked bough behind the door. Tar went over all, the better to deny the Null anything and incinerate a few meanwhile.

From the surrounding land came in the last harvest of all things edible: what was not portable was spoilt. The fleetest Null would stand amidst an arid landscape.

They were not long delayed. Pausing for short breath after the battle of the Downs, they sent their youths on in advance. The castle did not waste shot on them and the slim purple forms stood to regard the high walls unmolested. Behind them in the distance a similarly-coloured sea poured down the valley where Guildford ought to be.

The mass musketry training was suspended to allow the warriors to behold them. Blades hung a few who quailed at the sight. Their swinging in the breeze and stiffening stiffened the remainder's resolve. More 'harsh necessity', he comforted himself. Like so many things it was a shame. One of them had been a quite passable poet.

The Null were learning. They wanted to make things easy for themselves. The snares and explosions that greeted them in deserted New-Godalming town engendered caution. Mankind could still bite. Thus, finding the gates of the castle barred and the *meat* within resistant, they opted for subtler courses than frontal assault. That would not always have been so. Even teetering on the precipice, upraised humanity was accorded some respect.

Whether the recipients would see things that way was another matter. The Null had taken prisoners. To taunt and provoke they tortured and ate them, one by one, in full view of the castle walls. The screaming meal went on for a day and night and was eventually ignored – till Jezebel was told that her son had been brought forth. She hastened to the scene, a manic missile, all black silk and white face.

Emperor Blades was likewise drawn rushing to the walls, to prevent some madness on her part. He need not have feared. Jezebel proved her mettle – and earned her queenship – that day.

Standing on the very parapet, she blessed her child and cursed the Null. Realising their luck, the beasts then gave sign that were she to come forth or open the gates they might spare him the teeth and fangs and slow descent into the dark.

She was magnificent: an epitome of the proud spirit of mankind-off-its-knees. Drawing up that black gown she exposed herself to the onlooking monsters.

'From here came one fine son,' she told them. 'Behold the mould for making more!'

The Null understood – and proceeded to dine.

'And then there's Arthur – and, of course, Stilicho and Aetius, my two sons by Jezebel's sister . . .'

'Called?' Silas seemed more interested in the minutiae of his nieces and nephews and sisters-in-law than the broader picture being told.

'er . . . Sappho – that's it: I'd moved on to poets by that stage in the namings. Listless sort of woman but she came with the Jezebel package.'

'Well, one more wife couldn't do much harm, could it?'

'I thought not.'

'Not amongst so many.'

Time was when Curate Blades would have recognised irony, especially from blood family. That time was past.

'No. There was ample room in the harem.'

'Oh well, that's all right then.'

Blades fiddled with the bread knife, twirling it on the rough table with long, slim fingers. 'Of course, I have to differentiate between them.'

'Of course.'

'Otherwise there'd be disruption – and even more conspiracy. They're split into circles one to three, one being the closest.'

'You mean to the centre of all things: yourself like?'

'Exactly. I won't tire you with all the signs and symbols of each. There's separate uniforms and titles and such: endless diversions for them to worry about. Suffice to say it keeps them aspiring to rise rather than anything more harmful.'

'Aren't you troubled with favouritism? Isn't there just one you prefer to cuddle on a cold night?'

Blades gave his brother a *look*. Silas's settled happy marriage had always been an unspoken issue between them. He studied hard but could detect no mockery.

'Not really. Boudicca, I suppose. I call her just for her company sometimes.'

'The one with the wonky leg, her?'

That was a test. Thomas Blades failed it. Silas saw the brief lightning flash of murder in his brother's eyes.

'God saw fit to frame her imperfect. I don't mention it – nor should you.'

Silas bowed languid apology from his chair. He didn't mean it.

'No children off her, then?'

'No.'

'So there's some things you can't command . . .'

Blades pointedly surveyed the entirety of Silas's workshop and abode. It didn't take long.

'I command enough – and can live with the balance. How about you?'

Silas smiled and puffed his pipe.

'You've grown waspish, brother.'

'It's in the blood.'

Silas conceded that by an amused burying of the mouth in his tankard. When he surfaced all was forgotten.

'You were recounting your offspring.'

For his part, Blades had forgiven nothing.

'I tire of that litany: t'would take too long.'

'Your loins have streamed forth too prodigious, I understand. Well then, am I not to meet this unsuspected horde?'

The Emperor-Curate was gladly blunt.

'No. That's my other purpose here. I've come to close the portal of communication.'

That did slip the knife in. Though loath to show it, Silas had genuine feeling for his kin.

'And so we'll meet no more?'

'Never.'

Silas tried to engage his brother's eye but it would not be caught. Blades still had shame enough not to want the glee to show.

'How? Why?'

'A case of grenadoes is brought over with me. They'll more than suffice for one old clock. By tonight it will be splinters. I dare say the goldsmith's bullion will survive, though his cellar be scarred. You see? Grand as I've risen, I'll do no man harm unless I have to.'

Blades did not see, probably no longer could see, the hurt he wrought by his blitheness. It is a hard and heavy thing to truly lose a brother – especially when he still breathes – but Silas shouldered the load, face unaltered.

'You forgot the "*why?*" portion, Thomas.'

Blades leant back, a happy Emperor once again; convinced that mercilessness was merely his right.

'I do not want the Null in *this* world, I suppose there is that. Once, I thought you – us – merely fortunately in being free of them.'

'No,' said Silas. ''tis thanks to God's loving kindness.'

Blades frowned. 'But that accuses Him of malignity elsewhere. No, now I perceive the work of human hands. Doubtless they *were* here . . .'

'Genesis 6, 4: "*There were giants in the earth in those days*",' said Silas.

'Exactly. But their present absence plainly indicates they drowned in the Flood. Noah must have set his face against them and all the other monsters my new world retains. I applaud that decision and wish it to be final. The closing of the portal removes all danger of thwarting the Prophet.'

Silas chewed on it, unconvinced. 'Hmmm. And the truth?'

Blades considered – and then graciously allowed that his brother deserved that much as a leaving present.

'I long for . . . severance. Memory of the past is distasteful: a shaming contrast. When the portal is blasted into death tonight I shall also kill that history. I will be beyond its shabby reach. I will deny it.'

'Even to yourself?'

'Even so.'

Silas thought on, looking for loopholes as he did with the tithe laws.

'But does an Emperor's mind obey his own decrees?'

Blades conceded the cavil with a pause.

''tis one's least tractable subject, I confess, but in time it will heed the voice of command.'

'We shall be dead to you, then.'

'In effect – and I to you.'

'And even the memory of Mum and Dad?'

Blades did not answer. The silence grew – in both length and strength.

Finally, Silas accepted his cold conclusions.

'I hope,' he said, evenly, 'that you were this hard with the *Null*.'

The Emperor was suddenly wreathed in smiles, reliving happier days.

'Oh that we were, brother. We were that hard that they *broke* themselves upon us.'

Silas studied the stranger before him and found it easy to believe.

'Fiery fire in Old Jewry – Papists suspected'

'. . . *blazed to the ground, though timely blasting of fire-gaps in the adjacent streets by sailors of the fleet saved them from likewise ruin. As to the reports of mighty explosions from his strongroom as the*

105

source of conflagration; the goldsmith thrice denied (as false St Peter, first POPE, did Our Lord) before the magistrates that his property served as a secret Jesuit academy and store of munitions. Says THIS WRITER that if ten thousand armed Jesuits skulk beneath fair LONDON awaiting the POPE's sign – as divers good Christian witnesses do affirm – that they must be somewhere stored and by their signs shall ye know them. Said goldsmith is taken to the Tower that his memory might be refreshed . . .'

'The Protestant Flail & Gazette' 23 March 1702

When he mounted up the mob dared to lay hands on him. They dragged him from the saddle and held him tight. He had never been so glad to be unhorsed.

That relief could not be shown, of course. For form's sake and the future he had to be outraged and order the foremost punished. He was soft-hearted, though; a flogging rather than mutilation or death. They'd been doing him a favour.

Reluctantly, and in time even graciously, he accepted the spontaneous verdict of his people. They did not wish for him to ever leave again. They thought it was his presence, rather than their own sweat, that had thrown the Null back from the walls. There was every good reason to let them retain that childlike faith. At present they had little else to sustain them.

So, when the sortie streaked like an arrow from the postern gate, he was not at its head. A galaxy of his sons from the second and third circles formed its spearhead and faced the Null throwing themselves at the horsemen. Nevertheless, Emperor Blades accompanied them in spirit, even braving the cold breeze on the ramparts to urge them on. He was not sanguine about their chances – hence the withholding of first circle offspring – but wished them well. Since the People were watching, he made his feelings manifest, weaving his hands and chanting in the semblance of a spell.

Though insincere, it must have worked. There proved to be

sufficient warriors to win through, thanks to their speed and carelessness. The monsters peeled off the formation's outer leaves, bringing down man and steed alike with tooth and claw, but the core pressed on, closing their ears to the cries. In time, though much diminished, they were on their way and lost to the horizon.

And according to *their* way, the Null tracked them with looks of hatred. Then, reacting as to some unheard signal, they collectively forgot the horsemen and turned to their meals, some of which were still feebly quivering. They were right to take thought of husbanding their strength. Soon, it would be fully dawn and time to assault the castle once more.

Emperor Blades retired to breakfast – on dry bread and water just like the rest of the population (through perhaps a little finer grained and cleaner and sherbet flavoured). Later, like any other soldier of the beleaguered fortress, he would take his gold plated musket to his well-appointed sniper's tower. True, there were servants to reload for him, human shields to protect him and expert lip-maidens to entertain meanwhile – but Blades *would* play his part.

He was his people's hope, which was a heavy, lonely burden, but now had a portion of that same precious substance himself, to lighten his war-booted step. Contrary to honest expectation, the sortie had won through. So, it wasn't entirely beyond belief they might actually make it back with the cannon.

They were still there; mute symbols of human aspiration, arrayed in battery lines just as they were overrun. Freed at last – in gnawed skeletal form – from their chains, the slave teams nevertheless remained loyally with their charges in death. The leather harnesses hung slack over scattered shoulder blades and skulls. Even they had been chewed in anger.

The sortie came upon the great battlefield at dusk, which was a mercy. Even the victorious Null host could not consume such a bountiful larder. They had eaten what they could and toyed with the rest. Overhead Parliaments circled, creaked and cawed, disturbed off the leftovers. The cavalrymen kept their eyes front.

Against the cannon themselves the Null's fury had run up against their lack of imagination. A few were overturned, some of the larger bores had human remains rammed down their muzzles. Arms and legs protruded from the brazen mouths, an insulting outrage silhouetted against the dying sun. The removal of those was the first distasteful task, delegated to slaves brought along for just such reasons. Fortunately, their feelings did not matter for they were not returning. Their horses were now required for more pressing tasks.

Otherwise the *far-death-speakers* were unharmed. A team of artisans inspected each and pronounced them well. Stilicho, the most senior Blades-son present, draped his silken arm around the nearest, resting his head against its carved cold iron, giving thanks to Blades. Aetius, his brother, joined him and together they gave the order.

Gagging against the stink of death, slaves tied ropes to mankind's last hope.

. . . Pilgrims then proceed through Castle gate into Courtyard Five and make obeisance to the Pillar of Henry (peace and blessings be upon him) the fifth God-king incarnation, who on that sacred spot conceived his firstson, Redallen, builder of the rose-crystal temple of the One God, accounted one of the wonders of the world and the centre of worship for all mankind. Henry (peace and blessings be upon him) subsequently razed all trace of his former apartments after the betrayal of Gunnislake (may she be cursed and burn for eternity) but this monument was erected in his memory by his general and confessor, Eric Null-bane, fourth-circle son of . . .

. . . Courtyard Twelve is hallowed by the memory of the first God-king's favour for it. Whilst walking there attend that your steps remain only on the raised blocks at all times, bearing reverently in mind that HIS (He needs not our blessing) feet may have trodden here. Observe the granite-faced minarets of Michaelstow III festooned with ancient Null heads on bell chains of silver. Passing zephyrs urge them into a fitting perpetual lament of remorse.

Now cast four pebbles (provided) at the titanic rock effigies, one at the Null-mother, three at the Professor (may he be cursed and burn for eternity) and then proceed in silence. It is a capital crime to express DOUBT in the Courtyard of Blades (He needs not our blessing).

. . . The pilgrims, having divested their garments and being now adorned in a simple wrap of purest white, approach the climax of the pilgrimage and draw near to the orifice of grace. At the famous dozen doors of the Cathedral of First-Entry, all touch their brows to the earth seven times and frame their thanks in the most sweetest of prayers and thoughts. Note the glossy smoothness of the pavement, worn to a marble sheen by the piety of generations.

Be advised. Our faith tells us that those who pass these portals without truest sincerity draw down doom upon themselves within the twelve-month. Testimonials of awful deaths and pleas for their averting, pepper the Cathedral's Wall of Supplication.

If your purity of intention is not established upon a rock then turn back and approach another year. It is better to endure repeated travel than earn unalterable damnation.

. . . the more leisured and pious pilgrims add one day to their itinerary and visit Artillery Plaza after their night-long Cathedral vigil. Here they may pray on the actual site of the miracle. A few of the cannon — alas, ravaged by the ages — still remain to be viewed under glass canopies.

A tradition recounted in the sayings-book of the great-grandson of Firstmet (may he smile on us from Paradise) states that HE (He needs not our blessing) himself stood here on that glorious day when HE (He needs not our blessing) LIT THE TOUCH . . .

'A Pilgrim's Compendium of Wisdom for those who would Glorify their Earthly Life with the Jewels of Piety and the Silken Raiment of Prayer'

Thane Brixi of New-Compton in the Province of Wessex, United England. In the Year of Our Deliverance 457 A.B.

They came back in a wide circle, the guns at their centre, sacrificing the outer shell to secure the inner pearl.

The Castle came out to meet them, there being no purpose in holding back. Without the cannon more days of life were only pointless prolongation. The bread bins were empty, the wells dry. The summer days reeked of cloves and sweat, Null saliva and human suffering.

When they came it was night but there was no hiding the cacophony of hooves, the wild bump and career of the harnessed guns. Some bucked so high that they overturned, dragging team and outriders to ruin with them. They were left to the rapidly arriving Null.

The scouts and fanatics, those foremost in the rush from Castle Blades, said the monsters unpeeled themselves from the sleeping piles like tomatoes over a flame. Their young were with them and joined the onslaught. Only the fat mothers remained, thinly coated with warriors, in their camp, to peer into the dark and noise with protuberant eyes.

Blades thought of them even amidst all other distractions – which was why he was en route to god-head and no other. Teams of the most wild or expendable, their torches unlit, swung round the main struggle, seeking the fertile wombs that fast-bred mankind's enemy. They'd not return but would provide valuable service, distracting the Null army back and aborting Null brood yet-to-come.

Most had gone on before, but the best fed and armed, his own huscarls and first-circle sons, remained with him at the postern gate. Even the Emperor's stomach had rumbled for hunger that pre-dawn morning, not satisfied with the scant breakfast assembled. Everyone else was in worse plight. Blades had had to issue decrees enforcing modesty in dress, lest the citizens should distress themselves with the counting of ribs.

They were hungry and thirsty and dirty. The level of service in the Palace had gone right down. It wasn't that the spirits weren't willing but that the unfed flesh was weak. Blades didn't want to live on like this; it wasn't how he considered an Emperor should be. Accordingly, he'd come forth in his armour of gold.

The night hid all but the tumult coming ever closer; a good sign in present poor circumstances. The screams of horses and men was mixed with the liquid call of the Null. Straining his ear, the Emperor discerned the rumble of wheels above all. It was the defining moment.

Did he *belong* here or not? Now was time for honest, final, answer.

In fact, he'd already answered that question definitively some while back.

On that occasion, there'd been a tongue of flame from the Goldsmith's fiery cellar and its hot following breath – and then nothing. It was the last message from the old world. Whatever particles of air had come with it spread, progressively diluted, into those of this new universe. *Here* was the true reality now, any admixture was negligible.

Blades had looked – and then double and triple checked. Where the portal had hung there was now only this world. Still uncertain, he'd waited until all the lingering dust and smoke had cleared.

Then he'd dusted himself down and stood up straight to face the future, like a man leaving his – moderately missed – parents' funeral: newly independent and warming to the role.

'*I am*,' he'd congratulated himself, '*no longer a foreigner. I'm here. For good. For better or for worse, for richer or for poorer, in sickness and in health . . .*'

He'd paused to consider the parallels those words suggested – and found himself well pleased to say '*I will*'.

Now, once again that same stark query: pondered in the cold dawn before the postern gate, the sounds of havoc from the dying night his only encouragement. Again, he barely needed to consider. Emperor Blades spurred his horse and raised his sabre, leading the way.

The *Angel* sensed the portal's death, a pinprick diminution in the *possibilities* of her universe . She'd known it, crossed it, long ago, before evolving wings with which to glide and grace creation. She recognised it even after destruction.

Somewhen along the line a coat of wood had been attached: the housing for a minute-measuring machine which had captured one drifting terminus. A time-dweller's effort: primitive but a charmingly naive enhancement. Worth preserving.

Not only that, but bonds of affection remained with the last *solid-home*. The loss blemished the distant memory. A pity. Sentimental attachment revived even after so long: a deliciously naughty nostalgia. So she resurrected the lost thing, painstakingly collecting and reassembling all the component atoms. That occupied an otherwise dull era.

The 'goldsmith' who'd owned the clock-clothed portal didn't want it back, that could be sensed clearly. Time-dwellers were often fretful about damage to their nests and the goldsmith resented it in that respect. So, out of loving kindness, she gave it instead to the previous custodian, a three-dimensional just slightly blurred into the slipstream at the moment – an unusual, and therefore interesting, animal.

Yet since it was he who'd murdered the gate and fully expected the thing gone forever, the *Angel* replaced it a few years down the line, again through kindness, just to minimise the shock.

Some 'time' later she met the Angel-of-death-in-the-ditch. They fought and then bred a family and then ate them and then conversed. The coincidence of their separate dealings with Blades came up for discussion.

Things were definitely afoot in that little rut-world, they agreed. It merited closer attention.

His leading arm sling-bound in cloth-of-gold, Blades's wrong hand had to be pressed into service. It was still equal to undemanding tasks. Bowing low, the artilleryman passed him the taper.

Even now, not all propriety had been lost. The glowing cord was grasped in miniature tongs of silver. The Emperor accepted the charge and studied its scarlet tip, seeking warmth for his pale face as he thought his own thoughts and the Null rushed headlong on.

Mounting the cannon on the walls added richly to the cost in lives of retrieving them. There was no time for care or economy of effort. Massed muscle-power and ropes heaved the guns aloft. Elderly hearts gave out, dozens fell or were crushed, or failed to clear quick enough when loopholes were blasted. No one took much account, for in the last stand of humanity every hand was busy at the oars.

Some guns were still outside – and their crews were with them forever. They had faltered or stumbled or been detained and the gates were closed in their faces. Even then, some Null had entered in, streaming in with the returnees, and any celebration had to be postponed till they were put down. That mad knife and powder-smoke struggle in the gatehouse was made worse by the hammering on the doors. Null and excluded human alike battered feverishly for entrance. Of course, the human component of the chorus soon diminished to nothing . . .

The diversion assault on the Null mothers helped. Just when the maelstrom in the half closed gate was coagulating, the Null had heard a second call. Some – enough – rushed away and the clot could be cleared. The doors slammed shut on reaching arms and intervening heads. Slaves toiled on the gears to hold them fast and great bars were slammed down to make sure of it. None of the raiding party ever came back but they'd bought their comrades a respite.

At the time that seemed the wrong word for the hours that followed; a haze of pain and effort. Only the artillerymen and the Emperor and a pregnant first-circle wife or two were excused the toil. The guns *had* to be aloft before the dawn and the daily onslaught.

And so they were, slick with sweat and blood and the marks of myriad human hands. Their servers did the loading, sighting and ranging, and then all was ready. The first light of day slanted over the horizon and the Null came on with it.

They had no need of ladders or scaling equipment. Their talons could gain them purchase on the walls; their steel-like muscles moving below grape-purple skin could haul them aloft. Once fastened on they were the devil to scour away, resistant even to heated sand or boiling water poured down the walls. The soldiers had to lean far out to fire or jab at the ascending foe, rendering themselves vulnerable to a sweeping claw.

The pressing need was to prevent them gaining the ramparts and a foothold where they could stand upright and utilise their superior strength. It had already happened twice during the siege and they had only been thrown back with great sacrifice. That was when the defenders were fresher and better fed, when powder and shot weren't in short supply. Now, it was a weary and depleted garrison that watched the incoming purple tide.

What reserves they had were lavished upon the cannon; unlike the musketeers they would not go short of their desires. It was tacit recognition that here was the last hope. Why husband supplies for a tomorrow no one would see?

They were waiting for him. The great array of guns hung upon his word, the master artillerymen's hands poised over the touch-holes. The first Null had already passed the agreed stop-line.

Emperor Blades looked around a final time, savouring the moment of decision, relishing history's eye upon him.

He said a swift prayer and lowered his right hand. For a second the world was all noise and smoke. There was a pause – the slightest sliver of silence – and then the song was repeated all along the line.

'Fire!' The two cannon fired perfectly together, putting on a show for the visiting royalty. The water erupted, was stained with red. One of the sea-beasts boomed in pain and sank. Terrified parliaments flapped away from their fishing.

Emperor Blades led the applause. He merely troubled his hands with a brief flap or two, relying on the glittering array around him to take up the task with vigour.

'*Middle Tudor*,' he thought, '*not quite Good Queen Bess yet, but on our way.*'

The shining brace of culverins, and the complicated *lunette* battery they stood in, indicated that he was making a conservative judgement, but the sprawling, brawling mob all around dragged the scene back down the timescale. The youngest princes and princesses were fighting over the food. The rest, older in aims and wisdom, were eyeing each up for love bouts and alliances. The spirit of the Borgias met and mated with the spirit of the farmyard.

'Come forward, man; receive our blessing.'

The master gunner, doubtless harsh monarch of his own little world down here on the coast, was abashed. He had to be led forward, eyes downcast, by one the lesser chamberlains. The gold and black of the royal party made way for his scarlet soldier's coat but they looked down their long noses at him. Blades noted it and disapproved. Just because he got his hands dirty and lived in the back of nowhere . . . Again the Emperor resolved to send some princelings out against the Null, just to let them appreciate how the other 99.9 percent lived. Last time he had abandoned the plan under seductive lobbying from the darling boys' mothers. This time he'd be firmer; close his ears against the shrills.

'Cannon-master, how often are our realms assaulted by the sea-Null?'

The man mumbled something into his chest. He was already on his knees; the sound hadn't far to go to sink into the ground.

'He says,' Firstmet interpreted, 'less often now that your benevolence has provided these weapons.'

More humble mumbles.

'And in depriving them of this bay whence they come to feed, he says there is hope of their extermination.'

That was good news. The strange marine creatures, flat, white, house-sized things, armed with stings and razor teeth, were not actually 'Null' as best he knew, but it suited Blades to term them thus. Though flabby and floating-corpse-like to look at, they were a mild risk to the incautious onshore; they raided coastal villages, attacked boats and probably competed with man for fish. They'd had the sea to themselves too long whilst mankind remained under the heel. Now that particular foot was off and elsewhere, it was time to teach other species the proper order of things. Tuition was provided as and when they came to notice. The sea-devourers had positively surged up the beach and begged for education.

Bullets bounced off their ghostly hide but shore batteries were another matter. The great guns were diverted from their watch against the true Null. Coming in with the tide to feed – on whatever it was they ate – their shoals were a sitting target.

The bigger remnants could then be harvested by brave boys in row boats and use made of their blubber and bone. Already it was reported the numbers were not so great as hitherto: sure sign of humanity's success. Likewise their land-cousins; ragged slab creatures that lurked at the bottom of shallow pools and then *leapt*. These 'mud-monsters' were become rarer still.

'We are pleased. Take this symbol of our favour.'

Blades signalled to the Keeper of the Purse: three fingers. That meant a gold *Tom*, heavy and ornate, his head adorning both sides. The gunner took it and cleaved it to his heart. The Emperor doubted it would ever be spent.

Blades caught the slipstream of a black look. Prince Sennacherib, constrained by his iron collar, had been too slow in the turn. His hungry look was converted into a white smile. No matter how much honey he poured, the oiled ringlets and heavy beard prevented sweetening of his face. It was all menace, veiled or no.

That was his choice. Fed on half-grasped Bible stories and history from his father, the first circle son had locked upon the example of the Assyrians. Careless of other studies and learning, he wanted to hear all that could be recollected – or made up – about the Kings of Nineveh. He'd made them his model and dressed his followers in iron helms and coats of mail. With such protection the more mettlesome of them even dared to wrestle with Null and thus Sennacherib's inner retinue self-selected itself.

Actually, it wasn't so strange. Another honoured son, Arthur – and again it was the father's fault – took his name to heart and was recreating Camelot in Canterbury. He was forbidden a 'round table' to castrate any monarchical developments but otherwise chivalry ruled the roost in Kent-reborn. Blades indulged him as he did 'Assyria'. He could think of worse historical revivals to take root. Henry VIII, for instance. He deliberately never mentioned him.

Sennacherib's mother, Jezebel, had accompanied the Royal progress, casually inviting herself along. Blades *knew* her though, knew that she was ambition lightly encased in flesh. As soon as they reached the Pevensey enclave her beauty became sharpness, her face turned thin. She was all vigilance and approval, observing her husband's every facial twitch. Even now, when dining, her gaze was on him. It made him mischievous.

'My dear,' he told her, across the length of the dining divan, over all the heads of the courtiers, 'I see you have begun the entertainment early.'

There were always *scop*-singers and jugglers and such for the digestion spell, but Queens were not called upon to perform – not that early in proceedings anyway.

'How so, majesty?' she replied, a frozen smile plastered all over her sudden caution.

'Why, with your famous bird impressions, of course.'

That smile broadened. It would reach her ears soon: her head would fall off.

'I was not aware of it, my Lord . . .'

Blades liked a bloodless *coup de grace*. It made him feel imperial and merciful at the same time.

'No? Well, you're certainly watching me like a hawk . . .'

Even Sennacherib laughed – at first – and thus all the rest could join him. Amusement even rode atop Jezebel's sighs of relief.

Both Emperor and Empress knew. The boy was building his own nobility, his own client network. Blades could see that, but made no protest. He was his third – or was it fourth? – born after all. Sennacherib – self chosen in preference to his given *Augustus* – was given his own enclave to play with. Assyria was reborn on the coast of what Blades would always think of as Sussex.

And maybe it would be Sussex again one day, free and independent. Its new prince had scowled to see favours accepted by one of *his* people from another, even the sublime Emperor himself. He was developing regal unreasonableness to a promising degree. Blades could only approve. The enclaves might be cut off from New-Wessex for weeks at a time when the Null summer offensives came. It required strong men and women to hold the walls against that tide. If one son chose to do so dressed up as a Biblical terror amidst the mist and drainage channels of the Pevensey Levels then that signified nothing. A king must be allowed to play in order that he might work.

Still, Blades rather hoped the artilleryman wouldn't come to grief through his Emperor's blessing; that was none of his intention. He was a good man – and useful, which was the same thing in New-Wessex under siege. The servers of cannons were held in high esteem and ought not be dispensed with lightly.

After all, it was they who'd saved the day at Castle Blades. The Null had broken themselves upon the guns' welcome, wasted themselves in waves upon the walls. Back then, the beasts still did not have the measure of massed artillery safely emplaced. Time and again they'd charged, but it was flesh – purple, heavy muscled flesh, true: but still flesh – against metal. And when that flesh grew weak the defenders had time to vary the metal menu. It could be heated red-hot or fired in chain-linked pairs, the better to swing and scythe through the oncoming ranks.

The Null were not to know it was a race between their persistence and the powder supply. They did not understand the workings of the far-killers. In the event, they blinked first, a mere two or three charges away from seeing the guns fall silent. The Null swarm retired just as the gunners had to lean far in to scrape their barrels, pursuing the powder remnant round and round with unburdened scoops.

They left behind twitching middens of the dead and dying

and a sound that would never be forgotten by those who heard it. The howling anger of those leaving unfed mixed with the sobs and rattles of their brethren departing more permanently. At the end, its lower registers were augmented by human cheers.

After that, it was fair to say that Castle Blades – which was all of New-Wessex for the moment – would not fall. Its inhabitants might grow skinny some summers but the Null could not enter in.

The succeeding years saw mankind press outwards and found new castles. Early on, Blades employed the formations that had survived the *Great Defeat*, in the interest of using up those whose faith might have been over-tested. To bolster resolve and remind them of their cause, brazen statues of himself were borne on palanquins before their march. He'd got the idea from the Roman legions and their eagles. It soon became accounted a regiment's deepest shame to lose their '*inspiration*'. The Null perceived that and buried captured examples deep within their sleeping clusters, snuggling obscenely up to and around them. During the day they would bear the mistreated trophy ahead of their random, hunting, progress. It was a calculated affront – they were beginning to learn from their former livestock.

For those who'd mislaid their emblem all honour went with it. Their sole path back to society lay in regrouping and recovery. They ceased to be counted on the army roll meanwhile and wives grew disdainful, children sullen. There was every incentive to face the risks of excavation into a Null night-swarm and some – a few – even emerged triumphant. Emperor Blades thought the system worked rather well.

The same applied to the '*marcher territory*' strategy; the castle-by-castle clawing back of land. Some survived the precarious first campaign season, some didn't. The following year's expedition might find a wrecked and silent 'motte and bailey', and signs of a consumed garrison. If not, then the women and children would join their men. Life would begin anew. Slow but sure, the liberated zone grew again.

Pevensey was one such area. Defended by the sea on one side and the marshy Levels on most others, it was a natural first choice for a settlement out of the citadel Downs. The People were amazed that the Emperor should even know of its existence: further proof of his modestly concealed omnipotence. He would draw marks on paper and direct his expeditions and lo, they would find hills and rivers and sea just as he had predicted! Amongst the devout it began to be said that their deliverer was creator of the world and thus naturally familiar with his handiwork.

'More drink for my father! May his lip never grow dry.'

Even the hand-servants wore tokens of iron and swathes of chain mail. As best these allowed they scurried to obey. It was clear Sennacherib had things well in hand.

Just for a second, Blades wondered whether to accept the drinking horn. The Prince wasn't usually so solicitous over others. That moment would come sooner or later: the poisoned draught, the knife in the dim-lit corridor. He did not seek to avoid but merely survive it. How else would he know who was his worthy successor?

Assuming his own guards were as good as he thought, the culprit could be chastised – and then groomed. Mankind deserved a protector who was up to the task. It was his heavy burden to run the risk of seeking him out.

He looked at Firstmet. Firstmet was looking at his household eyes and ears, his spider's web of spies. Their nods were relayed back. Emperor Blades – who was actually quite thirsty – drank. He then pondered on a tempting tray of oysters. They looked lovely but Sennacherib had not sampled them yet. The Emperor wavered, saliva rich.

It was not a relaxing repast.

'In Heastings we have two new burghs at the enclave

boundary. I shall see if they survive the next invasion.'

'Hastings.'

'Your pardon, father?'

'It's pronounced *Hastings*.'

'We pronounce it "Heastings". Such is our usage.' At this early stage raised eyebrows were enough to call him to order. Even after five years in his own enclave it was doubtful he had men he could command against the Emperor. 'But we welcome your wise correction. In *Hastings*, as I say, we have extended our boundaries to the border you decree as *Kent*. If they hold, then I next envisage the incorporation of *Pevensey Sluice* and *Battle*. Since we have you here – and are honoured thereby – may I ask what battle is expected there?'

Blades shouldn't have been surprised to find so grotesque a growth – he had done nothing to discourage it – but stumbling over casual faith in his knowledge of the future drew the breath out of him.

'There is no bat . . . do you not think if I fore-knew the weave of things to come I would have ventured the Great Defeat – or . . . married your mother? How do you reconcile my omnipotence with my mistakes?

They were in private, his son could have spoken freely – but he had not even heard. Thought of Imperial fallibility bounced off him like bullets off the sea-Null.

'I do not think of it. The matter is a paradox: irreconcilable. But tell me of this *Battle*.'

Blades sighed – but not all that sadly. He frowned, unhappy – but not as much as he ought to be. His conscience itched.

'It is – was – a small market town, with a large and glorious Abbey – and will be again. A great . . . battle was won there.'

Sennacherib glowed at this success foretold: assured.

'Amen!' he said, and drank deep in celebration.

The Null youth relished his occasional breakfasts before the *meat*-towns. The *meat* were preoccupied. Those who had worked through the night on mysterious tasks beyond the walls were at their least watchful. Unwary servitors, fear-tasty escaping slaves, even the odd sleepy sentry were there for the taking by the brave. It meant risk, it meant longer travel than before. It entailed a night away from the sleep-swarm and individuality – cold loneliness under the stars – but it was worth it. The alternative was scurrying furry beasts or cowardly four-legs: little meals. Biped *meat* was better than anything: they put good muscle on the bones of a warrior. The elders also said that if you could gulp the still-beating heart of a slaughtered *meat* you absorbed their mettle, their tricksomeness, alongside its juicy goodness. If so, then he ought to be replete with the *meat*'s better qualities.

He was brave, did not fear travel or trouble – and was often lucky. Previously he'd seized sustenance from under the walls of New-Godalming itself – though that was no longer so advisable. Nowadays, the Null youth chanced his arm outside the minor settlements. They were more vigilant but not so heavy in sheer *meat* numbers. The animals were still on the defensive there. You could dine well and live to tell the Null mothers of it.

He didn't know this wet-land's name; it had none in the Null tongue. One sleeping, feeding, playful place was the same as another to them. They followed the prey and did not take much thought. Only after the *meat* rebellion were they obliged to think of terms of discrete geographies: zones where all was as before, others that were not safe. That riled them as well. They did not like to have to delineate their world. A Null's anger did not subside but remained with them in lighter sleep and vicious hungers. If unassuaged, it mounted and mounted to end in fury turned blindly upon those nearest – or even self-destruction. That wasn't unknown just lately and the older Null, adrift in a new world, had shook their heads in sadness.

He himself was not happy to be splashing in mud just to find good game. Hunt-cunning was all very well, laudable even, but the young warrior would not delude himself. It was not craft that confined him to these water-channels but wariness of the *meat*. When he heard voices raised he splashed into cover, staying put till silence returned. There he'd graze on the small beasts that made their homes in the banks, the fish that brushed his pillar-legs, even passing insects, and he would hunger, dreaming of richer mouthfuls. Solitary *meat* he'd take without hesitation but where there were herds there were also firesticks. Alone, he dared not risk it.

When the channels deepened he swam; easy, powerful strokes propelling him swiftly with the tide. Other times he waded, periodically raising his sleek head to take bearings. The stone *meat*-house was drawing close, the centre of all these green portioned bits of land the creatures grew plants on. There he had hope of his heart's desire: a solitary but exalted *meat*, not one of the stringy types they put to work on the land but a plumpened elder; *meat* nicely flavoured by the flesh it itself had lived on. The *meat* seemed to mourn those losses more than others of their kind and that only made it sweeter.

He looked over a lowered section of the bank, a place trampled down by four-legged food when they came to drink. His even pulse flickered, urged on by joy. There was his wish, there his body's desire. Saliva came, the stomach gaped: he could not think so clearly as before.

The *meat* was alone and distracted. It sat by a channel and all its attention was upon the thing it held. The Null had heard of but not seen this before. Some of the *meat* were said to look into these square objects for long periods. From time to time they would move the flimsy white sheets within but otherwise say or do nothing. Clearly it was akin to the effect on some animals of certain herbs and fungi or fermented fruit. Indeed, the Null themselves would occasionally frolic under the influence of the red-capped mushroom, seeing visions and falling into orgies – though that had been more frequent *before*, when they didn't need to be heedful. They saw no wrong in it – or much wrong in anything at all – but the *meat*'s peculiar addiction did nothing for them. They'd captured some of the square objects from time to time, saving examples from ravaged farmsteads or taken castles, but could squeeze no pleasure out of them. They'd sniffed the puzzling mark-covered contents, they tasted the firmer bindings, but derived no goodness. Their only use was found to be in the torment of *meat* captives. They seemed distressed to witness misuse of the thicker, black-covered examples of the square things. As with all *meat* matters, it was a contemptible paradox.

It was also opportunity. The scarlet-clad breakfast was deep into its indulgence; its back was turned, no fire-stick could be seen. Unless the Null wished so, it would not even feel the transition between life and . . . whatever lay beyond for lesser species.

He left the water, lithe and low. The fluid was allowed to drain from his limbs so that, close to, there should be no betraying liquidity. When required, his race could display patience: the poised statue remained at the water's-edge until dry and ready. Only then did he move, skimming across the turf, a smooth repetition of legs and outstretched arms.

At the last the target screeched, perhaps sensing him through the pounded grass. It half rose but then his claws were upon it. They pierced the scarlet coat, shredding the shoulders, freezing the contents with fear. One talon reached to caress its head, completing the convenient turn. It was a model kill, the neck stretched just right, a perfect target for the descending jaw. The teeth met resistance, closed and met. There was just one great shudder, stronger even than a Null grip, and then life let go, surrendering itself to sustain a better.

He raised the body in his mouth, shaking it in the traditional gesture of victory – and met resistance. For a second he thought he had not killed – but then realised this was more than *meat* strength. He released the limp meal and it fell with improper sound, with clanking and rattles.

It had been tethered – with links of the hard, shiny material that the *meat* made. The end of the restraint was deep nailed into the ground. Now he understood the strange sluggishness of its blood. This beast had been drugged and left out for him to find. It had been a sacrifice: more *meat* mystery – or was it cunning?

Cunning. The Null looked around and found that answer in

124

the hedgerows. They were now *meat*-lined and prickly with fire-sticks. He had been tracked and lured; his life was over.

None were much nearer than the rest: any would do. He charged at the first to catch his glowing eye, wanting to *bite*, if only once, before the fire-sticks tore. It saddened him that no elder would see, no Null mother hear. He finally accepted that they had been right to curse *individuals*.

His death-day was also one of high strangeness. The *meat* did not make the smoke that killed. They awaited him. Some even came forward. That was not their usual, animal, way. This was more Null behaviour, a worrying sign not just for him but his race. When lesser breeds copied higher then they were *aspiring* . . .

They strode through a hurdle-gate in the hedge, three bold *meat* clad in the hard shiny material. They held sharp lengths of the same stuff but no fire-sticks. There was hope. He closed quickly, scenting the sickly oils this portion of beastdom liked to put on their tight curls. There would be pleasure in having *their* taste on his cub-lips at the next rebirth.

A blur of assured motion, he fell amongst the would-be noblemen.

'One down. The beast's claw has shredded his breastplate – at the cost of its talons. He rises . . . no, down again. He lies still.'

The wind whistled across Pevensey Castle's battlements but Sennacherib did not have to raise his voice. Everyone hung upon his lightest word.

'Who?'

He could have had a perspective-glass the same as the rest, but was too grand to work for his entertainment. A courtier quizzed the scene and commentated for him.

'Shalmaneser, your majesty . . . I think.'

'Don't *think*, tell!'

The poor man was terrified but fear could not add to his powers of vision. The field was far off, the combatants well covered.

'I . . .'

'It was the one introduced to me as Shal-whatever,' intervened Emperor Blades, to save him, setting down his glass. 'Our first and last encounter, I suspect.'

The anticipated regret didn't arrive: Sennacherib was unmoved. Even when not atop high towers he was still exalted above ordinary feelings. More '*harsh necessity*' he'd earlier told his father – and recognition had made him wince.

'He fell too soon. No, a mere soldier he remains – but let his clan keep his estate.'

He expected such munificence to earn an imperial smile but Blades had turned back to the fray.

The courtier was excited at having good news to tell.

'Ah! It falls, a broken sword between its ribs. It flails and snaps but cannot reach. Shamshi-Adad steps back, one arm is limp. I cannot see his face for blood . . .'

'It is not yet done,' snarled Sennacherib. 'He has no right . . .'

'Kutmuhi hacks its face: it sinks. He lops a beseeching hand and . . .'

'*Enough!*'

Even the King of Pevensey-Levels jumped at an imperative word from the Emperor. Everyone around the tower waited.

'Put the damned glasses down!'

They did. Out of clumsiness one went over the parapet. The postponed crash and tinkle far below did not lighten the atmosphere.

A sunburst was spreading out into searing life within the imperial chest. He had worn the abrasiveness of this visit, he'd made no comment on all the Assyrian archaisms, unmoderated by Christian mildness. He'd even overlooked the matter of the tethered man-bait, because this was his son's realm and they so wanted to display their vaunted Null vigilance. This one had been followed since the South Downs, monitored and allowed to make his way close to put on a show for their majesties. The soldier-shepherd he'd dined on at New-Wilmington had been thought a price worth paying. The Emperor had even bitten his lip about that – as though the People he'd raised up were just *toys* for the using.

126

Come to think of it, he recollected that there were many things about which he'd held his peace lately. There was no good reason why an Emperor should have to do that but he had. The acid in his stomach had no business being there. Apparently, even absolute Emperors got to be bossed about. He was just too considerate of others' feelings – that was his trouble. It was time to rebel.

'I could make all three *Levels-lords*,' offered Sennacherib. His voice was not used to placatory tones; it was no good at them. 'Even the one that failed . . .'

Emperor Blades stood up. He waved away the slave who rushed to move his chair. The poor crushed creature almost backed over the battlements. The Emperor's perspective-glass went sailing to join its dead colleague.

'Do you know,' Blades asked the company, 'what I don't *like* about you ?'

They didn't, and if they did the glittering array would have changed it. But Blades knew – and he knew it was too late to change. Even worse, it was all his fault.

The court looked at him and he at them. The wind got up, taking away the residual sounds of distant battle drawing to a close.

'Do you think it's your callousness?' he asked. They had no idea. It was Sennacherib's job to answer but no one wanted to catch his eye. He was glowering, a thwarted brat on the edge of a precipice whose Dad wouldn't take his hand. Even Jezebel saw the wisdom of remaining still, leaving him to it.

'Or maybe it's your cowardice? I don't see you lot down there baring your arse to the Null!'

Some of the concubines present might have done, if ordered to, but they didn't think that's what he meant.

'Or your sheer God-cursed spoiledness?'

Still no consensus. They didn't deny any of it: they were just raised to think it didn't matter.

Blades stared at each in turn, his thinning locks raging above the iron crown, courtesy of the breeze. It was their unassailable . . . innocence that got to him. He'd created them: part of his rage was against himself.

No one, not even wives and children, held his look. They sensed he was cursing the world he'd made.

'No, I'll tell you. I'll tell you *exactly* what I don't like about you and all this – and that's your *relish* for it!'

Journal of Tom Blades Esq. Emperor of New-Wessex.

May ye third: Ye Year of Our Salvation 1702, Our 22nd year of work in this world.

. . . In the morn about 5.30, with Firstmet and the Huscarls and sundry wives to New-Pevensey through New-haven – though 'tis not New or any kind of haven yet, but a project for future times, may I be spared. At Ripe we were met by Sennacherib and his Aysrrian hordes all clad in gleaming iron and they did obeisance to me – though Sennacherib with a shamed-face. Queen Jezebel was very distant to her boy but I know her thoughts like I do her parts. They are but mere years from attempting something . . .

. . . with all the caravanserai to Pevensey Castle and thence to the sea. The Levels are quite as I recall them, Neptune having freely given back the land that generations past slaved to reclaim by human might. Therein is a lesson for those that would see. There are heads on stakes, dotted over the Levels and adorning the castle walls: Null and human-traitors intermixed. Also, New-Assyria drowns its lesser felons in the channel called 'Deadwater' which runs behind the castle. The worst sort are staked below high tide mark for a slower watery death – unless it be they catch the sea-Nulls' fancy first. There is, I am gratified to say, always a trial first.

After breakfast we walked down to the beach where we entertained ourselves very agreeably an hour or 2. We also had the pleasure to see a new lunette battery erected there against the sea-Null and its two guns, 18-pounders, in action against their incoming tide. There is a very neat house and magazine belonging to the fort and a gunner resident there. 'tis a very lonely and dismal place, flat and water-logged and mist afflicted.

In the afternoon and armed, we explored the dreary hinterlands, probing its shallow pools and gravel pits for the unimaginatively termed 'mud monsters'. None obliged by presenting themselves for our instruction and target practice. I think I should like to see one — from a distance – before the breed is finally extirpated.

I told the hunters that in the old Sussex dialect the beasts would be called knuckers – from the knucker-holes in which they dwell – or else Grendels or Afanc, equally ancient namings. They nodded but were not converted. These are a very practical people and I would wish for more lightness and fancy to them.

We dined in the castle court as follows: legs of lamb, boiled; hot baked egg puddings, gooseberry pies and tenderly fine lobsters with green salad and white cabbage. Sennacherib's inner guard affect to feed on raw meat to demonstrate their savage vigour – but I caught one a-picking at our dainty left-overs. I forbore to report the poor mortified wretch . . .

May ye sixth Ye Year of Our Salvation 1702, Our 22nd year of work in this world.

Today I had occasion to roundly rebuke my family, speaking sternly to them during the tournament against a lured Null. They have strayed from the path of wisdom and have grown unused to correction. Doubtless the fault is all mine but it came as a revelation: one foul moment when I saw them true. They have become knife-faced, smirking creatures: Null in human form. I told them so. We were poor company thereafter . . .

. . . Pheasants (well established now the Null may not feed), cheese-bread, blood-puddings and spit-roasted Pevensey-fish – which tasted all the sweeter for being denied the sea-Null. These last were so fresh plucked from their ocean home I declare their dead eyes did not reproach me, so recent had been the parting from life. Would that the company was as tasty. Then arrived the pastries and tartlets . . .

. . . but at length we were replete, and a poor, languid audience for the dancers who could neither raise our parts or acclamation. I reflected that had Jezebel been mistress of this feast we should have dined on naught but tongue-pie and cold shoulder. Such are the only rations she has served these last days. But no matter, she chooses to accompany her son on his adventure: distance shall soon make her shrieks and curses inaudible.

. . . my family continue out of sorts with me but I know I am in the right. Jezebel is mistaken: I do sincerely wish Sennacherrib well against the Null. He may even return to Pevensey one day.

I think I will found a town where Lewes should be. We have a regiment to spare.

No one is speaking to me: they are (servants) fearful or (family) full of bile . . .

July ye twelfth Ye Year of Our Salvation 1702, Our 22nd year of work in this world.

. . . The summer expeditions are to depart today. The Null's impetuous breeding-time incursions are everywhere weathered, harvest is yet to come. Now is our time. We will expand even as they rest from their madness. The army shall press far into Berkshire and as far West as where Blandford Forum should be – and will be again, G*d willing.

I have drawn a map, as best my memory will serve, and more skilled hands have transcribed it on to the finest stretched vellum. It now hangs in my private library and I oft-times find myself in a study before it, contemplating the patterns I have weaved upon the land. We have done well. If this year does not bring reversal then we shall be close to linkage with the Cornish enclave, hitherto only succoured by sea. Then my ambitions reach to crossing the flat lands of east Anglia to see what prodigies this world has bred in the Fens. Mayhap I could resettle my family there, amidst malaria and monsters, so that they could relearn gratitude . . .

Such musings prompt recollection of happier times. I call to mind a summer residence once high in my favour in Devonshire. This was in the early times: before complexity and betrayal; when the Null were the sole serpent in this garden. I recall happiness there, simple pleasures in its humble walls in those pre-palace days – and peace in observing the sun descend to rest over the Cove. The Null took it, along with all the broad swathe from Bristol down to the Channel, but they have been masters there overlong. They must be made to vomit up this place of refreshment. The Emperor of New-Wessex wishes to behold it, to benefit from it, again.

Thinking on – 'twas there affection first bloomed between

Boudicca and I. She is one of the few: she has not changed. Nor does she assault my ears, dawn to dusk. She has no brood to promote. Her infirmity has engendered sweetness in her. What once was shall be again. Like Christ my content will rise again.

Blandford Forum re-born can await another year. Tomorrow we shall leave – and in martial company. I will divert men to Lulworth and then we will go on holiday . . .

Before he left New-Assyria the Emperor had some more to learn – about himself and the world in general. Pevensey proved to be an instructive place all round. He lived and learned.

Blades just chanced to be passing, on the very day of departure. The incident gave him pause but, in the end, he was thankful for the delay. Otherwise he might have remained in ignorance for further decades.

John, the new-ish captain of the huscarls, frowned at the hubbub, as he did at all lapses from perfection. To start with he'd had no surname, like most of the People, but it had amused the Emperor to distinguish and 'christen' him *John Lilburne* for his querulousness. Quite like his radical namesake from the old World, the man was burly and surly, not much to Blades's taste, but unquestionably brave and good at what he did. Generally, the Emperor preferred he did it out of sight. Today, Lilburne's eternal vigilance awoke the Imperial interest from a light doze: it being a slow morning, post-concubines, pre-council meeting and pre-packing. Blades ordered the palanquin to halt.

'What is that disturbance?' An Emperor is freed from the tedium of targeting queries to the most applicable. They are leapt upon by the hungriest. Imperials and Pevensey men alike opened their mouths.

'It is over,' said Lilburne, the first, but barely civil. 'It never was.' He was already directing fleet huscarls in that direction with finger flicks.

'I wish to see.'

Likewise, no one ever contradicted Emperors, but a pause was the next best thing.

''tis an unpleasantness,' said the bundle of melancholy-masked-by-violence. 'I will deal with it for you.' There was also devotion there, a softening admixture that only baffled the whole into more anger.

'No, I shall.' And that sufficed.

They bore him towards the noise, down the broad tree-fringed avenues of Pevensey's Imperial quarter. At the edges it grew ragged and less sedate, with taverns and barracks and, most relevant to the moment, the municipal impaling stakes.

They'd been his own – drunken – bright idea, though he blushed to admit it: an innovation, now repeated throughout civilised humandom. It was stolen from the Turks of his old world, though the People were not to know that. At the time, strong red wine had helped paint it as a quick way of dealing with the worst crimes, a practical way of showing society's lip-curling disapproval of some felons. 'A *public entertainment*,' he'd announced, through swirling wine fumes and slurring speech, '*with a moral – and a hundred percent record of reform*.' They'd applauded – as they always did.

It had caught on, too rapid and popular to repent of. There were some things even an Emperor struggles to rescind. So, he tried not to think of it, or else restrict it to captured Null or the very dregs of humanity, and though the bodies were left on display, in New-Godalming and other Imperial fiefs, they were thoughtfully sited downwind of the Palace. He rarely went to watch.

Today there was no choice. A mob of tipsy New-Assyrian musketeers on celebration-leave for the most part, were trying to sit a man on a vacant stake. He didn't want to go. They'd just had more luck with another victim. The Emperor averted his eyes.

'Stop them.' It was calmly issued but heartfelt: an offering for the times he hadn't been there. Some day, when he was *really* secure, he'd have the wooden fingers hoicked out, grassed over, and put a church on the site. Then he recalled he hadn't built a new church in the Empire for years. His thoughts rushed on, embarrassed.

John Lilburne obeyed. He moved among them and asked pressing questions whilst Firstmet eavesdropped. The mob were abashed. Strictly speaking, only Pevensey law applied here but no one raised the point, nor were they consulted. The Emperor had arrived and all established custom melted away before his whims.

There were some sore faces but no fatalities, since Lilburne knew he was under the eye. The mob prostrated themselves before the Imperial presence and their would-be victim was brought to Blades, though well past any explaining duties. The point had gone partway in. He was bleeding.

Firstmet had said nothing so far. He was grooming the new security man, letting him earn his spurs. Blades noted unanswered concerns mounting in the one remaining eye – and approved. A quizzical expression to this best-of-lieutenants was sufficient to break the drought of counsel.

'Rough justice,' he told his Emperor, 'but justice all the same. Miracles belong to you alone.'

Blades considered. On safety grounds alone that sounded like a wise precept. Non-interference in his children's games was a time-honoured policy. Likewise, he'd long ago desisted from pouring cold water on his subjects' wild expectations of him. If they wanted miracles, it was best he held the monopoly.

And yet . . . This poor, penetrated, wretch looked like no threat to anyone – and certainly no miracle worker. The man's presumed companion now stared sightless to the sky, past threatening anybody. If, after all, the survivor proved deserving, he could always rejoin his friend.

'Nevertheless' – he rarely went against Firstmet's advice, the pill had to be sweetened – 'one is curious. Have him revived, mended and brought to me. I wish to get to the bottom of this.'

Some so far forgot themselves as to snigger at that. In a second revelatory moment, lit by inner lightening, he again saw the landscape clearly – and again hated it and them and all he'd made.

'Do that again.'

The 'wretch', having been to the door of death, seemed to have left most of his fear there, for later collection.

'It is draining, Majesty, but I will try.'

Amidst all the other wonders this sturdiness was additional worry. If the man should care to *reflect* . . . Emperor Blades wasn't having it and slapped him down with good old irony.

'Yes, if it's not *too* much trouble . . .'

Firstmet and his cohorts picked up on it and moved, ever so slightly, forward. Sennacherib – temporarily displaced into a side throne – radiated displeasure. His '*Iron Council*' likewise. Jointly, the message went home.

The man concentrated. Another distant window shattered: each and every tiny diamond pane. Seconds later came token of their fall into the moat far below. The sound carried easily in the silenced throne room.

The Emperor could not afford to be fazed or even vaguely moved. He treated it as he would a mildly amusing sleight of hand.

'You are a . . . destructive subject.' It was said with a smile, not as condemnation. 'Now amuse us.'

The man thought and then with one wave raised the skirts of the court ladies. There was an alarm of rustling silk and frantic petticoats, soon subsiding into mere cruel merriment. That some of the guards and nobles were kilted but not similarly troubled was very instructive. As was the sight itself. In deference to their married status, Blades had withheld his hand – and other parts – from some of these females, though many were *damned* tempting. Generally, he waited until invited, unless the need grew urgent. Now his curiosity was simultaneously satisfied and roused.

The wizard maintained the trick whilst his Emperor had an eyeful and enjoyed the shrieks. Even Sennacherib laughed.

Eventually, Blades signalled he should desist and it clearly came as relief. The man was breathing heavily, though not for the most obvious reason. That much was encouraging.

'You are in our favour and under our protection. Rest, feed, recover your strength. You shall remain with me and divert us further. Some other time.'

And then the man, who was only a mere carpenter after all, was wreathed in smiles. He would not die but live – and there might be respite from planing wood and spear-shafting and annual Null campaigns for him.

Following all the lengthy associated ceremonial the Emperor withdrew. A door behind the polished sea-pebble throne led into a smaller chamber used for robing and private audiences. He signalled that the inner retinue and Sennacherib should follow. The polished floor thundered as the court rose from its bellies.

The room was of dark varnished oak, obscurely lit and cornered, the centre only in clear view. Blades held that space, hunched and thinking. They did not suspect. Laughter could still be heard outside.

But when the door was shut he turned on them – and his face was all executions.

'Why was I not *told*?'

The Garden of the Mind and the Cultivation Thereof.
A Primer for Mages

Produced under Imperial license. Eremuth Press. John Dee Academy. New-Yarmouth, Vectis. The Year of Walking Aloft 202.

Nihil Obstat. The honourable Hopton Hoptono. Procurator for Ideological Vigilance. New-England beyond-the-Seas

Introduction and a Pious Preamble.
. . . that you may so boundlessly *convince* yourself that your word shall BE is proof that you share – in some minuscule way – in

135

the godhead of the Imperium. At the moment of conception a drifting thought from HE mayhap rested upon your parents' roof and blessed the act, adding a precious golden drop to the conjugal act. Or perchance HE or HIS passed by their abode when desire stirred in their hearts or, just then, HE considered their province and gilded the moment. In this life we shall not know, but doubt not, even as you must doubt not your lordly convictions, that you are *raised*, a step or two, up the mountain that leads to HE.

Be honoured even as you are humbled by this intelligence!

Behold, you are a chosen people, sheltered amongst the bosom of the People, a royal priesthood, a few, a precious crust. The Imperial spirit has seen fit to let you see clear that nothing is true and fixed save HE. All else is given to you to amend.

BELIEVE and you shall wreak great works to the greater glory of the G*d that permits you to rearrange his handiwork.

. . . 3) Basic Training – and how came you here today?
. . . a leavening of perhaps 2 percent in each generation, boy or girl, strong or feeble, has that lack of doubt wherein to say that '*what I will shall* be' – and lo, it happens! Herein is proof that the stuff of the universe is malleable and held, complete and perfect, only in the mind of the IMPERIAL SPIRIT, from second to second and age to age – may he never forget or doubt us as we might wickedly doubt his eternal self.

Your tuition shall be long and arduous. Your faculty must be trained and extended even as your limbs and breath are. To some is given much in the way of *belief* and others little. Where some may perform the inexplicable three or four times in one single day, for others even the failing attempt will prostrate them for weeks. In a few nature will yield to their invisible fingertips only on random occasion. Yet all these, from the most puissant to the weakest brethren, are partakers in a *gift* – and knowing the source of that gift we reverence them all.

For your ease, the wisdom of preceding generations has been accumulated into the grimoires which shall be your closest companions in the years to come. Therein are the tried and trusted mental formulations held most likely to produce the desired effects. You shall learn these spells in their ascending divisions until they be as much a part of you as your G*d-given soul. And learn also this: be you Prince of the First Circle or beyond-Downs dirt farmer you shall not leave us till you hold these spells, pristine and efficacious, ever-shining in the weapon we shall make of your mind.

To conserve the required clarity of thought, contact with blood relatives, tribal brothers or spouses is not permitted for the duration of initial training. After the third year this stipulation may be relaxed but special application must be made to . . .

There had been also been *mind-warpers* in the time of the 'Angels', or so it was said; probably raised up by those same elusive beings. During that lost age, if ever it existed in truth, men supposedly walked the Downs and, under *angelic* tutelage, challenged the Null with the powers of the mind, not Blades's 'far-killer' sticks of smoke and fire.

The effect had been the same. No wonder the Null coveted human flesh above and beyond its luscious taste. There must have been a time of standing erect, of burying the honoured dead in long-barrows, of getting used to sunlight and fearlessness. That confidence and the power to mould reality were probably intertwined.

Then something must have happened – if it ever happened at all. The *Angels* went away, and the confidence went with them. The People went below ground again, forgot how to make their thoughts manifest. There were still the tales, told in the starless nights beneath the earth. And there remained a few, a very few, maybe descended from the greater mages of long before, who could cause trifling effects, but the backbone had gone out of them. It was trivial stuff, hardly worth mentioning beside the miracles wrought by Emperor Blades. Later, it appeared nigh-on blasphemous to venture into territory *He* had made his own. Everyone knew – like they knew that Downs grass was green and the Null were purple. Sennacherib knew it, Boudicca and Jezebel knew it; the humblest stableboy in Humandom knew it but never thought about it. No one said. Everyone assumed *He* knew everything – as he knew where 'Pevensey' was and where 'brimstone' might be found.

For his part, Blades now learned that he had been told only what they wanted to tell him, or what they thought he would approve of. It was productive of a few restless nights and for a while after the world he'd made seemed a jot less . . . well-fitting than before. Yet, once he had thought it though, opportunist as ever, sure enough the sun came out again.

He realised that they'd meant well. There was flattery in the realisation that it was he who'd brought their confidence back, and with it – to a few – such self-belief that thoughts could be made real. If they'd had kept it to themselves, or used it in sneaking ways, close to criminality, he saw their point. The information was withheld out of civility. The upright members of the People had no need of such powers, or so they thought.

Emperor Blades begged to differ – after he had finished raging and demoting. He issued an Empire-wide proclamation to all of the hidden *mages*, taking them under his wing and, to the best of his ability, putting an end to the pious persecutions. Special academies would be set up, on islands and in remote places to develop their skills. The Isle of Wight sprang straight to mind – and rioted therein like magic itself. They already had a toe-hold on its western tip. A mage-led expedition to burst out of the New-Yarmouth enclave would be interesting, an experiment to see if wizardry could scour away the Null as well as musketry. Learning whilst on the job, so to speak. Sink or swim; the proving of a new blade. Then, an academy based on Yarmouth castle and a Yar canal to Freshwater, converting west Wight to a island in its own right, as in his former world. A mysterious thaumaturgic isle brooding just over the Solent. The idea appealed. Emperor Blades jotted a reminder – a couple of scrawled words to change the world – that it should be done.

He leant back, momentarily entranced by visions of a doubly golden age for humans of . . . wider understanding.

And if he could not replicate their skills or generate such self belief, try as he might, then it was only embarrassing to himself. He clearly came from a lesser breed. Boudicca did not conceive, Firstmet's eyesocket remained empty. It was no *loss*, as such; matters remained just as they were.

Anyway, the experiments were conducted out of sight and in odd solitary hours. The Emperor kept quiet about it and his subjects were none the wiser. He had still learned: he had lived and learned.

That very night, a dozen men and women went to feed the Sea-Null, staked out on Pevensey beach at dusk to await the tide.

Their hands were clipped, their tongues torn out. Sennacherib did not want them performing any little tricks or reciting a valediction. Mages were notoriously hard to kill.

They were – had been – the unsuspected best, the most accomplished of mages, and useful in so many ways. Sennacherib flattered himself no one else owned such well honed tools, ready to unleash. They'd been his secret collection, painstakingly accumulated, talent-spotted from amongst the Assyrians or tempted in from further afield. Now they had to go. He could not risk the Emperor's surprise again.

So, painfully they'd come and now painfully they went. It was a shame. Sennacherib bade personal farewell to each, whispering solace into their frantic ears.

He also cursed the uncollected wildcard that had alerted his father, a 'high mage' lurking unknown under his nose, wasting himself with planks and nails. Someone's hide would smart for missing *him*. In their different ways, neither Sennacherib or his father had expected the man. He'd descended as a revelation on the heads of two divine rulers.

And that was yet another puzzle in itself. Why the Emperor's astonishment? Why should an all-knowing intellect feign great areas of ignorance? It was enough to set your own mind thinking . . .

As his estranged father's great convoy headed west, bent on some senile 'holiday', Sennacherib braved the evening chill to watch the waters engulf his lost elite. He needed to make sure. Then the sea-Null came in with the tide and the noises left no room for doubt.

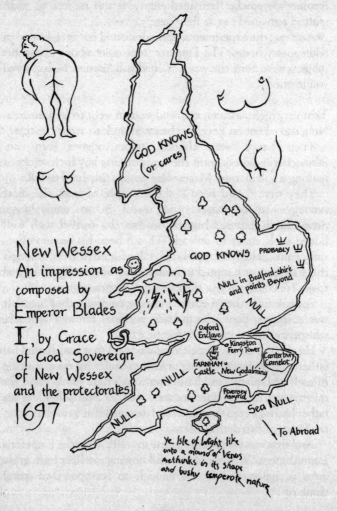

The high-tide of human advance could hardly have been plainer. Blades's road builders had driven a track almost all the way down towards Lulworth Cove, the basis of something grander when time permitted. It never had. Everything had been sacrificed to the great Null invasion, every cherished project dropped. The roadsmen, if they still lived, were patrolling a castle wall now, or else building new ones. There wasn't yet sufficient intercourse between enclaves to merit Roman-style roads. The Downs heartlands were criss-crossed with acceptable trade paths and that sufficed. The rest could wait.

Emperor Blades wasn't feeling so patient. He swept aside the advice of Nebuchadnezzar, the general who'd recovered this area and who now was all faintheart about its occupation. He'd even been curt to Firstmet who wanted to sweep every wood and covert before allowing his Emperor access. There was such a thing as knowing when to *lead*, when to show an example. He and his glittering entourage had swept in not far behind the victorious regiments; days before work could start on a new – in one sense, and first in another – Lulworth Castle.

'A few more minutes,' he told Boudicca, who was glued, wide-eyed, to the carriage window, 'over the next rise.'

And so it was, two stories of local grey stone, dating from before his architects were instructed in the baroque. Nestled humbly amidst its own fields it might have passed for any middling Downs-Country farmer's abode, save for the attendant rose garden and maze.

That the house was still there was welcome but small surprise: the Null did not go in for destruction of the inanimate. They had plainly defiled it though, sensing in their black and purple swirling thoughts some value attached to it by the insurrectionary meat-animals.

From a distance they saw penetrations in the thatch roof and blood sprays on its upper reaches. Cat-like, the Null must have toyed with some prey up there. Likewise, it was clear where the enemy had rolled and cavorted in the flower beds. Through spite or impatience they had burst through the hedge walls of the maze Blades insisted upon in each of his residences. A Null sleep-swarm had obviously centred itself atop his favourite statue of himself. It was all streaked and chipped now. They had used it as a claw scratcher and then a latrine.

Doubtless every room was similarly marked with droppings or the tokens of lavishly enjoyed kills. It wasn't much of a welcome to a holiday home – but the only one on offer. All was silence: marked contrast to the imagined symphonies of death now playing in the head of each arrival .

There'd been a skeleton house-staff when the Null arrived – and there still was, their white bones jammed in rage into the bricks and mortar or fashioned into a mocking avenue, protruding up from the pleasure garden. Plainly, the Null had feasted well there, too – and at painstaking leisure.

The horsemen, chariots and carriages swept down the mere farmtrack to the house, a cloud of raucous activity dispelling the cloud of quiet. Hares and rabbits scattered across the shaggy fields but otherwise there was no sign of life.

Such was his zeal that Blades descended without assistance, too quick even for the hastening body-servants. He was pleased. His weight was on the flagstones; he'd come into his own again: the past was there for recapture.

The Emperor took in the blank, staring windows, he drank in the scene – and paused. For one moment there was . . . anticipation, an air-borne spice of unease. His feet froze; he vainly sought it again. Nothing: only neglect and the scent of straw. Perhaps he'd picked up the house's final exhalation of the evil it had held. New life had arrived: the past fled.

'Start with the parlour and one bedroom. Till they're cleaned we'll take our meals outside.'

He was long unused to such fiddling considerations but had brought the burden on himself. The Emperor had travelled light: the minimum of body-servants, caterers and huscarls, a wife or three, some poets and entertainers, a few favoured children of recent arrival, the Mage of Pevensey. He had to descend to thinking through his own arrangements.

'I saw some sheep when we arrived, over by that spinney.

142

Also myriad rabbits by the trackside. They'll suffice for this evening.'

The designated foragers set off, as directed. He would have liked to ride with them but did not feel guilty. The rabbit matter allowed Blades to feel as though he were actively contributing. They were an early introduction of his to this new world and a wildly successful one.

He knew the place had been traversed, top to bottom, by Firstmet's operatives but Blades still felt like a conquering hero crossing the threshold of his recovered home. He was glad he had come: there was respite in petty actions, a holiday from being oneself, just as much as in a change of location. He felt refreshed already.

'Boudicca! To me!'

She swung her legs out of the fortified coach. It was a long way down and her maids had to assist.

The Emperor waited at the door, recalling a tradition from the old world.

'I forgot to do this when you first entered the palace. Position makes you remiss. You lose out on the good things of life – the little things. I suppose the wedding robes were too bulky to permit it in any case . . .'

She didn't understand him but that was so common as to be normal. He often mused away like that: it was passed over in a smile. One of the things that made him warm to her was precisely that quiet acceptance of the abyss between them. Right now Jezebel would be firing questions, seeking explanation, rooting around in the allotment of knowledge, trying to harvest advantage.

But even Boudicca reacted when he swept her up. Her shorter leg made her hyperconscious of balance. A frightened shriek turned into laughter and the Emperor was gladdened. She was no featherweight and he no young, lusty, newly-wed, but he was determined not to be robbed of his gesture. The courtiers gaped and then applauded.

'Better late than never,' he told his puzzled, giggling, bride-of-long-standing, and then bestowed a kiss as he bore her over the threshold into the house of death. Cleansing sunlight followed them in.

The first night. Three bottles in.

'And I'll tell you *this* for nothing; beforehand, it was a place of peace, all mildness and high learning. The kings were reasonable, listening to their councillors. Like there was this thing called a *Witan*, right? Parliament grew out of that. The kings consulted it – had to: couldn't order the early English about too much.'

The Emperor took another long drink and then, slowly, precisely, set the goblet down. Wine still slopped over the brim but wasn't noticed. He lolled back in his travelling throne. Night in the garden was falling amidst the sweet fragrance of roses. The gnats were held at bay with slow-burning brimstone coils. He'd set all tasks and plans and worries aside; this was holiday; he was relaxing. All was well.

'And another thing, you wouldn't find that across the water – or in Scotland, oh no! It was all divine-right, absolute monarchs with them . . .'

Some of the soldiers and courtiers exchanged glances. This was a revolutionary gospel they were absorbing tonight. Their thoughts couldn't keep up with it.

'Like the Church, too – no heavy hand like afterwards. They was *good* priests, true to their creed, not nagging after gold at deathbeds. I recall this vicar called Speed: terrible man. I'm not saying he was like that himself but he weren't much of a Christian either. No. Only cheeks he ever turned was his wife's. Lovely woman by the way – not unlike Boudicca in looks – in some lights.'

He used that same light, shed by blazing torches, to check, and saw it was so. There again, between the flattering illumination and the wine, all the women present were turning into goddesses.

'Same with a lot of you, actually: you two there – and you. What's your name, angel-face? What? No, doesn't matter, tell me later . . . Come to think of it, that's why you're here. Nice

144

rosy cheeks, above and below. One likes that. Where was I?'

No one knew or cared to say. They were too agog. It was rare beyond measure for the Emperor to hint, let alone rant on and on, about the *before place*. The scribes were scribbling away like there was no tomorrow. Even the sentinels around the walled garden neglected their duty and strained to hear.

'Oh yes, I know. The Anglo-Saxons: fine people, much maligned. The later kings got monks, Welsh monks, to write bad things about them – and that's what passes for history. Bah! I spit on their history books; I *piss* all over their handwritten, illuminated lies. Bloody Gildas? Bloody Gerald Cambrensis? Celtic mercenaries! My ancestors were all right, they were. You listen to this: a maiden, right? In them days a *maiden* bearing gems laden in her arms could pass from one end of the land to the other unmolested. I've seen that written down. We'd sorted the Vikings – seen them off; everything was going well. Scholars from all over came there. The Frankish lands, and the Germans, even the Italians looked up to us. Great things were coming, great things . . .'

He lapsed into inner soliloquy for a while and then suddenly jerked awake.

'But then the Normans swept over the peaceful land, visiting it with fire and sword. Listen to this, right? Of every ten Englishmen alive when William the Bastard landed at Pevensey Port only nine survived the years of his reign, borne off through war or famine. It's the truth! T'wasn't fair! Two armies to face – one up north – beat that, and then had to rush south; should have waited. Nearly won anyway. One afternoon's work and then all was lost. He *scourged* us, I tell you, scourged us with flails of fire. I don't know what God was thinking about . . .'

Indeed they didn't know what he was thinking about – but they were lapping it up. This was something to tell your grandchildren about.

Firstmet was fearless – save in one, focused field – and considered privileged besides. He dared to try and steer the monologue along a route of his own devising.

'Sire . . .'

'What? Oh, it's you. What? Speak up, don't be shy!'

Firstmet's single burning eye belied the tentative tone. From the zone of torch light the semi-circle of courtiers re-directed their gaze to him

'Why did not your King Arthur save the Eng-lish race from these *No-mans*? Why did you withhold your command from him?'

As Sennacherib had seized upon the Assyrians, so Firstmet latched on to *The Once and Future King*. He loved his Emperor's occasional half-remembered, half-made-up, tales of Camelot, the Round Table and chivalrous quests.

Blades faltered. It was brought home to him, yet again; the unbridgeable chasm between him and his people. His was a thickly textured past, however imperfectly recalled. Theirs was made up of burrows and then whatever scraps he doled out: misheard, misunderstood and twisted in the repeating between them. It was not his own world he was recreating here, but an unpredictable cross-breed of it.

Still, it was *his* chosen version, his the selection of the elements in that mating. He ought not to complain. Still on the upcurve of the wine-rush, he let himself be cheered.

'I never knew him, Firstmet. It was long before my time – and anyway, I weren't a king then . . .'

That got a round of gasps and, even under the cloud of strong wine brought from that same 'before place', he knew he'd staggered a pace too far. Though she understood – and cared – less than most, Boudicca knew it too. She took his arm.

'You are fatigued, my lord: the long ride . . .'

He squeezed her waist even as he allowed himself to be levered up.

'Maybe so,' he winked, 'but now I'm *longing* for another one . . .'

'Whose side where the Null on?' interrupted John Lilburne, the captain of the guard. They were his day and night obsession, his one known interest save for the welfare of his Lord. 'Did they aid the *No-mans* or the *Vikkings*?'

146

Blades allowed himself to be detained, his usual caution to be lulled. He blearily recalled the phrase 'in wine there is truth' – and thought it an order.

'John-boy, there *were* none there. We were free of 'em. Do you know what I think? They never made it on the Ark; all drowned in the Flood – but that's another story. And bloody good job too, or we'd be in the same pickle as here. I'd 'ave grown up shaggy in a burrow like you!'

Another collective intake of breath – but it went unnoticed. He'd risen, scattered a few gold *Toms* at them and then turned his back, heading with clumsy haste for the royal bed.

Emperor and Empress stumbled and his weight went on her crooked leg. She yelped before the pain could be suppressed.

'That's the spirit,' he misconstrued, 'want to hear lots of those . . .'

He turned to dismiss the gathering with a wave and then noticed two of the more forward serving-maids; all long loose hair and slack lips.

Blades considered – but only for a brief span.

'You as well,' he ordered, beckoning them with a palm full of Toms. 'We are on holiday: tonight we shall be *inventive*.'

Some scrambled for the coins he'd strewn but others forbore; more than usual. Of those who watched him go, the sterner soldiers of his guard, the unchosen wives, the younger and so less grateful nobles, there were not a few who looked – and looked – emulating their Emperor, thinking inventive thoughts indeed.

'Wheat.'

'No, bearded barley.'

Boudicca couldn't see the point of distinction. The waving fields supplied grain of some or other sort – unavoidably mixed with invader poppies and cornflower. It was all she needed to know: the servants would bring what was required.

'Father says barley,' she told the tottering infant. '*Barley*,' –

and then instantly forgot. Likewise, the child didn't hear and it didn't matter. A prince by birth, he had better things to learn and wandered off to join the other junior royalty. The Mage was conjuring pressed patterns in the crop for them.

Boudicca mothered the more fertile wives' children as though they were her own – save that she surrendered them back without rancour at afternoon's end. Blades could have ordered a son or two to be delivered up to her but it was not asked for. He knew she would have, had she wanted. It was just like her not to buy joy with the tears of others.

The Imperial head and bowels were still troubled by the excesses of the previous night, throbbing with the impurities within a vintage grown under the sun of another world. Stocks of old-earth wine were growing thin now, even in New-Godalming, and were fetched up only for high and holy days. Those bottles of genuine Portuguese port had been too much for him to resist, just like the shameless serving maids. Each reeked too much of *play* to withhold his lips – and hands and parts – from.

Now he regretted – not the act itself but being caught. Boudicca told him that he had also said too much – but then could not explain how. However, he saw confirmation of it in some of the new looks he got, where before there had been unvaried awe. Noah's sons had beheld his nakedness; though Blades – dimly – recalled the Bible held *them* to blame for that, even though it was the old man who was sprawled out smashed. Hitherto, he'd reckoned that as rough justice – but now appreciated the mysterious wisdom of Scripture.

Be that as it may, somehow – and thankfully only for some – he'd briefly alighted from the dais of divinity, becoming a mere man such as they. A few were now measuring him against themselves – and since he recruited only the finest in every field, that was not reassuring.

'I must walk – my head is clouded.'

Boudicca nodded and resumed her reading. 'I'm not surprised.'

He transcended the wifely rebuke. He approved of her

absorption. She liked plays, she devoured Shakespeare over and over. Making her literate had been one of his better investments of time. Jezebel could write scathing letters on a daily basis but the books he gave her were destined to be mere doorsteps and dust-gatherers.

'A more moderate feast tonight I think . . .'

It was a hybrid between order and suggestion.

'And a less crowded bed?'

'Definitely.'

'Then I'll join you.'

There were paths trodden in the barley; servant trails wending to the sea. He took the nearest, leaving the Imperial family to their own devices before the house. A half dozen huscarls and the ever-present Firstmet trotted after him. After all this time they could practically read his mind and remained a few paces behind, permitting him the freedom to think and recover. He strode on without looking back, never doubting they were there.

The Mage was summoned too. There might be occasion to talk; a chance to locate some better role for him than children's conjurer.

Soon enough the slope of the land and the few scrubby trees at the garden's edge took them out of view. Behind, all that was now visible were the chimney-stacks. The sound of infants at play went as swiftly. He felt happily alone – for the guards were so usual as to be invisible. The sun was getting up, bringing every sign of a broiling hot day to come. For the moment though there was the occasional refreshing breeze, right in his face from off the sea. He drank it in and pleasure made an appearance on the frontiers of his discontent.

The crop was chest to shoulder high, waving in unison to those same salt zephyrs. There would be no one to it harvest this year and no call to do so. This was still frontier, marcher, land where all efforts were directed to just maintaining a grip. Supplies came in from more secure areas like the Downs, the work of those with leisure to plough and reap. These fields, remnant work of those who'd thought themselves established, would have to await happier days, growing wild meanwhile. In this, only the third or fourth year of their freedom, they still kept mainly to the boundaries set by their dead masters. There remained, with the eye of faith, a delineation between wild and reclaimed; in a world barely clawed from the hand of cruel nature, people saw beauty in a pure straight line.

The Emperor walked on, following his nose and the dictates of the paths. The enclosing barley muffled all sound save their tread. From time to time there was a rustle in the nearby crop, the retreat of some small creature or the eruption of a nesting bird, but otherwise he'd found welcome silence. The inner pains were easing with each stride.

At a clearing by a field gate they regrouped to consult. The Emperor's memories of the ways had grown fuzzy, whereas Firstmet had trodden each, by lantern light in some cases, just as soon as he was happy with the house.

'There leads straight to the ocean, via a deep hollow. That way is to the main stables. This 'un heads for the far hills.'

He was one of a few permitted not to prefix everything with *my lord*, *highness*, *majesty* and the like. It made for swifter speech and appeased the former curate's residual democratic conscience.

'I remember now. There's a cove – and a curious archway worn by the sea.'

'Previous you gave it a name: *Durdle*.'

'Oh yes, Durdle Door. Was that one noted?'

On most of its perambulations the Imperial party were accompanied by cartographers who recorded each name as the Emperor recalled it or else made one up. Firstmet nodded confidently. He could be quite sure: he'd memorised the map.

'Oh good . . .' Sudden recollection crowded in upon Blades.

He'd been here before, during the previous life, on a cart trip with his brother and father, deep into worrying foreign lands where people spoke strangely and stared. They'd gone to Poole to fetch back Silas's bride, the daughter of a old carpenter friend of their father's. Whilst noisy negotiation went on they'd had time to poke around and see the sea for the first time. Blades recollected the amazement of that and how even Silas had been silenced. Whilst struck dumb by the wondrous view an old beach gleaner had come up to them and sympathised with their amazement.

'I know,' he'd told them. 'And I 'ear there's more of it along the coast beyond Swanage!'

Afterwards they'd meandered to evensong in Dorchester, still in a mood of thankfulness, but then Silas had been unbelievably rude to the parson and spoilt the mood . . .

The Emperor shook his head and his huscarls mistakenly thought it the aftermath of last night's wine. It was a hangover of some or other sort, true, but not the kind they had in mind. Too clear visions of a shewed-off life were disagreeable to him.

So, here the yawning gaps were fairly easy to fill in, the maps produced in New-Godalming reasonably complete. Elsewhere, his imagination was getting severely stretched and some places were getting uninspired christenings.

'Not the sea, I think; not today. Towards the hills: that direction, I haven't been there.'

Those of the guards who heard it disbelieved; disregarded. Their lord was all charming modesty. Of course, he'd been there; he'd been everywhere whilst he was creating the world.

''Tis a fair way and it'll be hot soon. Horses'll make it easier – bring some pleasure to it.'

Again, Firstmet was one of the very few permitted to amend Imperial suggestions. Anything emanating from him could be trusted to be only for the best.

'Very well. We shall call at the stables. In fact, I like your idea: mounted, we may cut across this confining crop. One tires of single file.'

Their hampered pace seemed less onerous now there was purpose to the tramp. An end was almost in sight.

They were halfway through the next field when all decisions were brusquely rescinded. There were screams from the house: powerful ones to be heard at such distance – screams cut short.

The party turned in confusion, faces tilted upward, scenting the air, straining for sounds. All they could study was the crop

151

and the sky. Pinioned between walls of barley they felt vulnerable, a long off from being useful.

There was another call; a ram's horn sounding hard, an agreed rallying sign. It too died before its proper time.

Unbidden, the huscarls shimmied round him so that men stood fore and aft between him and harm.

'Horses or straight back?' asked Firstmet. His voice lacked all inflection, as though enquiring about dinner.

Blades couldn't think. He'd been out of battle too long and snuggled amidst an army even then. Here there was just the inverted bowl of the sky and a few lost companions. The sun was suddenly searing, directed at him alone. The Emperor felt exposed: a pea on a drum, bouncing to some unseen other's tune.

Again the decision was taken out of his flapping hands. The Null rose from the barley.

They stood to a signal, though not one humans could hear. The cereal convulsed as they arose *en masse* and, as one, looked at the stranded party.

Firstmet's hand was disrespectfully upon the Imperial collar, dragging him along.

'To horse,' he explained to his lord – and then left it at that. Blades saw the wisdom of the decision and made it his own. No other words were required for the while. It was plain they would need every available reserve – and ample luck – to win free.

For the most part the Null were content just to shadow them. They kept pace parallel to the humans, crashing with ease through the barley. Occasionally, one of the nearest would veer in, or an unsuspected beast would rear up right alongside, and the two forces would brush. The huscarls were at additional disadvantage apart from numbers, surprise and strength. They were hindered in the use of their favoured great axe by lack of space. Several were peeled off and then killed, unseen but well heard, amidst the crops.

They died to some purpose. Each loss allowed the shrinking projectile of humans a little lull in which to draw nearer their target. Nor was the killing all one way. From time to time a whirling axe head met and sliced its aim. Those blows made the Null yowl their shrill hurt-song in earnest and led to the end of all interest in proceedings. Now the sprays of red upon the barley were not only human. The Null hated the great axe almost as much as the 'far-killers'. Swung well, the six-foot shaft and weighted blade made puny man the fleeting equal of his predator.

Firstmet had brought a brace of pistols but he husbanded them, knowing that they were for story's end, not the chase that would precede that end. An occasional pointed wave of one gun bought them an enemy's change of direction and extra seconds. The timber rectangle of the stable block was now in sight, tunnel-seen through an avenue of stems.

They knew. A Null, an upper-end-of-the-scale specimen, cleared the crop and stood four-square in the path. Blades was all faith and did not slow his headlong sprint. Sure enough, a huscarl hurtled past him to occupy those poised claws. Then, whilst he was being redly brushed aside, another hacked the monster down. It took two grunting blows for the thing to be made still. Undelayed, the Emperor took the carcass with a leap.

Then they were clear and into the stableyard. There was reluctance in issuing out of the field – for at least it softened sight of the full facts. In the open their unedited predicament was spread out for them, plain as a whore in bed. The Null had kept pace and arrived as they did – but in numbers and full of joy.

Firstmet used a pistol then. He was known to double charge his weapons: at the cost of wildness over distance it transformed them into argument-stoppers. The nearest Null was lifted up and back and broken.

It gave the rest pause. They were known to be both frightened and fascinated by the stick weapons, vainly torturing human prisoners to teach them how the magic worked. Failing in that they killed captured musketeers by impaling them upon their weapons: a mark of both respect and its opposite.

The humans knew of that and so there was no reason for

them to be moderate. They hurtled across the cobbled court-yard, using the sound and smoke of the discharge as their ticket of release. To either side the Null were near claw-reach, a soft-sighing, smiling mob, undaunted, finally confident of their feast. Also, they knew they had the *meat*-leader. The older, scrawny Null at the back were pointing at him. They thought they had the ending of a shameful episode in their grasp – and jaws and guts.

The rows of stable double-doors were closed but that could soon be remedied. There were horse noises aplenty from within and so their quest still had purpose. Firstmet gestured a man back to buy them time.

He – true huscarl – did not hesitate. The great axe might not have all the deadly force of an overhand blow when swung like a scythe, but it was good for securing solitude. The incoming horde leant back from its path – one of them insufficiently. The razor-edge parted its stomach, the purple flesh peeled and gaped, giving up its tight-packed load.

That angered them: they did not care to be reminded that they were also just bags of *meat*. The Null flung themselves on the axe-man and swallowed him up.

The Pevensey-Mage was next. Desperation made him reveal all his cards: not stylish play, but effective. Two exclamations, two passes of the hands and the same number of Null fell bubbling. Then they were on him and twisted his gifted head off. The Emperor learned the type's full potential too late.

Firstmet, though now no youngster and grown grey in his Emperor's service, lived up to his name and was foremost to a door. Its iron handles obliged, the latch did not fight. He slung the barriers aside – only to reveal more waiting Null.

Those equine sounds they'd heard and taken as hope had been panic and death-throes. Some mounts remained alive, rearing and kicking to postpone the inevitable – emulating their masters in that respect – but they were too few and scattered and wild.

These new Null must have been younger braves. It was still not clear, even after so long a war, whether the Null took and issued orders like men, or acted jointly on pure instinct. In the brief time allowed to him, Blades doubted it could be part of their design to dine upon slaughtered horses and stableboys. Surely that could have waited?

Negligent or no, the monsters blinked at the sudden light like the beasts they were – and Blades had never hated them as much as at that moment.

The remnant humans shot in amongst them – for there was nowhere else to go – whilst they were still squatting, red-mawed, amongst the dead. Axes added to their number. A narrow gap was cleared. The place reeked to the roof of gore and straw and fear.

Firstmet trod on dead men and Null to get to a cornered steed. Its eyes were white-showing, rolled upwards. Foam was all over its lips. He secured its bridle and hung on, though flung back and forth like a doll, whispering to it, seeking its ear.

The Null were of their party now, intermixed. Despairing of axe-work in that clinch, the remaining huscarls had drawn hand-choppers and the stiletto blades that costly experience had found best for penetrating Null musculature. It would be token resistance at best. Man for man – or beast, Humanity could only match the Null when in serried ranks or shieldwall. In individual duels they reverted to the old status of uncooperative meat.

Emperor Blades bore no arms; in recent years it had been thought beneath him. So he stood useless and vulnerable, like the proverbial oiled boy before the Turk, whilst others made sacrifice and gathered company for judgement. If he hadn't been so busy and fastidious he would have fouled himself: a farewell gesture to make his consumption less pleasant.

Amidst the swirl the final huscarl went down, still attached through a buried stiletto to his Null. Then the Emperor thought himself alone and the last of men. He said a swift – sincere – sorry to the God he'd rather neglected of late and spread his arms. A clear path given to the chest and throat was the easiest parting from the world via a Null – he'd seen that on staked-out criminals left for their attention. There was an implausible second of silence; he even caught a snatch of birdsong. In the circumstances it was not consolation but cruelty.

Given these distractions, and being so quiet, Firstmet had been forgotten or assumed dead. He resurrected himself with a pistol placed in the Imperial hand, a taut bridle thrust before his face.

'Save yourself!' he said above the resumed Null noise – but really it was a plea, his own last prayer. It could have been his horse already but he'd forgone both it and life.

Emperor Blades still – just – had the decency to question that decision, but only for so long as sight of the first Null claw. He even brushed his saviour aside to fling himself atop the mount.

Horse and rider were trampling Null before they could properly read events. One minute there were two *sweet-meat* cowering behind a four-leg *tough-meat*, and the next, one had abandoned the other just to gain a little more life. It took them aback. Such things could not happen amongst them, for they were brethren and children of the same mothers. They did and died together. Because of this spirit within they were not *meat*.

Blades wasn't so inhibited. He did not even look back as he ducked through the stable door. A captain of the Null who blocked his way was shot full in the face, decapitating him. Then luck and desperation found a path away from the place ordained for his end. The Null had bunched in the doorway, expecting to be spectators only, excluded by numbers from the death. They were unready. A crunching brush, a raking of horse-flesh and then he was free.

The older and wiser Null lamented that, knowing he was the pre-eminent *meat* and that they had missed him. Even the fleetest Null-youth could not outpace a *four-leg* in its fear. They were saddened – but only for a brief space, according to their kind.

The rest, blissful in lack of thought, their appetites raised, were crowding into the stable. The elders gleefully joined them, for within there was still work to do.

He crossed the fields to the house. Happily, the crop concealed neither pothole or Null. At the gallop the first would be more lethal than the second. He would have trampled a mere monster down like he did the treacherous barley.

The Emperor knew in his heart of hearts what to expect but still hoped to help. Then, at the brow of the rising land, there was the expected, but no less painful for it, chest-stab of disappointment. The Null were making merry in his house.

Some of the human inhabitants survived but only to be toyed with. When they had leisure and were replete the Null were known to rape, regardless of sex, and, by their greater size and persistence, kill that way. There were some such scenes now, in the garden where he had sat with his children. Blades had to force himself to look. He saw familiar faces, both dead and – presently – alive, but, happily, no one foremost in his heart. He scanned further afield.

The hastily repaired maze was being misused. Ill-advised fugitives had sought refuge there or perhaps been driven inside to spin things out. From his vantage point Blades could see the tops of speeding heads, both pursuers and prey. They were making parody of his indulgence, perverting its proper purpose. Small insult added to mortal injury.

Shutting his ears to cries from upper windows, Emperor Blades looked and looked and did not know whether to desire or fear failure. In the long run, thinking of the years ahead when he must recall and wonder, it would be for the best if they'd had a quick death. If they should appear and appeal to his impotence he'd take a wound that would ever fester. *What the eye didn't see, the heart couldn't grieve*, his Cromwellian grandma used to say. A harsh but true bit of wisdom. He decided he didn't *want* to see, he didn't wish the pain of too clear grief. The furniture of his mind was grotesque enough already.

But then, as always, when wise acceptance was almost there, cruel hope made its appearance. Just like in the old world, presiding Fate seemed to dislike things getting bad past any point in proceeding. It wanted people to stagger on to yet more dancing to its jerky tunes.

Inopportune hope came just as the Null in the house caught sight of him, gesturing and singing themselves into action. Till then, flight had been the only option. The monsters were inadvertently prompting him into the years to come. It would be no disgrace, not his fault. He might be tearful but he had good reason to move on.

Then the human soldiers appeared.

'Too late.'

Was that doubt in his eyes or thwarted ambition? Blades could not decide whether John Lilburne the huscarl doubted his decision or wished for expiation in death. He must not be permitted either.

'Do as I say! It would be to no avail. They are gone, and we must live to fight another day!'

He'd ridden hard to reach them before they got too far in. At that distance there was still time for withdrawal. The Null were preoccupied but not beyond the temptation of a dessert course. The Emperor ordered the formation *about-turn.*

And anyway, that was enough *explaining* of orders to underlings. Even a tearful, sweaty, Emperor should guard his mystique from over-familiarity. He wanted to praise Lilburne but found resistance within. The hard truth was that he, first generation out of the burrow, had behaved better than his Lord. That was the seed of the look he now saw. It was *doubt* and Blades did not approve. Doubt might canker into despising.

It was the Emperor who had set huscarls to fence repairs, who'd thus neglected security and allowed the Null in. Firstmet had warned, so had John Lilburne. The beasts had not been driven out but consciously withdrew, setting a trap. They'd mock-fled before the attacking legions of that summer and then infiltrated back round them; an unlooked-for, out-of-season incursion. Some scout must have sniffed out the chief human's presence or else the beasts were even more worryingly cunning, anticipating his impatient return.

Either way, he'd sauntered in, slept through all the signs and sealed their fate. Whereas it was John who had rallied his scattered men and then headed for the fight. But by then there was no fight, only consumption and torture, and the Null were too many for anything more than gestures. If things had been as they ought the incursion would have been detected early on. There could have been a fighting retreat, his loved ones at the centre of a hollow, protecting, square. But they weren't there and now it was too late. Even so, John the huscarl still attempted the right thing before his master stopped him. The lesser was teaching the greater. It riled.

It also came on to rain – in drenching buckets. All his courtiers and caretakers were gone but Blades was soon provided with a military cape of leather. Slumped in it he rode back to the frontier at New-Winchester.

The Emperor of Humanity: amidst a throng of soldiery – but lone and lonely.

Journal of Emperor Blades I, Downs-Lord Paramount, Emperor of New-Wessex and its dependencies, Protector of Assyria-in-Sussex, Despot of New Godalming and the Holy of Holies, Sultan of the Marches, General of Hosts, Firer of Cannon, Musket-Master, Keeper of the Citadel keys. Redemptor and Defender of the Faith. Bane of the Null.

. . . Thurs ye 3 of something or other. It matters not the year.

Now that everything – or nigh everything – I wish is mine to command, I wish only for that I cannot have. I miss the lurch of her shoulders, the flash of her eyes when I wrong . . .

I confine myself to the inner sanctum with bottles for company. I am inconsolable . . .

Saturday.

. . . John Lilburne the huscarl must go to another city – or Sicily. He says nothing but his face is an accusation, a reproach to me. Far away he may serve us profitably again. He will like the sun – and the solitude. I am being considerate to him. Caiaphas, his placement, is from afar: he knows not pharaoh . . .

Sunday.

. . . There were tears aplenty on our return, some genuine, a few for the right reason. I am surrounded by the pared-down, the ambitious and calculating. Even my own family – sharp faces all – supposedly my cushion against the howling storm outside, leave open the door to let it in. Without her kind words I am quite alone. Oh despair . . .

Monday. ye 7th July. The Year 22. The architects have come with plans for her memorial. There shall be five stories, encased in marble, and other polished stone, the tallest minaret in the city. Daily there will be a sacrifice of Null before her effigy. But it will be an empty place still, like my heart. SHE will not be there . . . SHE is in some monster's gullet. The new corps of mages were paraded for me but I sent them away unseen. They cannot work the only magic I require . . .

AN ELEGY TO LOVE THAT LINGERS ETERNAL

*A riven heart, ne'er shall heal
when the wounded victim picks its scab
day by day, day by day by day and day
and ofttime all night as well!
And of tears a Euphrates or a Tiber has worn
its bed down this long face
which now, dried and sterile,
is the sad daily wonder of my shaving mirror.
I study that map and think:
Should I follow its crack-ed map,
sad explorer through a blasted land?
Would I find my way to YOU?
Probably not, but try I must . . .*

*Wednesday ye 9th July ye year 22 . . . the new strawberries are a solace. The gardeners have quite bred the wildness out of them. But their sweetness reminds me of Boudicca and my lost children.
. . . The architects' proposals are preposterous. The stone they*

require would draw manpower from the frontiers for its gathering –
and what then? The Null would flood in. What price a grand
memorial that day? I asked for a tower, yes, but they have redesigned
Babel . . .

Friday ye 10th of July, ye year 22. I feel a lot better today though
naturally still stricken with grief. My Lords Belial and Judas have
invited me hunting tomorrow. I think, for my health's sake, I shall
accept. It is for the best: one has grown pallid moping indoors. I
scarce dare look in the mirror whilst trying new robes. No, sad as I
am, the sun's kiss is needed to assist me re-shoulder Imperial
responsibilities.

It is no material matter but I recall Belial's second youngest girl is
a lively piece. She makes me laugh again – and she is yet unwed . . .

Sunday – in haste. AN EMISSARY FROM THE NULL!

'Oh, quite considerate, really.'

'*So what were they like?*' It was the first question that each
successive interrogator posed. No one had ever returned from
the Null before.

The huscarl was surprisingly composed, a credit to his
species. The monsters had nipped off his fingers that he might
be no further danger to them, but otherwise he seemed
unscathed.

'They fed and watered us,' he explained to his Emperor, face
cast respectfully downwards, 'like dogs really – raw joints of
venison, escorted trips to lap at streams: we could survive.'

And *she* had survived, along with most of the royal
household. The soldier confirmed that he'd seen her only three
days back when he was driven out of the cave of confinement.

''Twas always their plan, I suspect,' he continued, without
prompting. Plainly he'd pondered little else on his lonely
journey back to humandom. The man had had to justify his
survival to himself. The court overlooked such forwardness

161

without rebuke, since unique specimens merited a little indulgence. 'Older Null came after the first wave: some really ancient, stiff-legged, stringy ones; no good for battle. They sniffed around whilst the normal beasts were still locked with us, pushing the perimeter back into the house. Their desire was you, majesty, but in your absence they made do. The old ones stopped the general slaughter, they made judgement in each case.'

Apparently not perfectly. Princes of the blood had been ripped up, presumably because they fought as soldiers. Conversely, some less-than-nothing jugglers and concubines were spared because they appeared high-status creatures of leisure. The Null's understanding of their prey's emerging society was still crude: slack-contemptuous. They had no parallels within their own streamlined lives to hang useable notions on.

Still, even the mere taking of prisoners was a development to be chewed (sic) over. That the Null could resist consuming a human bore interpretation two ways: as cheering indication of increased respect or else worrying evidence of subtlety. However, the one thing indisputable was that here was innovation: Null diplomacy!

To the People, a nation used to nothing but novelty, it came as no great shaking of certainties. Their fathers had skulked in holes, they carried muskets, and normality was nothing but a raging storm of change. This was just another wonder to take in their stride.

On their Emperor though, the effect was more profound. A beacon, thought definitively pissed upon and sodden, now flared into the light of hope. There was that side to it certainly.

On the other hand, sufficient of the defeated, timid, curate remained for him to balk at transformations. What was lost and mourned for was now unexpectedly back – or potentially so. The Null had resurrected her. And, as with Christ's resurrection, that wasn't unsullied good news to all sections of society. The consequent wifely promotions had already been decreed. And where *they* ascended some powerful noble houses came along too. Reversal and demotion would put noses out of joint. At best they'd sulk, at worst Caiaphas and his security service would have plots to abort – and then punish, prompting further feuds and so on and on . . .

From a personal point of view, what he'd suffered in the days just gone by didn't bear stringing out or – worst of all – repetition. Boudicca being alive meant he had to re-examine all his feelings for authenticity. There was the embarrassing danger of – final – absence having made the heart grow fonder.

It was too tender a spot to rub at. He settled for easier questions.

'And did they communicate in any way?'

Musings about the Null's life amongst themselves, 'at home' so to speak, were a perennial favourite amongst the reflective elements of New-Wessex. On winter nights round a warm fire they served as that world's equivalent of ghost stories. Higher military circles pretended to be at serious business even as they enjoyed the speculation. Hitherto though, it had all been merely that: speculation for lack of evidence. The problem was that dead Null had no comment and the live variety kept you otherwise occupied.

Now there was an English-speaking, amenable, source of information. It was too tempting a chance to miss. The nobility of New-Wessex had flocked to hear and rarely had a court levee been so well attended for its own sake.

The huscarl was a pious man and so drew no conclusions from the Emperor's lack of joy. Yet he did wonder at it even as he concentrated on supplying proper answers.

'No, majesty; no more than my father does to his sheep.'

'Could you observe their customs?'

'They blinded those who sought to pry.'

'Did you note their converse.'

'They kept their distance, Lord. I sensed we are distasteful to them save as food.'

Blades sighed.

'You stayed cooped up in a dark cave, didn't you?'

'Just so, majesty.'

'Thank you, soldier. You shall be rewarded for your fingers. Do not fear a dishonoured or hungry old age.'

163

In a world whose tone was set by the Null that was fortune indeed: grounds for lifelong loyalty.

'Majesty!'

Blades recognised the shyster transaction – and was disgusted by the way life was. He called the man back and felt free to be blunt.

'Why weren't you killed?'

He considered.

'I was lamenting my digits, but they did chime at me whilst they . . . bit. And . . . some of them gestured. I remember thinking they wanted me to come back.'

The huscarl paled at the very notion and Emperor Blades smiled reassuringly at him.

'Don't worry,' he said to the furrowed face, 'you have my word on it. There's no question of that.'

'Over there.' The maimed huscarl pointed with his truncated hand. 'The valley ends in an overhang. There's a cave underneath.'

'And a trap in front,' added the general. That was off his own back, for he'd never been here before. Few had, save scouts and escaped slaves and – according to his testimony – one unique former prisoner of the Null.

'Probably,' that man agreed. 'It was teeming with 'em before. We came through a purple sea to get to that cave.' For a moment he stumbled in recollection, reliving the moment, whey-faced. 'They hissed at us as we passed. They licked their lips.'

The huscarl was as much admired by the expedition as he was shunned: the former for courage in returning, resolute, to where his fingers still were, and the latter, unfairly, for being some favourite of the Null. He had not escaped but been let go; therefore some taint of theirs remained on him. He ate – clumsily – alone.

General Antiochus studied the narrow defile and tried to

hold that image of perversion in mind. It might look green and tranquil now but the hills above could hold a tidal wave of Null waiting to roll. This was beyond-human land, beautiful to the sight on occasion, maybe, but false beneath. It awaited conversion.

There was nothing else for it but to advance and see. They had not been ordered out of Wessex to practise caution. They had a mission, received from HIS lips themselves: there were no two interpretations to it.

Mouthing a prayer to the One God and his Prophet on earth, General Antiochus Kingston-Child waved his mailed cavalry forward.

The idyllic valley was dead, killed in humanity's eyes by tokens of its former inhabitants. They'd left bones and worse.

There was not even the chance of contact with wild, burrow, mankind. They were getting rare now. In the lands the Null still held they rooted them out lest they too should ascend like their unguessed-at brethren. Beyond the sight and knowledge of New-Wessex a hunting genocide was underway. What the Emperor had gathered to himself was now all there was likely to be.

No monsters launched from the hilltops, they had gone elsewhere, taking their darkness with them. The sunlight no longer alighted on abomination. Even the birds had come back to sing, making the place falsely sweet. Yet the soldiers were not deceived, the new day did not charm. They were in a tunnel; should the Null reappear to block it night would swift return.

At the end there was a cave, just as the huscarl had recounted. He revisited its deep shadows lost in thought, leaving others to the search. They found good news – in the prevailing abysmal context. There were recent signs of human, in number, alive. They had not been slaughtered, not here anyway.

The greater wonder was at the cave mouth, deep etched into a broad, flat, rock. It took and absorbed all their attention. Gap-mouthed, General Antiochus gestured for his scribes. They too paused in wonder before speeding their pens to copying work.

To date no one had suspected the Null of map-making skills.

'Then you will wheel at the river bank and gallop, in column, to your mustering spot. Do not stir from there unless the wind-tubes blow thrice. If they do, take any Null landing in the flank.'

Emperor Blades was enjoying himself, choreographing the array of humanity. As a special honour, that they might remember the day, the colonels lined up to receive their orders in person.

Considering the disaster of the 'Great Defeat', mankind could still put on a respectable show. On the high ground above the river stood a token line of cannon, though the majority of their brethren remained in the citadels, in case of treachery.

Below, there were the blocks of foot, each a porcupine of pikemen in black-leaded armour between two clumps of musketeers. He'd set them out in the complex chequers-board formation used by Fairfax at Naseby. Blades recalled the boy he had been poring over a print of the battle, aching to have viewed the reality for himself. Now he had his wish and a bigger army than Parliament's New Model of 1645 to play with – and one a sight more colourful, too. Blades looked – and saw that it was good.

This was their first real joint outing, the gathered mobile armies and the gleanings of all the garrisons. There were small signs, if you searched for them, that it was not yet one force, melded into humanity's clenched fist. At speed things were prone to grow ragged, each officer retaining his own ways of doing things. Happily it didn't matter if the deployment proved over-subtle for immediate use. Neither side envisaged bloodshed that day.

To either flank were the cavalry, the brazen *cataphracti* nearer in, then lancers and pistoliers and finally clouds of pony skirmishers. He intended them to sweep in, regiment by regiment, past the faces of the Null, giving them the scent of insolent *meat* and denying them it at the same time. This was meant to be a defeat, a humiliation. The enemy would look for, ardently expect, a degree of face-saving. Blades wanted them lulled. Lulled Null. Despite himself, the Emperor chuckled – and fate wasn't having that . . .

'*Why* am I not foremost?'

Sennacherib had denuded Pevensey of its iron soldiers to show his loyalty. Now he expected proper thanks. He was misguided enough to think the family reconciliation as a once and for all thing.

Blades leaned back into his throne. Even thus exalted, it was difficult to maintain proper status against a horseman looming high above. The boy should have dismounted. The grim Imperial mages sensed the tension better than any. They drew closer.

'Because I say so. And because your iron-clad Assyrians will make more impression as the final troop. Their image will be that which remains in the almond eyes. Recall how the Null hate flesh clad in fang-proof wrappings.'

The prince was unplacated. A brief spell as an East Anglian marcher lord had failed to teach him wisdom.

'Then where is Arthur and his Kentish men? He covers his knights in slabs of metal. Let him take the hindest place.'

'He and they are unable to be present.'

'So you'll have me wait, will you, watching the arse-ends of some shepherd-boy light cavalry?'

The two linked glances, the elder's tilted upwards, the younger's straight down.

'I *will*, yes.'

A pause, then: 'The Emperor knows best,' said Sennacherib, without irony as best Blades could tell. The Neo-Assyrian bowed in the saddle and raised a dust storm riding away.

That phrase was taken from Firstmet; it had been his watchword and invariable advice. Blades missed him. He would have known what to say – or do – about impatient sons.

Because the immediate vicinity had been soured Blades took in the wider view. Across the broad river Thames were the Null.

167

They already lined the bank, ten or twenty deep, unnaturally still for the most part, at other times swaying in unison amidst communal chant.

Blades knew what temptation that sight must present to his artillerymen, a clumped target of malignity begging for case-shot. He felt it himself, but likewise knew he could trust them. This was all a show, a puffing up of chests for both sides. They did not come to cause death but to prevent it. This was the dawning day of an *arrangement*; victory and defeat snuggled in the same parcel.

The Null had come south in peace, that familiar purple river flowing round – not over – the works of man, for once. Their full array passed the outlying settlements without violence. They put the taste of death in their mouths, true; they called out unkindnesses to the humans, but they also failed to assault any walls.

Amongst mankind, only Emperor Blades *believed* the Null – but that sufficed. He withheld the mailed fist, he ordered the far-flung farmers, salt-panners, trappers and quarrymen to stay put. Some – most, even – had faith in him and obeyed. And if others did not, if a stream of refugees poured into New-Wessex, he was indulgent with them. In any case, they were ideal people, knowledgeable and motivated, for another, parallel, project he had in mind.

His every mood and move was scrutinised by loyal eyes. A mere languid gesture sufficed to set the forces of humanity-militant in motion. Blades's whim was translated, grossly magnified, into trumpet blasts and sent all along the line. The infantry's dragon wind-pipes took it up; kettledrums amongst the cavalry repeated it further out. To blaring music mankind began to march.

The horse went first, as per his dictate; line upon line of mailed men – and Amazons – and mounts. As they drew near the river, pennoned lances were lowered as though upon the charge. For a spell they cantered, then galloped as if to cross the water by speed and commitment alone. Only at the last moment did each troop wheel away and file off to take up position along the Surrey bank. The Null took the point and radiated hatred.

From his throned perspective above, Blades adjudged it impressive. And well it might be, for they'd practised long enough for days before, well out of Null sight in the great muster camp where Ewell village ought to be.

Sennacherib and his Assyrians were the final word, as ordered. The Emperor looked hard but failed to detect the slightest sign of mutiny. If anything, they mock-charged more convincingly than any other. Final decision on the boy's longevity was postponed yet again.

The rank and file infantry of New-Wessex were scarlet-coated: a sentimental indulgence brought from 'home'. Likewise, they drilled as well as anything Cromwell's New Model ever put out. They too '*knew what they loved and loved what they knew*', but had even stronger inspiration via the prospect of defeat. At worst, the Parliamentarians had absolute monarchy and Anglicanism to fear, not extermination and consumption. Thoughts such as that put a snap into manoeuvres like nothing else. A bronze-Blades 'inspiration' preceded each regiment.

The private regiments of the nobility, the marcher legions and scouting formations, were more dour or flamboyant according to the whim of their creator. The last-named were as green as the landscape they blended into, whereas the marchers matched their '*here-I-am-do-something-about-it*' masters. Likewise, the town militias of New-Godalming, New-Winchester et al, were peacocks dressed to express civic pride. The Empire encouraged rivalry in dress, desiring leakage of that same spirit into battle.

Unit by unit, they marched to prearranged positions in two columns, at length forming an avenue down to the river.

Last came the corps of huscarls, half musketmen, half bearers of the great axe, tall contemptuous men chosen for height and bearing or earlier prowess in lesser formations. A dedicated mage was assigned to each band, clad in Blades's idea of wizards' garb. Their pointy-hatted, scarlet-purple melange stood out alone from ranks of burnished chainmail that put Sennacherib's Neo-Assyrians to shame. Together they moved in slow step down the avenue of troops, symbolically barring the way to the facing central Null. The Emperor's personal standard – the woolpack of Godalming topped by a golden wyvern windsock pennant – went before them.

The Emperor followed on in glorious isolation, one man but the representative of all, down the avenue of soldiery. His progress was stately; leisured; his path plain and clear but powerless to impose urgency. The ferry to row him to the island in the Thames, today glorified with cloth-of-gold and fringed with Imperial marines, would await his pleasure. Meanwhile, the order was that silence be observed.

What the nearest ranks also observed was the broad smile on his face. They presumed it to be outward manifestation of his god-like confidence but, as so often in its dealings with former Curate Blades, consensus presumed wrong.

It *amused* him that all this was a show, as life itself was but a show – though, granted, like life, an absorbing one. Also, knowing that the real action was elsewhere merited a thin grin.

The full smirk that came to birth, though, was more than the sum of amusement and cunning. He wore that in homage to the goddess of Irony.

It was surely her divine intervention, he concluded, that led the Null – in their blindness – to choose Runnymede, of all places, in which to draft this new *Magna Carta*.

The Null spoke: a chiming and ascending of scales. It meant everything and nothing. All their discourse sounded the same and like hunger, varying only in the urgency of appetite.

'I don't understand you. Don't you have anyone who speaks English?'

But he did understand – only too well. And they did have English speakers: that was the sole reason he allowed himself dragged here.

The grass of Runnymede was lush and – to Emperor Blades only – steeped in history. History's heavy hand was also on his shoulder and the sun, Zeus Unconquered, shone overhead direct upon his crown. An army awaited either side of him. There was no shortage of aids to concentration but all he found himself thinking of were the little things.

His 'Grandma Ironside' had said you needed a long spoon to sup with the Devil. Maybe so, since much else she said, except regarding *papists*, was spot-on true. Right now Emperor Blades thought of her as he wished for a longer stick to parley with the Null. The present one put him within claw range.

What would his old black-clad granny had done? He tried imagining the Null elite as cavaliers. The vision obligingly arrived, heavy and deadly as Cromwell's cavalry.

'Get back, vermin – you make me nervous.'

A poke with the stick made the nearest monster leap back as though scalded. The few humans allowed to accompany him laughed.

It didn't like that – either the jab or the *meat*-amusement. It raged even higher up the octaves.

'Yes, yes, *yes* . . .' he dismissed the protest. And that was a joke too, for it had all been *no, no no* up to now. The monsters knew they were negotiating from strength.

The Emperor's voice had only simulated weariness for he was braced for retaliation. He almost wished for it, since the artillery had orders to sweep the island clean of life at first sign of treachery. At least that would have been an end to endless trouble.

Yet no cleaving claw came. He had to live on and concentrate upon their map.

The Null were no cartographers, though their earlier effort in the western valley had got him to Runnymede well enough. This example was better but still crude: the southern half of England in outline, with rivers marked in, as best as fresh dirt allowed. Four young Null had peeled off an expanse of turf and then a wizened elder arrived to draw.

The humans had been permitted time to study the finished result and reflect. What it lacked in detail it gained in simplicity. Their demands were made abundantly clear, their ambitions for the Earth etched upon its face.

'No. No, definitely no.'

The Null recognised a negative if nothing else. The chief spokesbeast went from ease to fury in a single breath. That too was their way; sign of their uncomplicated black and white universe.

Growling, howling, it jabbed its own crude pointer into the soil, erasing Blades's amendments, removing another symbolic human enclave. Displaced soil flew up in Blades's face.

It was informative that in this depiction humanity was represented by the shaded, scuffed-up parts. The Null's own, exclusive, areas were those left blank.

In the Null wish-picture mankind was confined between the Downs and the sea. Right to the chalk highlands, a great swathe south of the Thames was ceded away. The land north of there was not even mentioned; was just presumed Null-home inviolate.

Over one portion the head-speaker waved the stick and enounced a sound like '*Null*'. Over the other came a swallowing, lapping, dismissal. Blades supplied his own translation, acquiring his first word of Null, all the vocabulary this proposed future would need. Human = *meat*. Confirmation, if any were needed, of their wishes and intentions.

The Emperor imagined dismantling Castle Blades and firing New-Godalming and all the other blood-won places. Then the wailing wagon-trek south: whipped out, thoughts drifting back to burrows again. They'd be beach-remnants, clinging on to a fringe of land, broken spirited once more and forever, waiting for the Null to finish the job. The next generation – should there be one – would face unappetising options: like whether to turn aquatic or be happy hole dwellers and passive Null feed.

As futures went they were fairly vomitous: certainly not meriting a smile. The Emperor had to suppress that grin. The Null mustn't know.

They thought they already did. A *no* from cattle was mere impertinence, nothing more than that, soon yielding to the goad.

And the monsters knew where to lay on that goad. They'd

172

found – when they'd got beyond considering man as mere sustenance – that the breed had sensitive spots. Pressure was easily applied, taming not that difficult.

Scouts had already reported the human-corral up in the Chilterns. They'd suggested raiding it, rescuing their own and then replying to Null proposals out of cannon mouths. The Emperor liked the idea, even daydreamed the image as he vetoed it, confident that the Null would joyfully slaughter their reprieved larder the minute one trooper hoved into sight. He had to allow them their treasured trump card.

The council of humanity, his senior advisors and generals, the more intelligent sons, had been fed the notion that this bartering was the highest flattery. To be 'spoken' to at all was an honour. Those dark areas on their map represented a concession of world-changing extent to the Null.

The men in metal didn't say anything but neither did they buy it – which was genuinely encouraging.

When the hostages were brought forward a silence fell. The monsters did not bother with cords and chains when they could allocate a Null apiece. They were paraded at a distance, roughly treated to raise screams that floated back to their paused brethren. The Null negotiators stood back to let the effect sink in.

The Emperor had anticipated this. He didn't demean himself with his perspective-glass – but others further back had been delegated the task. There were agreed signals.

He allowed them a space and then turned for the message, his stomach a schoolboy clench of acid. The designated flags dipped and waved. He interpreted, waited for the repeat, and only then accepted.

There was Boudicca, there were all the important children, there was even Firstmet – which was a real surprise. The Emperor resurrected him in his thoughts and was glad. He said his first true, non-begging prayer for some time.

They had them, they would not surrender them, but neither would they be harmed – yet. His love for them was their ticket of survival, the seal on the arrangement to be made today. The abominations might not understand it but they'd use it. Certain *meat* had inexplicable status, nothing to do with texture or flavour. That much comprehension sufficed.

Fair enough, concluded Blades. If they only felt sympathy for their own kind he was absolved to act the same, conscience clear. That wind of freedom felt quite exhilarating: *do as you're done by* – but do it first and worst.

The Null thought he'd had long enough. One of the oldest threw up his stringy arms. They were up to prearranged signs as well.

Way off they began to kill the humans, more slowly than was their nature, their inclination. It was a show.

Blades understood; even appreciated their clarity of purpose. There was much humans – or the leaders of humans – could learn from the Null. They hadn't put a millennia-long foot on humanity's face for nothing. Yet he couldn't just stand by and admire. He was being watched – and the beasts' understanding was crude. Doubtless they were using up the lower grade prisoners but they might easily make mistakes. A crook-legged woman might not be accounted much in their eyes.

'Mercy, mercy,' – plus placating hands and bowed head, the Null understood those well enough. The same wiry purple limbs as before went aloft and the murders stopped direct.

He'd fully intended to beg time in which to draw his further-flung subjects south to safety – but there'd been the risk inherent in delay. A claw might be poised over *her*. Now it was too late: the opportunity gone – just like some of the Null army. Quick off the mark, they'd already whooped delight and started to peel away, racing to ravage the – settled – lands ceded to them. Those '*of little faith*' refugees had been right after all.

Emperor Blades took a step back, then another, commencing the retreat of humanity.

'Charge!'

The horse gunners took up the call first, scrambling down the valley sides. They needed level ground for their trick. The remainder, the pistoliers, the pike and cage men, followed on in slower, dependable blocks. Round all weaved a cloud of aristocratic cavalry, directing operations, ready to sacrifice themselves should developments slow.

So far north the Null did not bother with sentries. The few early feeders already peeled off the sleep pile were ridden down, too late, too surprised, to raise proper alarm. Still groggy, the great tumulus of Null unravelled with all haste – but far too slowly. The oncoming humans were more than willing to assist them up to speed.

The horse guns were the idea of a Swedish gunner, fortuitously kidnapped in one of the old-world slave raids. To save himself from field work the man had absolutely unfolded with invention – and blossomed. Unlike old Christendom, New-Wessex positively welcomed wild ideas. It lacked the sodden cloak of precedent and tradition that choked innovation. The Swede proposed, he drew and lo, the thing – even if only a prototype – was made. He was free now, a nobleman no less, and thought himself no longer a Swede but a son of Wessex.

His best notion was one-use 'leather-guns', only lightly banded with iron. Strung between two specially-trained horses they could be rushed right up to an enemy and discharged in their face. Then, the supporting cords loosed, the spent tube fallen away, the bearers were plain cavalrymen again, and almost on top of their blackened victims.

There'd been a trial run on an out of the way Cornish Null tribe, one sufficiently remote not to pass on the tactic should it fail. The gunners went by ship and made landfall on St Michael's Mount. The next day, in a hollow where the village of Ludgvan ought to have been, it was found there was nothing better for getting to the heart of the Null issue. They'd charged so close the blasts of case-shot had penetrated the outer beasts to kill the inner mother. That drove the survivors wild – or wilder – and there were casualties and empty horses and ample space on the homecoming ship. Yet there were also Null tokens nailed the entire length of the rails and the mother-monster's carcass as a new figurehead. They got a hero's reception when they docked at Pevensey. The former Swede got his freedom and a harem.

'Fire!'

Prince Arthur was with the gunners, right beside them as they rode in. They now knew the best distance at which to discharge, the optimum point of aim; they had already started to consider themselves an elite. His actual command was just expected New-Wessex etiquette. Shared blood with the Imperium and a coat of silver braid gave the right to at least the semblance of control.

Some cannon never got to fire. More sprightly Null perceived their significance and went for the horses, diving beneath and between the hooves to open their bellies with raking claws. Then the team would crash in tangled ruin and take no further interest in proceedings.

But not all were so used, not even most. The rest spoke and their not-to-be-denied word received due attention. They did not want to kill the mother as in Cornwall, and so applied the taper a little further out. The bee-swarm of shot met advancing, separated Null; it embraced them and carried them back to meet their still entangled kin. Together they were stripped of flesh and another layer levered from the pile.

Where they could the horsemen peeled away to left and right, restricting their interest to Null standing in disaster-puzzled and deafened isolation. Sometimes they were not given the option and a delegation from the Null pile drew them into its most voracious interior.

Close behind them came the pistoliers, 'reiters' as the old European armies (where Blades had taken the idea from) called them. They advanced at the slow trot, in tight knee-to-knee formation. Each front rank would come to pistol range, discharge their brace of weapons and then wheel back, reloading in the saddle, whilst the next row had a go. Like a slow machine gun, they tore caverns in the purple hill.

Finally, when the reiters were in danger of embroilment,

they made way for the clumps of pikemen. Porcupine-like, already at the sprint, their eighteen-foot shafts impaled all before them. They trod on and over the dead and dying to impale the still snarling mound.

After that it was all up to individual skills, putting down the survivors – which was when, within claw and fang range, the humans suffered most. However, by this stage they had done their work and had the blessing of numbers: the issue was not in doubt.

From start to finish, from unspoilt dawn to smoky victory, the action had occupied fifteen busy minutes. Soon, the only Null remaining were those expiring on the pile, a few making doomed stands and – wonder of wonders and sweet novelty – a number fleeing before mere *meat*-beasts.

There were voices raised in other than pain or struggle. Already the *scops* and tale-weavers were recounting first drafts of the legend-to-be, interwoven with musical praise of the Imperium. Likewise, the wind-tubists were sounding, taunting the scampering Null on their way.

It was heady stuff, even for a prince of the first circle and thus used to glory, but Arthur recalled his duty, the main purpose of the day, still unfulfilled.

He'd remained in the forefront throughout. He had directed the cannoneers, shot with the reiters and got stuck in with a pike whose owner no longer needed it. Then, remounting, he busied himself in aborting the impulse to pursue.

When all was safely gathered in and the soldiers circled all around, he could focus attention to the hill of Null. It was gently quaking, for the breed tended to quiver when on the brink of death. Their zest for life was such that they did not surrender it easily.

Thereagain, nor did their former prey. That had come as a shock to Arthur after his first engagement. He'd always assumed that battlefields would be still places when the day was done. But they were not: they were full of jerky movement.

He shook off his soft musings and called to mind that a prince was here to court a queen. It was not as though they had

177

all the time in the world. This was *their* territory, beyond contesting. Those Null fugitives hadn't gone away to weep but to fetch friends.

At Arthur's command, well-practised teams abandoned their pikes and fetched even longer shafted hooks, the sort used to haul down thatch from burning buildings. They set to clawing at the Null swarm, dragging off the dead in search of its inner portions. The clove stench came with them, in choking waves.

She had not been seen to flee: she must be in there somewhere. A few Null, perhaps her special bodyguards, proved to be dissembling death and had to be granted the real thing. The soldiers had seen this behaviour before and musketeers were standing ready. Each time the powder smoke was given time to clear. They didn't want to miss her.

Then finally there was one purple carcass that would not be fetched out, even though the hooks bit deep. It screeched and shifted but was too gross to be moved.

The soldiers spat even as they acclaimed the find, greeting the great womb of all their troubles. Two precious mages, held out of harm's way in reserve, now rushed up to seek and bind her mind. Their sensitive faces registered horror with each invisible probe.

Arthur was not so involved, he did not have to get so close. Therefore his feelings could all be pleasure. She could be added to the others. That was five now!

High above on the valley's edge the cage teams were waiting. He jubilantly beckoned them forward.

Rain had attacked them as they tacked around the coastline for first sight of a new sea – a bad omen on a grey day. Even the refugees from the Null advance, *far-dwellers* all and brought along for that reason, were out of their knowledge here. And yet there it had been, 'Anglesey' – just as the Emperor had predicted. Green and grey, mountain topped, apparently lifeless, *He* had known of it before ever mankind set eye upon it.

It was ideal: an island arrayed for their convenience: a

harbour, a base; opportunity to test their mission in moderate fashion. The place might support two, or three Null bands at most: maybe none – the Null were no mariners.

Starting in Anglesey in a small way they could then move on, well drilled, to what it pleased his Imperial Highness to call 'the Welsh mainland'. Even there, if luck held, they might find the enemy depleted. Scouts' tales said that the bulk of the abominations were gone south to the great parley

With their attention thus distracted, Blades decreed that mankind should show just what they thought of the racial enemy. Prince Arthur was dispatched by ship to go and molest their mothers.

Cages, strong and specially-forged for them, rattled a song in the hold below.

'And would you honour *me* in the same way?'

As she spoke she paced the throne room, anxious energy diverted from face to feet. The bustling servants were ignored or brushed aside.

Her husband's hesitation was all the answer Jezebel required. It undermined the lies that sped out in compensation.

'Of course. You are all equally precious to me. Besides, it's not only Boudicca they hold.'

'No, you're right.'

There was no telling at the moment. Jezebel might be concurring or it might be just a rally before the next volley went in. She'd been strangely controlled since her return: disturbingly even-tempered. On balance, Blades thought he preferred the tantrums. You knew where you were with them.

'They have Lord Firstmet, young children of all three inner circles, most of my household staff, Maxted the jester . . .'

'Oh, *well*, then . . .' she 'agreed' again. 'That's different: I *see* now: all kinds of *precious* people. We can't afford to lose our jester – well worth sacrificing the outer provinces and all the Marcherdoms for.'

It was true many of the Marcher people wore disgruntled faces. They'd been doing well, were undefeated, and now felt confined back in shrunken humandom, perhaps even a trifle betrayed. Yet, for herself, Jezebel had shot back at the first sound of recall, rejoicing.

'They shall be recovered. There are matters afoot.' Blades's voice could be firm when he felt justified. That much he sincerely meant.

'As shall *she*.'

He grimaced. Sooner flying crockery than word-games.

'Such is our fondest hope, for Boudicca, for Firstmet, for . . . Clute the flunky who shines the piss-pots. All of them: equally. We love our people.'

She came to a sudden halt directly before him. Her fingers took over the frantic activity ceded by her feet. They writhed round and round each other like worms.

'Some are loved more frequently. *Our* bed is grown cold. The cracked-legged one's is like an oven.'

'She is not in it so I don't see how that can be . . .'

'In your heart; in your dreamings it is still warm with her. You are still between her twisted legs . . .'

She'd dared to interrupt – and in front of his barber and manicurist. They pretended to be deaf, they feigned absorption, but he knew what they were really absorbing. A certain righteous anger was excusable. He hadn't dared hope for that assistance.

'Woman, you *chose* to accompany Sennacherib to his new Marcher land. You *moaned* while there. You are back, he has Pevensey again and yet still you protest! Don't you know any other songs? Sweeter ones? Listen, I tell you solemnly, I tire of you!'

There was horrible pause. Jezebel shook as though under a blow. Some inner seismic shift had occurred. She needlessly dusted down her raven-black, slashed, gown and drew breath.

'Husband, I can surely sing the song of *duty*. Henceforth you'll hear no other tune from me.'

180

Her smile and gracious departure was more worrying than Null through the window.

The Null clapped hands to its ears and mimicked distress. The Emperor was all grinning indifference. Silence was not his to command in any case.

The army's blood was up, it scented that victory was on her way and sang to greet the fickle mistress. The organised survivors from Middlesex, Berkshire and points north who swelled their ranks were especially loud and tuneful.

Blades shrugged his shoulders. The Null would have to lump it. Having played the long game, now in sight of the home straight, he could indulge himself. They should know the years ahead held only humble pie for them. They ought to get used to relishing those rations right now.

The Runnymede turf still bore marks of their last visit. With the eye of faith, even the Null's map could be discerned, a stripped square etched with residual marks the summer rains had not washed away. This time human hands made it legible, eager helpers amending it to tell a very different story.

Blades's pointer scratched the combed earth and threw the Null back into the Midlands. He dug them out of Cornwall. South of where Watling Street should be, from Wroxeter to the Thames, there should be none of them. The downtrodden curate from Godalming had replicated that England freed by Alfred the Great from the Vikings, had liberated it from an even fiercer enemy.

The vision drew hisses and gentle bubbling-throat sounds that were nevertheless boiling anger. He did not even look up, using the same stick to brush all protest aside.

It was their turn to be fixed on sights beyond an immediate tormentor. The cages of Null mothers were set on the skyline. A cannon sat behind each: there was no prospect of rescue. From time to time pikemen caused the prisoners to screech their misery.

That music entered every Null heart all right. There proved to be a way into those tigerish citadels. The Null loved their mothers.

Blades indicated the map, indicated the human prisoners. He showed the caged mothers their children and beckoned them forward. But of course, they could not come, not yet. Their laments rolled down the slope to the Thames.

The Null had been summoned in the manner they pioneered. A prisoner, mutilated to be beyond further use, was sent back to its brood. A simple map, a phase of the moon, were tattooed on its back, clear message to those who would see. The army of mankind then advanced north – in flagrant breach of the Runnymede treaty – to wait.

Up to that moment it had not been known that male Null could weep. That had not been observed before, even under the cruellest tortures. The Emperor drank in those tears, memorising the scene to be a solace in his dotage. The monsters were a constant source of surprise to their pupils.

Thrusting self-indulgence aside, Blades returned to harrying his tutors in mercilessness. The Null elders' attention was redirected to the map. He become insistent, jabbing and growling after their own fashion – a sort of pigeon-Null.

This phase was most important, as valuable to the overall war as casualties, maybe more so. He wanted their spirits broken as the burrow-men's had been broken. If that could be achieved then the struggle was effectively won and there remained only a warfare of detail. He basked in the prospect. He wanted to behold the last Null before he died. Amongst his people he was accounted a moderate in that respect.

Thoughts sometimes seemed to pass collectively amongst the beasts: a relic perhaps of a hive mind. Human scholars had noted before that the experience of one could soon be common knowledge to all. It wasn't always so but often enough to be worrying. Another reason to kill the lot.

That faculty seemed in operation now. The elders and spokesmonsters groaned and doubled up as though struck on their flat stomachs. They expelled breath and pain rode upon it.

Simultaneously, the Thames-side host whistled and piped their anguish.

Humanity had never heard sweeter music. They applauded it.

The chief Null, an old specimen but still stretch-skinned with corded muscle, leapt forward. The Emperor's huscarls hefted their axes and guns. They need not have worried: the creature intended no harm, however much he might wish it. With savage strength he impaled his pointer stick deep, *deep* into the map.

Blades estimated its point of impact as York. They were conceding. There they would stay. He knew it meant nothing, that they'd no more honour their 'word' to him than he would a sentimental reprieve to a fatted calf. Yet this day was still important.

The Null had trodden another mile along the road to humility. Former Curate Blades no longer believed the meek would inherit the earth: on the contrary, he laughed at the insidious notion. He knew the humble and easily put-upon inherited just enough earth to lay their bodies in. The unmeek remained alive to tread the soil down. Thus he hungered and thirsted for the day that the Null became *meek*, as the Bible told man to be, ill-advisedly. Let them adopt the gospel first and see where it got them.

Quite properly, there was no trust between them. The hostages were released progressively; one purple mother for a dozen or so humans. A few, the biggest, the most matriarchal looking, were retained for insurance purposes. The Null did the same, holding on to a troupe of erotic dancers mistakenly thought important. Each group bewailed the death of hope and their abandonment, but were ignored.

The ferry boat was busy, plying back and forth. Runnymede grew crowded with the liberated. None of the returnees were in good shape, for they had holidayed with inconsiderate hosts. Emperor Blades saw Firstmet, beheld the stumbling figure of Boudicca, but held himself aloof. They understood. The time to translate his leaping spirits into action was not yet come. An Emperor was not for himself but an icon for the present, a story for posterity. There was not a single public moment when he need not consider that.

There was also that lack of *trust*. The presiding huscarls ensured that each batch of prisoners was ferried back safely to the bosom of the army before the next was received. They did not want to risk a crowd-for-slaughter, jammed upon the island. It became a slow business but they had the patience. Mankind now had all the time it required. It had the future – which is ample time.

The Null mothers would not endure a second more of *meat*-company. They ignored the offered ferry and slid-slithered down to the river themselves, mooing pain. In the water, a purple flotilla, they were surprising graceful, the river buoying up and dignifying the bulbous collection of udders and orifices. Null warriors splashed into the tide to meet each successive release, to bear them up and away from every indignity. They too were crying and Blades coldly noted it. Another chink.

The two species were drawing back, their business concluded. Strictly speaking the humans need not have done so, for this was their land now, undisputed, yet the urge to be out of sight was strong. They wished to be wholeheartedly joyful and that was still not possible in sight of the Null. Mankind also needed further convincing of its true status, and Emperor Blades noted that too.

He was last off the island, a kingly gesture; one matched by the senior Null. Blades paused at the lip of the ferry and looked. The Null likewise before he dived in. They stared until it drew anxious comment from the huscarls who feared the evil eye. They were waved to silence.

That gaze was maintained, without rancour, until both recognised, at the same time, the impossibility of communication. The fleeting opportunity passed and there was nothing more to say, nothing that could be said, ever again.

The one boarded, the other swam, moving directly away from each other.

If the Null intended celebrating, as he certainly did, then

184

Emperor Blades wished them well – they'd have precious few excuses for it in time to come.

Thereagain, given that their pleasures were sodomy and slow-feeding on live things, he immediately repented of his blessing. Rather, they ought to mourn and be miserable and get in fit state for extermination. He thought they should – in fact he *knew* they would. He could be positively sure of it. He'd taken steps to guarantee any Null happiness be short-lived.

The day before they were released, before it was even certain they would be, each Null mother was fed on slow poison. Those who wouldn't cooperate had it stuffed up them anyway – there being no shortage of avenues for the purpose.

First tested on ordinary Null captives, the dosage proportionally increased, their end was certain, though delayed. They'd linger on, quite well at first, though vaguely troubled. There followed weakening, then haemorrhage, then acceleration into spectacular dissolution and departure from the world. Certainly, they'd breed no more, but only abort and spew out stillbirths. Blades smiled at the thought.

No mercy to the merciless! Humanity were roaring-boys now, an unanswerable avalanche. Their eyes were alight.

The Emperor raised a cup to toast the returnees – and then paused, silenced by a thought. *What if*, he wondered, *the Null were as wicked as he*?

'The thing I'm saying is . . . well, you know there are others but that doesn't mean that someone can't be, well, I suppose I mean, *pre-eminent*. I'm not downgrading the rest but while you were away, I realised – was made to realise – that someone can become indispensable. I thought you were dead, I mourned you: ask the body-servants, they'll confirm that. And then I felt guilty about not saving you – and then I learned you were still alive and there was the chance to go back and try again. That's not often granted, is it? You were dead and then you lived again. It brought it all home to me: how much I . . . well, *like*

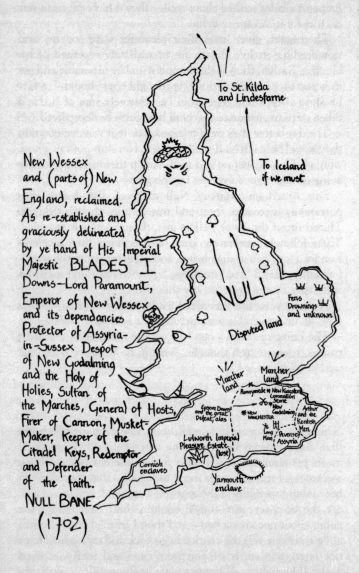

To St. Kilda
and Lindesfarne

To Iceland
if we must

New Wessex
and (parts of) New
England, reclaimed.
As re-established and
graciously delineated
by ye hand of His Imperial
Majestic BLADES I
Downs—Lord Paramount,
Emperor of New Wessex
and its dependancies
Protector of Assyria-
in-Sussex Despot
of New Godalming
and the Holy of
Holies, Sultan of
the Marches, General of Hosts,
Firer of Cannon, Musket=
Maker, Keeper of the
Citadel Keys, Redemptor
and Defender
of the faith.
NULL BANE
(1702)

NULL

Fens
Drownings
and unknown

Disputed land

Marcher
land

Marcher
land

Runnymede & New Kingston
Coronation
Stone
New
Godalming
Epsom Downs
and the great
Defeat, alas

NEW
WINCHESTER

Ye
Long
Man

Arthur
and the
Kentish
Men

Pevensey
Assyria

Lulworth Imperial
Pleasure Estate
(lost)

Cornish
enclaves

Yarmouth
enclave

you and miss your company: especially when I was bickering with the rest. You don't have their glee: you don't smirk at harsh things. I don't know how but you're not from the same mould as them. So . . . I mean, if you've followed me till now you'll know what I'm trying to tell you. You above all should see. You see beneath all this *Emperor* and *Imperium* stuff; you're a solid point of reference. I can lay down the crown in your company knowing you won't misuse the access that gives – will you? No, not that I'm actually asking you that – I already know the answer. It's a rhetorical question.'

Blades ceased his pacing back and forth. He drew a deep breath.

'Look, you see the difficulties I'm in: meet me halfway. What I'm trying to give you is a protestation of love. What do you say?'

From behind the privy door came ferocious sound: a tiger being backed unwillingly into a confined space.

Earlier, Blades had gnawed upon a grisly notion amidst his meal of contentment. Suppose the Null had had the poison idea, too? They were certainly unsporting enough. The returnees were hurriedly gathered together for counter-measures.

'Boudicca, did you hear me? Boudicca?'

The Queen had not, could not. As the powerful emetics took hold, she and all the other rescued hostages had other things to bother about, not knowing know which way to turn. Rump aloft, her universe had telescoped down to the space between face and privy – grasped firm between two hands – and then the long drop into the moat.

For whole hours to come, it and it alone would have her undivided attention.

There *was* poison abroad that season, but not the Null's: it was all of human making.

Whilst the monster mothers were gradually drooping down to death, far away in their remaining fastnesses, whilst resurgent humanity spread out like a stain across the map, gifts arrived at

187

the camp. Alongside all the other supplies from the Downs heartlands there came celebratory food. Cider and sausage for the soldiers, dainties for more fastidious palates. After victory they were both welcome and irresistible.

The Emperor adored strawberries and best of all those whose roots sank into soil he knew. The punnets bore the emblem of the Imperial market gardens at New-Binscombe, the fruit had been individually selected and one could feed at ease, without fear of mould or canker or anything distasteful. They knew his tastes to the last degree; the berries had been de-stemmed and lightly rained over with honey-water. They knew his mood at that moment would naturally incline towards indulgence. That Boudicca and his other concubines chanced to be spewing and voiding their guts out was just happenstance but still power to the donor's elbow. The Emperor of Mankind was easy prey for substitute solace.

It was that very *solicitude* that gave him pause, the exaggerated care to please. You could take it one of two ways; as a token of love or an arrow straight at you. Blades had to ask himself which was more likely from his family.

The first strawberry was halfway to his mouth before he *reconsidered*. Likewise, a fruit was poised over Boudicca's full lips when he leapt to knock it away. She'd pronounced herself almost recovered and willing to join him in the joyous treat. Their gold cups and platters went flying. She looked more disappointed than frightened.

Food-tasters, even a team of them, cannot sample every portion of a healthy input, but that day the Emperor insisted each and every strawberry was vetted and nibbled. The men and women, both slaves and pious volunteers, perished horribly, without dignity.

As they did so the Emperor watched and triumph soured in his mouth, as foul tasting, if not so deadly, as any venom.

An hour passed when he recalled little save shouting but, after that initial nova of fury, he finally found himself able to . . . set it aside. Moderation and proportionality prevailed. Only the carters were impaled – though they protested their innocence right until the point went in. Then, fleet horsemen departed to make an example of the supplying farm, taking ample stakes with them. That would suffice.

It was the first purely *human* affront against him; the first shocking tear in their unity. He could either draw attention to it or mend it and pass on. At the time the latter struck him as the path of wisdom. Least mentioned, soonest forgotten.

That happily coincided with the part of him which was still milk-and-water Godalming curate. The easy life, the postponed decision, retained their temptress appeal.

Half suspecting their final destination but refusing to think of it, Emperor Blades imperially declined to trace the strawberry vine to its roots. Fortunately, there were brighter things to dwell on, memories to harvest for old age. He allowed himself to be distracted.

During the great return he had her only: constantly, even to the exclusion of the troupe of wonderfully trained 'maidens of the passing moment' hurried up from New-Godalming.

They made round of her three portals; they clung to each other in the night, made one by shared warmth. They left marks on each other. He'd never known such honest passion. She was sweet to the nose, the tongue and the heart, without the slightest lingering Null taint. The two wearied themselves together, then began again and, for whole moments at a time, almost made contact.

And if he saw the puzzlement, even mockery, in others' half-caught glances, he found himself able to forgive. The courtiers and warrior-nobility of mankind could not understand him cleaving to the less than perfect when any number of straight legs were his for the commanding. For once he left them in their ignorance, their loss. This brief time was just for himself.

There was no secret, no mystery to it. What was lost was found again, in her and in himself. He'd feared the death of feeling, as much if not more than he did *her* death. Its springing from the grave was greeted with according joy. The slipping in and out of her was only a symbol.

Other wives looked on with fish-cold eyes but he knew

they could be placated. He also knew there would be trouble with Jezebel but that thought bounced off the armoured happiness of those days and nights. Any price was a good price for those.

Both sparkling jewel and sprawling convoy, the Imperial court and its hundreds of pennoned carriages and wagons and chariots, all set amidst the almost as glittering army of humanity, made its way back over the green Downs towards the heartlands and peace.

'*Do* it!'

The maid did so and slackly took her position with the rest. Competing shadows from the huge fireplaces in each wall played across their wonderful pink nakedness.

'Further over!'

They obeyed as one, synchronised by her voice. Their shuffling topped and tailed the echoing of her commands. There couldn't be certainty, but it did seem she'd *held* them all.

Jezebel liked them thin, to the point of skinny-ribbedness. These were perfectly chosen: long-haired, base-born. She was gleeful. There was the looked-for tightness, between her legs, in her guts. Of the few things left to her that she might hope for, each had arrived. Though still poor seconds, the addition of wine made them suffice.

The Queen's tutors had counselled against imperiousness in command, for then there could be no distinction between success and simple obedience. Right now, excitement and habit combined made that advice hard to recall.

She had not sought instruction in the fullness of the art, just those parts that would console her. Even so, the lessons had been strenuous, especially given her other distractions. Also, they were oft-times impertinent. One mage-instructor's head adorned a spike atop the Castle because he had taken too much upon himself. Queens – even queenly novices – are not to be admonished; not by *anyone*. Not even *him*. The very thought made her mind squirm again in memory. There was pain. She lashed out.

He'd admonished her. He had not cared. He was all around her, in one shape or form. *He'd* commissioned portraits of himself and his brats and all his supposed ancestors. Alternated by mounted stag's heads they nigh covered the walls. They still did: they hung there, but more limply than before. She'd flayed them all into ribbons.

Some of her accomplices, chosen for height and physique, were in Null costumes, genuine purple hide fresh peeled off dead beasts or prisoners; tanned and fitted and topped with cunning masks. In the half light of the Castle's great hall they looked marvellously sinister. She waved them onstage, replica spiky Null cocks accusingly foremost.

The maids could not fail to see the approach: specially provided mirrors faced the whole length of the long banqueting table they were draped over. Yet still they did not squeal or rise. Jezebel's magecraft *must* have worked.

The awakening of her mind was still fresh to her. Sennacherib's chief mage had urged her to believe and believe – and believe again until there was nothing in her mind but belief in belief. He'd licked his lips with nervousness then, warning there were but few who could rise to *awareness*. He had advised she steel herself against disappointment. *That*, she told him, in ice-tones, *she was well qualified to do*. And *steel* was one thing she had no shortage of. Inside and outside she was nothing but steel. Her sharp edges cut – herself and anyone else who approached.

Once before, in the long ago time, Jezebel had been a single-minded girl. She'd dared offer herself to the golden stranger and bathed in his favour and her daring. There'd been a period of ease – almost relaxation. It seemed long ago now – and silly. Displaced from that effulgence of light, she'd frozen. Out in the cold it was easy to become one focused thought. The universe was a simple place; black and white, amendable by will. When it arrived, the magic had come easy. She *believed*.

Her first word of power, unexpected early success, had

splintered a door, wounding the innocent guard beyond. That set the tone.

She'd progressed since then, in virulence and reach. She had it under control – when it suited – and if all her spells were mangling, controlling ones they only mirrored the inner mood. The mage tutor was no longer there to extend or correct her repertoire. He was dismissed, job done, back to hunting *mud-monsters* in Pevensey-Assyria.

The cries attracted her like a shark to a spray of blood. The pseudo-Null were ordered to disengage. They left their prey raw and whimpering, the latter sure sign the compulsion grew weak. Jezebel *clamped down* on them. Silence returned save for the crackling of the fires and her own heavy breath.

She loved it best when their sweet lips – fore and aft – were the only pristine parts. The Null-men knew to assault other avenues. Then, so that all else should be angry red and interlaced, she liked to complete their scourging herself, with every painstaking care. A whip was already placed to hand. She considered it and gloated.

There was all evening and no hurry, no possible reason for haste when life itself was drained of meaning. Consummation could be as far away as she wanted it to be and sometimes she found she did not want it all. That didn't matter: nothing did – but it did pass the time.

Jezebel felt laughter coming on and stifled it, knowing the difficulty there might be in stopping. She tried to concentrate on the matter – the matters – in hand.

Grasping the back-proffered valleys a pair at a time, she checked. All was well: fear-dryness, which was soon changed, and aquamarine musk were on her fingertips. She softened into smirks and exultation. The girls bucked and reared under her probing talons but could not cry out. She held them. They were hers.

One day the answering thrill might not come but for the moment it was an essential reminder of continuing life. Something that important justified any amount of horror.

Whip and dildo to hand, Jezebel surveyed the five feminine

behinds and giggled convulsively.

'This is good, being a god,' she thought. 'And I'm so much better at it than *him*.'

They took it leisurely, just a few miles a day and along a wandering route at that. This was a triumph, a sin to spoil with haste. Wherever they lingered, whatever they consumed, he paid liberally with gold *Toms*. Like an aura, joy followed them and was spread around.

The progress favoured New-Chertsey, then New-Weybridge: typical Blades-dictated *Bargate* stone constructions: Surrey-style meets Gothic meets Saracenic. His spirits rose further at the sight, as well they might, since he'd designed each, from street plan to defences. Fortunately, all the thatch rendered the fearsome whole homely and bearable, and would do for some time yet. Imperial expeditions were years off securing a steady supply of Welsh slate.

In each town they feasted on untold oxen, picnicking by the bank of the Thames. They later learned the roasting fires were seen as far off as New-Dorking and New-Coulsdon; celebration starring the dark night.

At New-Kingston they paused by the fortified bridge, no longer a redoubt against incursion, but the pathway to an expansive future. There was a ceremony astride the river, formally opening the way. Within days new settlers would be heading across.

Blades recalled that, back in the first world, Kingston-upon-Thames had held the ancient coronation stone of England. Great Athelstan and Alfred's son and half a dozen other Old-English Kings had set foot on it to accept the crown. On impulse he decreed it should be so again. A suitable sandstone block was hurriedly found – a press-ganged mounting block – and Blades blessed it. He promised that his sons ever after should come there to inherit. To christen it with use, Blades stood atop to dub Firstmet a *Knight of the Round Table*. It was an empty gesture; there'd be no companion *knights*, no *Round Table* even, but New-Wessex had never witnessed so broad a grin. Blades worried the top of the man's head might topple off – but need not have feared. He was simply happy: they all were. The justified-Arthurian's mood caught on. The Kingstonians, the whole army, went wild – wilder.

On the Downs at Epsom, scene of the *Great Defeat*, they held horse races. It was a sunny day, yet bracing. Firstmet's fifth son won three events on a chestnut yearling and was feted around the impromptu course. Emperor Blades watched and wondered. No one seemed inhibited by the shaming field of bones not far away. Regularly repeated, such jollities might exorcise the place of taint. He recollected again and instituted the meet as a yearly event, a *Derby*. Slowly but surely, he was reforming his world into recognisable and comforting patterns.

The Marcher Lords departed one by one; Arthur to Kent, Sennacherib and his Assyrians to Pevensey, each severally off to their far reaches. All the refugee units, armed and militant, from the lost, now regained, northern provinces had already gone. What remained were the core New-Wessex men and even their numbers dwindled, leaving an ever purer Imperial remnant.

Regiments peeled away as each neared their home towns. The inhabitants turned out to whoop them back. That some wives and husbands rushed to laughingly mount one another, in full view of everyone, was a throw-back to burrow days. Blades had never seen the way to drum modesty into them and now didn't care to. Having given it some thought he'd years ago concluded that guilt was one thing best not imported over from the old world. Humanity needed more humans, the more the merrier. If they should also be merry humans then he, for one, was glad.

The harvest was nigh. Everywhere, the great caravan progressed between ripe fields and orchards. The amateur army of mankind knew at best a week or so separated them from stripping off their soldier scarlet and the frenzied hard work of harvest home. They were minded to celebrate. The barrels were drained.

Fireworks were a recent innovation: a sign of healthy powder supplies. When they lingered anywhere after dusk, the sky was lit up for them with huge rockets and *Wessex-Rousers*. License romped over the Downs under their light and there was an innocence to it that positively forbade frowns.

From New-Leatherhead to New-Dorking, quite densely settled land, crowds ribboned the road, flinging themselves to the turf as *he* passed, then rising again to let loose with air-tubes and pipes and voices. It was music that Pan himself would have approved of and gambolled to.

At Box Hill there was another massive feast, the winter slaughter arriving early for myriad beasts. Blades stood, separated, at the highest part of this high point of the North Downs, watching the smoke of their cooking ascend. His thoughts went with it, over the Mole Valley, into the Weald and beyond. He looked down in his mind's eye – and concluded it was good.

The Emperor took in all the fields and farms and foundries, the plantations and orchards, all the signs of industry by hand and mind, that now adorned the previous wilderness. If you met the notion halfway, it was as if the Null had never been.

He had achieved that and made his children happy. He could hear their happiness coming to him in voices borne up from the festivities below. He had not laboured in vain. They were grateful. This was *his* moment, the apex of triumph.

Blades called for Boudicca to join him on that clifftop and, when a screen had been placed around them, he had her every way and for hours. He could not explain it except as some consummation or other. The sun went down on them as he did on her.

The whole army were late in rising the next morning, slack and slow, thick-headed and sore-groined. Firstmet would have had people flogged for it until Blades forbade him. Even with sight of the spires of New-Godalming, home and heartland and hub of the Empire, as inspiration, they didn't set off till gone noon.

They need not have hurried. Their welcome there was musketry.

'Forward.'

'No, back!'

'Do you *dare* to . . .'

He did. Firstmet dared to manhandle the Emperor of humanity, his own personal King Arthur, away from further stretching their outrageous luck. The volleys had stripped away many of their companions. Each departed with an '*ooff*', a final expelling of air that carried the life-force with it. The shot fell like hail on the courtyard gravel, churning it around their feet, spitting it up to sting their shocked faces.

It was only later they learned that many had shot high or low, unwilling to risk damnation. Only the fanatics, Jezebel's own and some Pevensey-Assyrians, tried to aim true.

The barred gate, the cold faces at the apertures had stunned them. They'd stood like doomed oxen to take the first shots. It had started slow but once the die was cast others joined in from the walls. The Imperial party's only retaliation was their look of betrayal. Bullets took no notice of it.

Lord Firstmet dragged the Emperor out of range of his faithless children.

Immediately before the old Castle main-gate, now long since swallowed up and made redundant by the citadel's expansion, is THE WICKED PLACE, remembered in infamy. Here HE (HE needs not our blessing) stood and was sorrowed.

Pilgrims should, for their own sake, tarry and say the prayer of expiation. Sincerely recited, it absolves those who may have had an ancestor-participant in THE WICKEDNESS.

The great crucible of boiling lead over THE WICKED PLACE is kept in perpetual ferment to symbolise the eternal fate of the sinners involved. It is a virtuous act to cast some precious object to destruction within.

'A Pilgrim's Compendium of Wisdom for those who would

Glorify their Earthly Life with the Jewels of Piety and the Silken Raiment of Prayer'

Thane Brixi of New-Compton in the Province of Wessex, United England. In the Year of Our Deliverance 457 A.B.

Issued this day,
the Seventy-seventh such
of the siege of **RIGHTEOUSNESS**.
Be it known that it is ordered, directed and decreed
by **HER IMPERIAL HIGHNESS**
Jezebel
Empress of New-Wessex, Protectrix of the Out-Provinces,
True-wife, Mother of Princes, Witch-Bane, Null-Bane,
Defender of the Faith.
that *this day shall be a further day of* FASTING
to the great glory of **G*D** *and the Imperium.*
That this day, no dweller in the Realm of **RIGHTEOUSNESS**
shall consume greater than:
Two cupped handfuls of barley or oat meal
and
One Imperial-standard flask of water.
Infants, for their better disciplining and education,
shall consume nothing at all.
And further:
Any soldier of **RIGHTEOUSNESS** *discharging more than six*
cartridges save by specific permission
shall speedily learn to fly and
be delivered to damnation and the enemy by the speediest route.
With love, to her loving subjects
Herewith, her seal
Queen Jezebel I

The first ranks fell silently. Spouting erect little bolts in head and chest, they laid themselves down to rest. The Neo-Assyrians were well known to be crossbow-fiends: the ideal tool for dealing murder without disturbing the quiet of Pevensey Levels. At that range, in those hands, weapons rested comfortably on the Castle parapets, every shot found a home. That was as well: after twelve weeks of siege, supplies of projectiles were running low.

The besiegers had no such problems. They had the broad expanse of New-Wessex and the loyalty of its people behind them. Harvest permitting, goods and men poured in their direction.

That too was just as well. Assaulting Castle Blades on a weekly basis had become expensive. Each costly failure was a tribute to the defences' designer who sat outside to watch each rout. The Emperor on his luxury observation dais ruefully considered he'd done rather well there. If it could keep the Null out it was certainly up to his half-hearted mob.

To start with he hadn't the stomach for a bombardment. There'd been such love and labour lavished on New-Godalming it seemed wicked to tear it down. Besides which, *they* had most of the cannon. Humanity had learned its lesson from *The Great Defeat*: the artillery always stayed in the towns. That way they might lose a battle but not the war.

The soldiery shared his reservations. This was the first inter-human strife, save for a few burrow tribes who'd resisted civilisation. There weren't so many humans yet that any could be cheerfully wasted. Fast breeding was an Imperial decree, the fecund were rewarded and honoured, and yet thanks to the Null and disease and hard work total numbers didn't exactly leap ahead. Blades had seen them fight the monsters and now he watched them run in against the Castle. There was no comparison.

The enemy, by contrast, were full of conviction. Those who weren't had their bones broken till they could be tied into a ball. In that shape they were flung at the besiegers from the war catapults. It was amazing how little measures like that could forge unity in a faction. His admiration for Queen Jezebel grew daily.

Those front ranks were fanatics from the wilder regions, lightly armed and lightly regarded. They were good for taking casualties and not complaining of it. Then, whilst the traitors did their worst to these expendables, behind advanced the line regiments and huscarls with ladders and battering rams. It should have worked well, but Blades could observe their lack of zeal through his perspective-glass. When the Castle cannon were in full shout he could see his best men deciding in their hearts to put on a fair show and then retreat. You could make that sort of attack until Doomsday and still not get anywhere. It was as much meaningless ritual as one of Sam Speed's services.

Unable to wean the People off their weird sounding wind-tubes, Blades had customised them to grate less. Made gigantic, requiring a team of three to hold and pump and play, they almost reminded him of the church organs of dimming memory. A bank of them stood behind his divan, ready to convey his thoughts on proceedings. The Emperor ordered them to perform the 'come home'.

The recipients were quicker about that than they were in going forward and that was a sign for those who would see. Blades saw and learned.

As the former army and neo-rabble streamed back it occurred to Emperor Blades that one – a recklessly brave *one* – might succeed where a multitude failed. Then he studied the loop-holed, cannon-studded, walls of New-Godalming and decided against. A bombardment it would have to be.

Issued this day,
the eighth such
of the siege of **RIGHTEOUSNESS**.
Be it known, and daily repeated
that **HER IMPERIAL HIGHNESS**
Jezebel
Empress of New-Wessex, Protectrix of the Out-Provinces,
True-wife, Mother of Princes, Witch-Bane, Null-Bane,
Defender of the Faith,
decrees that:

Any, whatsoever their estate or previous service,
who shall deliver this realm and its ruler
from the sorcerous servitude and seductions of the
Witch ~~BOUDICCA~~,
by any and all means,
shall be granted fortune, not less than his or her weight in gold
Jezebels, and a life without care in this world
and the Sweet Gardens of Paradise in the Next.

'Thou shalt not suffer a witch to live'
The Book of Blades, Exodus 22, 18.
'There shall not be found among you a witch'
The Book of Blades, Deuteronomy 18, 10

The tunnel failed, even employing the expertise of years-before kidnapped Cornish miners and their sons. The idea was to undermine a main tower, pack the excavation with straw and tar and then fire the lot, burning away the supports and causing a collapse, tumbling all to ruin. Massed cavalry, on horse or captured Null lizard-steeds, were held poised to rush in and carry the shocked defenders away. In the event they ought to have brought a book, for they waited to no purpose, a mere target for cannon snipers.

Alas, the defenders were canny. They set bowls of water all round the base of the walls. Closely studied, ripples therein betrayed the miners' work and then they could set to countermining. The poor Cornish were washed away with tides of molten sand and lead. Or else there was desperate battle in the dark underground as mine broke into counter-mine. That was dramatic, the very stuff of future bard material, but no way forward.

So, one promising avenue closed off, it was back to weekly massed assaults, assisted by giant '*belfries*' which were trundled forward to surmount the walls. The Emperor had no faith in them but went through the motions for want of better ideas.

Their construction gave the army something distracting to do meanwhiles.

Then, when enough oaks were murdered and moulded into use, he stood to watch each belfry perish in flames, for all their soaked ox-hide protection, or else be toppled over by long poles or reduced to matchwood by a point-blank cannon. The battering rams went the same way, squashed by boulders from above, drenched with boiling water or de-manned by musketry. They laboured in vain, in any case. He knew how much stone had gone into those walls. Ironically, he was the one who'd decreed them made ram-proof.

It was very frustrating when all he wanted to do was get into his house and talk to his wife.

'And then she sorcerously enhanced her lips and bum, the better to bewitch the Imperial prick. They were rendered more welcoming, more serviceable. I saw it done; there can be no dispute.'

Indeed there couldn't. Axe-bearing Assyrians lined the walls to abort any debate. Queen Jezebel's daily consciousness-raising sessions with the New-Godalming elite were strictly monologues.

'She has him in thrall, led glaze-eyed by the nose – or parts, more like. If he shows signs of waking or asks for me she enspells him again in coma. Is that not so?'

The captured huscarls mumbled agreement, nodding their ill-treated heads. They'd been drawn off the belfries with hooks or netted from the ground and then rough handled till rendered reliable. Jezebel deluded herself their prior reputation gilded their testimony. She didn't otherwise take prisoners.

'And she serves the Null. I have it from her own pouting lips. She wished to press them to mine but I spurned her perversity. That is why she hates me. She says she was their prisoner but I know she went willingly. Boudicca accepted their cocks and bore their babies. She has Null spawn: I've seen them. They travel with her in a closed carriage. She grooms a Null son to be King. And . . . and she danced for them when she was their prisoner – to incite them to lust. And war dances. That's how she wounded her leg . . .'

'The audience is ended,' said Sennacherib, advancing on his mother, cloth in hand. Her spittle was flying, out of control: like the rest of her.

'*It is not!*' she commanded – and sent him, involuntarily, back till the wall curtailed him. He paled under the rebuke and magic.

This was none of his intention. He'd envisaged an orderly regentship – and the throne in due course of time. His father was to have been honoured, cared for in retirement, not shifted the far side of anarchy and magic and civil war. The total price should have been poor Aunt Boudicca swallowing a stake the hard way: an absolute bargain, considering. Now it was all going wrong. Sennacherib knew no apology was going to dig him out of this venture.

Pinned to the throne-room wall, he wondered what his namesake, or maybe the great Sargon of Nineveh, would have done in his place – and for the life of him could think of no answer. *She* was not some plain and simple mother you could just murder. Her will, and his troops, were the only things keeping this going. His head and hers stayed on or came off together, now part of the same transaction.

The assembled officers and nobles gasped disbelief – and since they hadn't been asked to, Jezebel sent guardsmen in amongst them. She didn't like being interrupted – any more than they liked being hit with axes. The room quietened, save for the noises of the dying. They alone were excused.

'*He* will not be free, I say – nor this land either, while *she* trails her fingers in his mind. Lop them off! Slice them away! Bury swords in her eyes and cunt! Rescue him – us! *Why* do you not do it?

The answer was because Boudicca was the other side of a wall that was their only safeguard, behind an army of their kith and kin, standing beside the man to whom they owed all, someone strongly suspected of links to the godhead, that was why. But they wisely said nothing.

For just a moment Jezebel was at the precipice of tears. They

202

hoped she might fall in and drown there, but just in time, their Queen drew back. There had suddenly arrived inner solace: realisation she could make a whole day *go away* with her harem.

The room was dismissed and blessed with the sweetest of smiles.

'That's all, thank you.'

Trapped between two furies, timely alarm bells called the conscripts back to the parapets. Another onslaught had begun.

Boudicca sighed. He didn't like that and paused in unwrapping her.

'What's the matter?'

She languidly fell from his arms back on to the opulent bed, shedding loosened garments, sinking into its white luxury. Wire-rimmed spectacles regarded him.

'Nothing that can be remedied.'

As an Emperor and despot – and as a man – Blades took that for a challenge.

'I doubt that. You'd be surprised what I can do.'

Boudicca shook her head. Lustrous red fanned across the deep pillow. She hennaed her hair now, giving recent bedtimes a whole new lease of life.

'Not this. Not even you cannot turn back time.'

True enough. He frowned, not caring to be reminded of his few limitations.

'Tell all.'

She was not denying him; she never did. Even as they spoke her hands worked at the trickier man-proof fastenings of her bodice. Only the glasses would be left for him, a task he liked to leave till last.

'There is nothing you can do . . .'

'Try me.'

'I do, constantly. I shall, any second. Be content.'

'Contentment is not my destiny.'

That stopped her hands and speech and eyes. She looked up at him; truly studied her husband as though for the first time. The awful pause was unmanning.

'Very well,' she said eventually, in distant, unconsoled tone. 'Learn the answer if you must. I lamented that the best was past.'

He reeled it in, stunned and bagged it but still didn't know what it was. That was not a proper position for an Emperor to be in, even a trouserless one.

'Explain.' An imperial command.

'It can never be better than when I returned. First there was you, then the Null, then you again: unexpected. It can never be better than our reunion.'

'What, vomiting and all?'

He'd misjudged her depth of conviction. A bottomless look shut him up.

'*Never* better,' she repeated.

He knew this had the potential to be some climactic moment. She might even want it to be, though he'd had to drag the thing from her. It was his for the taking and yet the outcome was opaque, unforeseeable. He considered – and then stamped on its fingertips till the dangerous moment fell away . . . The spell broke.

Boudicca seemed not to mind, passing on without regret.

'It's me they want: I am the problem.'

That was both truth and falsity together. Blades knew what Jezebel and her crew wanted and it wasn't the woman before him. She was the mere shell of excuse.

Heralded by trumpet and wind-tube, the evening bombardment commenced: the thump of trebuchets and *vox dei* of cannon. Its percussion penetrated the grim-carved multiple stockades round the Imperial compound and the rich stuff of the pavilion itself. Cries and orders even tracked round the cunningly offset entrances, unabsorbed by the gaping mouths of the totems. Soon enough New-Godalming answered in kind. The ribs of the earth were pounded. He missed some words.

'. . . it is me. You could just turn me over to them.'

'Eh?'

'That would be an end to it. I would not mind. You could just turn me over.'

204

That got the stiff-making blood flowing. He was mettlesome again in seconds, hands diving into the cloud of raven overskirts and white petticoats, flipping her face down.

'And turned over you shall be,' he whooped. 'That was always my plan.'

The cannons' *crump* and catapults' slam blessed them with a rhythm. He felt god-like and ploughed away to their accompaniment.

Boudicca's face, as best as he could tell, when he bothered to enquire, was once again a seat of tranquillity.

'How can you have *types* of slave? They are slaves; they slave: there it ends.'

Jezebel thought herself magnanimous in passing over her son's intervention in silence. Anyone else would have earned themselves an axe.

'There shall be sixteen grades in ascending order, from latrine slave to philosopher-tutor. You will devise a title for each, Sennacherib; concoct Assyrian terms if you wish. We do not mind.'

Her mind was much on *his* mind of late. She was ascending into some place where he could not follow, even had he wished to. The kingdom she was planning was not of this earth but somewhere other. It would need to be elsewhere for it to work. He'd protested as much as he dared. The terrified courtiers and councillors dared not protest at all. They scribbled notes and scurried off to implement the impossible. And all this whilst a siege prevailed and failed to prosper.

'There may be progress between the castes, by merit or education, but at no faster pace than one stage per lifetime.'

'Manure-man to sage in sixteen generations,' commented Sennacherib. 'A . . . stately progress.'

Queen Jezebel had become de-sensitised beyond detecting irony, or even sarcasm. Sennacherib relied on it. Unfortunately, her other sharp faculties were heightened in compensation.

'Fifteen generations.'

'Pardon, mother?'

'Fifteen generations. You miscalculate. He or she starts at one. Ultimate progression therefore takes *fifteen* generations.'

'Ahh, I see . . . Yes, you are right. All is well, then.'

'Though I doubt we shall see it often.'

'*We* shall not see it at all. We shall be dust by then.'

She did not care to be reminded of mortality. The best victory she looked for was simple outliving. His contradiction was wordlessly frozen to death.

'Each slave type shall wear a different colour, from . . . dun brown to . . . pure white. And there shall be a college of recorders of status.'

'A seventeenth caste of slave, perhaps?' queried her son, quill exaggeratedly poised. ' "*Scribe-bureaucrat*"?'

She took the suggestion at face value, even if the rest of the council did not. They were looking longingly at the door.

'No. Slaves cannot be trusted to account for themselves. They would cheat and forge. The college shall comprise only free-men. There must be order.'

It seemed odd to talk of '*order*' when the walls shook to cannon fire. Mere minutes into the evening bombardment, a light dusting of ceiling plaster adorned them all.

That powdered grey on his perfumed black curls emboldened Sennacherib to haul her back to earth.

'Indeed, mother, and it shall be done. Meanwhile, cast your regal eye over this.'

He slid a broad sheaf across the council table to her. She did not look down. He waited. Still she ignored it. Others read *for* her nowadays. Before the silence became dangerous Sennacherib had to oblige.

'The armourer says we're low on powder; "*perilous low*".'

Her expression remained frigid: fixed amusement from somewhere or other but not there or then.

'We are *not* spoken to thus. Deal with him.'

'Mother, he merely presents the numbers: I interpreted them.'

206

For a moment he thought she might have reached her limit with him. Her eyes, suddenly twitched his way, were round and glassy. Then came signs of recognition. His iron-banded stomach unclenched: she spoke.

And for that brief moment he almost believed that she was bigger than Blades, that she really could replace him – until the tower shook again and he noticed their own return-fire rate was restrained; diminished.

'The matter is already resolved,' she told them. 'We have written to Sicily.'

To the commanders and servants of New-Wessex.
A General and Binding Proclamation.
Issued this day, the Fiftieth such
of the reign of **RIGHTEOUSNESS**.
Be it known that it is ordered, directed and decreed
by **HER IMPERIAL HIGHNESS**
Jezebel
Regent-Empress of New-Wessex, Protectrix of the Out-Provinces,
Knight-Commander of New-Sicily,
First-wife, Mother of Princes, Witch-Bane, Null-Bane,
Defender of the Faith.
that, *to the great glory of* **G*D** *and the Imperium,*
is instituted a new realm of
RIGHTEOUSNESS.
Such that
all who swear fealty and shew forth sweet loyalty to it
shall not die but live
and
pass to life everlasting
(where there is no Null nor weeping or strife.)
Wherefore, and with good reason,
you should surrender to and obey the bearer of this notice.
Thank you.
With love, to her loving subjects
Herewith, her seal
Queen Jezebel I

And there was even a personal note:

Favoured-slave John Lilburne
We do not forget that you delivered the Boudicca-witch to the Null
at Lulworth and we love you the better for it. The Emperor, in his
dotage, sent you away to weird climes but we would have you home,
in order for you to bathe in our smile. Be assured, you will not find
the new regime's weather so inclement.

Bring with you all the gunpowder at your disposal – and soldiers.
Destroy all that is left behind, including those that you adjudge love
us not. Or else leave them in the ruins to await the Null. Come
home. Leave Sicily to quiet wildness.

There has arrived a fresh dispensation. You are the last of the
powder-bearers. When your stock is exhausted, man shall face the
Null with the righteous strength of his arm, not wicked far-killing. I
have decided that is the better way.

We hunger and thirst to see you; my appetite rises. Therefore
tarry not.

Your Sovereign-Lady, G*d-wife and Empress

Jezebel I
Her Seal

They'd met before. Years ago, as a young pirate, John had
helped hijack his ship and kidnap him to another world. If
there was recognition or grudge the Sea-captain didn't show it.
He was all business and averted eyes, not actually in New-Sicily
at all.

'How soon can you load?'

Lilburne looked up from the quayside. The captain hadn't
even disembarked, sign of his impatience and discomfort. The
Imperial missives had been tossed down to him and time given
for barely one scan. Those slights made answer easy.

'What makes you think I will?'

Sea-captain – his only name now – didn't even have to pause.

'That and this and these.' He indicated the Queen's summons, slapped *The Lady Bridget*'s rail and threw down a shower of coin. Lilburne caught one. The familiar gold *Tom* was crudely overstamped with a stylised female profile.

'She's sent 'ee a barrel of them *Jezebels*, for what it's worth,' the captain told him as he looked. 'But listen 'ere to weightier considerations. I catch tomorrow's tide, be 'ee with I or no. I misdoubt there'll be more ships. Here will become mighty lonely. No more provisions, no more letters. Tell your people that: see what they think. Then get loading.'

John Lilburne remembered Jezebel: no worse than the other lordly ladies. He still couldn't credit her as ruler of the world.

'Oh, she *has* you, don't she?' he accused the captain. More provocation: he needed more clues.

'She has my wives and little 'uns in New Godalming. That's the same. I'm expected back. If I return with you or your curse, it's the same to I.'

'She might not be so easy going. The Queen requires brimstone.'

'And we'll have it: fight you for it if need be.'

This was more Lilburne's line. In a conflict everything was out in the open, clear cut, courage against courage. You barely needed to think.

'We outnumber you.' He also liked bald statements of fact.

'And we 'ave cannon. Do y' think I've given no *consideration*? Boy, there's little else to do in the coast hop here. You hardly need captainship and navigation. No, our plans are laid firm: try and thwart me and I'll stand off and blow your defence walls down. Then when the Null have 'ad their feed we'll return and help ourselves. Think on. Be sweet and personable. Come home nice like.'

You couldn't really say fairer than that so Lilburne didn't try. Turning on his booted heel, he strode away, leaving Sea-captain calling after him. He didn't listen or reply. A little mystification would buy him time.

'Holiday!'

The labourers knew that word even if the rest of their English was rudimentary. Before Governor Lilburne arrived they'd been slaves; native burrow-Sicilians rounded up to be taught brimstone shovelling and little else. One of his first acts was to free them.

True, they still worked all day for not much but at least it wasn't under the whip. Right from the start he'd thrust dignity and the rudiments of speech in their very midst. They were no longer to be beasts with spades, no longer expected to be eternally grateful rescued Null-meat. He had them shaved and made to resemble men. When they arose to rub the liberated skin and feel the sun's first kiss upon it, new notions already showed in their eyes.

John firmly intended to incorporate them amongst the People – and straightaway, not gradually as the slavery apologists advocated. It was one of his new ideals; one of many. He had plenty more, books full, but his People were not to know that yet. They'd be allowed to show their face bit by bit in order not to shock.

By now, the first-met aborigines were already musket-toters and conversation-starters. They rather *liked* Mr Lilburne; almost as much as these things called *holidays* he'd invented.

Like the children they mostly still were, the horde downed tools directly and streamed past him, instantly, delicately, happy. Soon enough their whooping momentum would have them on to the pontoon ferry and then back to the main island, past regrouping. He let them go, waving the worried overseers back, careless of production targets. There were more important things in life. Lilburne wanted a bit of solitude to consider them.

Brimstone Island was high on the nose: a downside to it being nigh on pure stuff, the gift and offspring of a quiescent volcano. An occasional fuming vent cautioned against affection or ownership, timely reminder of the transience of the place and its true parentage. Offerings and sacrifice were made to the sleeping spirit beneath their feet – whilst meanwhile they robbed it like fury.

The noon-day sun smote yellow vapours from the island and you could practically scoop the precious stuff off the surface. It was enough to just pile and fire the pumice boulders to make the brimstone flow, running it into waiting wooden moulds. They didn't even have to think of mining yet.

By contrast, just across the strait on Sicily proper, was the farming enclave: fields of cereals and root crops ringed by powder mills and beehive huts of baked brick. There was now little space between them and the great double ditch and wall that held the Null out. Their years of successfully performing that duty had allowed the settlement to grow and encroach right to them. Maybe half of the population had been born here and knew nowhere else.

At the moment though, real change still arrived from outside. For a long time there had only been the beehive huts, some grander than others, some for work, some for sleep, but basically the same. It was Lilburne who varied the skyline of New-Syracuse with a whitewashed church and a domed *Court of Justice*. He laboured mightily to ensure what went on in both was meaningful.

Convincing them about an omnipotent Father-Deity proved easy going compared to explaining the jury system to the People, natives and Wessex-men alike. He'd persevered. It was drummed into them that they were judges of both fact *and* law, not judge-puppets like in the world the Emperor described. If they had hats he forbade them being doffed before the magistrate and what the sentence-givers never had they never missed. He'd stamped on the very first sign of *lawyers*, as autocratic as any god-king, enforcing rough and ready elections for court officers till the system just seemed natural, acquiring a life of its own. All in all, he flattered himself he'd squeezed a fair amount of justice out of a world not keen on it.

Other things would never change. Silhouetted against the clear blue atop the massive wall, black against distant, smoking Etna, stood the cannons. Early on, the Sicilian Null had been easy prey to them, learning the wary cunning of their English

211

brethren the hard way. Then, when the beasts grew shy, the newcomers went in search of them, luring them into clear fields of fire with tethered felons and unsatisfactory workers. On empty beaches or in confining coves they were drawn in and then slaughtered by the tribe. Ranks of men stood just offshore on rafts or atop high hills and fired away to their hearts' contents, till the guns grew too hot to touch and powder was exhausted. The earliest incorporated burrow-Sicilians were corralled up and conscripted along to watch, to be impressed and learn wisdom. Their love and obedience was thus secured. At first they wailed and wet themselves but within weeks they were cheering. It was heartening to find that here, as every-where, mankind needed little persuasion to get up off its knees.

And, as a useful by-product, it was discovered that rotting Null, well mulched, made good saltpetre. Whereas as fertiliser they poisoned whatever they were spread upon. Therein was a lesson for those who would see.

Meanwhile, Sicilian humanity gained a breathing space in which to stand aloft and build. The wall went up to cut off an isthmus of safety, a stream was diverted to power the mills and work started on Brimstone Island. With the construction of a quay, soon enough the cargo ships began their schedule. By year three New-Wessex's first overseas possession had attained a degree of permanence. Though now rebred and wiser, the Null might hurl themselves on defended New-Syracuse as much as they pleased, the more the merrier.

Beyond the wall and guns, beyond a narrow, scorched zone to thwart surprise attacks, there was the dark, stunted, forest and it went on forever. The Emperor assured them Sicily was an island but Lilburne hadn't seen that with his own eyes. It looked pretty eternal to him.

Lilburne took those miles of useless trees and thorn-scrub as a reproach and bursting out of this tiny childish cupboard as his next priority. They were dwarfish, twisted growths, dry and acidic smelling: unpleasing freaks compared to the noble growths of home. It was the shelter of Null and Parliament and unfeasibly large lizards. One day a troop of monstrous, four-legged beasts with snaky noses and sickle tusks, had emerged from the forest to butt the wall with their heads until persuaded to *go away* with musketry. Lilburne had no patience with any such excesses of Nature. He'd vowed an axe and torch to their olive green hiding place and fully intended to keep his promise.

Yet now the process was turned on its head. He was ordered home and the forest invited in! One Imperial thought put on to paper and lo, the Null were to be restored to their birthright. Cautious at first, crab-like up the quiet wall, they'd explore. Then the triumph call, the spitting at the departing sails. Soon they'd be striding round, jerking their sleek heads back and forth to stare at the meat-creature's strange creations. Then they'd defile what wasn't already destroyed. Lilburne had observed what they'd done with captured parts of New-Wessex.

He raised clenched eyes to the hot sun, hoping the light would purge the sudden sickness he felt. It didn't. It went down and through to his toes without the slightest warming. When he looked again, spots danced before him, obscuring the view — and he was glad of that mercy.

The new *Lady Bridget* had put out to sea, was watching, awaiting his decision.

It was no decision. John Lilburne, formerly just plain John-the-huscarl, a true son of New-Wessex, had no real choice. He *believed*, he truly did. He had read and now he believed.

Every eminence in New-Syracuse was topped with an effigy of the Emperor. Orthodoxy had it that nowhere should be entirely deprived of his remembrance. From the brazen, twice life-size *Blades Militant* astride the city wall, to the modest figurines on the larger huts, he presided over all, and all in turn saw him. The gracious Emperor of Humanity was never out of their thoughts, just as he, allegedly, constantly treasured every soul in his.

The best Brimstone Island could boast were some jagged spires of black, glassy rock, but they sufficed to hold a gilded-plaster *Him*, overlooking their hard work from the very edge of the mute fire-mountain, back turned to the sea way below. John

Lilburne tramped over to it, raising puffs of yellow with his boots.

There was the danger that the *Lady Bridget* might see, training a perspective-glass on the focus of uncertainty, and then all pretence would be in vain. Yet still he needed to act, to jump the internal divide. There was no longer any merit or honour in remaining still. That he might not reach the other side, and plunge forever into an abyss, was a possibility – but he had to find out. Equally, there had to be outward sign.

The Emperor was surrounded by offerings of cacti flowers and unusually shaped pumice. They were kicked aside. The painted-plaster Blades proved to be bolted home with rods of iron. Lilburne did not test them but put faith in all the months of doubt and anger. Flowing at last along their proper course, that sudden flood gave him strength. Both the inner and outer John Lilburne heaved. There was resistance but only a little. Something gave.

'Traitor!' the statue was told. Settled, calm, tones. 'False god!'

Emperor Blades went down in stately somersault to meet the waves and sea-Null.

Before he'd left, been cast aside, Blades had shown guilty kindness to Lilburne. He would repent of it – as he would all his best and worst deeds.

'I'm sure there are references to the island in my library,' he'd said; one of their last conversations. 'If you find any you may take them.'

That was his careless mistake. In the wrong – and right – hands books are deadlier than bombs.

At that stage, clinging on to belief, John seized the slightest sign of Imperial favour like a drowning man. Also he prized his literacy as much as he did his wives and tribe. In those days he proxy thanked the Emperor for that as well and entered the great *Cyclopedium* with pride. . .

The New-Wessex printing presses had been in operation for years now and so there were native works of value on the shelves as well as reprints. These were well-ordered and catalogued and easy of access, but for what Lilburne required he had to enquire of the random pilfered volumes of early days. Almost as an afterthought, when most else was gathered in, Blades had set his 'shaggy men' on some minor colleges and pillaged their collections. Since the succeeding years held other distractions for him, and because the sanctity of their other-world origin put off pious scholars, they were mostly left untroubled save for blind rote-copying. Lilburne was faced with wavering, dusty piles of neglected wisdom.

Undaunted and with nothing better to do, he attacked them, eventually learning all sorts of interesting things. Some weren't relevant to his plight – though still thought provoking – but others went straight to the point.

It was very *interesting*, for instance, to find Diodorus Siculus's *Bibliotheca Historica*, in translation. His world history mentioned Sicily a fair bit, and dwelt on the two great *Servile Wars* fought there in 'ancient times' – whenever they might be. The risen slaves had rebelled against their brutal 'Roman' masters and defeated whole armies, liberating cities and great swathes of the island. Amongst them had arisen slave heroes like Eunus, the magician-king *Antiochus*, and Achaeus and Cleon and Athenion and Salvius, *King Tryphon*. The worst treated of mankind had behaved well, won battles, struck their own coins and founded *The Kingdom Of Justice*. Finally defeated by overwhelming might, the last prisoners died gloriously by their own hands, in the heart of the beast in Rome, rather than fight as *gladiators* to please the Romans. The final victory was theirs, really, sort of.

Then he found Appian's Roman history and read all about Spartacus. That capped it and made a lot of things clear.

Later, to his utter amazement, he found bound pamphlets with 'his' name on them, for all the world as though *he'd* written them. Not knowing they were Blades's half-disapproving, half whimsical purchase, and assuming he *hadn't* written them and

215

then forgotten, John naturally dived in.

This other, firebrand, *John Lilburne* had penned 'The Agreement of the People' and 'Come out of Her My People' and 'England's Birthright', arguing with dauntless courage against tyrants. Soon enough, mere pages in, the New-Wessex Lilburne knew that if he hadn't written them then he could have and should have. The old he was swept away. Here was a new and better identity, pre-destined by name, just waiting for him to slip into.

Blades's collection, when Lilburne ceased savaging it, was left gap-toothed: ominously injured. When he finally sailed for New-Sicily certain volumes were clutched to his chest or committed to memory, sailing to a new world in more than one sense. He had indeed found the references he wanted – only he'd never dreamed they'd be personally addressed.

The huts were already afire, covering all New-Syracuse with yellowy smoke. The brimstone barrels were piled by the quay. It was all the Sea-captain's desire and he hoved back in to shore.

John Lilburne was beside the brimstone formations. He made no protest at his loss or their loading. The dockside cranes swung away, arranging them on deck.

'And yes, I *did* recognise you,' said Sea-captain to him. 'You were a shaggyman, weren't you?'

Lilburne neither confirmed or denied it. That was another life: he carried no burdens from it. The man seemed lost in contemplating his fired dreams.

'I lost my ship a'cause of you – though you see I now have her miraculous back again.' Once more he lovingly stroked *The Lady Bridget*. 'You're losing something precious. So now we're quits. Fret not, soldier. Happen you'll be as lucky with *your* heart's desire."

Lilburne deigned to take notice of him. He looked away from the pall of smoke.

'I've decided to come back,' he said, not especially to Sea-captain, 'but this is all too precious to leave. So I'm bringing it back with me.'

That earned a laugh from up on deck.

'In your dreams, maybe . . .'

Lilburne shook his head.

'No. In your nightmares – certainly.'

A hand signal – then a single cannon fired from the wall. The barrels aboard jack-in-the-boxed to life, their loose caps flipping up to release musketeers. They had overwhelming numbers, swarming across the deck. The sailors were scattered, busy with ropes and duties. A few shots, several cries, then quiet.

'Betrayed!' said Sea-captain. Tears stood in his slitted eyes.

'We are *all* betrayed,' answered Lilburne firmly – though gentle on the man's grief. 'I shall explain that to you on the journey. Meanwhile, the gangplank, if you please. Your new captain wishes to come aboard.'

Sea-captain readily obeyed, recognising authority and spiteful destiny when he saw them. And in any case, surrender was becoming easier with habit.

As *The Lady Bridget* changed hands yet again, the readied teams rushed round New-Syracuse dousing all the damp-straw fires. Besides some smoky unsightliness and a few scorched huts they'd caused little lasting damage to the Sicilian Utopia. Hopeful Null who'd gathered at the sight were blasted back into the forest. Soon enough everything was as before and developing nicely.

In their Governor's absence, elected delegates to the *Committee of Public Safety* held their inaugural solo meeting. The streets were quiet; well ordered. Though there was no compulsion, work resumed, on the brimstone and barley fields alike. Lilburne had left his experiment in safe hands.

The man himself stood high on the wall to look – and thought he glimpsed a new and better civilisation in the making.

He sailed at dawn and in confidence, taking his stolen

collection of stolen books with him, ferrying that priceless old-new knowledge back home.

The cannonade continued; inadequately answered. The would-be Emperor was trapped between his father's artillery and his mother's mad stare. He very nearly wished to turn back time and be a Pevensey philosopher-prince again.

A solitary pearl of sweat escaped the greenhouse of Sennacherib's helm. It tracked down his brow, slow moving to death and oblivion amidst the curls of his beard. He did not reach up to it, did not wish to draw attention to his fright. The other councillors had their own concerns but he felt sure every gaze was riveted on to the traitorous bead.

'Then, mother, if all our gunpowder needs are thus sorted, there remains only the issue of supplies. I'm sure . . .'

Jezebel's eyes were glaring at, through and beyond him, into some other place better than this. Her son wondered what superior-to-reality visions she saw there. Whatever they might be, at least she hadn't observed his tidal perspiration.

'How bad?'

That was a lucid, concerned, question. She was back. He could answer from the heart.

'Bad. It's rats and horses soon. Then each other.'

'How *soon*?'

'Weeks – perchance a month if we chew slowly. After that we either feed on righteousness or sally out for one last thrust.'

She *evaluated* him. Sennacherib saw what his father had once seen.

'Desperate measures . . .' she said. It could be either query or statement.

'Not promising,' he *agreed*.

Jezebel turned her presence on them all. Even the guards harkened.

'We have a heavy responsibility,' she said: mere presentation of fact. 'And a threatening prospect. Null before us, a duped

Emperor behind. We are at *risk*. We, the righteous, are a *vulnerable* vanguard.'

There was no contesting that. A lucky swathe of chain-linked shot penetrated some nearby slit windows. The adjoining chamber blossomed with screams, slowly diminishing into faltering, repeated, sobs.

Jezebel magnificently ignored it and them.

'We have *sworn* to serve the Emperor's true best interests, *sworn* to do him no harm, *sworn* to safeguard his life and liberty with ours – yet still the people do not come in to Righteousness . . .'

The pounded wall shook again and their tower with it.

'I know,' mused Sennacherib, 'amazing isn't it . . .'

She overlooked that too, as a gracious Queen might choose to without loss of face. She continued.

'But given the price of our failure; an eternal night of loss and error, we feel justified in taking *any* course to succeed. Humanity demands it. History demands it. *You* should demand it!'

She rose and studied each man and woman in turn, right from favoured son to frozen-faced axe-guard, drawing them in, implicating and involving them. They took their cue and gave their support. For many it was a sincere acclamation. Something told them they – or she – had reached a moment which was kill or cure to all their ills. It swept them along.

This was Queen Jezebel at her calmest, her best. Sennacherib then learned that he'd been wrong to doubt, that his dear mother was not mad. For a while there'd been fever and the ranting that came with it, but now, at the further end, she'd acquired precious clarity of vision.

'We have *sworn*,' she concluded, 'and given our oh-so solemnest word. And now we shall break it and him.'

'It must be from your own mouth, Lord.'

'Write!' snapped Firstmet, his concern overriding all propriety. 'Write instead. Sign it. Attach imperial seals!'

Caiaphas, chief huscarl and presiding general of the siege, shook his shaven, tattooed head.

'No. When we spoke he was adamant – by the Emperor's own mouth. Besides, I knew him. He cannot read.'

Another indictment, another cause for Emperor Blades to feel shame, one more helping of burning coals on his head. He was barred from his own capital and his own chief doorman – no mean figure in New-Wessex society – was illiterate. The man was half willing to admit him but couldn't read an instruction to do it or understand notice of his forgiveness. His Lord had been so busy pleasing himself he'd neglected his children's education. Now, quite properly, that selfishness rebounded right at him.

Emperor Blades waved the Babel of dispute to silence. He was weary and rested his head back on the throne.

'It seems to me,' he said to one and all, retaining with effort the observances of Imperial-speak, 'that we have done little enough for our subjects. That is one reason why some have spurned our friendship. We shall make amends. A prodigal son offers to return. The very least we can do is to talk to him . . .'

More cacophony. He knew they only had his best interests at heart but they were *crossing* him once more. There was that irritable, stretched feeling inside again, everything being just that bit more trouble than it was worth; the heart wanting to rend. It worried him but when it had passed it gave him strength. He shocked them. They hadn't realised a god-emperor could swear like a ruffian.

That shut them up. They stared, gap mouthed.

'And talk to him we shall,' he said, sweet-voiced again. 'In person. Arrange it!'

Once upon a time, New-Godalming was beautiful by night. He'd decreed tar-beacons along the walls, and belled chain-trails of enamelled Null heads to catch the moonlight and make music. Now the place just looked angry – and dark – and ravaged. All his own doing. He repented the unwelcoming sight.

Gatekeeper had sent word that should Blades himself supply pardon, the drawbridge would be surrendered to him. A party to hold it went with the Emperor, the whole army covertly stood-to behind.

Two Master-mages, hot-eyed, dishevelled types just like their lesser brethren, stood shoulder to shoulder with him, testing the air, detecting and standing between him and any ill-will. There was open ground before them and the towering Main Gate, and absolute quiet, by Imperial order. Some designated soldiers performed routine tasks in the besiegers' camp lest the hush be untoward, but otherwise they did not want the rebel sentries alerted. Leather creaked and armour grated but these were small sounds, far outweighed by night animals and nature's general mumblings. They got close.

Tall towers stood either side of the entrance; jet black and innocent of motion. Blades could almost imagine his world to be at peace and had to slap that Judas notion down.

The mages reached forward, outward symbol of their questing thoughts. They exchanged looks and found only agreement.

'There is just one,' the older reported. 'I think it is he – and I sense preparation. He's arranged things. Matters are as he promised.'

'Just one?' hissed Firstmet, made savage by worry. 'Be sure!'

Because he was who he was they tried again.

'One spark, one soul,' it was confirmed. 'Waiting.'

'We go,' ordered Blades – and that was it. He set aside his black hood to reveal himself and be recognised.

'I see him!' whispered one of the foremost, shot-absorbing, huscarls. 'Left, middle left window. I recognise . . .'

There was indeed a pale blob at the relevant slit but the painfully slow descent of the drawbridge was all the confirmation they really needed. Gatekeeper had not only wanted pardon but also word of the 'truth' about the Emperor and

Boudicca. Blades wasn't sure what exactly he could say to convince, but was willing to converse for the time it took to secure the gate. For that they had to meet since, whatever else the devout might think, he could not walk across the moat. A level drawbridge, a raised portcullis, were the price for setting Gatekeeper's mind at rest.

With a rattle of boots – including even the Emperor's silver-shod pair – they ran across.

In fact, Gatekeeper's mind was already at rest – and eternally so. Stuck on a spear it still served to appear at a window and deceive. The portcullis rattled down behind them.

Jezebel let go the spell of exclusion and all the constrained thoughts exploded out of its burst bubble. Being forged in fiercer fires, her skills were stronger than others. Whereas she merely staggered, the Imperial mages were caught by the hours of stockpiled energies and recoiled. One recoiled still further when Firstmet put a knife between his third and fourth rib.

'Traitor!' he told him, misunderstanding – but the unjust curse was lost on the dying man, swallowed up in the greater chaos.

Shot poured down through the murder-holes above the gate, then spears, then red-hot sand. Loyal servitors took that portion intended for Blades and so he survived to re-meet his wife.

He'd heard the rumours seeping out of the beleaguered city, tales of her amazing new powers and the uses to which she put them. He'd been intrigued, but never thought to experience them for himself.

She was clearly visible, amidst an array of Assyrians, looking down on him as a tired bird might a worm. He did not know how his gaze appeared to her – like a frightened rabbit's most probably.

His mind was seized, his body frozen. He fought back but his strength was as a child's compared to a mage's inner con-victions. Like it or no he experienced exactly what he'd inflicted on her. Therefore Emperor Blades felt very unhappy indeed. The white-hot needle jabs of her . . . disappointment rained down again and again. It would have been some – small – comfort to squirm and scream if he could, but she would not permit it.

Whilst her troops scoured away the remainder of his following, Queen Jezebel silently explained to her husband just exactly how she felt. It was made clear that at the end of the story she would kill him; administering a final, cathartic, *bite*. There'd be not a mark but inside he'd be as dead and shrivelled as her – only he'd not be moving any more. Whereas *she* could carry that burden and still live. She was the stronger.

Speaking of strength, Lord Firstmet survived to join his master. His thick night-coat of black fur had saved him from the burning sand. Luck alone preserved him from sturdier missiles. Looking up, he removed two Assyrians with his brace of pistols and that clouded the issue somewhat. Under the cover of their smoke he tackled the Emperor away from the bewitchment, little guessing it took more than mere yards to detach Jezebel's grapples from her prey. Blades's body went with Firstmet but his stricken mind lagged behind.

Blissfully ignorant, Firstmet was content with what he had. He knew, as only he and the Emperor and very few others knew, that the castle architects had constructed cunning ways to riddle the thick walls. Those architects were long gone, sent to hazardous outposts against the Null, and thus the circle of knowledge was shrunk – as fully intended. Lord Firstmet remained one of the few aware that New-Godalming's outer gate hid a private tunnel to safety and that its door was almost in reach. He deluded himself he could reach it.

He was quite wrong of course. Three Assyrian muskets were trained on his broad back at that very moment. They could not all have missed. Emperor Blades would have been left to Jezebel's mercy – and she had none.

Happily though, the Angel then intervened and saved them all.

. . . and plucking an air-elemental from those dimensions known only to him, the first God-King (HE needs not our blessing) removed himself and his disciples from the betrayal intended by the satanic witch-queen.

The site, now made redundant by the City's expansion, is left untrodden, in hallowed remembrance that there HE (HE needs not our blessing) thrust his holy hands into realms we may not presently see. And who knows but that some lingering perfume of that day does not adhere to the old Castle Gate to sanctify those who pause in faith?

On the easy assumption that HE (HE needs not our blessing) would not leave his children quite without comfort till they meet again, this site is designated as the twenty-third station of the minor pilgrimage wherein some essence of our Saviour may be perceived. Two prayer cycles are prescribed by the Great Missal but this writer never favours it with less than four and has oft been correspondingly rewarded with grace.

Through this Holy place also poured the ranks of the repentant during the Day of Mercy . . .

A Pilgrim's Compendium of Wisdom for those who would Glorify their Earthly Life with the Jewels of Piety and the Silken Raiment of Prayer'

Thane Brixi of New-Compton in the Province of Wessex, United England. In the Year of Our Deliverance 457 A.B.

Because he or she detected some warm feelings for them, the Angel also saved Firstmet and Caiaphas and a few surviving – quite ordinary – soldiers too. They were taken through the lowered portcullis, penetrated the raised drawbridge and carried over the inky moat. On the further side the Angel protected them from the shocked fury of the rebels and Jezebel's wickedest spells. He or she then deposited them at the gate of their camp. One and all they were too shocked to say thank you.

Only Blades saw the entirety of their saviour – because that was the way he or she wished it. The rest glimpsed only shimmering white wings and enfolding arms, and even that only intermittently. By the time the camp was reached they'd simplified things and declared it all Blades's doing. Nor were they backward in telling the tale.

And so the war was won.

'*First instincts are best,*' he thought to himself. '*I ought to have done this straightaway.*'

New-Godalming looked awfully close but, by day, no longer quite so awful. He recognised it better, close by, in the light; even recognised some of the armed men on the walls. This time he was not approaching like some thief in the night, but as an Emperor should: boldly coming into his own.

He declined to analyse earlier events and his continued survival, refused even to consider them. Quite the foxy, opportunist curate again, for the present it was enough to take advantage.

The City was left to stew for a day, time enough for rumours to spread and fester but too short a span for counter measures. He revelled in the certain knowledge that somewhere in the sullen, smoking, City, his lady wife was furiously revising her opinion of him – mere steps ahead of her subjects. The ending of any counter-bombardment was outward sign of that process. The Emperor lapped it up.

Boudicca caught the glint of glee in his eyes and misinterpreted. On her knees, she begged mercy for the people of New-Godalming and he was rascal enough to pretend to waver and extract a quite astounding night of passion (again mostly on her knees) from her as the price for – had she but known it – already granted forgiveness.

Then, on the morning of the second day after his deliverance, ragged but grinning broadly, he stepped forward to tell his wayward children the good news.

Firstmet, now doubly in awe – if such a thing were possible – of his Lord, arranged for heavy, musket-proof, mantlets to be wheeled along but Blades waved them away. For one thing, he did not wish to confront his wandering sheep cowering behind, peeping out from, evil-smelling ox-hide and oak protection. Secondly, he felt confident of some better, if invisible, guardian.

There was a little bombardment, the siege equivalent of a parental cuff round the ear. He did not want them to think they'd totally escaped his displeasure, but it was not for long, nor the worse they could do. Blades ordered it concentrated on the opinion-forming sections of City society, knowing there the spine was weakest, the flesh least tolerant of blows.

Then, on the opposite side to himself, along the valley of the little river Ock, there was a diversionary attack. That would occupy the entrenched malignants, the Assyrians and most-expectant-of-an-impaling-stake, who might actually grind on with all this fighting business. Whilst they were busy killing and being killed, Emperor Blades could address the more rational majority in peace.

It was still a risk. That was why he'd rejected the option early on in the siege, despite watching the umpteenth rout back from the walls. There only needed to be one wretch with a musket and good luck and that was that.

Blades booted the disabling thought aside and stepped forward. Pages took his cloak and then there was no mistaking him in the full Imperial purple. People were lining the wall, and more of them by the minute as news spread. He looked at them and they at him.

Some of them had muskets but declined to shoulder them. The range was such that they could almost have chucked stones had they been so minded – but apparently none were.

He hadn't been totally reckless. The keenest shots in New-Wessex stood by, supplied with the best its armoury could provide in terms of long barrelled rifles and fowling pieces. There was a fair chance they would get a shot in at the first hostile inclined rebel. Conversely, to give Blades his due, there was a fair chance they wouldn't.

The rest of the army were really up for it. They'd heard the stories and had had time to embroider them. Stood-to in deep formation not far behind they audibly bubbled with anxiety to participate. Even at purely visual distance you could tell they were champing at the bit. That too was fully intended. It was good to make clear that the only thing standing between them and the fiery sack of New-Godalming was the lone figure in the mid-ground. Therefore it wouldn't be wise to antagonise or fell him.

Enough time for thought. As smoke plumes ascended over the far side of the City and the distant sound of strife travelled to them, he acted. The Emperor raised his hands to his people, silently beseeching them, embracing them. He gave every sign he wanted them to come home.

For a long while there was no response. His arms began to tire: there was the appalling danger of appearing ridiculous. If that happened he'd have to raze the place and everyone in it and start again.

Then he and they were saved. Slow at first, but fast accelerating, weapons were cast over the wall. Voices called out to him in piteous tones. He again lifted his spread hands, encouraging them. They responded till the wall was nothing but a chorus of repentance. Only a few, perhaps the most guilty or embarrassed, disappeared off to arrange their own salvation.

Others went to take more practical steps. A flurry of shots in the Gate of recent mixed memories was followed by the lowering of the bridge. A trickle, then a stream and finally a mighty river of penitents came flooding out.

Only then did he sniff the air for any sign of Angelic guardianship. He detected none and the realisation caused his brow to chill. Still, it was over now, the guns were cast aside. In humans a risk survived is a risk forgotten. He turned to fresh considerations.

The tear in their unity had been a scandal, he knew that; a disgrace to the very idea of *humanity*. Its ripping of the tapestry he'd made had been audible to the extremes of the liberated world. Even the chastened Null had heard and grown venturesome. There'd been border incursions despite the Runnymede treaty.

Blades also knew a little history. He'd been unable to swerve it as part of his theological studies. Reading about the antics of the Kings of Israel and the sordid birth of the Church of England had dragged in useable stuff alongside all the mandatory learning. He'd observed that empires more often fell through disunity than external threat, that mighty oaks should fear rot more than axe or lightning. Accordingly, he ought to have had kinder feelings for the Null than the people now at his feet.

But because they were his children, and because he'd promised Boudicca – and because he retained a small portion of Curate Blades's kind heart – the Emperor welcomed them all with open – if aching – arms.

Then he raised them up, wiped away their tears and told them to never do it again.

Together, reunited, at the centre of a ecstatic mob, Thomas Blades entered the capital of his species, showering compassion.

Of course, he was only human. For some there could be no forgiveness. Upon reaching the Palace they played murder from room to room, rough guessing who was on whose side. Though no spring chicken, Blades took part, leaping balustrades like a young warrior, finding homes for the imperial sword in ungrateful servants. But even then he found the capacity for clemency: the prettier female offenders were let off with just a spanking.

When that palled, there followed a whole afternoon of in-house assassinations and slapdash trials. Even some third and lesser circle children got the axe or stake as, with Herod-like impartiality, he dispensed rough justice. The bodies were dumped on the Palace steps to show the ordinary folk he was harsher still upon his own.

As to the rest, Blades was as good as his – unspoken – word. Even the Assyrians were spared, once they surrendered and bowed the ironclad head. The fires were put out and repair work started. Normality made a way ahead of schedule appearance.

Business as before was the watchword: his consistent and humane policy. He didn't even make a proclamation. Another proverb of his old Cromwellian Granny came to mind: '*Least said soonest mended.*'

Except for Queen Jezebel. No escape *for* her, or from speech *to* her – even if only to whisper *goodbye*.

They found her in her harem, the former Great Dining Hall, taking final solace. It was thought best that the Emperor not be amongst the first arrivals – and wisely so. Her rampaging magic accounted for the foremost huscarls and the mage who led them. Plaited together, they went all up one wall.

Then, as the pleasure-maids screamed and scattered, released from mind-bondage, a lucky loyalist got his axe-shaft to Jezebel's head. Royal eyes widened even further and she rushed to meet upcoming night.

Blades entered just as the rough soldiery were binding and gagging her and copping a covert feel. The first two measures were pre-ordered, the third on their own initiative. He didn't blame them. They'd risked all to obey him and were naturally curious about how the other 0.000001 percent lived. Even spark out and with a purple bruise spreading across her brow, the Queen was still a beautiful – regal – woman. Another chance like that might never come to them again. He coughed and they desisted.

'*Poor Jezebel,*' he thought. '*Mad and angry and manhandled. It's not the end I would have predicted.*'

Then he recalled that her 'end' had yet to be arranged and that difficult decision was his alone. The Emperor of all Humanity postponed it by ordering her away and secured. A cage and shackles were ready and waiting.

Things quietened a shade once the soldiers hustled their burden off before she could wake. If you ignored the scarlet splurge of former huscarls adhering to one wall, there was almost the illusion of peace. The City was already heading that way. No distressing noises came from outside to correct his wishful thinking.

The harem girls shared in the general calming. They'd rallied in a far corner to passively await developments – all part of Jezebel's training – and Blades noticed them for the first time, right in the midst of tut-tutting the shredded portraits. His head swivelled. He called them over.

'And what do *you* do?'

The dresses they almost wore, their battle wounds, should have told him, clear as speaking. But since the long table and facing mirror were still there, they demonstrated as well.

When he'd finished admiring the view – and only then – a degree of shock was allowed room. He hadn't anticipated his wife's erotic repertoire would expand as riotously as her ambitions. Perhaps one and the other went together. For a moment he was tempted to keep her by him. Then he was prey to other, less dangerous, temptations.

There was still pressing work to do, the battle not quite over. He found easy excuses to dismiss – most – of the company.

'Not you, ladies. Stay as you were.'

Just as mad and bad as she was, Emperor Blades decided to be *kind* to himself after so much hardship and bravery. Not every innovation of Queen Jezebel's short reign needed to be immediately swept away.

'The prisoner *must* reply!'

But she wouldn't. Jezebel would say nothing – and maintained that stance as if it would last forever. Her side of the story had been told when she'd held her husband's mind in the Gatehouse. Further comment was superfluous.

The highest judge in all New-Wessex looked to the Emperor for assistance. There were ways of obliging defendants to plead – hefty stone slabs laid on until they reflected anew – but the '*press*' might not be quite the way forward here. The court waited.

Blades was no help to his judiciary. He had his own problems. The Queen was tightly bound to constrain her magic but her eyes were left free to roam. They chose not to but rested on the Emperor alone and had done since the trial began. He couldn't withstand their wild accusation. It was becoming difficult to find a place to put his gaze.

Boudicca was a comfort, as ever. He'd not asked, but she'd accompanied him anyway, resting her hand on his during the painful parts of the indictment. Doubtless that was like a red rag to a bull for Jezebel but her tastes no longer commanded their old weight. The soothing of his wounds took priority.

Sennacherib was alongside his mother in the dock, minus armour and thus a strange sight, but still bristling and defiant. Blades was pervertedly proud of him. Another shame, another waste . . .

He'd been found where he should have been: amidst his Assyrians, with an axe like anyone else's, preparing for a glorious last stand. Brought to the sight, the Emperor had approved and withheld the waiting cannons' voice. Humanity had need of spirits like that. He humbled and then forgave them, sending them back to their marshes and mud-monsters.

That pattern was general. He'd been free with his death penalties, arranged the stakes and gallows, let the condemned contemplate them during a long night, and then reprieved the lot at the last moment, just as their necks and behinds were being arranged. Now he had them for life. A life for a life: fair exchange.

Sennacherib could not be included in the general amnesty for he'd been too far up and in. On the other hand, nor could he quietly join the other worse offenders in their fresh shallow graves: he was too prominent. Accordingly, the boy had to have his day in court. He looked neither distraught nor pleased about it – entirely the right attitude to take.

The only others ones to get to trial were Jezebel's menagerie of pseudo-Null, the ox-like youths who had dressed up to enliven her orgies. They were put on display because they reflected badly on the Queen and had intrinsic entertainment value. In the course of a few hours the point was well made, the costumes and the wooden cocks held up for all to see, though Jezebel did not so much as blush. Her eyes never left the Emperor so that it was he that reddened instead. Perhaps that explained the setting aside of New-Wessex legal norms that followed. The circus were spared noose or stake, instead being set, sewn into their play-garb, down amongst real Null prisoners. At first the Null did not know what to make of them, but soon enough made them dinner. It was a messy feast watched by thousands.

'I shall record that as *not guilty*,' said the Judge, and the clerk and scribes dutifully noted away. He was getting to rather like this giving instructions to royalty: a dangerous taste to acquire but oh-so-sweet and heady stuff. He already felt like more.

'Now, Madame. A further charge: namely that you improperly levied taxation on both the core and out provinces, using the Imperial name, and misappropriated those revenues found, at that time, in the New-Godalming Treasury for your own fell purposes, viz.: the raising and arming of rebellious formations to the furtherance of your own blasphemous ambitions. How do you plead?'

She didn't. That hadn't changed all morning and now wasn't likely to.

'Very well. Let that also be recorded as denial. Similarly, what say you to the graver charge that you wickedly attempted the life of our beloved and most sacred Emperor, firstly in the provision of poisoned fruit, to wit, punnets of strawberries, intending that . . .'

Blades felt Boudicca's arm slip from his. He wasn't at all concerned until she stood.

'No,' she announced. 'I did that. It was my doing'

The earth opened beneath him. He saw an abyss gaping there and then fell into it forever.

She looked back and down at him. His denial was writ plain on a silent-screaming face.

'*Oh, yes I did,*' she contradicted him.

Everyone heard. And so now there would have to be a new trial, another defendant, some feminine company for the Queen in the dock.

Jezebel smiled.

'I *told* you once before when I offered to solve all this. It can never be better than when I returned. There was you, then the Null, then you again: un-looked for joy! How can it ever be as good again as our reunion?'

Boudicca was on her knees: quite literally – he'd put her there. He'd so far forgot himself as to strike her bad leg with his stick. Then at least pain might prompt some tears in her dry eyes to match his own.

'It was kindness,' she explained patiently. 'It was love! I sought to end our story beautifully.'

He had no answer to that. Though their vocabulary was the same, though he fondly imagined he'd passed that tongue on, it transpired he did not speak the language. His silence was like Jezebel's.

'I had a strawberry to my own lips,' she said, uncomplaining, patient as ever with him, 'until you knocked it away. And then I was so sad. There could have been that moment forever. We would have walked into the night *together.*'

She looked up into his eyes and her melancholy matched his, though for entirely different reasons.

'Now there's only decline, and ageing and fading memory. We shall not scale that mountain peak again.'

Emperor Blades raised his stick. She did not flinch, not then nor when he hurled it furiously away.

To understand all is to forgive all, but it need not follow that understanding is sweet. She was mad; they all were. It wasn't her fault.

He reached down and lifted her up. Then he tenderly kissed her for the last time.

He scattered them to the winds, choosing their new homes from the edges of stolen Admiralty charts; sketchy information looted out of hijacked ships. St Kilda for Jezebel, Lindisfarne for Boudicca. Firstmet would see them safely there. They'd have a few volunteer companions, some supplies. It might go well. It was all they or Blades were good for.

Only Sennacherib was still of use to himself or anyone. He spared him, after a fashion.

'What shall I do with you?' he asked, in open court, the play-act of judge and jury overruled.

'Kill me, I'm dangerous,' was the honest reply; the only one that could have saved him.

'Spoken like an Assyrian. To the west of us you will find a place called Ireland. Go and see about it.'

He'd sailed the next day, alongside some die-hard Pevensey men, without so much as a goodbye. And that was probably the end of him. From a hidden vantage point, Blades watched him go.

Then the Emperor was free to take to his bed and bottle.

He thought he'd created a real world, a even-better-than-before copy of the old one, but it turned out he'd laboured and shed blood in vain. This was only an indulgent parody: a mere patina, a thin laminate. Crack that and you were staring into a bottomless pit. Beneath, they were still the blank-palate burrow people. There was no *history* to them, no depth. Only he had that stratigraphy of culture that comes from inherited thousands of years and he couldn't just hand it on, try as he might.

Dining on that was a blow almost as bad as all the others. He stayed inebriated and bed-ridden for days, whilst his wives and senior son sailed without farewell. Hour after hour he added his own stumbling laps to the fruitless pursuit of mankind's favourite conundrum. How could anything so well-intentioned go so very *wrong*?

234

The watching Angel overheard it and inaudibly chuckled. How many times, he or she wondered, had they heard that whine?

'We're not delivering, we're trading.'

That would do. Pevensey-Assyria was awaiting the axe of imperial vengeance, knowing they'd lost but not that they'd been spared. Gunpowder from any source or means was welcome.

The harbour-master looked up from his rowboat to the brown-tanned men leaning over the *Lady Bridget*'s rail.

'How much?'

They said. He nearly fell back.

'That's ten-fold normal!'

'Twelve, actually,' John Lilburne informed him. 'I forgot to mention that. We also bring news of new arrangements. Take it or leave it.'

There'd be a lot of huffing and puffing but the final answer wasn't in question. The world was turned upside down, mankind divided. A bit of independent trading was only to be expected amidst so much temptation. Sicily had the monopoly of the brimstone trade and there was no decent powder without brimstone. The Null were only waiting for the day the firesticks fell silent.

Whilst the haggling ritual was observed, they entertained the Harbourmaster and the Assyrian governor of Pevensey Castle, plus other dignitaries, on board. Once having clanked up the side, fiery Sicilian wine soon flowed and considering they were desperate men being skinned, things got quite convivial. Lilburne, merely the first among equals aboard, absented himself till they were in receptive mood. He trusted his colleagues for the less imaginative transactions – but only he had read and understood the *books*.

'We don't just take payment in supplies,' he then told them, entering when they were rubicund and unjacketed, cosy in his cabin. 'You might get a better price by a different method. Dover did.'

That intrigued them. Not only did they dislike emptying their barns and larders but anything the rival port possessed was hard-felt loss for Pevensey. Already there more piracy than alliance between them.

'Tell me more,' said the Castle governor. He had an impressive ability to be instantly sober.

Lilburne steepled his hands.

'We accept land and protection as well as goods. We saw some along the coast that would suit us.'

The chart was laid out ready. He pointed and drew a perimeter.

'Exclusive possession, plus mutual defence, equals as much powder as you can shoot. We might even have to deprive Dover a bit.'

He'd said the same to Dover port, just changing the names. They'd guess as much but it still prodded all the right parts.

'Pevensey-Sluice? That's waste, that is,' said Harbourmaster, who didn't just know his own little ship-shelter. 'She's barely drained: only mud-men and lizards: no use to anyone.'

He'd declared his hand; had already sold the place, though it was not his to give. It might have been Lord Sennacherib's once but he was probably gone and past caring. No one lived there and what was no one's was anyone's and welcome to it.

'We can use it,' said Lilburne, and he and his friends were so smiley and confident that the Assyrians believed them.

Only the Governor still held back. Life with Sennacherib had made him that way.

'What on earth do you want it for?' he asked

Lilburne passed over a sheaf of papers.

'This'll explain,' he replied. 'And when you've done reading, pass 'em on.'

A notice
to all Emperors, Kings, Queens, Monarchs,
pretended gods and little lordlings.

From:
the free *PEOPLE* of the Earth,
earnestly desiring the glory of G*d,
the freedom of the Common-wealth,
and the peace of all men.
Together with:
An arrow against all tyrants and tyranny,
shot into the bowels of arbitrary Government.

We, the people,

the working, soldiering, child-raising People of New-Wessex, the out-provinces, New Sicily, and all those lands prised from the Null, and yea, even those places still to be so prised, say:

that the poorest he that is of us hath a life to live as much as the greatest he. Wherefore, it surely follows by light of reason that man should submit only to that government instituted and maintained by his own consent.

Further, nor do we find anything in the word of G*d, the holy Bible or their child, the light of reason, that one man shall choose for all and a plain man choose nothing. We say most solemnly, we find no such thing in the law of nature nor in the law of God, nor in the law of nations.

And therefore: designing to live with dignity, with decency, and in freedom from fear, in such manner that honours our intelligence and birthright, we accordingly cast off our yoke and declare ourselves, from first breath unto last, henceforth:
Free men and women
Signed and promulgated, this twenty-third day of March,
Year 23 of the Common Era
New-Syracuse Citadel, Sicily.

. . . *no originals of the incomparable, 'Arrow into the Bowels' (better known to us as the Declaration of Emancipation) are known to survive, since they were often the victim of attacks by the unenlightened lackeys of autocracy; serving as scapegoat for the vengeance they were unable to visit on the sturdy authors of the text.*

Therefore, this copy dates only from either the third or fourth edition of the Declaration. Even so, its uniqueness lies in its purported identity as the very first copy to emanate from the illicit Leveller printing presses of mainland New-Wessex, as opposed to New-Sicily or freshly established Freeport-Sussex. As such, it is our foremost and most valued exhibit. However, well-attested legend also has it that this is the very Declaration that was nailed to the Cathedral door in New-Godalming, on the eve of Emperor Day in 35 C.E.

The subsequent riots and loss of life . . .

'A Guide to the Antiquities and Curiosities of Freeport-Wadebridge, New-Kernow.'

Text by Sophie Amon-Ra Nettle, illustrations by Jane O. Williams.

An Gof Press. Mousehole. New-Kernow. 105 C.E.

'Where are you, dammit? You shouldn't flash the furry hoop if you're not going to . . .'

There *had* been a girl, he was sure of it. He'd have sworn on the . . . well, he'd have sworn anyway, that a minx had raised her skirts at him, accompanied by a look that tightened the trousers, only to skip off down the corridor from the Imperial bedroom.

He'd been minded to sleep – if only! – alone but the girl had sewn fresh thoughts. Now, if she'd wickedly eluded him, he was doubly troubled: a frustrated, restless night awaited instead of just the normal tossing and turning.

If he'd been bothered or able to think, if he'd been less prickled and randy, Emperor Blades would have reflected that this girl must have a noteworthy turn of speed to clear the long corridor before he poked his head round the doorway. He'd have queried what she was doing in the well-secured palace and marvelled at her courage in teasing a tetchy absolute ruler. However, straight thinking wasn't much on the menu of late.

For instance, he *ought* to have given more thought to his recent Angelic salvation, but was not in the mood for that or anything. There were too many distractions. Neither was he particularly grateful for continued existence. It seemed to bring just that bit more trouble than it was worth.

Accordingly, his feet had to be directed for him. He really did think he saw a flirtatious girl . . .

Just as he was about to give up, just as he was going to call some huscarls to do the chasing, she provided a sighting, a clean pair of heels, a departing back, even a flashed bum when he lagged behind, to urge him on, to convince him to settle this himself. He didn't fear ambush, even as he suspected he was being led. There was more soldiery than sunshine in Castle Blades and all his enemies were dead, departed or cowed. She was just some court lady overdoing it, about to earn herself some sore parts to match his sore feet.

It proved quite a walk but only at the Cathedral door did he pause, libido grappling with the first tendrils of unease. Libido won hands down. He marched on. Then, when he'd traversed the great candle canyon of the nave, querying the fitness of consummation in consecrated ground and still losing sight of her, a bolt from the old world hit him, redundant knowledge lurching from a dusty cupboard.

St Paul's letter to the Hebrews, Chapter 13, verse 2: '*For thereby some entertained angels unawares*'.

The inner Blades had tried to save him, but too late. The door to the Holy of Holies was swinging open. A glow came from within where no glow had been for years.

A slim, white, girl's hand beckoned. It reeled him in, protesting.

They had met before. The door slammed like judgement.

'It was soooooooooooooooooo beautiful. You shouldn't have hurt it. You shouldn't have hurt it. You shouldn't have hurt it.'

She – though Blades only *decided* she was a she – was so beautiful too, the sole reason he'd dared enter in. She looked down on him, far taller, far better, than he. The Emperor had no answer for her.

'*I* knew it. *I* mended it,' the Angel continued, 'and sent it forward. In your time it reappeared tonight. You should look.'

He would do, when he could, in due course.

It was the eyes. Blades couldn't tear himself away from them, a few furtive seconds at a time: as much as he could abide. Old, mischief-rich eyes set in a pale young face. He'd never seen anything so wonderfully, deservedly, selfish. The fleeting glimpses of wings, the coruscating white of her gown, were mere dullard's-talk compared to those eyes.

'Speak!'

'I . . .'

'*Yes*!' The creature was satisfied, replete with all she'd taken from his astonishment. The harshness of the command receded infinitely far away – and then returned just as speedily.

'Look!'

Her will hit him, swept him up and pushed his face into the returned portal. The force of it brought tears. The Emperor did not want her to be violent with him, he really didn't.

His wide eyes were dried by the sights beyond. First dusty dark, then light abundant through a tiny door. A pendulum rhythmically split the view. The clock was whole again, loudly counting off the seconds above his head. He'd quite forgotten Silas's yard, along with Silas's world. There was no one about. It looked bright morning in old Godalming.

He drank in the air, his face protruding into that world like a man peeping into a rockpool. A whole wealth of recollected scents would have entertained him in any other circumstances.

She drew him back, a fierce tug on the night-shirt coming from no discernible movement on her part. He slammed against the far wall.

The Angel smiled. She meant no harm; he saw that. He also saw her entire lack of concern. The door to the Holy of Holies had thundered shut: obeying the mere slipstream of her desire. They were alone. Blades wondered, as he recovered his breath, whether she regarded herself so. Did he count as company?

'*Would* you?' she asked, all amusement and wider-still eyes. 'Impudent youth!'

And somehow she'd caught his speeding thought of how he'd like to take her. Faster even than that, she granted an

240

impression. She licked her lips over his lifetime experience – which lasted barely a flicker – and then moved on to his secret ambitions and fantasies. Blades felt himself spiralling away down an irresistible waterspout. There was only dark at its centre and he'd arrive there shortly. His store of sexuality didn't last her long. She gobbled it all up. Then she had mercy, and sicked the morsel back.

From man to husk and back again had taken a second but it wouldn't be forgotten so soon. He gulped like a stranded fish.

'*You.*'

He acknowledged her word, because he was frightened not to, but could not reply, not remotely knowing what to say. Blades had already surrendered without being asked.

'I know.' She was nodding – but to what? 'I saw. What you've done. Many of us did. Congratulations.'

She didn't mean it. The eyes and the smile said all. It was praise of a child's valiant attempt.

'Thank you.' He forced the words out but they didn't suit. She frowned. He flinched. The cloud then just as swiftly passed.

'You,' she repeated. 'You did this. We don't mind. We're glad. Carry on.'

Because he was floundering she let him *understand.* Even her briefest enlightening burned. Blades screamed and clutched his head.

She'd meant the world and his works upon it. It had been theirs once and then they'd left it. Later, squatters came to stake a claim. He was allowed to appreciate their indifference. He'd amused them. They approved. She even detected his dismay and left a little consolation.

'You may be our viceroy – until the game is complex enough for us to play again. Drive this chariot faster – mould the game to our refined tastes. Make it . . .'

She'd forgotten him – or been distracted by something else. She looked into an elsewhere his eyes couldn't pierce, even had he wanted to. He was lost in her white arms and legs and her better-than-possible totality. They were like that for a full five minutes or more.

241

Then she was back, suddenly, seamlessly.

'. . . ready.'

The Angel pointed to the revived portal.

'Don't be bad again.'

The Emperor signalled he wouldn't.

She looked around. He had no notion how much or how far she was seeing. Whatever the sights, she approved. He was granted a broad smile. It was castrated by the oval eyes above.

'Thank youuuuuuuuuuuuuuuuuuuuuuuuuu . . .' she said – and left; taking all his certainties with her.

'Mebbe I could 'ave rode the one thing; oh aye, I'm no milksop.' Long lost country accents were surfacing along with all the other honesty. 'But not two. You try losing new-found love; cruelly snatched away, like, *and* have the rug tugged from under y' feet at the same time . . .'

Head down, mumbling away, Emperor Blades awaited a wave of sympathy which never came. So he pressed on, meandering to a weak conclusion. 'S'too much for one man, so it 'tis.'

His brother agreed. 'Far too much,' said Silas, taking advantage of a pause in the flood of words. He removed the cider jug from the table. It was long since empty, although – as a direct consequence – Blades was having trouble appreciating that. Twice in the last few moments he'd upended it in vain.

The candle was guttering low and Silas's patience likewise. Supper had been one long tail-chasing circle of his brother's woes, lubricated and impassioned by drink. Come to think of it, he'd emerged from the grandfather already well-oiled and hadn't stopping sipping since.

'Why not talk about it?' asked Silas, in his driest tones. 'Sometimes it helps to talk about it . . .'

Blades was well past heeding voice inflections.

'You're right, I will . . .'

'Oh, Lord . . .'

The possibly-former Emperor lolled back, still chastened to

be back in a Godalming that wasn't a metropolis and his to command. He looked for more cider, even rattled his tankard, but the brash signals were ignored. Men of Silas's party disapproved of drink unsanctioned by thirst.

'S'right,' Blades went on, abandoning – or forgetting – the quest for refreshment. 'Talk's the thing. Work it all out, we shall.'

For a second Silas looked alarmed – a raised eyebrow no less, wild panic by his standards, but his brother failed to notice.

'Did I tell 'ee about Boudicca?' He leered up at Silas, through squinting, fringe-obscured eyes. 'Did I say about 'er?'

'I believe you may 'ave, Thomas, once or twice . . .'

'Bitch! False-loving whore of Babylon, she was!'

'I reckon that's overstating the . . .'

'Tried to poison I! Out of *mutual affection* she says. Madness says I!'

Silas was struggling here, torn between Christian charity, filial feeling and speaking his mind.

'Love and hate: they say 'tis a thin line dividing them. Mebbe she went funny . . .'

It was just a noise: he might as well have described what he had for breakfast. He didn't mean it, his brother wasn't listening.

'You 'ave a care,' warned Blades, as frightening at that moment as a growling sheep. 'That's my wife you're talking about . . .'

Silas sighed and looked to Heaven.

By coincidence, all offence forgotten, Blades was now appealing to the same quarter.

'I mean,' he quavered, raising outstretched hands to Paradise – or somewhere, 'what *can* you do?'

'What indeed?'

The Curate-Emperor slewed back his chair and, like a man moving through deep water, made unsteady progress to the window.

From their upstairs location, there was a fine view of Godalming and the Wey valley – or would be when the Sun rose again. Blades looked out at the little lights of distant

Binscombe and Loseley and tried to come to terms with the fact that they were not bastions of a great city – and never had been *here*. He knew, should he care to go and look, that he would find only hamlets of thatch and subsistence farming. For the first time since his flight he found himself thinking the other side had the best of the bargain.

That in turn prompted reflection on what else he'd left behind: order in the Empire but chaos in his heart. There'd not been enough bottles and bottoms to drown out remembrance of it. So he ran away – only to find spectral reminders and a cold reception.

Silas hadn't turned a hair when his long-lost brother emerged, drunk and dishevelled, into his yard.

'*Hello, bad penny. Didn't think you'd be long behind the clock,*' was his only comment, followed by a gesture towards to the kitchen pump whilst he finished a chair.

Two days of decent sleep and meals had put some spirit back into Thomas Blades, only to be undone by him topping up with spirits of another kind. Silas's tolerance stretched but never quite broke.

Nor did he enquire or probe the pain, but bravely endured the nightly flow of woe. Blades's pack of troubles was wordily unloaded into his lap – though it seemed to grow no lighter. Bit by bit, the story emerged.

'I mean,' Emperor Blades told the night, 'it weren't as though I were a *bad* man . . .'

One moment the town timepiece, the next a new world. The newcomer applauded such novelty. The great municipal winding key was pocketed and forgotten.

There was a sudden bath of warmth, the tinge of salt upon the air. The new arrival spread his arms to encompass the sun and sea and sand and thank them. Truly, life was glorious and proof positive that God loved man, requiring only that he enjoy himself. It was the same point made by wine – and just as intoxicating, though cheaper.

He walked a while, leaving footprints on the virgin beach. That too was fine for a spell but, being a civilised man he began to hunger for community. Joy wasn't joy in its fullest sense if not shared.

As though scripted, he saw figures along the far fringe of dunes. The newcomer called and beckoned. They met him halfway.

A staunch republican, he deplored their propensity to bow and scrape, but in those innocent smiles found speechless welcome enough. He was content – and lulled-misled. Permitting himself to be passed from place to place along the line that led to New-Godalming, he discovered friendly faces in short supply there.

'Hang him. No, impale him – that's surer. No, wait, take out his tongue now, *then* impale him. Good. That's that settled . . .'

It certainly was. Once the god-king had made up his divine mind there were still no shortage of people to transform wish into deed. The poor stranger was dealt with then and there in the throne room. Terrible, distressing mess. And a pity. Up till then he'd looked the soul of affability.

No one else had understood his warm greeting, save Blades. No one else could, for he was the only person in that world with the slightest knowledge of French. Memories of unhappy schooldays were now dim but he could still distinguish the essence of a fulsome hello. On the off chance the newcomer also parlayed some *Anglais* it seemed best to abort even the possibility of lucid converse.

The Emperor required no news from *over there* – though intriguingly enough, the stranger's dress suggested he came from after the Bladian epoch. He might have had some interesting updates to tell but even that prospect failed to melt the icy wall of indifference. His cheery '*Hello, how are you? Nice to be here,*' bounced off it. The only reply was first pincers and then a sharp stake. Gallic protests and pleas ended in bubbling and then bundling away.

In the unequal struggle a large clock key fell from his coat. It clattered to the mosaic floor but no one dared attend to it. The Emperor pretended not to notice. 'So that explains that', he thought to himself.

For a few moments more the two men had a deal in common: a shared history and origin and all that went with them. Only nationality and mother-tongue and ownership of a tongue distinguished them. Blades felt a wave of fellow feeling but ignored it till the thing died for lack of attention.

Unlike most of his old world contemporaries, Blades did not hate the French. He held no strong feelings about them at all, save a general antipathy for visitors.

The Emperor later enquired of the peasants who'd found the future Frenchman and escorted him off Dungeness beach. He extracted from them exactly where the portal had flashed into life, and a full description of its shape and form. He gained the very clearest picture of the arrival that their rustic minds could frame. Then he ordered Firstmet forth with scarce gunpowder to deal with it.

He was in no mood for guests, however affable; not inclined to extend the hand of friendship to foreigners. Be they Angels or just plain human blow-ins, and taking the long view and his own sad example, they were a danger to the world and themselves. Witness his own distress! Plainly, it was for the best – for himself, themselves, for everyone – to cauterise the wound the short way.

'We want no more of his sort,' he explained to the mildly curious courtiers. And, still assuming he knew best, that sufficed.

The rude interruption past, Emperor Blades readdressed his wine.

'It just came back one day. Here.'

The two brothers stood admiring the grandfather in the yard. Silas had constructed a little shelter over it to fend off the elements.

'Didn't you query that?' Blades had always envied Silas his

lack of curiosity. It made for a so much happier life.

The carpenter applied his yellow polishing cloth to an imagined blemish on the casing.

'After all you told me? Was I going to choke on swallowing one more marvel? It went, it came back, it don't trouble I: that's all I ask.'

Blades moved to open its little door. Silas's hawser-like hand shot out to prevent him.

'And I don't trouble it,' he said firmly. 'That's our little agreement. I winds it once a day, I keeps the rain off it, it keeps off my back. Then we rub along just fine, see?'

Blades indicated he did. Only then was his hand released.

'But weren't you ever curious? I mean, just to poke your head through and have a lookee?'

'Nope!'

Blades wished he was as sure of just one thing, anything, as Silas was of everything. He sought in vain for the secret.

'Why not?'

'I know me own destiny,' came the unusable reply. 'And that's both me strength and me weakness. Yours has yet to fall on you or be recognised.'

The Curate-Emperor abandoned the fool's quest. In silence they studied the ticking enigma.

''tis a fine piece though,' Silas eventually conceded. 'She keeps good time, too. Have you made the like in your world yet?'

For some reason that touched a sore point. The one consistent thread in Blades's *apologia* over the last week was the poor harvest reaped by his sweet and reasonable regime. Only last night he recalled slurring *'if I'd ploughed a bit harder then mebbe we'd not have raised so many weeds . . .'*

Now, with sobriety, it came back to haunt him.

He'd been scrupulously truthful with Silas so far. All being equal he wanted to keep it up.

'No,' he said. 'We tell the time by other means.'

There hadn't been a similar case for ages. The Emperor happened to be passing. He was bored. He dropped in.

'Heaven knows,' he told the tribunal, 'I don't wish to restrain the ingenuity of the People. Invent away as you will but *abide by the rules*. They're few enough, after all.'

The clockmaker, a Leveller-Lilburnite in any case – a fact that had sealed his fate in advance of the hearing – dared to argue.

'But why?' he roared from the dock, rattling his manacles. 'Why fetter the imagination that comes from God? Why load it with chains every bit as real as these? Just tell me why and I shall be conten . . .'

Contentment drew still further away from him courtesy of a court guard's elbow. He was felled below the level of the dock, though his protests could still be heard.

Blades felt the eyes of his children upon him and the unlooked-for weight of a crucial moment. He was in no mood for eloquence or explanation, but after so many years, a degree of Emperorship came naturally. A stitch in time might save nine Levellers later.

'There is nothing *wrong* with innovation,' he told them. The scribes and *scops* and scripturalists who accompanied him everywhere sprang into action to immortalise that wisdom. 'There is nothing evil or vicious or unhealthy to it – as such. In almost every aspect I say to invention: flourish! Go where you will! Enhance the life of my People, make their time easier, their speculations better informed. Find better ways to kill the Null. Invade the realm of ignorance and push back its frontiers by any means. Observe no treaties with stupidity!'

He was carrying them with him, he could see that. From the tribunalists to humblest clerk they were his so far. Now the tricky bit. He raised his voice.

'*All* I ask is that *one* tree in the orchard remain untouched. Withhold your hands from that fruit alone. It is forbidden. That is my simple command.'

With a shock he realised what mantle he'd casually draped upon his shoulders. What on earth had possessed him? Latterly it wasn't overly encouraged or else heavily interpreted, but almost from the earliest days, they'd had the Bible. They all knew about Adam and Eve and the garden of God. He could see from all the widened eyes they'd grasped his metaphor. Apparently though, it was tricky to swallow whole. Even Firstmet looked embarrassed. The Emperor strode on, also metaphorically speaking, but now walked alone. His temper, hangover-fuelled, flared.

'Was he taken red-handed?'

The prosecutor nodded. 'It was near completion, Lord,' he confirmed.

'Does he deny his hand in the construction?'

The angry prisoner would have dearly liked to but stubborn honesty would not permit it.

'Then *what* is the problem? Convict him. Then hang him.'

They had their orders, they set to, but Blades detected a new reluctance, a dragging of heels. Even absolute Emperors can overreach themselves.

That just annoyed him afresh. The anger now permanently coiled within lashed out, commandeering his tongue.

'God knows I don't ask much of you,' he screamed at them – and they flinched, 'but I will *not* permit clocks!'

I, the undersigned, having read – or being unlettered, having had read to me – this contract, do by my signature or mark signify my free agreement, that whilst I reside in, trade with or have any intercourse with any Freeport or Leveller undertaking, I shall abide by the letter and spirit of the foundation ordinances, to wit:

1) That all men are equal, insofar that they are universally sentient sparks brought into being by the will of the Almighty. Accordingly, there shall be no distinctions between them other than those instituted by the will of the People and regularly reviewed by those same People.

2) And that therefore no magistracy, office or position shall be hereditary or borne as of right.

3) And that a man's business and mind be his own matter, save that they prejudice no other man, and so it follows that none shall walk in another's thoughts to regulate them.

4) And since it pleases Almighty G*d that men should hold a diversity of conceptions of his Divine stewardship, no man should make enquiry of another's opinion, save it be volunteered, beyond these principles which we hold as self evident:

That there is one G*d and no other.

That therefore G*d is just and G*d is justice.

Wherefore there is a life beyond this, a full and fair settlement of accounts, and that we may reasonably hope for happiness in it.

And that therefore religious duties consist in doing justice, loving mercy, and endeavouring to make our fellow creatures happy.

And thus we should do unto others as we would have them do unto ourselves.

5) That no Freeport citizen or resident shall trade combustive powder other than to those cities and powers deemed worthy of its possession by the decision of the Parliament of Freeport and the Leveller Confederation. A list of said approved parties shall be posted in a prominent place in each Freeport on the first day of each month. The penalty for illegal supply shall be loss of citizenship or residency and forfeiture of property on the first offence and shooting unto death upon the second.

6) That men may divide and record and mark time in any manner they think fit or useful or convenient to their unfettered judgement. Wherefore clocks and timepieces are the mark of a free man and are freely permitted.

Any person presently residing within the bounds or protection of Freeport-Hastings – plain Hastings, as was – shall supply their uncoerced agreement to the above and have the same witnessed by a Leveller magistrate before two accredited Leveller witnesses, and shall bear a copy of same at all times, available for inspection, WITHIN THREE DAYS OF THE DATE OF THIS NOTICE or else depart FOREVER with what they may carry, by sunset of the *third day. Failing which they shall be expelled by force with forfeiture of property.*

Proclaimed this 10th day of August.
Year 1 of the Days of Freedom (DF)
Leveller Governor Freeport-Hastings.
Pericles Overton

'And New-Brighton also.'

Talebearer, mouthpiece of the Council of Scouts, looked warily up.

He'd hardly expected his news to be welcome but the Emperor was already in a fizzing-fuse sort of mood. He earnestly wished to say his piece and be gone before the explosion.

'Leastways, we may – no, must – assume so from the lack of communication. Thus all the ports in the region are Leveller fallen.'

Emperor Blades's burning stare could be taken any way you liked but Talebearer didn't care for any of them.

'If the situation is to be restored, then an expedition against the offenders must be launched soon. Our powder supply is curtailed and they will not trade more save on ruinous terms – and with embarrassing undertakings. Nevertheless, the opportunity is there. One Freeport will trade against another. We must strike whilst the iron . . .'

'You're a scout,' said Blades, evidently hearing him for the first time, 'the head one, I believe?'

Talebearer took a mental step back, bracing himself for the worst.

'I have that honour, Lord . . .'

'So you must keep the maps – our own and the stolen ones.'

'Archivist knows better than . . .' he caught the Emperor's reaction and changed testimony on the hoof. 'I claim perfect acquaintance with them, Lord.'

'Good. Then tell me, do we have much on St Kilda? Or Lindisfarne? Decent scale, enough to let you visualise . . .?'

To see an Emperor swig from a bottle, just like any street tippler, is a shocking thing. Talebearer had been forewarned, but to actually witness it for yourself . . .

'No, Lord. Until your recent revelation of their existence, they were beyond – well beyond – our ken. Now that ships have returned hence we have better particulars but . . .'

Blades *fixed* on him, as though he was the focus of all disappointments.

'A simple no would have sufficed.'

Talebearer swallowed audibly.

'Then no, Lord. They remain but specks on our charts. I could obtain testimony from those who delivered . . .'

'No.'

After that, Talebearer was happy to steer back into even wreck and shoal infested waters.

'And the Leveller rebels, Lord? The taken towns?'

His Emperor didn't have to consider. The easiest path now commanded his slip-sliding feet.

'Pay them what they ask,' he ordered, 'even up to thirty pieces of silver.'

'Silas, what do you know of Lindisfarne – or St Kilda?'

'Who?'

'They're islands – off the coast of Scotland.'

'Are they now? Well, I try not to let 'em dominate me life . . .'

'You've not even heard of them?'

Silas looked up from his platter of fat bacon.

'Of course I haven't. Why should I? The only way I was ever going to Scotland was in the army and I'm past that now. You're the one who should know; you had the more schooling.'

From somewhere, Blades had secured cider for breakfast. He downed some to his brother's disapproval. Once it was gulped, he wiped the residue from his slack lips and returned to the attack.

'So have you got any maps or do you know where I can buy . . .'

Silas slammed his scarred hand on the board and made the cider jar jump.

'Enough! Too much! I wasn't going to say but by God you've worn my consideration thin. Why was Molly weeping?'

Thirst had given sudden way to ravening hunger. Blades was stuffing a cottage roll in his mouth. Round, over and through it he tried to reply.

'Who?'

Silas sighed but didn't disengage his stare, refusing to play out any more line.

'Molly the maid, the wench who does for us and has tidied your mess this last fortnight. You know as well as I.'

'Crying, was she?'

'She was. We heard her in the night.'

'Strangely refined little thing.' The mouthful safely down, Blades was now musing to himself rather than replying. 'More gentry sensitivities than slave thoughts . . .'

Silas's suspicions leapt out of bed.

'What have you . . .?'

'I'm only human,' came a glib reply. 'She has rounded parts that match my needs. I merely ordered her prone for five minutes but, do you know, she *wouldn't* oblige – even after sight of my manhood rampant. Don't concern yourself, Silas, I recalled the disparity between here and the other place. She was not chastised for her frustrating refusal.'

Too far gone with either drink or grandeur, Blades didn't register his brother's gaping maw.

'Speaking of which,' he continued, 'where is the nearest whorehouse nowadays?'

Silas – silently, word by word – put his first response away. To cover the painful process he carried on with breakfast. Unsteady in his chair, Blades queried the quiet with raised eyebrows.

'Sorry?' he said. 'Did I miss something?'

'Yes, you did,' came the swift and not-to-be-gainsaid reply. 'You've missed a great deal. But we shan't miss you: not one bit in present state. You don't belong here any more. Go home. Go to the cacky bed you've made and lie in it!'

That put some pseudo-spine back in him, but it fooled no one, neither Silas or himself.

'I don't have a home,' he said, stiff-backed, pain-faced.

'No, brother, you don't. Not here anyhow. Be gone by tonight or be driven out.'

'You couldn't . . .'

Silas's militia sword hung over the fireplace. Not needing to look, he indicated it with a backward jerk of the thumb.

'You wouldn't . . .'

That lacked all conviction. The word wasn't even credited by its creator.

'By tonight,' Silas repeated, calm as a stranger.

Blades looked round as though for support and, for the first time, realised the extent of his aloneness. Molly was hardly likely to weigh in on his side. Then, despairing of help, he made a snap decision to settle for company. There was wildness in his voice.

'Come with me. You be Emperor: you'd be better at it than me.'

Silas shook his head.

'And become what you have? No thankee.'

'A regentship then; first minister, chief advisor . . .'

The same easy answer.

' "*Get thee behind me, Satan*", with your feeble temptations.'

Blades felt the return of the settled panic that had driven him from his realm. It squeezed out any remaining dignity.

'Don't send me back there alone.' He hated the wheedling tone and wished death on all who'd heard it – himself included.

Silas owned a deep well of pity that he didn't care to publicise for fear everyone would want some. Now he was driven to draw.

'You shall not go alone,' he said, leaning forward to lay a hand on his brother's quaking shoulder.

'No?' Hope and fear warred on his face.

'No. I shall send something with you.'

Blades wondered what he would wish for – and found he no longer knew his own mind. He hadn't strength to dip into the whirlpool of possibilities to extract a decision.

'What?'

'Not maps, not company or guns but the one thing you do lack.'

'Which is?'

'Good advice.'

The very air in the Holy of Holies was proof of something or other. It was frowsty and stagnant; showing no one had enquired within all the time he'd been away. Either they didn't dare or care. The answer was only the other side of a thick-ish door. One twist of its handle and he'd know one way or the other.

He paused. It was an odd thought that the farewell party, Silas and Kate, his wife, and even Molly, were still just beyond the glowing portal but also unknown leagues away. He could probably push his head through and catch them as they turned back to work and normality. But that would be the very sea-bottom of humiliation, like saying long goodbyes to a crowded room and then having to return for your hat. He hadn't sunken quite that far down, or maybe – a spark of hope – just maybe he'd started the long ascent back . . .

The door handle beckoned, became the whole focus of his attention. He'd never paid it much heed before: a bronze Null-in-agony standing between him and a whole world. That served as excuse for delay. After so long away he didn't care to grasp the monstrosity.

To justify procrastination, he retrieved the letter. The portal's stepped podium served as a seat.

It had a candlewax seal: rare formality amongst family. He cracked it and read.

Being a schedule of counsel to Thomas Blades, Curate of the Church 'by Law Established' and also Emperor of a foreign realm.

By his still loving brother, Silas Blades, Carpenter.

Item:

1) Intercourse with all pretended 'Angels' and the like.

Ignore them as if they were not, until such time, if ever, you find the means to DEAL with them.

2) John Lilburne and his Levellers.
Make peace with them and incorporate their sweet ideals and precepts into your own Empire for its better instruction.

3) Pray.

4) Read Scripture.

5) Never run after women or coaches. There will be another along in a moment.

6) You may judge a man by his SHOES.

7) Take it out on the NULL.

8) Never go to bed till you're glad of it.

9) Sort yourself out.

> *'What does the Lord require of thee but to do justly,*
> *love mercy and walk humbly with thy G*d'.*
> *(Micah, 5, 3)*

As dictated by Silas Blades to his wife, Katherine and truly
reported by her.
Herewith his mark
X

'Fair enough,' Blades said to himself, and headed for the door.
It transpired he still had an empire – albeit a smaller one.

' . . . *and the thirtieth miracle of the first god-king (HE needs not our*

256

blessing) is that after The Days Of Betrayal (may they be blotted out), He withdrew his love and guidance from us and adjourned to those realms that He and only He knows. The Empire lay bereft and wicked men seized the day to spread their gospels of doubt and rebellion.

Then, after three black weeks, He returned to us from the Holy of Holies, full of loving kindness and as He ever was, though no vittles or drink had passed beyond the door in all that time. The waiting hordes of the faithful rejoiced and even rioted in exultation. Those buildings damaged were never restored as tokens of remembrance of a day of joy. A few such remnants may still be seen in the older parts of the City.

The god-king's health and prosperity flowed swiftly forth to restore his disconsolate children. He shared out his miraculous well-being and all was well.

Even today the pious fast each year during these three weeks and humbly emulate their Lord by padding their apparel to dissemble satiety.

The thirty-first miracle of the first god-king (H.N.N.O.B.) is the Deception of the Professor . . .'

'A Pilgrim's Compendium of Wisdom for those who would Glorify their Earthly Life with the Jewels of Piety and the Silken Raiment of Prayer.'

Thane Brixi of New-Compton in the Province of Wessex, United England. In the Year of Our Deliverance 457 A.B.

'Freeport Winchelsea is fallen.'

John Lilburne allowed the scroll to revert to shape and escape his pinching grip. 'Its new Imperial Governor bids us greeting and cordially invites us to roll his letter into a cone and sit on it.'

That got the thunder roll of anger he required to cover his dismay. A sharp wind over the parapet raised their hair and matched the mood.

'Freeport Ramsgate supplied 'em,' growled one of the Freegenerals. 'Traitors!'

'Or Freeport Dover,' suggested another. 'They're anyone's. A good price for their powder: one less trade rival. You can see the way it's going. Divide and conquer. They're rolling us up!'

'Listen to me!' roared Lilburne, seizing the helm again; hushing them by volume: as bad as any god-king.

He, the originator of the great idea, was often the rock they rallied on. The thought of that responsibility tempted him to caution in battle, not for himself but for their sakes. One bullet, one Null in the hedgerow, and he could see his project dying with him. At the same time, that meant he had to keep a savage eye on himself. The shoots of grandeur were subtle growers, not easily weeded.

Even so, it was wearying to always be the positive voice. He often didn't feel like it, since it wasn't his true nature. However, ever dogged, he soldiered on. Fortunately, there'd been another timely book out of Blades's library to sustain him. He'd devoured it and profited from its instruction.

For all it was written by a Roman – and a Roman emperor at that, Marcus Aurelius's *Meditations* had been a godsend. The ensuing days fitted the call to '*Stoicism*' like a glove, dictating Lilburne draw deep from the *Meditations*' well. Somewhere along the line he'd made invaluable peace with the world's imperfections. Life didn't last forever and then there'd be time for rest – and in the meanwhile: courage and dignity.

'Remember this,' he said, effectively *ordering* them, 'we shall be reinforced. There's always a spray of die-hards by land and sea from any fallen Freeport.'

'Oh joy!' laughed one of his right-hand men, a convert from the earliest Sicilian days, 'Maybe we should let *all* the outstations fall: then we'd be powerfully enhanced!'

It was a comfort that such insubordination remained. The core principles still marched alongside them, even amidst this unpromising terrain.

Thought of that made Lilburne look out over the Hastings levels. They'd done little with them yet, too busy with trade and survival for serious fencing or drainage. Outside of the broad noonday it was still monster territory: a playground for

258

mud-beasts and lizard steeds; as wild as the ocean behind them. There the sea-Null grazed free, unculled by cannon. Extermination or domestication were as yet untried projects.

It was all the blankest, the most promising of slates for them to write an uplifting story on – if only they were allowed to.

'When the refugees do arrive – as they shall, never fear, we'll have enough for an offensive. Enough of clinging on! Seaford looks shaky: thinly held. We'll have her back.'

It was a miscalculation; he was losing them. They were underwhelmed by Freeport Seaford reborn as their highest aspiration.

Nebuchadnezzar, one of the steadiest, the least-speaking, Freegenerals, voiced what were obviously his considered and settled thoughts. Quiet men are listened to. 'We recruited too wide: too easy.' He contorted his honest face, displeased with inner visions. 'Fair-weather Levellers . . .'

His lover, Diana, allowed a respectful pause before expanding.

'He's peeling us off' – Blades was still *He* to them, the parental yoke not yet completely off their shoulders – 'one by one, leisurely, like the wrappings on one of his concubines – slow pleasure on a summer's night. Finally, when he's done, when we're good and moist and ready, he'll thrust straight at us – and we'll be 'ad.'

'By then it'll just be us,' agreed Sea-captain, master once more of *The Lady Bridget* and admiral of the New-Syracuse run: a prize convert to the cause. 'Only true-believers and eccentrics left, cooped up in Hastings. He'll have enough powder from the fallen places. His guns'll pound us to dust. And anyway, who's to say there's not Imperial ships Sicily-bound as we speak? Mebbe it's we who should be husbanding our shot!'

Lilburne trod back and forth between the stepping-stones of Diana's erotic metaphor and Sea-captain's *no-hard-feelings* commonsense. He couldn't be sure which had flashed him with a wonderful notion.

He pursued it, waving the generals to silence, certain there'd been something worth keeping, if only he could recall. It remained *just* beyond his lunging fingertips and, in the spirit of these things, probably always would.

He retreated, ignoring the impatient company, feigning defeat. The thought-imp, slighted by the loss of interest, advanced a shade, confident of the closeness of its home – a mental cave to which no path led.

Lilburne flaunted his indifference, resolved to consider anything *but* the will o' the wisp. It grew careless, drawing close to torment again. He pounced and bit.

Leisurely . . . HE was leisurely . . .

It was the faun-like Diana's word that had jogged God's horn of plenty. Blessings showered down.

Leisurely . . .

As though to reward it for restraint, Lilburne's mind was permitted to move at flash-flood speed. Disparate wheels and cogs fell pell-mell together to make a complex working whole, just like some Blades-forbidden clock. It told him the precise time.

'He *has* been leisurely, hasn't he?'

He was addressing both himself and the Council. They'd been kept waiting long enough, growing restive, residual faith flaking sliver by sliver away.

'Blades can afford to be . . .'

A flick of the fingers hushed Sea-captain. He bore no grudge: Lilburne's eyes were alight.

'Oh no, he can't. He's not made that way. This is not him, not all this . . . a probe here, a bribe there. I've been beside the Emperor when he thinks. He's a bludgeon, just because he can be. Something is restraining his strong arm – or commanding caution.'

Nebuchadnezzar laughed – his first recorded example. It shocked them.

'Well, if so it 'ain't us . . .'

He waved his hairy hand to dismiss their collective endeavour: one shipload of idealists presently with a favourable trading position, against an empire suspected to be divine-led.

Lilburne smiled. That was another of their major advantages

that would lead to victory: they were honest amongst themselves.

'No, I agree. So, what is it that's sparing us? Fear or mercy?'

They didn't know. Nor did he. Therefore, there was only one logical solution.

Lilburne fell upon it, taking it by surprise, wrestling it to the ground. The wild idea was too shocked to offer resistance.

'*I think*,' Lilburne told the High Council of the world's remaining free men, 'we should invite the Emperor here to ask him!'

'Both.'

Lilburne couldn't believe his luck: straight answers, maybe even honesty, wedded to instant access to the fountain of all wisdom – and guaranteed safety beside!

Better still, he detected some prevailing restraint in the Imperial camp. Blades had accepted their invitation and had come in force, but Hastings-the-last-hope was not to be swept away: not today anyway. Lilburne's cup ranneth over.

'*Both?* How so?'

The Emperor cleared his throat, apparently diffident about such rare clarity.

'*Fear or mercy?* Well, fear, because even a gnat's bite will fester if picked at. I shan't indulge you with martyrdom. Oh no, what I have in mind's far worse. I'm condemning you to the compromises dictated by time. Fire and sword would only magnify your memory and sanctify it. Your lot shall be the passing years. They'll render your cause sordid like any other.'

Lilburne's stalled reply showed the awful truth had struck home. Emperor Blades smiled as they strolled on together. To him fell the final, telling word.

'Oh yes, continued life can often be the cruellest option, believe me. And as to mercy, well, my brother asked it for you. I shall oblige him.'

Two shocks in ten seconds compelled Lilburne to renewed

thought. Recent adventures had led him to forget Blades was an *Emperor* amongst men, as well as emperor, false-god and tyrant. There were moments – lightning flashes of revelation – when he revealed his insight. He was imperial by right as well as fortune.

The coastal path was uneven to the point of treachery; the wind off the brisk sea just the wrong side of bracing. Away from the glorious, tent-strewn, *Field of Truce* it did not need the clatter of escort hoofs to either side to remind them this was no *holiday*.

Blades resumed the abortive conversation, betraying no sign of having been its murderer.

'You walked with me before, John,' he said, a mere statement of matter of factness. Then the tone softened. 'It could be so again . . .'

The Imperial forces had arrived looking like an invasion, for all their prior assurances. Aside from an artillery train everything was there, the full glittering array of New-Wessex. For a second, Lilburne recalled that sight, their steady line over the Levels: all flags and lancers and scarlet hedgehogs of pike. Even their encampment before Free-Hastings was a choreographed riot of colour: the Emperor's pavilion of cloth-of-gold, his surrounding huscarls a circle of purple and silver. They were a show, a pointed lesson achieved without strain. He envied them that ease. He thought himself back with them again, a prized cog in the wonderful machine that manu-factured civilisation.

The glory of this brazen day-dream naturally marched up to make comparison with his actual present – and quite put it to shame. His companions were dowdy and full of talk of *ideals*. And yet their private discourse seemed permanently tethered to the barter price of brimstone. Already, they were en-route to being merchant-accountants, all style leached away.

Temptation hung there like a spell, shimmering for his eyes alone in the salt-thick air. It required effort to brush it aside; a triumph of the will.

'No. Thanks all the same. I've seen finer things to put on: better fitting things than your scarlet coats . . .'

Emperor Blades was not offended. No sign of anything crossed his pale face – but there again, it rarely did since the Boudicca incident.

'As you wish. I just thought I'd offer.'

'You're most reasonable . . . frig! I don't know what to call you now: *my Lord*? Hardly, for you're not. *Majesty*? Never: else what was all this for? Yet I'm still so damned conditioned that *Mr Blades* gets caught in my teeth . . .'

'Is that so? Well, well. Then, out of earshot, feel free to call me Thomas. That's my Christian name, if I can still claim that title.'

Lilburne fretted at his chin stubble; outward sign of inner unease. From the corner of his eye, Blades noted it and smirked. The Leveller was compelled to rise to that challenge.

'I'll have a go – but you trained us well to the contrary . . . Thomas.'

Blades took the familiarity as promised, entirely without concern. The headmaster might appoint a new prefect but their relative positions were in no way disturbed.

'There, that wasn't so bad, was it, John?'

Lilburne stopped and turned on his former Emperor. Unheeded, despite all the solemn promises, two sets of body-guards *prepared*. Discreet, sleeve-obscured pistols and crossbows were levelled. Mage lips framed *passivity* spells. Firstmet positively strained at the bit.

'*Why* so reasonable?' demanded the Leveller, angrily. 'You're making it hard to hate. That's not kind. Our purpose is to ruin you. You know that. We need an iron spirit, not conciliation.'

Blades carried on walking. Lilburne had to hurry to catch up – in more ways than one.

'You're no leader of men,' the Emperor coldly informed him when he arrived, 'if you require just cause to destroy. Think on or else I've won already.'

Lilburne bridled afresh.

'We'll win – without becoming like you!' Lilburne's voice found the settled confidence it had prayed for. 'We *shall* bury you.'

Blades was still unimpressed.

'You can't.' The confidence was unscalable. Lilburne tried even so.

'We have a stranglehold! If we but *squeeze* . . .'

'Sicily alone is insufficient foundation to uphold your dreams. I'll ensure it never will be, or else build a fleet to reconquer it.'

'But the mariners are ours.'

'They are businessmen, John, as all men are. They will strike deals, just like your sister *Freeports*. Heaven knows, dear man, *they* sold themselves to me like whores.'

Lilburne could hardly deny that embarrassing fact. So he retired to his one unassailable advantage – only to find it assailable.

'Without powder you . . .'

'Look, John, I'll be as open and obliging to you as your allies were to me. There's an alternative supply of brimstone. You won't have heard of Iceland, I don't think. It's an inhospitable place: probably Null-free but tricky to get to. So far we haven't ventured its chill shores – but if the alternative's your anarchy and facing the Null with knives, well, we'll find a way, never fear.'

Here, arriving like cannon-fire, was another of the Emperor's inhibiting advantages: the infinite knowledge drawn from . . . elsewhere. He'd everlastingly have that. They were children to his teacher in that respect and always would be.

Lilburne ground his teeth even as he dined on the sour meal set before him. It would be mere indulgence to call it a bluff. He felt the ground slowly shift beneath him, like an ebb tide running fast beneath the sand.

'You think you 'ave us every way, don't you . . . Thomas?'

Blades allowed his face to be almost apologetic. They'd barely got into their stride yet but he'd already won without a shot. He'd planned on it taking at least until St Leonard's or even Cooden.

'I'm rather afraid I *do*, John. But, look, let's stop this school-yard fracas of boast and counter-boast. It's undignified. I'm an

Emperor and you're a head of state now: you must remember that. So hear this: my brother has underwritten your survival and that's all there is to it. Take the fact as your short-term comfort: sell it to your ungrateful rabble. You shan't be swinging from the flagpole you so richly deserve: not tonight – or not through any of my doing, anyway. No, your inevitable nemesis lays a long way off yet: even though its seeds are sewn today.'

As illustration he cast an invisible handful into the unpromising field of sand and tussock-grass. Lilburne's eyes followed its unseen trajectory.

He now had something to cling to: an insubstantial, inexplicable, straw bobbing amidst the wreckage.

'We never knew you had a br . . .'

For the first time, and without trying, a barb penetrated the Imperial skin. Blades grimaced with impatience – and something else; unidentified but worth remembrance later.

'That doesn't matter,' snapped the Emperor. 'Just know that the sides are drawn: enlightened despotism versus your chaotic circus. Gratitude versus childish rebellion. Now let the most fitting prevail.'

Lilburne puffed out his chest.

'I'll settle for that. I've faith in my ideals.'

Blades laughed: a bitter, barking, sound. He raised his face to the sky and fingers to his lips, blew a kiss.

'God be praised,' he said, 'for leaving some innocence in the world. God forgive me when I *grind* it beneath my heel . . .'

They both had the same idea from the same place but at different times; great minds thinking alike.

Beside the Imperial pavilion there was a rack of lances, red or purple gaudy weapons for the cream of his knights. Lilburne saw them in passing and the Emperor saw him see them.

It was only later that he interpreted the Leveller's look and so knew what the morrow would bring. Thanks to his razor-like distrust he had time to prepare and pray.

'I challenge you!'

'Very well.'

Lilburne and his guards and generals hadn't been expecting that. Emperor Blades could at least have indulged them with a moment's shock and pause.

'To a duel; a joust.' Lilburne clarified. 'Single combat. To the death; to settle this thing now.'

It was unnecessary. Blades understood the first time. He underlined the enemy's cloddishness with a frown.

'I know. I've already said yes.'

By now his courtiers were up to speed and protesting. Firstmet was screaming '*Let me do it! Let me!*' and had to be held back. The Leveller had years upon their Lord and other all-too-evident – embarrassing to refer to – advantages. The Emperor waved them to silence.

'When? Now?'

That really did have them. The rebels looked to each other. They hadn't expected acceptance, let alone zeal.

'But my armour is back at the castle . . .'

He heard how feeble that sounded. It was all going wrong.

'We've got more harness than horseshoes,' Blades told his breakfast visitors. 'Take your pick: borrow mine if you like. Unless, of course, you've thought better of . . .'

'No!'

That interruption drew scandalised gasps from the throne-gathered ranks. Again he pacified them.

'Amongst ourselves, quarrels are settled less barbarously. But still, we are in *your* realm now. Tell us about *your* customs . . .'

He could as easily have been querying their pottery styles or stabling arrangements. For a split second Lilburne was tempted to take the Emperor's tacit – if ironic – recognition of their secession and settle for that. Then rallying, he firmly overrode that weakness, tramping it down with mental hoofs – just as he dearly wished to the Emperor himself.

Lilburne tried to sound like the spokesman or even exemplar of a realm, as Blades had enticed him to.

'Amongst the Freemen, in our own Levels land, irreconcilable differences are ended on those same marshes. Two enter, one returns.'

'No,' said the Emperor, resolutely – and cowardly hope flared briefly in Lilburne's heart. 'I have said I will not harm you and I shall not. Do what you will but unhorsing will be the worse you shall suffer from me – and mayhap a bruise or two in consequence. I have sentenced you to the corroding years. You are under protection, and that doom remains.'

He was gaining all the points here and the Freemen hated it. By contrast, the Imperials were on the crest of a wave. They now dared to urge their master on, inciting him to wipe the floor with the opposition. Even without that support he was doing well.

'Harness up!' he commanded, and things were such that some of the Leveller party turned to obey. Then, at the door they were called back.

'But do please try to be quick,' he said, a kindly, if over-busied, father. 'I'd also planned a little sea-swim for today.'

The proto-proletarians went on their way, shoulders slumped, dismissed like boys to bath time.

Such aplomb. Such fatalism. Such justified confidence. Blades did not know whether to feel a fraud or not. Yet surely his foresight deserved a little self-forgiveness? He rather thought so. So the god-king confessed everything and then absolved himself, all in the space of a second.

As soon as the danger reared its head, he'd dispatched fast riders to New-Godalming. The deputising high-priest and his most trusted acolytes were authorised into the Cathedral's Holy of Holies, there to ill-treat the portal with rods and other indignities.

Response was swift. Two of the men vaporised, the balance

stumbled out in no condition to be wicked any more. Then, as the smoke cleared and the grieving relatives grieved, the Angel came to see the author of their misfortunes.

Blades was prepared, as best one may for supernatural visitations. He'd put his oldest gown on, was sitting comfortably. The pavilion had been stripped of witnesses and sharp objects.

He or she was incandescent. The shining white of its gown competed with the fresh-milk sheen of its face.

'*Bad!*' it said, and the word caused the sides of the great tent to billow.

Emperor Blades gripped the arms of his throne, resumed control of teeth and bowels and tried to explain his predicament. He even quoted scripture but the Angel proved not to know it. The human had to expound and then interpret.

'*Luke* 4. 10. "*For it is written, He shall give his angels charge over thee, to keep thee; and in their hands they shall bear thee up, lest at any time thou dash thy foot against a stone.*" Christ said that of himself. Even Satan believed it. I'd like a similar assurance – for a while; just for a spell.'

The Angel cocked its head; a jerky, doll-like expression of bewilderment. Blades had to clarify further.

'Lilburne will have a lance. A bruised foot could be the least of my problems.'

Now she understood. She widened her eyes. Their joint hopes were threatened. She showed him what she would do. It was far too much. Wildly overdone.

'No, no!' he protested. 'Not necessary . . . please.'

He'd never seen so much blood, nor wished to again: an abattoir world.

'Only this.'

He visualised what he had in mind. She pounced to snap it up, almost too small a morsel for her to grasp. It went down, was promised to him, in no time. Not a word was said.

Then the blast of her departure shredded the tent of cloth-of-gold, requiring a wealth of darning and explanation.

'It's not fair!'

'Only to me. It's also no skin off your nose. I'm not complaining.'

'You should. You must. I want to win this fair and square. Put your armour on.'

Emperor Blades shook his unprotected head.

'No, it's too sunny. And there's an end to it. Mount up or not as you wish but I'm going.'

There was such a thing as confidence but that degree of nonchalance was insulting. Alas, Lilburne had no choice but to go along with it. In the time it took for the metal-clad Leveller to clank to his horse, Blades was in the saddle and away.

Certain channels and streams were declared the boundaries to the contest but other than that the two were free to roam. Sooner or later they'd encounter each other in the flat wastes, assuming the natural fauna didn't intervene. For the Levels were still home to mud-monsters, stray Null and lizard-steeds; respectively unspeakable, inimical and inedible. Sometimes they were the presumed settlers of duels, when one party never got to sight the other. That was considered to be a best result, less productive of resentment and feud between the survivor and bereaved family.

Today though, there'd be witnesses, an apostolic dozen riders per entrant, sworn to silence and observation only. Both parties were too precious, the issue too weighty, to risk a mystery outcome.

Emperor Blades, who'd not been astride anything livelier than a harem-girl for years, trotted his warhorse to the approximate centre. He didn't even venture the risk of leaping intervening *guts*, but sought the safer route of tracking round the little sea-bound channels. Once there he dismounted and rested against a valiant bush, all twisted by its struggle against the prevailing salt-wind.

The view was sere, flat and boring and – purely temporary –

oblivion seemed greatly preferable. Therefore he arranged his armourless, past-prime, limbs for a little doze, and as his eyes closed on the scene, all he could hear was the scribble, scribble, scribble of the *scops*, high praising his amazing cool; the sound of future songs in the making. In his drowsy mind's-eye his yet-to-be descendants were with the witnesses, gap-mouthed in admiration also – and as per those of Abraham's: *'numbered like the stars in the sky'*.

Provoked out of all normality, stripped of all subtlety, Lilburne came on like a famished Null. His attendants were honour bound not to raise the alarm, but even on the sodden turf Lilburne's horse-transmitted fury was wake-up call enough. With angelic confidence Blades arose.

The charge drew even greater momentum from clearing a minor gut at the gallop. The lance was pointed undeviatingly at the Emperor's heart. He barely had time to coax his own steed into a walk to meet the headlong assault. All his concern was diverted to holding on to his faith, rather than his reins.

He received his reward for constancy and lack of doubt. At just the right moment the Angel moved him aside, better and more sinuously than his own slow muscles could ever command.

Lilburne missed, overshot and looked ridiculous. As he looked back to try and make sense of it, the Emperor playfully gave him half of a rough haircut, slashing with the wicked pinnacle of his lance. The shorn long locks were gossamered into the air by the horses' thunderous passing.

Blades laughed aloud: pleasure mixed with relief.

'Have we started yet?' he asked, and his amusement got stifled reinforcement from the supposedly mute witnesses. Lilburne wheeled his mount.

The next approach was more controlled, not that it did him any good. The Emperor shimmied out of harm's way, more dextrous than any mortal horse and rider has business to be. This time the Leveller lost an eyebrow.

Finally, Blades bestirred himself to a proper go. He felt so relaxed, so very confident, that the Angel's aid might not have been required but she gave some anyway. Her strong arm strengthened his.

The Emperor's shield took Lilburne's lance and broke it spectacularly. The Leveller rose like a pole vaulter on its impaled length and left horse and world far behind. An angelic wing aided him to improbable heights. Eventually he landed, stunned, undignified and arse uppermost.

Blades circled round to where Lilburne lay, posed catamite-fashion, and directed his blooded lance at the man's neck. There was nothing to stop him.

Breath was held by both sides until the Emperor graciously lifted the point, granting mercy. He had just won a second victory, unappreciated by the audience. He had overcome the Angel's frantic incitements, whispered hotly in his ear.

Even some of the Freemen could not forebear to applaud. The courtiers were less restrained.

'He did his best,' smiled the Emperor, condescending, from his high horse. And that was worse than taking the poor man's head off.

Then it was his turn to have his face amended. The unbecoming smirk fled away. Angels proved themselves to be broader-stroke creatures than mankind, less blessed with taste and proportion. *Mud-monsters*, a pack of the normally solitary lizard steeds, wheeling parliaments, and even a lost, immature Null, converged straight for the clump of armed men, in exactly the way they normally wouldn't. She was over-egging it.

Emperor Blades was, of course, angelically enhanced. Thus guided like a hand puppet, he remote-speared several of the ragged, leech-like mud-things, and when his horse was taken out from under him, fought on with a battle-axe – which appeared from nowhere. Using it he sliced bits off a reptile twice his height until at last it lay still.

The observers had firearms, which made things easier for them – if not for the things trying to kill and eat them. A few humans perished in close-quarter tooth and claw encounters, requiring Blades to come over and clear up.

When silence finally returned, they were in awe – even the

revived Lilburne. No one wanted to be the first to speak. The Emperor himself was embarrassed into peace by insider knowledge of his marionette miracles. But only he knew they were bogus – and was hardly likely to tell.

The unseen Angel looked around the little, diminished circle of men. She saw and approved and left them to it. A few, the most sensitive, felt some obscure loss in the passing of those wings, but even they attributed it to the shrouding of Blades's glory. He'd become a mere middle-aged man again but they – mistakenly – thought they'd been granted a glimpse of the richer reality.

They turned for Hastings and home.

Strangely, that proved not the end of Death's business there that day. Justice, ever contrary, allowed matters to be tipped as topsy-turvy as Lilburne had been.

On their way, sated with experience, the two parties barely noticed one Leveller slip behind. He had been thinking his own thoughts all the way and, within sight of Hastings Castle, came to the conclusion that one God was enough for any universe. He drew his pistol on the Emperor's unguarded back.

There was a shot, but not his. Lilburne felled his own man.

The father of the deed was not capitulation but his inviolate sense of honour. He had given his word and nothing, not even victory and a wiping away of shame, was worth the loss of that. It took some explaining but the finer there, of either side, saw the truth of it.

And so, contrary to all expectations, Lilburne won the day.

Emperor Blades's mercy and indulgence were lauded, even as stories of his prowess spread. For once they required no *scop*'s embroidering. They also justified his curious moderation in settling with the abashed Levellers. If HE wanted to leave an untidy fringe to his empire that was his business and no one – now – would question it.

And so the Imperialists departed with the next sunrise, cocksure and burdened with tribute, bearing a one-sided trade treaty. Never again would they want for powder, so long as the

Levellers were left a coastal strip in which to play their little games. The god-emperor had John Lilburne's word on it and – now – that was good enough for anyone.

He and Nebuchadnezzar and Sea-captain and all the other Leveller luminaries watched them go from the battlements of Freeport-Hastings's hasty motte-and-bailey castle, poor bastion of a chastened utopia. They were not to know it but Freeport-Dover and Freeport-Portchester's humble applications to rejoin the Empire were already being composed.

'So that's that,' said the sailor to the retreating scarlet ranks. 'The start of the end. A slow farewell to a brave notion.'

Lilburne had suffered worse than any there, in his person and essential self, but he still found cause to smile.

'Oh no, I think not,' he said, and his confidence caused heads to turn.

He was recalling the things he'd seen: the unparalleled intercourse, Levellers and Imperialists intermingled, in conversation and drinking, in wrestling and shooting contests. He'd noted plain faces chewing on fresh notions. They'd been infected with thoughts and there was no known surgical instrument to extract them. He'd seen and he believed. Ideas would prove to be deadlier weapons than anything you shot or stabbed with.

'No, no,' he expanded. 'Trust me. It might take centuries to show, but we won the war today. They're taking our eventual victory back with them.'

And later, those who reflected well on it, came to realise he was right, recognising with joy they could now relax, treating the rest of life as mere celebration.

'It's always been there.'

Emperor Blades looked at the hillside effigy. Featureless, it still contrived to stare enigmatically back at him. The bright day deprived it of menace but he had imagination enough to bring on the night and inwardly shiver.

'That is not possible. Everything has a beginning.'

He repented of the statement even as it crossed his lips. Now things were going to turn theological. The *scops* were already jotting.

The Pevensey-Assyrian Lordlings hid some puzzlement. Reincorporated into the Empire and yet weirdly permitted to keep their heads, they were eager to please. Sometimes though, the god-king made it an uphill struggle to be obsequious.

'Oh . . .' said the senior, and thus spokesman, an iron-bound and coiffeured monster. 'Really?'

'Yes.' A simple reply but one taken as definitive and all-encompassing. It was written down for posterity before its sound abated.

The little clump of men and mistresses stood in homage before the hill figure, imperially abandoned to their own thoughts. The sun on the Downs cheered them like the happy and innocent animals most were. They would be as pleased with life at the next stop and the next, whatever it might be. They were alive, clothed and fed, and that was good. Only Blades and the more sophisticated minority managed to squeeze melancholia from the scene.

He still refused to release the giant's eyeless stare.

'So what do people say of him? Who? Who by? When?'

Spokesman, a noted and imaginative torturer of Null, showed he'd not left his ingenuity at home. He politely phrased the disappointment of all.

'Actually, we rather thought it was of and by you . . .'

Blades broke off the pointless contest and turned on the Assyrian.

'Does it *look* like me? Am I slim-hipped, noseless and androgynous? Do I habitually carry two staves?'

The answer to all those was no. Middle-age had made him a man of the world at the price of an expanded equator. His snout was of typical Surrey-Saxon stock prominence (did they but know it) and no one doubted the rampant masculinity proven by a diaspora of children. Likewise, he never carried anything when there were slaves and lickspittles to do it for him.

'No, Majesty.' The correct and shortest – and thus safest – answer.

In fact, as always, he knew more than he was letting on. In a previous life he'd heard of the 'Green Man' or 'Long Man' massively occupying Windover Hill at Wilmington in Sussex. It was just a surprise to find it here also.

'When you were still burrow-people, you must have carved it then.'

'Just so, Majesty.' That was said smartly. They didn't like reminding of those days – before speech and armour and walking erect.

'And kept the outline scoured down to the chalk – otherwise it would grass over.'

'Doubtless.'

'So I wonder who they thought it was.'

Spokesman hadn't risen to heights under Sennacherib's acid regime for nothing. He was nimble footed for all the iron on him.

'Perhaps a premonition of you, Lord – and supplication for your swift coming.'

'And who can blame them?' purred Andromeda, Blades's favourite 'Night-wife' of the moment, a seventeen-year-old so wonderfully forward she'd lapped herself and all the other urge-slakers. 'He comes only at the right time to bestow sweet satisfaction to the people under him. I can vouch for it.'

She had nothing much to gain by non-bedtime lip-service: he'd lavishly rewarded her enough already. Yet, whilst still tenuously in favour, she took the trouble to leave good memories. Young people weren't often so considerate.

The legend of his titanic sexuality was another part of the Imperial mythology. Nowadays, alas, it was all 'do your best and be duly thankful' – or else the ceaseless search for, and diminishing returns of, novelty. So, though she lied and next year would find her gone, yet the tribute was kindly meant – and welcome.

Blades let the defusing sniggers die a natural death before continuing.

275

'Just so. But I still don't think it a good likeness . . .'

And then there was displayed the difference between stylish flattery and cringe-worthy crawling. A grizzled commander of Assyrian legions leapt in. 'Then it shall be erased – and re-cut, Majesty, the better to depict . . .'

'No.'

He found simple commands the best. They shut people up. Courtiers couldn't sink ambitious claws into imperatives.

'Leave it be. We like it as it is.'

For what it was worth he thought the figure showed a Null, a placatory image of the ever-winning foe. If so, it was sweet irony for him of all people to act as its protector.

The *Long Man* thus secured for another thousand years at least, Blades felt his debt for an hour's diversion had been repaid. He saluted the giant – creating yet another tradition – and then turned to go. Like ducklings the entourage went with him.

Thoughts of millennial spans prompted recollection of the ancient yew in the valley below. The worship of the burrow-folk in the pre-Blades time tended to centre round such long-lived successes: marked contrast to their own marginal and furtive lives. The Emperor emulated the wise practice of his former church by incorporating rather than suppressing such sites. A chapel – in messy transition phase between the Christian and Imperial faith, now sat beside the tree, sanctifying and sanctified by it.

The latest approved design substituted a crown for the steeple but Wilmington church was of the old style. Once-upon-a-time Curate Blades was of two minds about the change. The old look prompted both nostalgia and unease. For the moment the two feelings hung in the balance but one day resented guilt would outweigh fading faith. Then there'd be a clean break with what had gone before and universal change. A new religion required validation with a new type of holy house.

Unsure if he should address himself or God – and the point of doing either, Blades turned aside from Wilmington's house of prayer. He didn't want to think about that, or – increasingly – anything.

Not far off was Mount Caburn, Sussex's nearest answer to a peak. They'd passed it on the progress here but then he'd been in a dark mood and drawn the carriage screens. Now remembrance of it returned, forgiving, as a Godsend. Word was it was well worth ascending, to view the Downs and Levels and Weald, and survey where New-Lewes was taking shape. It would constitute quite a climb, eating up at least an hour or two: even more if they took it slowly.

He considered briefly and then decreed it so. Alternatives were an effort and first thoughts best. Under Lord Firstmet's direction, the Imperial party began to re-coalesce with the semblance of purpose.

In his New-Wessex there was no – safe – precision in telling the time. They were a long way away from the complex-as-they-could-be sundials of New Godalming. The Emperor of Humanity was obliged to consult the sun.

It was almost noon: knowledge greeted with a sigh of relief. He was doing well. They'd nearly filled half another day.

'I'm bored. I fancy something to read: something spicy, something stirring. Have you got anything like that?'

The Chamberlain consulted his folder of reports and news and miscellanies. From the speed with which he turned one page Emperor Blades knew that was the one for him. Obtaining it took some extraction. Chamberlain would never, ever, disobey, but he sailed precious close to it in economising on his Lord's distress.

Blades seized the screed from the shrinking fingers and read:

Think Well on't.

An Exaltation to the Unconsulted.

. . . And if, as we – often – hear, HE has such god-like power and is the bane of monsters and men-foes alike in easy combat, defeating

277

*them with flicks of his puissant arm; if HE is in consequence the Lord
of confident moderation unto his poor, weak children, THEN what
signifies it that:*

> *No opinion may be heard than his?*
> *No conduit for the Divine voice may be dug than his?*
> *No way of life be sweet unless he approve it so?*
> *No time be told save in the crude manner he permits it?*

*We say that a true father is relaxed after the ways of his little ones for
fear of raising puppets and poor imitations. And therefore might not
a true paragon of virtue and invention suffer his People to speak their
own mind on those sundry topics that most press them?*

*Wherefore we say CHILDHOOD'S END is come and there
dawns a day to put on adult things. To HE that made us a home we
say thank you kindly – but now comes a time to leave home. Father
– if such you truly be – DO NOT BAR THE WAY!*

Issued for the better pondering of all men and women

by

The Committee
The Campaign for Real Humanity

'All over New-Godalming, you say?' enquired the target of the
well-reasoned abuse.

The courtier was near to tears: the genuine affronted article.

'Not *all*,' he pleaded, wringing his hands. 'Just the major
thoroughfares, the Cathedral – again – some barracks, your
summer palace, the . . .'

'*Nearly* all then . . . And I'm not familiar with this "campaign". Another Leveller front organisation, I presume?'

'Yes, Majesty – cowardly wretches! I'm so very sorry,
Majesty.' And he really was: not frightened but offended for his
Emperor's sake. Blades put an end to his words and distress with
a kindly hand.

'It signifies nothing, Attila. We are unaffected.'

The faithful servant remained unconsoled.

'But on your holiday as well, Lord: the horror, the sheer . . .

278

inopportunity of it . . .'

'Water off a duck's back . . .'

Alas, that didn't do the trick either. He'd not made that particular saying general but kept it as a private metaphor. Accordingly poor Chamberlain Attila couldn't distinguish it from an Imperial instruction – the slightest of which his feet ran fast to accomplish. It wasn't beyond the realms of possibility that the Emperor wanted to see water poured over a duck. Blades had requested stranger things when the mood or the wine took him. His ways and whims were strange and naturally quite different from the common herd.

'Where are you going? I haven't dis . . . Oh, I see. No, cancel the duck, Attila. Put it from your mind, along with any unhappiness. Console yourself with occupation. Find a suitable home for these impudences.'

'I shall, Lord, I shall! And all its brethren gathered from the camp. Believe me I shall!'

That confidence piqued the Imperial curiosity. Its explanation when it came touched his desiccated heart. Some people still loved him.

'Attila. As a matter of interest, how *are* you going to dispose of them?'

The Chamberlain poised, vengeful-exultant at the tent flap.

'Quartered, Lord, if you'll excuse me, and then hung in the Null-keepers' privies.'

Blades smiled and was glad. His troubled conscience unclenched, if only for an instant. The world he'd created couldn't be all that bad, not as *structurally* wicked as its enemies made out. Observe, he told himself in the private desert of his heart, how even evil sentiments were passed on for absorption by their target audience.

The sunken garden was meant to be a place of pleasure, but after Blades had taken it he wanted to be left alone. '*After coitus all animals are sad*' – and none more so than he. The ladies and

279

instruments were shooed or cleared away.

Wine was the other, usually tandem, option, but a short term one. For every sparkling hour gained, he exchanged two dead ones and then doomsday in his head. The guilt produced by executions ordered whilst hungover was insupportable. So, just like his hermaphrodite concubine, the Emperor didn't know which way to turn. Beyond the oblivion of sex or intoxication he'd quite run out of ways to kill the day.

At least the garden's sunkenness took him out of sight and notice, which was some or other liberation. Its heady blooms beguiled two of his flailing senses and permanently laden beds and tables occupied odd corners to beguile the rest. When all else failed, a mini maze at one end supposedly offered opportunity to really lose himself. Unsurprisingly, it remained untrod after early discovery that he took himself in there also. Escape proved to be sturdily independent of human provision. Blades shifted on his divan, trying to find comfort. Even the thinnest of silk robes seemed to irritate him of late; gathering into Judas folds and bunches the moment he reclined. Tugging at it brought no relief. He wondered if people would laugh at the judicial impaling of a garment. Certainly it deserved it, but equally he couldn't be bothered.

The book he had been reading slipped from his hands but no slave was called to retrieve it. Let *The Anatomy of Melancholy* lie as it fell, like a Null-mother's legs: open but uninviting. Burton's masterwork had nothing to teach him.

Round the garden, top-to-toeing its walls, were charming – or so he first thought – terracotta tiles, warm-red, painted with intricate vistas of cherubs or nymphs alternated, promiscuously draped. They presented front or back, as appropriate, and were supposed to inspire him to fresh naughtiness. He studied their implicit stories with dull eyes.

The trouble was, when everything is yours to command, every which way, as often as you like, then nothing is 'naughty'. And passion without spice is no better than sneezing – or other more basic involuntary actions. The murals merely took him back to square one. He'd been there, done and taken that – twice this morning – and hadn't been all that excited the first time.

Lamb was still an elite foodstuff in his world. The Null and other lively fauna took such a toll of them, unlike the wild able-to-look-after-themselves unimproved cattle, that only the mutton and wool flocks were entrusted to the open hills. Till they reached expendable age sheep were kept in guarded pens and cherished even at the cost of human life. Nevertheless, they were still got at and no one much beyond the fourth circle got to taste younger, more tender specimens.

Emperor Blades thought of all that as he sampled the great plate of succulent meat set beside him. He'd purchased the honour of a virtuous Duchess with just a few lamb chops not long ago, but to him it was still the nothing-special dinner of wool-country Old-Godalming. He really did try to hold its peculiarity in his head as he chewed but his taste-buds were not persuaded. Like so many 'pleasures' of late, it refused to dance for him.

Then the answer occurred. What he required was something not self-referenced but a thing valued from *outside*. And then he naturally wondered, in a world entirely of his own making, what on earth could that be?

The conundrum was only given token chase. It was too difficult. He gave up and sought refuge in a doze but that, the easiest solace of his lowest slave, refused to attend the Emperor. He did not do enough to be tired: he was too 'tired' to do anything. Even the erotic murals could not bore him to sleep. Life. In general. It was on its way to being intolerable.

And so, as often happens – fearing it may have provoked too far – life allowed a consolation prize, just to keep him playing. Blaming his wretched garment, Blades tore at it and so discovered in one slim pocket the thing he sought. It was speedily dragged forth into the light, even at the cost of wounding the gown.

Here was what he'd wished for. Silas's letter certainly did not come from this – his – world. Its values and terms of reference were quintessentially 'other'. The Levellers' outpourings were either book-drawn or mere mirror images of Blades's

281

preferences, but this was the genuine perverse article.

Accordingly, he unfolded it with some reverence. In this world it was unique. Even the Bible, an oppositional document if ever there was one, could be *interpreted*, since its author chose not to defend its integrity. With this, though, he could hear it being spoken. He knew just what its creator had meant. Refreshingly, there could be no explaining away. He read. He adjudged. He tried to be honest.

1 : Angels. Easy, he'd done that. He'd done that well. Well done!

2 : Levellers. That too. He'd spared them. Not EXTERMINATED them. So that counted, sort of. It would be a lot of work to make and get a fleet to Sicily. Harder still to get brimstone flowing again after the likely devastation. Iceland could be held in reserve – which was the best place for it – to be reached out to only in dire need. Surviving to cant on was all they deserved and compromise enough. He couldn't personally agree with their *levelling* though – it tended towards anarchy and a hey-day for the Null. So he'd met Silas halfway *and* obeyed his conscience. Very commendable. Almost all that was asked of him.

3 : Prayer. Well, he spoke to himself a fair bit – and to a greater power when things felt desperate. That might scrape a yes.

4 : Bible reading. Hmmmmm.

5 : Women and coaches. He hadn't visited St Kilda or any other God-forsaken isle. Coaches waited for *him*. The precept had been honoured in both spirit and word.

6 : Shoes. He really did try to. But a lot of People didn't wear them.

7 : The Null. Couldn't be faulted there.

8 : Bed-time. Possibly a reference to the joys outlined round the walls. Or possibly not.

9 : Sortedness. Hmmmmm. Not for him to say.

Six or seven out of nine wasn't bad: wasn't bad at all – but should he push on for top marks? There was the question of motivation. What he needed, of course, was some outside opposition. Trouble was, in the world he'd striven so hard to make peaceful, that was – Angels aside – most unlikely.

One quarter it definitely wouldn't come from was the Royal household. Purged of perverse wives and sons, they were now so attuned to him it was difficult to see the joins. They knew his ways. For example, once the sunken garden was ordered cleared no one entered in for any reason. Sometimes he just wanted to relax. There was no telling what he might be doing. They'd never disobeyed him in that before.

Therefore, Attila and Caiaphas's arrival got black looks – until the significance both the intrusion and conjunction betokened sank in.

'Swive off, you . . . hang on, what do you want?'

Even they were conditioned enough to turn instantly at his dismissal. Likewise, Dick Whittington style, they turned again at his recall.

Caiaphas had something of the damn-your-eyes insolence of the early John Lilburne. Sadly, it went with efficient performance of his job. Blades just hoped the similarity ended there, otherwise the man would have to have an accident.

'Are you sure, Majesty? We don't wish to intrude . . .'

'Spit it out, man – no, no, not like that. Tell-me-what-you-want-to-say!'

Caiaphas stood still. The more intimidated Attila was two paces behind.

'You may recall, Majesty, that you have a corps of scouts.'

'I recall that New-Godalming's my capital, that the Null are purple: I recall lots of things. Get on with it.'

'Their finest, longest-serving, most daring, men have a joint message to convey. They wish to speak to you.'

Blades sighed.

'Is that really necessary? They spend their lives beyond knowledge of baths. Loneliness makes their discourse incoherent. Surely you have the gist of it from them.'

'I do.' Caiaphas had not only the face of a donkey but the temperament beside. Therefore he probably didn't much care that he might be earning early retirement.

'And it is?'

The soldier sucked in through his teeth.

'Both good and bad news, Majesty.'

Emperor Blades sighed.

'And they *are*?'

'The two things in the same sentence, my Lord. The Null have disappeared.'

DAY RETURN SHEET
DOVEDALE LINE
BASTION: 12 – Waterslacks TO Wetton

WEEK : 27

DAY:	Observed Null: Est.	Kills: Est.	Comments
1	4	1. 1 sore wounded	Raiding party
2	None	N/A	
3	3	Nil	Raiding party
4	6	1	Ditto
5	2	Nil	Ditto
...			

WEEK : 28

DAY:	Observed Null: Est.	Kills: Est.	Comments
1	6	2	Raiding party
2	8	1	Ditto
3	30	6	All juveniles. Unprecedented. Scouts?
4	1000?	50?	In force, as from a rampaging fire.
5	Morning: 1000?	50?	They by-pass us.
	Evening: 1000?	50?	
6	Thousands . . .	We are attacked.	

Records cease

DAY RETURN SHEET
DOVEDALE LINE
BASTION: 18 – Jacobs Ladder **TO** Tissington Spires

WEEK : 28

DAY:	Observed Null: Est.	Kills: Est.	Comments
4	In haste. 1000s.		The Castellan orders us withhold our fire to husband powder.
5	1000s.		They are bearing Null

			mothers with them. Unheard of. Even night does not abate them.
6	1000s.		In haste. They scale the walls.
7	Siege		

WEEK: 29

DAY:	Observed Null: Est.	Kills: Est.	*Comments*
1	500? returning	25?	We have survived. They return, lamenting.
2	500? returning	30?	The monsters do not heed our musketry, as though in despair.
3	100 returning	25	Returning stragglers.
4	25 returning	18	Ditto. Our army arrived.
5	Nothing		
6	Nothing		
7	Nothing		

*

286

First too many, then none at all. After the great Null offensive had been narrowly repulsed, the scouts of humanity recommenced their probes into monster-land. The only Null they found were past caring and bird and wolf-feed. Even daring forays into what the Emperor bade them call 'Northumbria' found not a sign of the living foe.

It was all a puzzle – though a pleasant one – and for the space of weeks the Empire didn't know whether to celebrate or brace themselves. With all the centuries of burrow-crouching still latent in their bones, the People weren't able to shrug off worry as easy as all that.

And then they found that caution, indeed pessimism, were fully justified. Answer came with gun and smile – and neither were for their benefit.

'And furthermore, he says you are a cad and a bounder, not deserving of the title of gentleman, nor fit for civilised intercourse, should your treatment of the fairer sex be indication of your general sympathies. Incidentally we have your poor cast-off family members in safe – or at least better than your own – keeping. Rescued, they now send their regards. Here.'

The herald drew out three sealed envelopes and cast them at Blades's feet. The Emperor did not take the bait; his eyes remained levelled.

'Suit yourself. And furthermore, the Professor says your ways and days are done, and unless you recognise that fact, you will be likewise. Geddit?'

Again that smile; more a smirk, as the herald lifted his eyes from the offensive message. His two companions matched it with a shift of the strange guns they cradled: arrogance personified. The Court had expected gratitude for allowing them to bear arms in the Imperial presence, for accepting without comment their unfamiliar swarthy skin and black hair. They didn't get it or *geddit*.

'And what, pray,' asked Blades, for fear one of the nearby

huscarls should explode all over the hostile silence, 'is a *cad*, or indeed, a *bounder?*'

He received a sigh instead of reply. With true Christian forbearance, he overlooked it and persevered.

'Is there something wrong in *bounding*? Why is that your culture dictates a man should not jump?'

There was that sigh again. This time the insolence could not be mistaken for anything else.

'*Your* culture, to quote the Professor,' countered their guest, 'is primitive. *You* are reactionary. It and you must go.'

As 'heralds' went, this one was less than courtly. Likewise, whilst the People's emissaries were peacock examples of their race, even when treating with the Null, these strangers were dressed as drab as the most mud-conversant New-Wessex peasant. They hadn't gone to any flattering effort, but dressed practically in garments of dun, hairy, cloth. Nor had they bothered to clarify their odd turns of speech. True, they spoke English, but it was a brusque and unfamiliar type, not the slow *ooo* and *ahhh* South-country dialect Blades brought along with him. That didn't seem to worry them though, even when their hosts were visibly straining to keep up. They rattled on at undiminished pace, without concession.

The reason became clearer by the moment. Somewhere along the line they'd been convinced that their way was best and the trio didn't trouble to conceal it. Even deep in the Imperial splendours of New-Godalming, dwarfed by Cathedral and Palace and monuments, they were invincibly superior. The very best they were shown produced only a curled lip. When he heard of it, Emperor Blades found that lack of zeal for friendship rather worrying.

' "Go" where?' Blades's grip on the throne threatened to leave fingerprints. Outside of the marital bed and Leveller zones, he hadn't been spoken to thus for years. He had gotten unfamiliar with disrespect.

'If I may finish . . .' said Herald, and lowered his noble hooked nose over the scroll again. 'Where was I? Oh yes, " . . . therefore, *out of propriety, for the furtherance of civilisation and liberal culture, in manumission of your ignorant misdeeds, and from a sincere desire to make reparations for the boorishness of that which you have built, you shall, within the succeeding fourteen days, dismantle the barbaric apparatus of empire, abdicate and relinquish your outdated rule and surrender to the authority of the district governor that will be dispatched to you." Sign here.'*

It was the obscurity of his language that saved him. If the court had both heard and understood he would have been torn to bloody shreds and his ribcage dangled to the – now pampered – captive zoo-Null.

He held out the long letter, together with a curious writing implement he'd failed to dip in ink, although that seemed not to dent his smooth assurance that it was ready for use.

The other end of the transaction was far from ready. The Emperor's desired reply was drowning in a whirlpool of fury, topped with a froth of fear. Yet it was that insubstantial decoration which stopped him from making his feelings clear and letting others act on them. He was prodded by ironic memories. Curate Blades had been as confident as this when he first walked with a musket amongst savages.

'Well?' prompted Herald, with minimal patience or respect. The document was shaken meaningfully. Even the slowest and most distant courtiers were picking up the nuances now. A communal growl was clawing its way up to audibility.

Blades had no answer – for the excellent reason no one had invented the right, scorching, words yet. In his mind's eye he was running through the rarer forms of execution. As a diplomat of sorts – the undiplomatic sort – Herald ought to have had his answer from looks alone.

He sighed for the third time, the loudest, most gratuitous, yet. The letter was reluctantly lowered. He nodded to his two copper-skinned companions. They ambled to the window and examined the courtyard scene below like hunters.

'Are they important?' one asked: his first speech since the scouts had presented him to the Palace. Emperor Blades twisted in his throne and tracked the gesture down.

As it happened the answer was yes. The flock wasn't just any old sheep, but the most cosseted, sweet-grass lambs that New-Wessex could provide. They were also doomed, being brought in to honour the visitors at a banquet that night, but Blades wouldn't tell him that. He had a feeling he was about as likely to enjoy the feast as the lambs were.

He replied in civil tones because the scene had acquired a horrible inevitability. They wanted to show, he wanted to see: destiny approved.

'Not really . . .'

The two showed what they thought by putting out the window panes with their gun barrels. In their own good time the shards of glass tinkled arrival on the paving beneath.

Because they were at heart practical folk, the People watched intently as the two men loaded and fired. There was infinitely less foreplay to it than with their own muzzle-loaders. These were charged with tiny brass cartridges slipped into the breech, an opening appearing there at the flip of a lever. From ammunition pouch to gun to shoulder to target there was very little to it. They rained down death at a furious rate.

Sheepish protest ascended up to the throne-room – but rapidly diminishing, and not for long. The strangers swiftly made their point – and then over-made it. They let some of the magic become mundane.

Amazingly, there was little smoke; just the slightest whiff from the muzzle and an even more spectral companion from the breech as one spent cartridge was flipped out and another tucked in. These men's battlefields would be clear-cut and rational things, cursed or blessed with seeing what you were doing. A moment's reflection was enough to realise New-Wessex soldiers might not be up to that.

They finished and stepped back, proud artists showing off their work. It didn't seem to occur to them to doubt the reviews.

'We were going to slaughter them anyway,' said Emperor Blades – and wished he hadn't, hearing how weak it sounded.

'There you are, then,' cut in Herald. 'We're here to save you work.' And then he cast the darkest of looks at Blades. 'Well, some of you anyway.'

290

The Emperor studied them and they he. The prolonged scrutiny told all. Evidently there would be no meeting of minds. Abandoning that hope, Blades let his gaze drop and the emissaries misunderstood.

'We know what you're thinkin',' leered Herald. 'You *could* copy the guns, maybe – given the time – which you won't be. Also, we've used all the shells. Deliberate. We only brought *just* enough to show you the new era's dawning. You'll not prolong the old one that way, no sirree.'

Actually, he hadn't been thinking that: though doubtless the notion wasn't far away. What Blades had occupied the silence with was daydreams of their messy demise. He was slowing down and losing his subtlety in old age. The screaming red images departed.

'Of course, *traditionally*,' said Emperor Blades, addressing the court now, not the visitors, in his instructional, this-is-for-your-benefit, tone, 'the persons of heralds are sacrosanct. The tenets of high diplomacy require that its practitioners should discourse without fear of retribution. *You* may well think these . . . blow-ins merit making love to an impaling stake. *You* may be right. In fact, and broadly speaking, we would probably have to agree with *you* in that opinion but, alas, we are not as free in our actions as the commonality . . .'

Now it was the strangers that were having trouble following the gist of it. New-Wessex courtly speech entered their heads imperfectly and required some filtering before it could be consumed. The effort – and the need for effort – made them grimace like lovers. Blades comically froze that gurning on their faces for a second by suddenly addressing them.

'What do *you* think?' he asked, uncle-friendly. 'What shall we *make* of you?'

Herald was the mouthpiece here, that was now clear. The others were gun-toters, their party-piece complete and thus forgettable. Blades turned his decades of absolute rule on the only important one and so won a little victory. A refreshing streamlet of fear broke ground along Herald's spine, liquefying his face before he wrested back control.

'We are inviolate,' he told the Emperor, commendably bold again.

Blades shrugged and smiled, letting it be known that he'd dispensed with *rules* long ago and was surprised to hear their feeble claims asserted.

'The zoo-Null won't have been fed yet,' suggested Firstmet, suppressed outrage bubbling up into voice and eyes. 'We could *make* their day: *make* dinner of these gentlemen . . .'

One of the riflemen slapped the stock of his gun.

'We know how to deal with Null. Ain't many left back home, nor here since *we* arrived.'

'But face to face, though,' said Firstmet, advancing on him, baleful and one-eyed, 'man to monster without your fire-stick?' He gently but firmly disengaged the weapon from the shocked soldier, like parting a bed-bound child from its toy. 'How then? Is your flesh better attached to its bones than ours, eh?'

Without releasing the poor man's gaze, face to face, almost exchanging breath, he kneaded the upper arm of his prisoner – and was not impressed.

'No,' he determined. 'I reckon it'll peel off a treat.'

With sudden violence he put a kink in the rifle's barrel, forcing the metal to conform to his knee. It had spoken its last. With mock sorrow Firstmet returned it.

'Not dinner,' he informed his Emperor. 'Maybe a snack.'

Blades wondered who'd they'd dealt with up to now. Clearly it had only just come home to them that they now faced people capable of anything. Herald's smile had become very fixed.

'I repeat my question,' he said, relishing recaptured status, even if was only to be temporary. 'What *is* to become of you?'

The answer, pre-considered, was spat out of Herald's waxy face.

'Honoured guests. We shan't impose for long. A couple of days at the most. The army will be here by then. They'd kinda like to find us alive and happy.'

'Limbs attached, privates intact, two eyes still: that sort of thing?' Blades's enquiry sounded solicitous.

'Right.'

'We'll see. And by the bye, we have an army of our own, you know.'

Herald's humour was distinctly unsettling.

'Yeah, we've seen . . .'

Blades made a decision that was no decision. Events were hurtling towards him as usual. Life was a raft without rudder or steersman. All you could do was sing cheerful shanties along the way – a more dignified response than wailing.

'And our guests you shall be,' he announced, descending from the quartz crystal throne to approach them. The unregarded family missives were ignored; trodden underfoot. 'Not Null food or mutilated, but whole and hearty till your friends arrive. We look forward to greeting this *Professor* of so much sound advice.'

Herald thought he'd won. His chest puffed out again.

'Good move,' he said. 'I'll see you all right under the new regime. A bit of fieldwork to toughen the hands, but then something easy: a nice desk job.'

Blades nodded gratefully. He didn't know what a *deskjob* was but he didn't like the sound of it.

'Now, first things first, our guests must be fed. Are you hungry?'

Herald was standing up to him now, his old self again, measuring himself against the Emperor. He was taller, better built: downward looking.

'Fairly.'

Blades snatched the bulky scroll off him and raised it to Herald's gaping mouth. He let the ice in his eyes be seen.

'Good. So eat this.'

Scouts had found them whilst searching for Null. The strangers were heading south, following a trail suggestive of human civilisation.

A chance encounter occurred in the far north, near where Blades hoped Carlisle would one day rise again. Apparently all was amicable. The two parties travelled back together, surprised and pleased just to be able to converse, eager to swop their very different stories.

After having 'crossed over the sea', the newcomers were in 'Scotland' and 'Ireland', too. They'd picked up Sennacherib and his little band of exiles there and held them in some or other security. Then, after treading the Irish Null underheel, they dealt out the same treatment to their Scottish and northern English cousins, stampeding them south to be repulsed by New-Wessex. Caught between that rock and a hard place, the monsters had to make alternative arrangements, taking refuge in death or hiding. The humans' joint return journey could therefore be a stroll, free and easy, devoid of tension. And so it was save in two small respects.

Firstly, the strangers refused to demonstrate their weird guns, however warmly pressed. They passed them off as something of no consequence. Likewise, though their every other word was 'the Professor' this and 'the Professor' that, just as their companions' talk was of Blades, they never imparted detail. Their companions eventually queried the reticence.

The Professor would explain all in due course, they were told – and firmly – just as he had to them.

The letters he rescued, though trodden and besmirched, unable to resist their siren calls. He excused his weakness by recognising this was an in-between time, a waiting era with nothing better to do.

Emperor Blades also recognised the handwriting and opened them in ascending order of risk.

Father.

I send you salutations. I have survived and learned many things. I fear the day fast approaches when you must learn them too.

. . . already, when we first sighted Ireland's shores, there were pyres of Null along the coast, the sweet clove-pork smell of their burning. We were met at landfall.

. . . you would have regained some pride in me. I resisted as long as my surviving partisans would obey. We barely got within musket shot of their line. I tell you most solemnly: they have wheeled guns, driven by one man, like unto hundreds of our poor weapons . . .

God saw fit to leave my left hand on the battlefield – if I may term such a one-sided converse thus. The Professor set his apothecaries to heal me and now we are affable. He promises me high office, once I am 're-educated'.

Mother is with me but not in best health. As well she may she sends you her regards. Doubtless I shall see you soon, so long as you do not resist.

your prodigal son

Sennacherib Aspour Maidenhead Sargon Blades (1st circle)

and:

Dear Peacock

St Kilda is a cold place. There are cliffs there and birds in multitudes. Their eggs are sweet but dangerous to procure. And there are cliffs there. Your face is upon them. I saw it when I climbed. I did and I did and I did

> and I did
>> and I did
>>> and I did

And I pushed my maid over. I could no longer find her pleasure spot. Yet my tongue is nimble, and fingers better. Therefore she does not have one. So what is the use of her? So I pushed her over and her head smashed and the seabirds pecked at her for days because you put her on a sharp rock out of reach of the sea. The waves would have cleaned her. That was bad. Why did you do that?

You can make houses out of turves, did you know that? Do you still know everything? I think the Professor knows more and I have asked him to kill you so that we can be together and

I must go now

your ever loving and first wife

JEZEBEL Blades

and:

My dear Thomas

How are you?
My spectacles were broken in a fall, I have no replacements.
Therefore, the darkness has returned. Yet alone of all the world I still
see you clearly.
I have never ceased to think of you.

Your ever-loving wife

Boudicca Blades
X

Well, *he* had – for whole hours at a time – and he didn't thank
her for reminding him. All that distancing practice and then
she yanked him back with a single tug on the thread of love.
Now he was returned to square one, crotch-kicked again, just as
a sea of troubles roared in.

Much obliged, Boudicca. So next time it wouldn't be
temperate Lindisfarne for her but somewhere even further out
of sight and mind. He'd see if she remained so attached to him
clinging on to Rockall with her fingertips . . .

DOVEDALE LINE
BASTION: 18 – Jacobs Ladder **TO** Tissington Spires

WEEK : 31
DAY RETURN SHEET

Observed Null: Est. Kills: Est.   **Comments**
DAY:
2 Nothing

3   Nothing

4   Nothing

5   Not Null. 200?   –   Strangers.
                                         Humans.
                                         Curious speech
                                         and uniforms.
                                         Parlay.
                                         Surrender
                                         demanded.
                                         Stoutly refused.

6   They fire. Their guns speak many times to our one! They
have artillery that patters our walls like hail. We cannot show
our heads. The bastion crumbles. Oh Blades have mercy on us
we pray.

7   The Castellan attempted parlay. They listened and then
shot him like a dog. Bombardment resumes.

                        Records cease.

'So tell me, boy, when did you know the game was up?'
    Ex-Emperor Blades was a vessel of terror and loathing. He
had to throttle both in their cradle if what he had in mind
was to come off. Survival was the only priority – for the
moment – until the glorious dawn. So he shut down any finer
feelings that might interfere with that. They whimpered
protest as the smothering pillow descended but he held it
there till silence fell. Only then was he ready to reply. If the
Professor held out hoops then he'd jump through them – with
a smile.
    'After the reports – or lack of them – from the Dovedale
Line. That had held the worst the Null could do but you walked
straight through it!'

The Professor leaned back and tinkled the ice in his long drink.

'We sure did, didn't we? Your boys didn't know what hit 'em.'

'Well, how could they?' Since they were getting on so well, Blades raised himself on one knee but the temerity was disapproved of. The Professor's frown sent him back down to the carpet. 'I mean, your weapons were . . .'

'Better. Yep! They *sure* were.' He was enjoying this, lolling in his comfy chair before a humbled emperor. He was minded to spin out the lovely moment with recollection. 'Why, I call to mind your bastions bursting out like an overripe melon!'

That was lost on Blades: he didn't know what a *melon* was – but there was no need for metaphor. The ex-Emperor had seen the real thing when the shells rained down on New-Godalming. He'd then found he could still weep after all.

'And may I tell you, sir,' the Professor leant forward, bushy mustache bristling. 'How I cursed you and all kings when you sent your poor dupes into hopeless battle. They were mown down like corn under the scythe.'

Blades remembered that sight too.

They *sure* were.

Because he had an inkling of what was to follow, and because – for all that he romantically thought himself frozen inside – he loved his People, Blades committed only a portion of his forces to the fray. The greater part were held in reserve, out of harm's way and hanging *waverers* and *traitors*.

The armed might of humanity had melted away into ruin once before, during *The Great Defeat* at the hands and claws of the Null. Any amount of suffering had stemmed from that day. They'd been set back years that would never be regained; maybe the very time in which they could have developed weapons to match the Professor's. Emperor Blades was determined any repetition should not be so final.

The turnout was still quite impressive: five infantry

298

regiments of the line, some not-bad cavalry, artillery the capital didn't want and all sorts of bits and bobs his generals had found hanging around on the army list, hoping no one would remember them.

To stiffen the array Blades brought half his huscarls, to shield his august, irreplaceable, body and also to deal a useful punch on the off-chance they got close. He tried to get to see each one personally, as a sort of thank you and goodbye.

The two armies met at a place that would have been called Swarkestone, had they been in the old world; not far from New-Ashbourne. The Professorial forces didn't even bother to scout – which was a bad sign. A lot of New-Wessex scouts failed to return at all – which was even worse.

Still, Emperor Blades doggedly steered that to the good. He got to know when and where they were coming and prepared, harvesting every little advantage. The best of the lie of the land was occupied against them when the enemy finally arrived; every hedge lined, each field wall loopholed. The artillery had ranged in to their entire satisfaction.

As it turned out he and they needn't have bothered, and many, for whom these were their last hours on earth, would have been better employed fulfilling some outstanding ambition. The closest they got to see their foes was a distant line of blue, casually unfurling. The Professor's men started firing – and took a toll – two musket-shots away. It was unanswerable. The New-Wessex cannon spoke once and then were *dealt* with in no uncertain manner. Concentrated fire, one by one, made each gun and crew dance in flame.

Blades ordered the advance, rightly thinking it best to close fast under such abuse, but men dislike to walk straight into hail, even of the water-ice type, let alone lead. Obedience and duty and all those kind of higher notions lasted a hundred paces for most. After that they made their own decisions, based on private calculations of odds.

The huscarls were twice the men their colleagues were: they got two hundred paces and under the lash of the machine guns before dissolving.

Even pelting straight back was not an easy option. The body piles and slickness underfoot made progress tricky. Many stumbled and fell and did not arise. Returning, men chanced upon dead and dying friends; brothers stumbled over brothers and they lingered to lament over them. Some got to stay permanently, joining their lost loved ones in the ultimate act of empathy.

For the enemy continued to fire with undiminished zeal as the army fled, well past doing any harm – and Blades thought that rather unsporting.

'. . . rather unsporting.'

'*"No mercy to the merciless"*,' quoted the Professor. 'I don't pussyfoot with *Empires*, no sir, believe me.'

'I would have thought that chivalry . . .'

'Chivalry! Don't prattle to me about chivalry, sir! I have the measure of you and it. Now attend.'

All the notetakers in the former throne-room poised pen over paper.

'Chivalry is the mythic sugar-coating over the stark facts of feudal exploitation. Outside of books and youngsters' longings it never existed. I've informed all my students of that and they've been the better for understanding it. *Chivalry*, sir, was the fine clean face – but a mask in reality I tell you – that justified *crusade* and social fossilisation, not to mention the institutionalised degradation of the fairer sex. Oh yes, sir, the chivalrous may say sweet things about the ladies – but only so long as they stay in their place. Then it's the scold's bridle and the ducking stool. And there you are, sir, that's explained your *chivalry* for you!'

'But . . .'

'But me no buts. And remain where you are. Emperors stay on their knees when they speak to me, sir. Stay in your place, I say. As you were! And speaking of which, where was I before being so rudely interrupted?'

'Chivalry, Professor,' said one of his drawling sycophants. 'You sure explained that one away.'

The good student got a beaming, fatherly, smile. Blades then received its mirror image.

'When I had it drawn to my attention,' the Professor pronounced, lapsing into lecture mode again now that the brief flash of passion was past, 'that a primitive culture had arisen in Europe, I thought to myself: "*I wonder if I shall find chivalry there? Will I find womenfolk exalted and fair play and Christian charity?*" He sneered in particular at the last. '*Shall I step into the pages of Tennyson and Malory and tread in Camelot? Why, fan my brow! I am surely excited! Let us go and see!*"'

His high command and invitees tittered. He'd waited for them to heed the cue.

'So go I did. And did I find any of those things? Did I hell! Excuse the language, ladies, but I am pro-*voked*! Well, you tell me, Mr Emperor? Do you think my pilgrimage was blessed? You of all people should know.'

Blades had been keeping a low profile, as befitted his abasement on the floor. Attend though he might, much of his captor's speech was obscure. Any answer he could give was perched atop a ramshackle edifice of guesswork.

'I . . . couldn't quite say,' he replied quietly.

By contrast, the Professor's voice was at a roar.

'Can't – or *won't*, is it? No quite so imperial now, are we, sir? No indeed. Well, since you're so tongue-tied, let me oblige you with the correct answer. Not something any good teacher likes to do, but experience sometimes tells you a student ain't ever gonna get there!'

That got the laugh he wanted. He smile-rewarded the audience again.

'What *I* found,' he explained, as though to a dull child, 'was womenfolk exploited: voteless, disregarded, the prey of any lustful hand. And shame on you, sir, I found womenfolk *abandoned*! Wives on re-mote islands, surplus to requirements, cast off with nary a thought to sink or swim as they may! What say you, sir?'

Blades shrugged.

'I had my reasons. They weren't killed . . .'

The Professor threw up his hands like a minstrel.

301

'Oh, paragon of mercy! Oh, prince of peace! You didn't murder them? Why, hush my mouth! I have ma-*ligned* you, sir. Can you ever forgive me?'

He cut short the show with a venomous look. It was then Blades, antennae questing, got the impression the Professor hadn't always been used to power and was making the most of it. The useful insight was stored away. The ex-Emperor still had hopes of greeting another day.

The toying-with went on.

'And as to *fair play* and the sublimities of religion?' He slapped his tweeded leg in overdone exasperation. 'No sir! What we found was systematic class-oppression, glossed over by an Emperor cult and a Christianity more forgotten and debased than even I'm used to. A Borgia pope would have heaved at the sight. So, tell me, Mr Emperor, aside from killing Null – and that little I'll grant you – what were you good for? Tell me, sir, I implore you.'

All Blades wanted was to bite the tormentor's neck and gulp his blood but he was forced to think of something else. Was it a clever or crushed answer that the man wanted? Pride masquerading as courage persuaded him to try the former.

'Constructing good harems?' he ventured.

The conspiratorial man-to-man smile met a frigid welcome but did the trick. The Professor both disapproved and was tempted. Two opposing opinions warred within – quite visibly to practised cynics like Blades – and shut him up at the price of a bit of bitterness.

'Chivalry, is it?' spat the Professor, covering his retreat on to firmer ground. 'Chivalry from Redcoats? Pah! And a whole lot of chivalry you showed when beaten in fair fight . . .'

The next idea was to exploit the invaders' arrogant lack of vigilance. They were around New-Aylesbury and New-Missenden, where the country got very scrubby, not yet as deforested as core New-Wessex. Prince Arthur held command.

302

With a clot of the cream of the cavalry, deep hidden in the abundant cover, he foresaw a fair chance of sweeping down on the scruffy bluecoats, of getting in amongst them with equalising lance and sabre. Emperor Blades agreed. A pretence at parlaying was the bait to draw the enemy in.

Alas, as in Dovedale and sundry other places, the invaders showed no recognition or respect for the white flag. The two sides proved to be as bad as one another.

The New-Wessex flag party was allowed into open ground and then hosed down with fire. The fury of the sight bestirred Arthur into action too early and that was the end of many knights. They sallied out whilst the copper-faced bluecoats were a way off, still chuckling over their cleverness and safe behind a stretch of open ground. The last charge of New-Wessex was a brave sight, all levelled lances and pennons and bloodcurdling cries – for a few seconds.

A knight on horseback is a very obliging target, ideal for bolstering a marksman's self-belief. Few bluecoats weren't oozing with confidence by the end of it.

Some survivors made it back into cover and then the Professor's army amused itself by standing off and pelting the concealing wood with fire, till autumn arrived early there. Leaves and branches obligingly rained down from the disrupted trees to bless the dead with decent burial. Borne back, dreadfully mauled, Prince Arthur looked his last on the world from under a shower of greenery.

They had no mercy but surrounded the place, like harvest hunters waiting for rabbits to bolt from vanishing corn. Occasionally a despairing figure or group would oblige them by running and the last sound each heard was laughter.

They were also patient as corpses, biding their time to the point of cowardice. Light was failing before they deemed the wood sufficiently pacified and free of danger. Only then did they sweep it and shoot the wounded.

'Treacherous Englishman!' commented the Professor. 'You don't change from one world to the next, do you?'

Swallowing the nasty medicine of that insult brought some benefit. Former Emperor Blades did not protest but smiled. He'd suspected that the be-suited chatterbox was a blow-in to this world like himself, but here was welcome confirmation from those boorish lips themselves.

He rebuked himself. Why the delay? There shouldn't have been any need to wait for proof. The evidence was all there, waiting, begging even, to be picked up and moulded into useful answers. If he could build an empire from nothing then he was well up to drawing a few radical conclusions . . .

For instance, the Professor was fair-skinned whereas many of his followers were not. Their speech was an admiring student's copy of his and they hung on its every word like revolting puppy-dogs. All became sickeningly clear. Blades and the Professor had trodden along the same road. They had things in common – which was good. That comradeship, that familiarity, might one day permit him close enough to slip the dagger in.

'Whatever you say, Professor.'

And that proved to be inspired: better than stroking his soft – or hard – parts. The man *loved* that phrase. Any student who said that was ensuring themselves a glittering future.

The insults continued but not so vehement, less intended to wound. Blades had bowed the neck and would be spared to say wonderful things again.

'Lickspittle Saxons . . . Norman footstools . . .' The Professor was showing off now, displaying his virtuoso vocabulary to the assembled protegees. They applauded without understanding.

'*And*,' the Professor swayed forward, finger pointing, to emphasise the point: something relevant that had just occurred and greatly pleased him, 'cowardly night-crawlers!'

A night attack was the classical prescription for outclassed armies. Surprise and darkness, agreed all the ancient writers, went a long way to evening out disparities in arms or numbers .

Indeed, and as the authors promised, they did better than before; killing the lackadaisical sentries in silence, and then getting close in, where musket and sword were almost as good as the rapid-firers. In fact it was all going rather well and New-Wessex hearts rose even as they stilled bluecoat ones – which only made disappointment all the more bitter.

Raised hopes were elbowed to the floor. Some unheard voice said *fiat lux* – and there was light.

They didn't understand the great hissing glass bubbles atop the tall poles, or the means and manner of them flaring into life. All they did know was that night was now made day – imperfect sickly-yellow day admittedly, but good enough for rallying and shooting purposes.

Whilst they were getting over that shock the tide began to turn. Ever strengthening volley fire knocked them back across the camp's edge. The lack of light outside began to look awfully tempting. A few more blasts and they succumbed to it. Welcome darkness embraced both the survivors and Emperor Blades's last great hope.

'. . . Back-alley coat-throats! Damn Redcoats! Twilight *thuggees*! Timid *guerrillas* . . .'

Blades had no idea what half those were, nor why a red coat should upset anyone. Guerrillas and gorillas were equally unknown to him, but he got the drift and couldn't forbear to protest. The perilous indiscipline manifested itself as a raised eyebrow. The Professor, who closely studied people's faces to check what they thought of him, noticed.

'Don't you *dare* bandy words with me, sir! Take the hat and wear it! Cowards forever forfeit the right to contest a slur. *Timid* I say, and timid you were. What say you, sir?'

Blades gulped and the thing – just – went down; another dose of poison for his queasy stomach.

'Very *timid*, Professor.'

It was still a result, given that the surrender was accepted. He'd had his say, self-respect's final stand – for you could take the reply either way: as concession or accusation.

Also he'd learned something more to his advantage. The torturer's voice grew in passion when he spoke of courage – or lack of it. He trod on shaky inner ground, unsure, raising the volume to convince himself and drown out doubt. This rotund, past-his-best, Achilles was proving to be all heels.

And whatever people thought, whether sincere or compelled, the *truth* remained, even if no one spoke it. The last free days of New-Wessex had not been *timid*.

Since lines of soldiers were mown down, Blades dispersed the army into a cloud around the enemy, descending on them when they could, retiring when the guns were brought to bear. It was only then, after letting slip the reins, that they had some days of success – but too late.

They enveloped them like a swarm of bees, stinging and dying, not lethal in themselves but cumulatively venomous. Every hedgerow spouted a musket, every path a wicked trap or ambush. Even the wells were tainted with corpses, the fields set alight. The countryside through which the invaders moved took on an evil and unwelcoming aspect. If they'd had further to go, if they'd dawdled, it might have gone badly with them. The Professor realised it and pressed on at a more sprightly pace.

He decreed any captured man as no longer a soldier but a *franc-tireur*, to be shot without ceremony. New-Wessex's last gasp got to hear of the title, even if they didn't understand, and adopted it with pride. Then, as the march became a slog and the toll increased, that category was widened to include civilians and women and children. What had been a progress grew ugly.

Enveloped in a buzzing haze of *franc-tireurs*, pestered into irritability by its bites and trailing an almost equal number of blue and scarlet-clad dead, the Professor's army arrived before the walls of New-Godalming.

'Blades! Blades! Blades! Blades! Blades! Blades!'

They called for him tirelessly, day and night, with relays of men using some sort of cone device to magnify their voice. Perhaps they wanted to talk – Blades didn't think they were acclaiming him – but he chose not to answer. In-between whiles there were bombardments.

The combination was very effective, putting the whole burden of the siege and harm on his – named – shoulders, but there was no question of him obeying. They had a type of chatter-gun, mounted on wheels and fired by turning a handle, that spat bullets even faster than their rifles. These periodically swept the walls clear of any defender. Emperor Blades wasn't going to commit himself to their tender mercies and an embarrassing, amusing, death by raising his head above the parapets. He knew with what respect the enemy treated a truce.

Whilst Lord Firstmet urged sallying forth in force, and the generals made brave noises, Emperor Blades said nothing and watched the love of his People ebb reluctantly away. They had already done and borne more than might legitimately be asked of them, and now incomprehensible destruction and hunger loomed. In the private chambers of their own minds they were now making accommodations with the forces ranged outside.

He didn't blame them. If he could have done the same he would have, but the way they shouted '*Blades*' suggested that was impossible. A few copper-faced men had been captured and they said – under torture, naturally – that the Professor didn't like Emperors and Kings and *gods*.

The picturesque, the fitting, way to go would have been with his huscarls, dying to a man amidst the burning ruins of the Palace. They were up to it – many were positively keen – but for that to happen the whole city would have had to fall first. Emperor Blades didn't want that, whether by storm and fire or treachery and betrayed gates. Only the egotist, who never really loved at all, is willing to take everything with him. In the end, his love was proved by him wanting something of his to remain, even if he did not.

He and his huscarls departed by night, without farewells, without dignity: faces blackened, armour and possessions left behind. They made it through the ring of sentries, leaving only a smatter of dead behind. The shots roused all the Professor's forces and, not understanding, they ignored the fugitives. Instead, standing to in scruffy ranks, they waited the revelatory light, unaware their nerves were needless and that dawn would show the bereaved city open – and ready – and willing.

And so all that Blades had built gave itself to a new master, and New-Wessex came to an end, without even a whimper.

'*Truly*,' Blades concluded through his tears as they force-marched out of Surrey, '*technology is the lord of all; easy master over even love and faith and loyalty*'.

And thus not *all* was disaster and loss. Along the road he'd learned a valuable lesson.

'The Levellers are a fighting force; one to be reckoned with. We can testify to that. Maybe – with inducements – they can be swung to our side.'

Firstmet was a simplistic, black and white and therefore happy, man. He heard Caiaphas's suggestion, looked away into middle distance and was straightaway calculating the addition to their arms.

'At least one regiment of good foot per Freeport,' he thought aloud. 'Plus cannon and decent light cavalry. And ships! We could harass them by sea! Find out were they come from, sail there and . . .'

Blades finally caught his eye and by his '*oh, come* on' look brought him to a halt.

'I *did* say with inducements,' clarified Caiaphas. 'Large ones: probably larger than we have left to offer.'

Sad but true. In this counsel of despair Emperor Blades – if that's what he still was – had already spoken of the need for *honesty*. Even so and not for the first time, he had to be their example.

'I don't doubt,' he said, as regally as was possible for a fugitive, 'that the Freeports are already approaching our enemy with honeyed words. I can't answer to the reception they'll get, but it'll be sweeter than the one we'd receive from them. Put that from your mind, Firstmet – *Firstmet!* I know when something's still lodged in your heart: I can read you like a book, so I can. Set it down and look for other hope.'

'Don't think there is any,' the man replied – and that was as much blunt *honesty* as you could wish for.

Blades was going to disagree but found – in pursuit of the same policy – that he couldn't. Silence fell.

That was unusual in Farnham Castle, for in normal times it was a busy citadel guarding the western approaches of the New-Wessex heartland. Now it was hushed, making calculations, awaiting a change of regime. The flow of travellers had almost ceased as the ripple of news spread through the Empire and people decided they should stay home and *think*. Even half the Castle staff had not reported for duty. Blades had become used to glittering receptions wherever he went. Here, now, there'd been just one ostler to hold his horse and a distracted-looking castellan. Truly the carpet had been whipped from under his feet.

Still more poignantly, there'd been a trickle rallying to the flag. None at all would have been better: more clear cut, less embarrassing to send away. This lot were too few to do anything with. Emperor Blades reviewed the thin ranks of farmboys and fanatics and then dismissed them home with a blessing. Their let-down looks of disappointment was another bitter memory to treasure.

Within the keep, insulated by six feet of stone from the doubts of the outer courtyard, it was still – just – possible to maintain the illusion. Messengers and flunkies came and went, the courtiers did whatever it was they pretended to do and the remaining soldiers reassured. For whole minutes at a time, Blades felt and acted the emperor. Yet it was the lack of messages for the messengers that betrayed all, the idleness of those used to purpose. This was a court with no one listening, a court that no one spoke to.

'We have the huscarls,' said Firstmet, sensing the need for his slowness to be their rallying point, 'and we shall never lose *them*. They'll do as a core. Then we can progress round the edges – avoiding battle, staying shy of the massed guns – and attract support. A sort of . . . sticky army, gathering stuff on our prickly spines – like a hedgehog, only more sprightly. When we've done the circuit a few times and got numbers and bases, we can start to raid. We'll get some of their weapons, copy 'em, practise a bit and see how they like it!'

He beamed wolfishly around the council table, already a victorious decade or so ahead of them. Then he raced on further still.

'*Meanwhile*, we could send ships: scouts, small ones to start with, to find out where they come from. We can raise a few fires there, take hostages: give those over here pains and distraction. Then we'll be well away!'

Again he looked around, an innocent with an invisible friend, puzzled no one else could see.

'So why the long faces? It won't be any more difficult than starting again against the Null. Well, will it?'

They didn't know. None of them could face treading even partway down *that* long road again. Lord Firstmet, acting with the very best of intentions, had demoralised them more fully than the arrival of fresh foes.

Then the fresh foes arrived to complete the job. They at least occupied the sad silence which followed the morale-boosting speech.

Gunfire – the rapid crack of the new enemy, plus, almost reassuring in the context, the thunder of old ones – came from nowhere: nothing to cacophony in a second. There were a lot of them.

This at least was something they could deal with: a welcome alternative to thought. The generals arose to arms.

Only Blades remained in his seat; relaxed, untroubled. That they all left the room without him or dismissal raised only a wry smile. He didn't take offence: it was only thoughtlessness, visible sign of things yet unspoken. The way of things to come. Firstmet's 'progress', his 'sticky army', wouldn't happen, nor would they work if they did. The Imperial magnetism being fatally weakened, no one would follow or adhere. Throughout the land, as just now in Farnham Castle, the Emperor was already discounted.

They came over the walls with clever contrivances of ropes and hooks. Blades admired their agility, the obvious fruit of practice, even as he read the end in it. The defence of Farnham Castle was broken-spirited, just as it had been in his 'own', old world's, Civil War. Its garrison saw the signs in the rate of fire and the derring-do of the storming parties. Most fired a few shots for honour's sake and then put on a friendlier face. Some, those nearest the Emperor at the time, had the decency to look embarrassed – but it didn't stop or delay them.

He was in the courtyard now, an unhurried amble later from the truncated last council of war. En route, he'd acquired a brace of pistols and stowed food – leftover banquet stuff – in a bag. That way both options; fight or flight, were covered. Emperor Blades hadn't yet made his mind up.

It was made up for him. Some of the annoyingly lithe attackers were already in the yard. He recognised New-Wessex traitors and copper-men mixed. One party of them – obviously specially detailed for the task – were fiddling with the castle gate. It seemed an insult: that was *his* gate, to *his* castle, in *his* world, and they had no business mucking round with any of them. So he shot one.

Being rather busy, they took no particular notice. So he shot another. That made them turn round and pay him some attention – and respect.

The madness past, Blades realised he didn't want that attention. He turned on his heels and headed off with a train of admirers in hot pursuit.

The generals and huscarls – bless them – were prisoners in a game of their own devising. Arrayed in a shield-wall, flanks conveniently secured, they'd at last found the place to acquire both death *and* glory.

Their Emperor was the final piece in the jigsaw, the essential foundation stone of any last stand. They called to him, even as the volleys hammered home and shook them.

He looked and thought – but only a second – and then waved cheerio as he departed. Their script was not his, nor his perceptions theirs. It was all very . . . sweet, the *oath* and *loyalty* things, but strictly for footsoldiers. Rulers had *responsibilities*.

Blades therefore took responsibility for a horse. Its former owner, a wavering trooper, hadn't been expecting that. The Emperor stilled his whinging quibbles with a pistol drawn from its saddle.

He made better time mounted. Pursuers left behind, he was out of Farnham Castle even before resistance ceased. The postern gate, once stormed, had been left agape. It was as inviting as Boudicca's legs similarly placed. He was through it in an equine blur, barely deigning to stoop. He decided to risk that final face-saver: there'd been enough stooping for one day.

Unfortunately, others knew him better than he did himself. He rode straight into a ring of patient greeters. Violent action, excluding all higher thoughts, just prevented him skewering his mount on the waiting pikes.

When stationary at last, after a split second of sheer gratitude for life, he finally had time to see. And there before him was answer to at least one question. They were Neo-Assyrians and Levellers, a flying column of them. He recognised their distinctive dress, their independent, cocky, faces; he saw their horse lines tethered not far away. Sub-contracted, it was his own rebellious children that had led the bluecoats here. The realisation must have registered on his face.

'That's right, father.'

It was Sennacherib, blue-coated and cockiest of all. Lilburne was beside him, merciful in his lack of expression.

With, he trusted, invisible difficulty Blades mastered himself, as he had his horse. He was not going to be out-styled by the once-infinitesimal product of his own balls.

'Hello, son' he said, smiling. 'How are you?'

Sennacherib didn't reply to that. Just as obstinate, a true chip off the old block, *he* was not going to have his great moment spoiled.

'You can't say you weren't warned,' he said, at maximum

gloat. 'I *did* tell you to kill me.'

Blades smiled again, but broader: tighter – the best he could manage. He had to speak from the heart or burst.

'You did,' he agreed. 'I should have.'

'So, where's your famed dignity now, sir?'

Blades kept pace as best he could.

'Around my ankles, Professor.'

Indeed it was, for that was where the shackles were. Blades's shambling gait came from them alone, not some less tangible surrender.

Remembrance of that both angered and abashed the victor. He tried to keep in mind all the chains royalty had clapped on in ages past but it didn't help the concrete moment. Thereafter he averted his eyes from the stoic suffering beside him and kept to purely lecture mode.

'Obscurantism, sir!' He meant the cathedral in its entirety, encompassing it all with a tweedy arm. 'Four walls to keep in the dark!'

The *Indoctorium* caught his particular attention; ascending row upon row of little pews where the children of the inner circles came – or had come – to learn their debt to God and the Emperor and have the dividing line blurred. Then there was the sacrificial altar, still Null and traitor dappled.

'Dust and darkness, sir! A shameful clinging on to infancy!'

Dust was a natural metaphor for him to seize on right then, for the flinging open of all the doors had caused it to rise everywhere in lazy spirals. Unaccustomed sunlight flooded into the great edifice, dispelling the mystery of all its odd corners and causing the air-borne motes to sparkle. There was a certain – last, unrepeatable – beauty to the moment.

For all the Professor might dally over certain special outrages, there was no mistaking his ultimate objective. His acolytes-of-uncertain-role crowded round him, goggle-eyed, on the path to the Holy of Holies. Dragging their heels yet horribly fascinated, a crowd of the New-Wessex elite followed on, ushered by disrespectful blue-coats.

313

Both the Professor and Blades were keenly aware of the historical precedents. Back in the old world, Alexander, Antiochus and Pompey, titans all, had penetrated the Temple's central secret. Prisoner and captor approached that recollection along different routes. The Professor was wondering if the mantle might fit and Blades gloated over each man's subsequent doom.

The seal on the sacred door proved tougher than the Professor expected: introducing a welcome comical note. He'd planned on dramatically rending it, conquering-hero style, but the seconds dragged on and people giggled. Ex-Emperor Blades hadn't had occasion to laugh for some time but even his neglected faculties stuttered into life. His enemy blessed him with an over-the-shoulder black look whilst continuing to wrestle with the wax-coated cord.

Eventually, red-faced and perspiring, he called a bluecoat forward to take a knife to it. That wasn't exactly the scene for posterity that he'd hoped for – but there was the consoling thought it could *still* be if he spoke to the reporters and corrected their memories.

The opening of the door killed all the nervous amusement stone dead and the Professor regained his poise. He was standing full in the path of all the holiness presumably flowing forth and yet seemed unaffected.

Some of the New-Wessex contingent, the slower-witted and/or more loyal, had cast themselves to the ground. Grinning bluecoats stirred them with boot and rifle butt back to their feet.

'See?' said the Professor, addressing all, arms spread. 'Nothing! Mumbo-jumbo!'

He had a curious turn of phrase that often outstripped them – rather like Blades in many respects. Both were always met halfway wherever possible and therefore 'Mumbo-jumbo' was taken to be a variant of 'nothing' – and they *really* did wish to agree with him. However, there was the troublesome evidence of their own eyes. Only the really promisingly sycophantic could overturn that.

The Professor heard the lack of acclaim and returned from bestriding history to the everyday. Their disbelief was reprimanded with a frown.

Normally that was all it took but wilful disobedience continued. The Professor was obliged to turn and follow their awed stares.

'Oh, *that*,' he chuckled, dismissing their wonder with a flick of one pale hand. 'They're nothing special. I've got one of *those*.'

The glowing portal continued to impress, but not so much now the ever-victorious victor beheld and treated it with such familiarity.

As to the Professor, he was now well pleased, noting the birth pangs of a more rational sensitivity in many an eye. The only wasp in the picnic was an unexpected smile on the humbled Emperor's face. That alone really shouldn't have been.

Blades saw he was seen and put it away. The Professor's baleful gaze became sunny and moved on.

The Curate, then Emperor, then whatever he was now, was again happy to dissemble – just as much as it would take, without limits. There was now renewed reason to smile and he would hug the cosy notion to his private self.

Apparently, only he had seen the Angel.

'Charles II.'

The Professor was plainly delighted to be able to snort derision. It was always pike-staff clear when he wanted to parade either his knowledge or ignorance.

'Where *I* come from, sir, we make no close study of your history: the fiddle-faddle of this king or that. We have our own story to recall and delight in – and may I say, sir, it is a mite less stomach-churning than your own. Be more specific!'

Actually, Blades's meagre stomach contents were much in his mind at that moment. For the umpteenth time they rose again in mutiny, refusing to obey orders or listen about

'Stoicism', and were – just – repulsed at the last line of the teeth. At this lowpoint in life he didn't want to imitate a waterfall in the presence of his enemies.

The summit of ambition now was solitude and stillness, and the liberty to be as sick as you like and then die. Both the constant noise and motion were unaccustomed: violence to his senses, conjoined awfulness without prospect of relief. Of himself, the Professor was just the vomit's acid aftertaste.

Some reply was urgently expected. Anything would do. Blades spat out everything in the wild hope *anything* would be amongst it.

'The eve of the twentieth year of King Charles's reign, the second of that name, son of the martyred Charles.'

The Professor, proud owner of good sea-legs, raised his eyes to amuse his students with a *'what* can *you do?'* expression. Some of them were a bit green round the gills themselves, but they laughed anyway.

'The *year* you came through, sir, the *year.'*

'1680. The year of our Lord 1680.'

The Professor screwed up his face. Its salt and pepper moustache twitched disapproval.

'There was no call to peddle your superstition alongside the required answer, sir. The mere numeral would have sufficed. *So,* you're quite the primitive, are you not? Mind you, having seen your little . . . empire, I don't know why I should register surprise. Primitive is as primitive does.'

He really did have the knack of getting under the skin, even of suffering, seasick men.

'Why?' Irritation helped Blades get the word out. 'When do you come from then?'

The man did so love knowing things no one else knew. Blades reckoned that back before he trod the portal, the Professor must have been an indifferent teacher.

'Later,' came the tart reply. 'Later than you, on another continent. From a later continent of the mind, as well.'

He leaned forward in his well-secured captain's chair and winked paternally at the older, shackled, man. All the thunder

316

and throb of the ship's engines below seemed his also; additions to his personal authority.

'And be thankful for it, sir. Once upon a time we would have your head off. But now the – what I suppose I must call *our* – species has grown more reasonable. I'm half minded to spare you, despite your crimes. In some lowly occupation and exposed as a salutary example to others, you could reform and come to see things our way. Yes, brace yourself, sir, you have several centuries to catch up on in a short time. The work will be hard – and lowly, as I've said. Minister for Labour, have we enough spit-turners? Or well-diggers?'

One – finer cut – bluecoat stepped forward to confirm they'd nowhere near enough.

'Well then, that's settled. But rest assured, sir, your rest-hours shall be more than filled with a proper modern and rational course of education, devised according to my very own system. You'll enjoy it and thank me . . . eventually. Years from now we may meet again and converse as almost-equals. How about that, eh? You see, there's the beauty of the society I've been privileged to nurture. Things circulate; air and light and ideas and people. They also *rise*, sir. Why, even the vilest can ascend to responsible citizenship.'

He leaned back again, misled, believing that his point was made.

'So then, what say you to that, mmm? Not too much though, pray: the untutored's talk can be mighty tedious and repetitious. A simple thank you will suffice . . .'

Blades couldn't say what he really thought but, even subject to his new resolution, he'd had had a gutful of this. He was blessed. A timely heave in the Irish Sea made him spill those same guts all over the Professor's bright clean shoes.

They met again on deck. Gulls and parliaments cawed overhead, the wind was blustery. Blades was chained in the spray-soaked fo'c'sle along with a select band of other New-Wessex exotica, destined for display. Without an audience to play to the Professor proved to be more colloquial – and far less merciful.

'Barbarian,' he called the ex-emperor, and followed that up with a – changed – boot to the ribs. 'English barbarian.'

Blades groaned as the air was shot out of him. Firstmet tried to rise but was held back by Blades's flailing arm. There were bluecoats present and the sense that an *example* would not be unwelcome.

The steamer's pounding racket didn't assist conversation, but the Professor's every word was crisp and clear and prior thought-out. Blades was readily able to follow him.

'Not so sure about all the schooling now.' This was the real Professor: chilly and desiccated: something sharp. 'Got me the feeling it might be wasted on you. So, boy, I'm gonna supply you a crash course.'

He took a weapon from one of the soldiers and hefted it lovingly in his hands.

'Here's your bottom line,' he said, and fittingly slapped the butt. 'Your gen-u-ine Martini-Henry, breech-loader. Twenty rounds a minute easy, deadly at three hundred yards and mighty fine for five hundred if you're also lucky. An English model, true, but you cain't have everything. The Confederacy bought plenty in the war and didn't do so bad. That's where I got it from: brought the pattern with me and we churn them out weekly by the thousands now: a whole factory that don't do nothing else. Look, learn and despair, boy.'

Blades did look, precisely because he wouldn't despair. He looked and studied but couldn't grasp the principle of the gun, of how it might come to fire and fire so well. But he knew people who might.

Since he lingered too long and purposefully, it was jerked away from under his nose.

'And that's aside from our Gatlings and Hotchkiss: more stuff courtesy of you goddam Brits. Never mind: it's ours now. Get used to that notion, boy. We've got more firepower than freckles and there's ain't nothing you can do about it.'

The Professor squatted, carefully, creakingly, down to Blades's level.

'You got superseded: in that world and now this one, too.

318

Boy, you're centuries behind the news. So listen up. I've annexed me a sorta thirty-sixth American state: though the rest don't know about it yet. It's kinda more to my pattern; ironing out the creases bad luck and bad government put in. We got votes for women, we took a firmer line on them Indians who won't play ball with civilisation. I only bought across settlers who think right: rational, can-do, folk. You won't find no churches in *my* America, no sir. We have *de*-spensed with that illusion. We walk jaunty style, without crutches. Are you with me so far, boy?'

Blades wasn't going anywhere else, so he had to be. Once again there were words and phrases that meant nothing but he nodded anyway. It seemed safest.

'Good. Right. Well, we're all straightened out at home now and everything's pretty hunky-dory and the Null are hiding in the swamps and mountains, keeping their heads down. We've proved you cain't slave 'em: black as they might be, so extermination is all they're fit for. The generals I left behind are seeing to that one. It's not clever work, just mopping up. *So*, I thinks to myself, Prof, ol' boy, what next? I ponders awhile and looks at my globe and then I think why not take a look at the old ancestral homes, where the folks originally came from? Go see how they're getting on in *the auld sod*. Well, here I am and lookee here, what *did* I find?'

Blades got the impression he actually hadn't been too impressed but felt obliged to show affection – like a Quaker married to the wrong sister.

'Mother Ireland was very fine. Yes, sir, very fine. Wet, though. I repaid her the little favour of de-Nulling, and found your cast-offs beside. Uh-huh, says I: those pesky English causing trouble all over again! So Scotland I approach more cautious but discover you're not there yet – save for your poor mad wives . . .'

Blades couldn't help himself; even less so than with his stomach contents.

'How are . . .?'

'Well.' The answer wasn't heartfelt, but the following of an ideal built on sand. At the moment it was convenient; no trouble. If that changed so would he. 'And shortly to go on before us. There's places back home that can help them. We find that once the hysteric female mind is calmed they're still capable of simple work: sewing uniforms and the like.'

Blades had once seen Bedlam in London. He thought even that wild freedom might be better than the invaders' cold charity.

'One's worse than the other.' Some twist in the Professor's full lips told Blades this was more personal. 'The one with the leg is less afflicted. She's also very loyal. You don't deserve it.'

So he'd attempted her and been rebuffed. Blades didn't know whether to feel angry or flattered, or just relief that she'd not just been savaged anyway, supreme ruler style. He settled on feeling nothing at all – for the moment.

'You'll be following on. There's one final role for you to play, before you start your new, more democratic, life. Dublin first, then Boston. Sadly, I don't think you'll enjoy either.'

That might be so but Blades simply loved the very next bit.

A rogue Irish wave surmounted the rail, surprising the Professor from behind. Strange and wonderful to relate, it contented itself with him alone, barely splashing anyone else but soaking him from head to arse.

Blades took that to heart, even more than the Professor did. He rallied within as much as the Professor raged.

The enemy might have the *Martini-Henry* and *Gatling*; they might be bright, right and rational; but that lovely, Godsent wave convinced Blades that destiny was on his side.

Accordingly, he became invincible.

Journey's end was a beautiful disc of shining sea, surrounded by rich green. The Professor's infant *industries* had barely started to blacken the shore, his strictly functional buildings remained few enough not to depress the spirit. Even the New-Wessex stocked slave pens could be overlooked if the spirit was willing.

The sun was shining and the harbour full of miracles. The fresh intake of captives didn't have the heart to rejoice but at least they were distracted.

If Dublin was just a temporary camp, as they were assured, then Professorial Boston might be a *miracle* too much to take. From the moment they first sighted it, Blades's jaw wanted to take up residence on his chest.

He managed to exercise control but other New-Wessex captives just let themselves go. The process of marginalising, of de-sacralising, him was near complete. Even his closest creations, save for Firstmet and a few other loyalists, were sliding down to treating him as mere partner in misfortune, just another prisoner like themselves. At the same time, they were being shown better things to worship.

The constant light would do to start with. When day failed it was artificially revived all around the harbour. Glass bubbles on poles, in turn cable-fed from mysterious brass cylinders, made pallid-yellow light islands of the type that had foiled the night attack. Bluecoats went about their business as though the hour meant nothing; an inconvenient detail now surmounted.

They'd thought the SS *Hegel* which carried them from New-Wessex a behemoth amongst ships, but in Dublin its bigger sister, the *Darwin*, awaited, all primed for the long haul across the Atlantic. Troops and coal and supplies were fed into it without cease, by day and negated night. A mountain of metal, powered by some force they did not understand, it was worth a won battle to the Professor's cause. The little knot of captives stood in its shadow and drew their own conclusions.

There were other wonders but Blades and his companions were not there to see but be seen. The Professor, something of a classical scholar apparently, intended they should form the centrepiece of a 'triumph'. Whilst he rode, laurel-wreath adorned and beaming, in a chariot, the conquered would be driven in chains before him. Instructive tableaux on floats, flower girls and all sorts of prodigies would follow on in procession.

Such Irish burrow-men that had already been gathered in

321

were to be specially assembled to look and learn. The bluecoats would be lining the harbour to cheer – and Dublin would be only the dress rehearsal for the real, post-Atlantic thing. God alone knew what they could put on over there.

Former Emperor Blades was no god but still thought he could make a fair guess. He'd read of such things during childhood battles with Julius Caesar's Latin; he got the picture. It was all too easily visualised in all its colour and glory and humiliation.

He likewise *knew* that he'd firmly resolved to be pliable, to bite his tongue and survive at all costs but, that first night in Dublin he discovered that there were limits; some *costs* that were just too damn expensive. He found he really, *really*, didn't want to be the amusing chained monkey in the Professor's show.

So he mentioned that in his prayers.

The Professor wasn't entirely bad. Both Boudicca and Jezebel had left letters for him and they were passed on. Lying unopened on the floor they were also pissed on – for the Professor's cells didn't run to sanitary facilities.

Blades didn't care. He hadn't the time or inclination to read them anyway. He was thinking – and praying – and since his belief in the Deity had grown spectral they amounted to the same thing.

He never knew if the real God heard him, and it was no use petitioning himself whatever his cultists might profess, but the Angel – that was another matter.

It was a path he'd hoped not to tread: a burning of the forest to fell one tree. His grand plan had been to endure and then exploit the fresh defects he found every day in his enemy. The tweeded-one might have weapons-of-wonder, but he was also a bladder of hot air and *principles*. His intellect was easily the less-handy tool; a glass hammer versus an elegant and versatile Blade(s). Left to themselves the ex-Emperor would have resumed his throne sooner or later.

However, the Professor's plans dammed and diverted that

stream of probability. Out of his element and made to dance, Blades would no longer be able to call events. In 'America', all dignity stripped away and kept busy, a spit-turner or well-digger he would become – and then remain. The Professor had inadvertently found a way round Blades's fox-clever mind and dished out a pill too gross for even him to swallow.

So, it had to be that night or never. Tomorrow would be the 'Triumph' and then the ocean. Those two things bisected his future and there'd be no crossing back over them once traversed.

Blades briefly considered the spiritual cliff-edge before him. He saw the danger but also no alternative. He leapt.

Because the psychic link was now well established, he didn't need to mistreat a portal to nudge the Angel. He didn't even get down on his knees, for the slick, slimy floor hardly invited it. Yet still she came and filled the stinking cell with white and wildness and wings.

They were alone but her coming disturbed the other inmates in some way they couldn't see or comprehend. There came myriad sounds of disturbed sleep and sudden bad dreams.

'Hello!'

This time she did not move her lips. The shrill, golden voice poured from everywhere and nowhere.

'Hello!'

Blades bowed – he'd had a lot of practice at that lately. He opened his mouth and drew breath. It proved sufficient. Answer to the unspoken words came swiftly.

'Another favour? No. Let the game progress naturally. We are in no hurry. You are becoming tiresome. You interrupted my virgins' orgy. I was the conductor. They were getting good. Tiresome. I don't like beggars. I don't like beggars. I don't like beggars. I don't like . . .'

He dared to interrupt. Her time was not as his; she might go on forever and he be spit-minding in America before she finished. He'd also foreseen this.

'I'm not begging but cooperating. Bear with me. Do you see a man called *the Professor*?'

She decided to tolerate the delay. Her sloe eyes bored into the middle distance, despite the confines of the tiny room. She was seeing something, that much was certain, straining after some detail like a giant seeking out one particular ant. Then suddenly she had what she wanted.

'Yes. Him. Well?'

'Spin the years forward.'

She apparently could.

'Ha ha ha ha ha ha ha ha ha ha ha ha ha ha ha ha ha ha. Tiresome. Yes, I see. Remarkable. Tiresome. So?'

'Is that what you really want?'

'Not ideal. Doesn't matter. We have many mansions. Can go somewhere else.'

She almost did. The wings unfurled, ignoring mere cell walls and transcending lines of brick. Her image went out of phase, fluttered on the cusp of it and only then returned to clarity.

Blades was shown with what abruptness she might depart, taking all the worth of his remaining years with her. He tried to keep the new urgency out of his voice but it still showed, even to his ears, in the higher note and quick-fire words.

'But this is home,' he reminded. 'First flight. Not just anywhere. Here should be a showcase mansion.'

She allowed he'd made a point just by remaining to hear more. It was all the encouragement he needed to weave a seamless robe of words to dress her in and make her stay. Blades gave his tongue free rein, shoving commonsense aside, uninvolved, to observe.

'*His* future will be boring. Reasonableness strips away magic. He brings factories and the timepiece and efficiency. His hedgeless fields won't have a border left for labourers to scrape their boots on at end of day. That's wasteful. Mystery's an enemy to him and his, something to be hunted down and ripped open for all to see. Everything will be mild and straightforward. Think dull! Think safe! Views will have signposts telling you what you're seeing and nature have a tight corset set on what's left of her. They won't like trees for fear children might climb and fall out of them! Quaysides will be labelled "*slippery when wet*"!'

He was raving now, in verbal freefall, and had to pause for breath. Yet still she was there, glorious milk face and sunburst hair tilted coquettish to one side. Her long spider-crab-like fingers propped up the pointed chin. He had her.

'And another thing: it'll all be ledger books and cold calculation with him and his descendants. Money will be their only God and conversation. You'd have more diversion out of watching sheep graze. Or a colloquy of misers! He won't have children taught of you, you know. He wants them filled only with facts: dust-biscuits for breakfast, tea and dinner! Oh yes, I grant you he might have bigger and better guns but to what end would he put them? *Pacifying* things, that's what: *pacifying* everything! He'll make sure everyone behaves, oh yes. He's just the man to do that. He's a marvellous mallet to the side of humanity's head! He's a merchant's caution made manifest!'

He would have had to stop for a gasp there but she was enjoying it. She gave him extra air, a lung-paining sudden draught of it, so that he could continue. That let him rise to desperate crescendo. He himself had no idea where it was going to end and listened in with keen interest.

'You want to visualise the human future if he prevails, do you? I'll tell you. Imagine a grey rainbow! Conjure up a slate sunrise! See a style-less, neat shined boot forever clamping down on imagination!'

As Blades collapsed over his heaving breast, the Angel clapped its hands together like a delighted child.

'Yes, yes, yes, yes, yes, yes, yes, yes, yes . . .'

She had loved it. Her pet had performed a trick.

Speech regained, Blades rose.

'So will you assist?' he asked, all placatory smiles and humbleness.

'No.'

He plummeted as far as he'd ascended. The landing was rough. He crumbled back on to the stone bench.

'Oh . . .'

She comforted him: a tomb-cold hand brushed along his

shoulder. The prison-shirt dissolved where she touched. Blades's hair and parts rose alarmingly.

'Sweet thing . . .' she crooned over him. 'Helpless lovely . . .'

There was the temptation to cry but with locks aloft and cocker rampant he knew it would make him look triply ridiculous. The urge was overwhelmed.

'Well, thank you anyway.'

Plain English courtesy had been drummed into him with countless childhood cuffed ears and '*what do you* say?''s, till now it was reflex. He barely registered it saving him.

The Angel looked guilty: an improper sight on something so beautiful.

'I haven't actually done anything . . .' she said.

'No.' Ever opportunist, even in the slough of despond, Blades sensed advantage. Sharpish, he threw grappling hooks at it. 'No, you haven't really, have you?'

The Angel had quite forgotten about pity: hadn't felt anything like it for untold ages. She rather enjoyed the reunion even as diamond tears tracked her sharp cheekbones. She bathed in the tepid sentiment and briefly grew indulgent.

'I shouldn't really . . .' She was smiling at him now and Blades knew that even if she *shouldn't* then she would.

'It's not good for you . . . contrary to the spirit of the game . . .'

He realised this was only mock reproof and happily bowed to it. Then came the flow of indulgence.

'There must be *some* effort on your part. Think on. You've already spoken the word he does not know and does not have, but you do. Think on and find it and speak aloud and I may well return . . . possibly.'

He hardly dared to speak or handle the gossamer-delicate salvation being offered him.

'And then . . .?'

She wondered, a capricious Father Christmas with some good, some not so good, toys to distribute.

'I'll do a little. I'll allow some of my full light to shine and bless you. You'll be amazed.'

He was already amazed but now he wanted to be more

326

amazed than anyone had ever been amazed before – because an Emperor deserving of the name ought to be in the forefront of everything.

A fighting chance was all he asked – given that victory-dumped-in-his-lap wasn't on the menu. So when she left he did not whine but sat down to *think* as bidden.

Their conversation was thoroughly regurgitated. Then, with the remains spread before his mind's eye, he set to work like a starving midden scavenger, picking at the pile. Even *hello* got relentless, time-consuming scrutiny before it was cast aside, and more subtle stuff was doggedly pursued right to its outermost meanings. Yet still nothing occurred.

Outside, visible through the high, barred window, dawn drew on, bringing with it the day and the *Triumph*, and thus final defeat. By its growing light, Thomas Blades sat and ate his words as never before.

'Magic! *Magic!*'

'Correct.'

The Angel was back even as he framed the jubilant words. She even replayed that portion of his discourse for him.

'His *future will be boring. Reasonableness strips away magic magic magic magic magic magic magic magic . . .*'

The fat slug in a suit didn't *know*. He and his had no magic, they never spoke of it, weren't aware, didn't realise. Mages and magic hadn't been mentioned to them just as they hadn't been mentioned to him for years. He'd found out himself by accident. The accident hadn't happened to *him* and them yet – or perhaps it had and he hadn't listened. Maybe Sennacherib had said something, or a Leveller, or if they'd only observed Jezebel in action. And yet . . . and yet . . .

Blades saw it now, and the Angel smiled on him, participating in his little mental sprint. The notion didn't fit in with the Professor's world view; he paid no heed to savages and mad women. He'd not have listened if they screamed it in his face. The prince of pompousness was hoist on his own *I-know-best* petard. There *was* a weapon he didn't know a thing about; something just as serviceable but less suspected than any *Martini-Henry*.

Blades stood up, god-like again despite the surroundings. Even the Angel edged back a little to make room for him.

'I want to enlighten him.'

And then she knew that this was no simple gift but a joint project. He was borrowing her unspoken vocabulary and plan, partaking in some small, millennia-to-go, way in the same nature. Distant affection stirred within her. They were remote kin in a manner the Professor was not and so she had done the right thing. The others would not be too angry.

'Enlighten!' she repeated and agreed, egging him on, hot-eyed, 'Light, light light light light light light . . .'

Then he saw that he had been mistaken and that she wore not a robe but a carapace. It started to crack and the light which poured from deep within was like a sun. The cell could not contain it, melting all things close by, bar she and Blades and those she chose to spare. The gaolers and guards vaporised, beyond even a shadow of ashes being found. Caught within the narrow radius selected, the harbour waters boiled.

Unscorched, not even dazzled, Blades stood free and alone. He looked around. She had gone – but before she went she had kissed him.

There was still the matter of the Dublin citadel, the barracks and the troops and the *Darwin*, with its cannon like chimneys. There was still the matter of the Professor. But she had kissed him, though just the lightest brushing of lips, and with it had come all he needed to know.

The combustion of his gaol had announced itself in a corona of smoke, the aroma of melted brick and a blast of heat that woke all. New-Dublin rose troubled to deal with the day's new problems. Already, bluecoats were issuing out of the fortress.

Blades only smiled on them and it.

Before the dawn, asleep or no, all mages dreamed. The Emperor they'd failed walked in their head and sweetly forgave them for their failings. Behind him, partly of him, was a great light, containing more power than they could conceive of.

In return for their renewed loyalty and love he graciously allowed some small portion of that power into them. Their abilities swelled till they feared they would burst, until he kindly abated the transfer. Then, as they lay unawake and afraid, he comforted and instructed them.

His full abilities would be withheld, he promised. They were too much even for a mage's mind. Then he let it be known their enhancement was temporary and he expected it to be well used. He'd put them to the test and they and all his children had failed him. Yet he was merciful and slow to wrath and swift with forgiveness and forgetfulness. Out of the goodness of his heart he was giving them a second chance. Would they take it?

And then in their myriad dreams he smiled on them and lightly touched their foreheads with his lips.

All over the former – and soon to-be-again – New-Wessex, amongst the captives in Ireland, mages woke as one. If only for a day, they were ten times the mages they'd been when they lay down to rest.

They awoke with a burning mission.

Taken to Dublin with the other New-Wessex miscellany was its High Council of Mages. They survived the prison-nova because the Angel desired it. The best of their kind in normal times, the new day found them glorified beyond comparison and powerfully impelled to serve their Emperor well. Their next course of action had been revealed to them in a dream – or so they always after swore. They'd readily assented to it and sworn to make up for previous lukewarmness.

Beforehand, the Professor and his bluecoats had assumed them to be just yet more gaudy nobility, haughty parasites vampiring on the peasantry's back. Accordingly they'd never enquired. The Professor had bequeathed a certain impatience, a basic lack of curiosity, about 'primitive' social structures. It was their loss. They – the mustering bluecoat soldiers, for instance – soon learned different.

The Mages found themselves able to seize scores of minds at one time, not just one at best, as before. They found themselves able to do terrible things to them. Suicides were inspired, then mass murders of their own. Entire units were suborned on to the other side. The bluecoats got to experience how it felt being hosed down with state of the art weaponry at close range. They tended not to like it.

For drama's sake, to undermine morale, some men were persuaded to leap from high places, screaming all the way down. Others made horrible examples of themselves with edged instruments not really up to the job. A few of those and the bluecoats were no longer so keen to rush into the fray.

By now all the other New-Wessex prisoners were about, self liberated from their cages and huts. Though not mages, the intended slaves made themselves useful. Some proved speedy learners on borrowed *Martini-Henrys;* others relied on good old fashioned swords and anger. The golden chariot, the floats and tableaux intended for that day's *Triumph*, went up in flames; the functional block buildings soon joined them. Between the rank and file and their more gifted brethren, embryonic New-Dublin died quite swiftly once things got going.

The Professor never learned the truth of it, nor even a portion thereof. He wouldn't have believed, anyway. Hearing a garbled version – and discounting it – but seeing the chaos ashore, he bounded up the *Darwin*'s gangplank and gave order to depart. The rearguard cordon of bluecoats round the quay began to thin.

Emperor Blades let him go. It was unclear if even the multiplied mages were capable of much harm to such thicknesses of steel. He contented himself with having the ship's guns swept clear of life. One set of crewmen departed the earth messily, then their replacements fared the same. After that they got the message. The Professor wouldn't even have the consolation of wreaking Parthian havoc ashore as he went.

The final – or almost final – indignity was his own beloved rifles being turned on him as the *Darwin* steamed up to leave. Bullets drummed on the hull like insistent callers and the scampering sailors had to crouch as they went about their frantic work. The cable was cut rather than loosened. Evidently they weren't coming back.

Furtive and dodging the whining trajectories, the Professor gained a memorable last sight of Ireland. His stars and stripes banner had been hauled down to be dishonoured with spit and worse.

Blades thought he spotted the puffy moon face of beloved memory, leaning over the rail, looking puzzledly back. It was a tempting target – but allowed to slip. He had other plans, promised him in an angel's kiss. What they were he didn't yet know, but the assurance was good enough for him, surely better than anything he could devise. The *Darwin* was permitted to chug towards the horizon.

As the victorious risen slaves gathered round their saviour, hailing the day and him, Blades, Spartacus reborn, gave the order for celebration. There was still scattered resistance, frightened bluecoats marooned to their doom, but he was in relaxed mood. The outcome wasn't in doubt, the *Darwin's* smoke trail an ever diminishing threat. Fruits of the Professorial civilisation remained to be plucked from the fire. His reconciled children ought to be allowed to play after their hard work and sincere *sorries*.

Come to that, he too wanted to play. It had been all work and thought and blows of late. How long was it since he'd eaten meat, ridden meat or put meat into meat? Likewise, he was well overdue clapping hands on something rounded and interesting; long owed a *holiday-from-life* excess of wine.

And yet more than that, it was essential he quickly tire himself out. For even more than indulgence, Emperor Blades just couldn't wait to sleep and dream.

The Professor first thought it was the storm, but it was Blades. He walked in his dreams and would not let him wake.

There was torture everlasting and horrible sights without

end, for in dreams time is elastic, at the mercy of the presiding intelligence. Normally that would be the Professor's much esteemed intellect – but not that night.

Blades showed him his destined grave, waxed about its loneliness and obscurity, the chill of it and the lack of any monument or marker. Worst of all he harped on the Professor's entire disbelief in any afterlife. It was not judgement he was going down to but oblivion. The Professor knew fear but could think his way out.

He was not the only thing going down. In the cinema of his mind, the poor Professor witnessed split-screen facsimiles of Blades going about the ship. Not understanding but under guidance, they opened the *Darwin*'s hatches and portals and sea-cocks. No one else saw: they wandered in the silence of the night. Similarly inky, the water of the mid-Atlantic flooded in: ravenous, devouring.

When it was too late, the Professor was released from one torment to another. He awoke to find his palatial cabin's floor awash and his most prized possessions afloat on it. From outside, along the sickeningly long corridors between him and the open night, came the sounds of screams – but further and further away, and fewer and fewer. Muffled steam horns trumpeted the *Darwin*'s distress.

Blades had said he'd tampered with the door and so it proved. Not *quite* enough as to make escape impossible, but sufficient for it to be delayed and undignified.

The timing was exquisite. The corridor was still lit, knee deep: empty but recognisable. Only the absence of people, the sense of abandonment, undermined its promise. He recognised this too might be Blades's doing, legacy of his predictions and threats. How the Professor wished he'd *dealt* with him as instinct first suggested. A noose, the sharpened pole, the Null: anything deadly and degrading. Then he'd not be in his present state; afflicted by black magic, lost and confused in the howling, sinking night.

The Professor shook off the horrid tendrils of his dream and sought for hope. He employed reason and felt the stronger for it: the wizard's grip ebbing astern. A wade away – a long wade away, admittedly – were steps, then open air, then servants and boats. When he got there, only then would he worry about the Atlantic waves and the chances of home.

The whole ship lurched under his feet and then righted. His sense of urgency renewed, he found he'd been loaned a young man's legs again – for a spell. He splashed along a few yards. The gas lights lining the wall flickered, rallied and then died. The darkness was absolute and full of distant noise.

The Professor cursed, treading on, and then blessed the lamps' sudden resurrection. Then he cursed again. They'd done him no favours.

Renewed light revealed the oncoming wave, floor to ceiling, come to take him to his new and permanent home.

He had a second or two, and his last thoughts were of Blades laughing about the power of 'reason'. He'd had no answer for him then, nor any now. The merciful cold water arrived to release him from his quandary.

Blades remained with him – and at the same time safely back in liberated New-Wessex, courtesy of the captured *Hegel*. In image he accompanied the Professor all the long way down to the sea bed, to the foretold, foreseen grave, eye to eye with him, keeping pace.

Long before they reached there the Professor had lost all interest, but Blades stayed right to the end, to see him safely in his proper place.

On the next day, the seventh as it happened, the restored god-king Blades rested – and ever after, really . . .

The latter-day god-king mistreated the ancient diary, ruffling its dry pages, careless of their death. Parchment flakes drifted to the floor like snow upon the Downs. It was only justice: the thing had failed him, like everything else. Parliaments put a song to his desolation, cawing outside the throne-room's high windows.

His attention wandered, the ceaseless prayer-supplications were no longer tuned out. Invocations from ordinary people continued, day in, day out, even though both he and they had new masters now. Logically speaking, the god-king reckoned they'd have been better served addressing them, not he, but tradition was the staff that kept the old ways walking. There was also the matter of approachability. Humanity was predisposed to pray to a god in human image

Random-arriving along the Castle's voice-tubes, snatches of some petitions once again made sense. People wanted children or curing, his blessing on a trade venture or curse on a foe. Standard stuff. He went through the motions of consciously willing each. Presumably it worked: no one ever came back to complain.

Then he wearied of them and they receded again, home to the blur of background. The great temptation returned in overwhelming strength. There was token resistance, the honour paid to his ancestors, but then all-too willing, with almost erotic abandon, the god-king succumbed. He wondered, without decent restraint.

'Hows – not whys': that was the cynical wisdom of the god-king's grandfather. When he'd taught the princes of the first circle, covertly eyeing them for his successor, that was always the opening refrain. Why's were befuddling, unanswerable questions, best left to bemuse the lower echelons. Ploughboys and Downs-shepherds had time to look to the blue sky and ponder purpose – to no purpose. Those that set them to their arduous hours should keep to the rules of the factual world; the levers and pulleys that made it dance.

The god-king had taken the lesson to heart and lived by it for long years. That wisdom had been the foundation of his success. Those who aimed for the throne but missed lived to regret it. Of all the declared candidates only the winner kept his eyes and tongue. No disputed successions and civil wars for the Downs-Lords! The god-king-to-be had had powerful incentives to listen to grandfather and believe.

And yet. And yet.

334

Why should the wise desire deliberate dulling of the world's glorious colour? How came it that the lowest spit-monkey in the Castle was free to embrace what his god-king had to spurn? It seemed topsy-turvy; a degrading self-restriction; worse even than the new rulers, worse than being a puppet-king.

The yearning for peasant-thought, that chase into fact-free cloud, was ever-present. It came running at the merest, inadvertent, crooking of a finger; was long-suffering and tolerant of rebuff. The struggle against its charms was wearing him down. Any clay-booted farmer could cast his thoughts into heaven but he, *he*, the spark of that same heaven, had to fasten speculation into shoes of lead. It both beckoned and repelled like some shameful lust.

There was no lack of strengthenings. The first god-king's diary was very proper. Its reading should have stiffened his resolve. It was full of facts, was replete with them: this province gained – forgotten names now – that city founded. The facts instructed, they accumulated, mounted up even – but he knew in advance they would never fly, never grow wings and soar to some splendid resolution.

The entries were only ever . . . just more of the same. Another day, another quick scrawl of ink and then no more. Like life.

Most importantly, there was no answer in it, not an inkling to the way free of current tribulations. The shocking possibility occurred that the first god-king had not even foreseen the present change in regime; let alone left a cure for it.

The god-king repented the delvers who'd perished fetching the book from its dark under-castle home. A weak thought, but heartfelt. They could have lived on to extract some coal or iron ore: better *facts* than this crumbling tome.

It seemed god-king-like, properly ruthless, to flip to its conclusion. Then he'd be done with it and striving – and that was some or other liberation: though not the one he was prayed to for – even prayed for himself. He'd done his best and mankind remained a subject race. Be reconciled to it. Things were no worse than under the Null.

Then he read – and across the centuries there was the lightning flash of understanding. Simultaneously, he was both undermined and consoled.

There'd been at least one other who'd thought as he. The very first god-king, Downsland's only begetter, had *wondered* too.

Final words, to a diary, the world or yourself, had weight. These summarised, they dared to frame, his inmost thoughts. Centuries on, unanswered still, they found echo in this god-king's heart.

It was a wonderful thing to no longer be alone. He read and read and rejoiced. Even as a portion of his city burned at the new masters' whim he was happy. The faded words danced before his not only smoke-moistened eyes. Blades had written:

'I am told that this is all there is – and it is not enough . . .'

The site of the ascension is not precisely known. However, since the Great Maze bounds the mystical and tragic spot, all within is deemed holy as the equally plausible divine departing point. Entry is thus forbidden save to accredited 'Priests of Perpetual Searching'. Nevertheless, the faithful may approach the outmost hedges and water them with their lamentations.

Note, if you will, the lushness of the turf underneath – proof if any were needed of the luxuriant tears shed upon it by succeeding generations. Pilgrims must don the provided slippers to tread the famous 'well-watered sward'.

The fortunate may perhaps glimpse some of the world-renowned 'Searching Priests' as they return to their task or else are borne, prostrate, from the maze. Neutered and de-fingered to prevent any possible occasion of sin, they alone are entrusted to search the Great Maze, without respite, in storm or shine, by night or day, alike. Their unending hunt is for any sign of Our Lord, any trace of his presence or – may it be in our time – his return.

The brothers and sisters wander, severally or alone, within the mysteries of the maze, calling for their Lord and God, and singing his praises so long as their strength and voice may bear them. Then, when finally overcome with exhaustion and hunger, those who have succumbed to the weakness of our present husk are taken forth by their comrades to recuperate for fresh endeavours. Not all are found in time but it is deemed a signal honour to thus die of thirst or exposure, mislaid within – as well as iron guarantee of Paradise. Accordingly, it is not uncommon to observe priests feebly re-attend the Maze on hands and knees, unrefreshed, so eager are they to be at their great mission once more.

The faithful should applaud that zeal on their behalf. Heaven forfend that He (He needs not our blessing) should favour us again and not find loyal worshippers awake to welcome him!

'A Pilgrim's Compendium of Wisdom for those who would Glorify their Earthly Life with the Jewels of Piety and the Silken Raiment of Prayer'
Thane Brixi of New-Compton in the Province of Wessex, United England. In the Year of Our Deliverance 457 A.B.

'He wanted to be alone – and went alone. I was not there with or for him. I repent but there is no forgiveness for it.'
Brother Firstmet. Founder Priest of the Brethren of Perpetual Search.

'He sent us away – to fresh things. We could not be there when his time was done. We must not repine but take his example with us as inspiration. I shall meet him again and make representations on behalf of all. Therefore you need fear nothing save disbelief.'
Second god-king Sennacherib I.

'He sent us away – but he is in Heaven now – and happy, I pray.'
Queen Boudicca I. 'Our Lady of Kindness' and First Consort to god-king Sennacherib.

From *The Book of Memorance and Comfort*

Compiled by High-Priest Green-Grimes-Deborah of New Godalming. AB year 32.

The Angels allowed the rituals to continue – though doubtless it was only time before some noticed and came to disrupt. They could be indifferent and capricious and angry all in the same moment. The wrong answer – or even none – might leave a trail of flame and death.

For the moment, though, the Priests still trod the Maze. The god-king took advantage of that precarious continuity to make his own communion. He was not a formal brother of Perpetual Search but the rules were still his to make and amend, even – for a while, probably – under the new dispensation.

A fingerless eunuch led him to the centre as directed and then left. The god-king waited for silence and solitude to return and solemnly raised his arms.

'Oh, Blades, I never knew,' he told the spirit who, he had faint hopes, was listening. 'I never knew that you were truly kin. Now I have read and I know. You and I both . . . yearn. The answer is now given to you, whereas I await. Be kind to your kinsman and send me the strength to endure. Grant likewise the wish to do so.'

He paused and considered. There was some spectral awakening of will. If the first and greatest god-king, the creator Blades, was permitted *whys* and wonder, then so might he. There was hope – or the hope of hope. He felt it within his breast – a tiny star of worth-waking mornings, flickering but diamond hard. It already shed light – a little light – into the deep dark of tomorrow.

'Return, oh Blades! Return! Come to free your people from servitude!'

For a second the god-king perceived some distant stirring in the transcendence he now felt free to consider. It was not here or even near, not in the tangible or width or breath or depth or time – but he felt free – freed – to believe it even so.

338

Maybe prayers were answered.

He was disappointed.

An Angel appeared above and told him to be quiet.

The god-king knelt and obeyed.

It should have been a time of triumph: no doubt about it. The succeeding years were nominally golden. All was well. No other conclusion was reasonable. Yet Emperor Blades stubbornly came to other conclusions.

He'd breakfasted well, he would dine well. He'd emerged from the orgy room having acquitted himself as best could be expected for a man his age. He'd widened a few eyes and other mucous membranes: they couldn't reasonably ask for more.

Now the sun shone on his morning walk – not that that was any of his doing, whatever the more pious might think, but it was a blessing anyway. He had a spell of free time before he must report to the Cathedral for the midday ceremony of permitting the sun to decline. In an earlier service he'd exhorted it to rise that morning, a further still would allow it to sleep that night.

The reacquired consensus of the People was that it was very good of him to labour so hard and exert his great authority on their behalf. They recompensed him with love and loyalty. The doubts and desertions of years past were never mentioned and the god-king Blades had kindly let the matter lie.

The Mages' magnification had been only temporary, a mere day's duration: enough to overwhelm the Professor's occupying forces in New-Wessex, as in Ireland, but not so prolonged as to give them ideas. In any case, they slavishly remembered he who they believed to be the source of that wild power. Blades had appeared as its emissary in all their dreams, the fountainhead of miraculous success. He'd tested them right to the last minute, probing their faith, and still forgave when it was found wanting. They'd not make that mistake again.

Blades let it be known he'd allowed the Professor some little success so that the People might be forged in the fire. It was a high risk strategy for any other than a genuine god-king, but that had been proven beyond all reasonable doubt now, and so no one quibbled.

The other official explanation was that the enemy had been human in outward form only and, in reality, smaller kin of the Null. That made the ensuing massacres, to the very last blue-coat, so much more palatable.

The years passed, as they do. The sense of relief faded, the anniversary celebrations grew less fervid, there were fresh troubles to distract. For instance, the Null had shown a revival of late, coming out in strength from wherever they'd hidden during the bad days. Clearly, the Professor had been less thorough than he'd boasted, just shooing them back more efficiently than before. If so, that moderately softened the blow of their turning up like hungry death's-heads at the feast: another detraction from the tweeded-one's memory. Latterly they'd even become a noticeable problem again, though the *Martini-Henry* copies now churned out in New-Wessex factories were more than equal to the challenge.

Emperor Blades almost blessed them for their welcome diversion even as he was too indolent to do much about it. A grumbling eternal guerrilla war up north wasn't perhaps the end of the world. It would at least keep his forces in fine mettle. He pretended to tolerate the Null resurrection for that reason, forever postponing schemes for final extermination.

And as for the Professorial realm, they heard no more. Deprived of its fountainhead of inspiration it may have imploded or, grief-stricken, fallen victim to Null and mountain-bear resurgence. Blades neither knew nor cared so long as they kept out of his – thinning – hair. Otherwise he'd deal with them the Professorial way, and not so gently this time. His experiences had rather soured him against Americans.

Thus, quiet and prosperity descended like a freshly laundered sheet upon New-Wessex , lulling them into amiable doze. Only now, when the growing population grew inconvenient were they minded to expand out to Ireland or the far north. Both were still Professor-tainted but their day could not be long postponed.

Sennacherib, thrice chastened now and very mild, was just the man for the job. He'd even been trusted to put Jezebel and Boudicca back where they belonged, taking all their unopened letters with them. And that was just another aspect of Blades's life that had been satisfactorily resolved. He had back the – respectful and distant – love of his family. The nervous survivors gathered quite close around him nowadays.

Alas, there were other days when he couldn't take their calculating faces and it was for just this that the *Great Maze* was built. He tried to resist its call but the appeal just grew and grew. He was spending too much – noticeable – time there. It beckoned now like sanctuary. For the moment he turned a deaf ear.

The problem was that again and again he'd reviewed his position and couldn't find the flaw that spoilt all. His daily recounted litany of paradise, the well worn inventory of blessings, still annoyingly failed to satisfy. Again today, even amidst sunshine and cloudless skies, he wondered afresh what on earth was missing – and today had the appalling misfortune to find it. Perhaps it was just his day of destiny. If so, he was well ready for it.

His unspoken-for hours were taken to the Imperial rose gardens. And there, though sitting perfectly still to outsider's eyes, he chased the same old quandary. Then, to his surprise, it slowed, maybe through age, showing signs of willingness to be caught. He had suddenly to consider if he really wanted to behold the face of the fugitive. There now seemed the distinct possibility it might be turned only to reveal a monstrous grin.

He too slowed the pace of the hunt and then, bit by bit, their roles were reversed. Emperor Blades sped off in terrified flight from one particular conclusion.

Come lunchtime he was hungry and lacked the strength to run any more. The one inescapable answer had to be embraced – even if it were a leprous bride.

What was missing was himself. Somewhere along the line *he*'d been left behind – but the empty shell had just kept right on walking. Assuming there were any, the man-overboard's piteous pleas had been ignored. Blades's – or what was left of him – stately voyage continued all the same.

It is indeed a bitter thing for a man to reach mature years and gain all his wishes but wake one morning and find himself empty. The experience both scarred and scared.

It also tripped some alarm left long ago. She or it or they had been waiting for this day. Blades sensed the arrival even if he did see it.

Like fallen Adam avoiding the footsteps of his creator in the cool of Eden, Blades looked for refuge. He knew it was in vain but was no longer answerable for himself. An extra few moments of non-acceptance would do. He turned his feet to the maze . . .

The huscarls and praisers and flunkies and strokers and *scops*, and all the rest of the ever-present cloud deemed essential, were dismissed. He scurried between the shady green hedges and was soon lost to their sight. Indeed, inside that refuge a whole regiment could get lost, let alone an ageing, tetchy, Emperor. Life-like Null statuary studded its blind corners to add fear to bewilderment – which was why he was hardly surprised to be met.

Then he realised who it was and would have settled for a real Null instead. His face reproached her. She might at least have granted him a last peaceful hour of wandering beforehand.

'Hellooooooooooooooooooo . . .'

He was brusque, no longer the solicitous lover. He had no need of favours now.

'Why? You weren't summoned . . .'

The Angel refused to bridle, was perhaps not capable of taking offence. Can a worm offend a plough?

'No. But we draw near to our time. You have made it imminent. We were right to spoil you. The new cities, the confusion, the noise, they become juicy meat and drink: most suitable. Tasty. Well done. You have achieved the critical mass without the Professor's aridity. We detect no *accountancy* here. The game is almost complex enough for us to play. We shall be more frequent visitors now. Do not release the reins – merely . . . *loosen* them. There's a good child.'

And he'd thought he'd permanently dispensed with them by making everything more rational, by tacking – as much as could be stomached – to the Professorial course. It transpired he was only playing – in fact, creating – their game. That was something of a sickener. When you considered the wilder options foregone . . .

She detected something of his underwhelment. Blades had come to believe they required the broadest of emotional strokes to sense anything. Therefore, that spoke volumes for his strength of opinion. So, he was still up to surprising himself! He'd not been aware of feeling anything much anymore, bar low level irritation. That was some feeble comfort.

He looked over the hedgetops at New-Godalming conurbation, and how it had swallowed New-Guildford and sundry other places. The dwellings of humanity now scaled the most implausible slopes of the Wey Valley. He saw how it all bustled and wondered if that frenzy was his doing. Presumably so.

Now someone else claimed it as their own and he found his grip on title strangely limp. Or maybe that was her doing. The same with the sudden change of view. Blades doubted she aimed to please in showing him the *scenes*.

Space and walls were nothing to the angelic classes. To please or plague him he was shown myriad vistas from various times. Sadly, they all looked fairly recent.

In innumerable homes Blades was the name to frighten children into obedience or sleep. Eyes slammed shut or grew tearful at the mention of his name.

'*Go to sleep or Blades the king will visit your dreams.*'
and
'*If you're not good, Blades will come to get you!*'

A hundred separate homes and voices and incidents: episodes presumably selected to please him. They did not. It had . . . simply never occurred to him.

'Enough! I didn't come here for that!'

'The maze?' she asked, solicitous by angelic standards.

'No, here, this land. I didn't work all this so that *innocents* should fear me.'

He suddenly recalled – and he didn't think it was her – that Curate Blades's one hit was with children. He hadn't talked down to them, they hadn't to worry. Sticks and cuffs were tools he always despised. He took to heart the not-until-today recalled exhortation to '*suffer the little children* . . .' That one bit of his religion he'd always been diligent about.

No longer apparently.

'Show me another text. Reveal those who rejoice in me.'

She obliged. He studied the – quite numerous – scenes. There was no one he wished to be associated with. Most would not get over a discerning threshold.

'No – not those weathervanes. Show me the unspoilt who think kindly. I want the blameless.'

She smiled, untroubled: a marked contrast to the god-king. Either she couldn't or there were none.

That was a blow: not an unexpected one, but a blow long postponed bracing for. It hurt grievously. All the pieces fitted, the jigsaw was complete – and disgusting.

At the last he saw himself true, revealed in a perfect mirror, and ardently wished to depart from it and the memory and himself.

So he fled her and the truth: neither easy tasks, even in a maze.

She was at every turn she wanted to be. She repeated the awful facts, not thinking them so awful. It was an enjoyable cat and mouse game whilst it lasted. Perhaps she truly thought her pet was enjoying itself. Then she tired and scratched him. The way was barred.

'It is the *truth*. Embrace it!'

There was impatience in that: a dangerous thing in an angel, but he no longer cared. He knew he could not outdistance her save in lack of interest. He said nothing, thought nothing, but fled like a boring, senseless, thing. Sure enough, she eventually grew weary of repetition. Fresh, false avenues ceased to be created; he was allowed to gain the exit.

Alas, the truth also awaited him there too, and could not be outrun.

The court children, his own amongst them, were passing by in convoy. As one they shrieked and sought refuge in the nurses' long skirts. Soon not even a peeping head continued to enquire.

The adults, though more masters of themselves, were also milky-faced. They bowed and then hastened to pass on. He delayed them, which caused some breasts to heave, but he was no longer interested in that or any other reaction, bar one.

'The child, madame. Draw it out.'

She did so, with difficulty, fearful for herself and her charge. This nurse was ambitious and so employed both pinches and kind words, whatever it took. At last she got her way and the little girl was face-front, shoulder-held in position.

Blades put on his friendliest, oldest and best remembered mien. He'd worn it most of the time once, long ago. Now it was no longer a comfortable fit. Forced out of their normal at-rest impatient scowl, his features already felt unnaturally stretched.

'Hello, my love. And what is your name?'

A child may well love God, will pray to him, but they soon detect that the all-knowing grown-ups fear Him as well. Their days of easy discourse with the Deity are short-lived, delicate creatures.

This one was well past them: seven or eight years old at least. She had nothing to say to this god but tears. He was frightening her ramrod stiff just by being.

Because he was at – well-buried – heart, still a good man, he tormented her no more and dismissed them all. The nemesis cortege resumed a sprightly pace and sped by, leaving him alone with veracity: an unsettling companion at the best of times.

Blades didn't wish for solitude. Any company would do: even the avenging Angel. He wished for her. She had been waiting for that, confident and sleek, and she came.

'This I did not wish,' he told her, now tear-streaked himself. 'This wasn't the summation I wanted.'

'No?' She doubted his plain word. 'Not respect? Not prominence? Not regard?'

'Not monsterdom. No, not that. I tell you: this world; this *game* – you're welcome to it . . .'

That presumptuous ceding was graciously passed over. It was

not his to give. No indeed. She knew it was hers for the taking anyway. She'd cultivated it like a farmer; an absentee one, admittedly, but still the proper owner.

'So was all that striving in vain?' The tone was unconcerned but mildly curious. This transient spark had his . . . unexpected moments. Content that he'd played his little part, she was still willing to hear the field mouse's squeak of protest at harvest.

'All. All. Now I see . . .'

'I could make you blind,' she offered, meaning well, 'if that would help . . .'

They were alarmingly literal; Blades knew that. He had to be hasty.

'No, but take me where I shall see no more. Grant me that one last mercy.'

For once he'd picked the wrong word and she grimaced. Amongst themselves, the angels strongly disapproved of *mercy*.

Even so, he'd earned her deaf ear. She obligingly overlooked this collapse and suddenly they were back at the centre of the maze. The great *Blades in Excelsis* monument, showing him triumphant over Null and family alike, was no longer there. A new portal was. It shimmered temptingly at her fingertips.

'Goodbye.' There was both farewell and curse in his tone – but she wouldn't have it.

'No.' Again that knowledgeable smile. 'Till the next time. It is not an end but another chapter. We shall meet again.'

He didn't – wouldn't – listen, seizing upon his distractions as excuse. Blades looked his last on the world he'd made – and shuddered.

She provided no information: thus he walked into the dark, all unknowing. But even if she had, he would still have marched, and willingly. Suddenly a burden lifted, a new spring appeared in old bones.

Without further rearward glance, the curate-become-god-king and soon-to-be Capresi beggar, stepped forward to a new career and freedom.